RAINBOW ROWELL

ANY WAY THE WIND BLOWS

MACMILLAN

First published in the US 2021 by St. Martin's Press
First published in the UK 2021 by Macmillan Children's Books

This paperback edition published in the UK 2022 by Macmillan Children's Books
an imprint of Pan Macmillan
The Smithson, 6 Briset Street, London EC1M 5NR
EU representative: Macmillan Publishers Ireland Ltd,
1st Floor, The Liffey Trust Centre, 117-126 Sheriff Street Upper
Dublin 1, DO1 YC43
Associated companies throughout the world
www.panmacmillan.com

ISBN 978-1-5290-3991-7

Text copyright © Rainbow Rowell 2021
Illustrations copyright © Jim Tierney 2021

The right of Rainbow Rowell and Jim Tierney to be identified as the
author and illustrator of this work has been asserted by them
in accordance with the Copyright, Designs and Patents Act 1988.

1 3 5 7 9 8 6 4 2

A CIP catalogue record for this book is available from the British Library.

Printed and bound by CPI Group (UK) Ltd, Croydon CR0 4YY

MIX
Paper | Supporting
responsible forestry
FSC® C116313

This book is for you.
Never let them tell you
you're not magic.

1

LADY RUTH

There's a candle in my window. Sputtering. Sizzling. Threatening to go out.

It won't. It hasn't. Not for twenty years.

I set a second candle beside it and point my wand at the wick—then hold my breath, hoping for fire.

The flame leaps up, warm under my palm. My tears finally come.

He lives, then. Jamie lives. Yes. Good. All right.

The flame is long and steady.

My son lives.

I reach for the decanter of Madeira by my bed. Cut glass. An antique. Andrew, my husband, wouldn't approve of this. Spirits so readily at hand. But Andrew had *me* close at hand. Until the day of his death. Someone to share the burden of his sorrows. I never expected to walk this path so long by myself.

I am not a melancholy woman.

I'm not spiteful, I don't hold grudges. There's no time for it—a grudge will eat up your whole life and leave you on your deathbed, realizing you never lifted your head to the sun or had a second piece of cake.

I let in the light. I eat the cake.

I was born on the Sabbath, you see. Blithe and bonny, good and gay. Oh, I was a golden girl, full of life—full of *magic*. I came into this world to find happiness. And I found it! In my husband and my own children. In Lucy, especially.

My Lucy, my daughter . . .

Everyone said she was the spitting image of me—but she was better, I think. With her father's sense of decency and my vigour. She was strong and stout and absolutely *pink* with life.

Until she met him.

The day the Mage died—has it been a year already? nearly two?—I took down a bottle of the *good* Madeira. I raised my glass. *"This one's for you, Davy. I drink to your death, you merciless bastard."*

That man twisted the life right out of my Lucy. Turned the girl's head till she could only parrot his paranoia and prophecy.

I told myself it was a mercy when she ran away, a blessing that she disappeared without a trace. Davy was the most powerful man in the World of Mages. How far did Lucy have to run to escape his long reach?

I imagine her in California, under the sun. Or in Siberia, warm by a fire. I imagine her walking down a dirt road and leaving no tracks.

I imagine the child.

I believe there was a child. I *hope* . . .

Well, I hoped that Lucy would reach out to me someday. A letter. A sign. (I've watched the skies for crows. I've checked the bottom of every teacup.)

But when would it have been safe? Davy was watching for her, too, I'm sure of it—his magic fiercer than mine and far more ruthless. Even the power of a mother's love couldn't match that man's capacity for violence and vengeance.

The thought of him finding her . . .

The thought of him finding *them* . . .

So many nights, I've stood at this window and cast spells into the sky.

"Hey, you've got to hide your love away!"

"Keep it secret, keep it safe!"

"Mum's the word, mum's the word!"

I imagined my words finding them, my daughter and her child, and acting as another blanket of protection pulled tight over their shoulders.

But now . . .

Now Davy is gone. The Mage is dead.

You can come home now, Lucy.

I stand over two candles, the old one flickering, the new one burning strong. I pour a glass of wine.

Come home, child, I need your help.

Come home to me.

Help me find your brother.

2

SIMON

"But . . . that can't be right. I *killed* the Mage."

I'm sitting in Dr. Wellbelove's study. When Agatha told her parents she was coming home, they insisted that I come, too, for dinner—and it's been proper awkward so far.

She and I sat in our old places—next to each other, on the same side of the table—and her mum kept looking at us like she couldn't decide whether to be disappointed or relieved that we aren't together anymore.

Agatha and I were supposed to be a sure thing. I think her mum had already planned our wedding.

But we were a sure thing back when *I* was a sure thing, back when I still had magic—when I still had *all* the magic—and a calling.

And before I got stuck with giant fucking dragon wings.

Mrs. Wellbelove was appalled when she asked for my jacket and saw what was lurking underneath. At least she didn't have to see the tail, too—I'd taken the time to wrap that down the leg of my jeans. (So uncomfortable. My leg gets chafed, and my tail goes numb, and I have to wear baggy jeans that make me look like someone's dad.)

Dinner was *endless*. Agatha refused to make small talk, and her parents didn't know where to start. Everything about me is something no one wants to talk about. Hard to ignore the elephant in the room when you're making chat *with* the elephant.

I finished my dessert, Eton mess, in three bites, then Dr. Wellbelove invited me into his study. That's where he likes to have serious talks. The Wellbeloves have been something like a surrogate family for me (something a little more distant than that—like a surrogate surrogate family) ever since I joined the World of Mages. They used to invite me here for school breaks and holidays, even before Agatha and I started dating. And Dr. Wellbelove has always tried to talk to me about father-son things. He sat me down in this very study when I was 12 to tell me about the birds and the bees. (Though I feel now that he left out some pretty crucial information.)

Tonight, he took the seat behind his big glass-topped desk and got a stack of papers out of a drawer. "Simon, I've been waiting to talk to you until all the legalities of the Mage's estate were sorted . . ."

Legalities. "Sir—am I being arrested?"

Dr. Wellbelove looked up from the papers. "Arrested?"

"For the Mage's death."

He took off his reading glasses. "Simon, no. No one is getting arrested. The Mage's death was an accident."

"Sort of . . ." I said.

"It was certainly self-defence."

I nodded, miserably.

Dr. Wellbelove put his glasses back on and looked down at the papers. "The Mage—Davy—*David*—"

"David?"

"His estate has been settled now."

I shook my head. "The Mage was called David?"

Dr. Wellbelove looked up at me. He cleared his throat. "David Cadwallader."

"Oh."

"There are relatives, of course. But the terms of his will are clear: The bulk of the estate is set aside for you."

"*Me?*"

Dr. Wellbelove cleared his throat again. "Yes."

"But . . . that can't be right," I said. "I *killed* the Mage."

"Well," Dr. Wellbelove said, straightening the papers, "that may be true. But, legally, it's irrelevant. You're still the Mage's heir."

The Mage's estate . . .

What does a man like the Mage leave behind? He already gave me a sword, but I'm not magickal enough to call it. He gave me his father's wand, and I left it at Watford. I think.

The Mage made me his heir to get me into Watford—only magicians could go to school there, and I wasn't one. I was a fluke. Killing the Mage was my last work of magic.

If Penny were here, she'd say that I *had* to kill the Mage, that *we* had to kill him. That it was the only way to stop him from killing me and who knows who else. It was already too late to stop him from killing Ebb.

If Penny were here, she'd say it wasn't my *fault*.

But they *were* my *words*.

I killed him.

I killed my . . . mentor, I'd guess you'd call him. My guardian. He never talked to me about father-son things, but I was in his charge. I was his blade, his not-so-secret weapon. I had a place at his right hand.

I never even knew he had a name . . .

"There are some personal effects," Dr. Wellbelove says, "furnishings. His wand and sword, a collection of daggers—"

"I don't want them."

"They're very rare."

"His family can have them. You said he had a family?"

"Cousins," Dr. Wellbelove says, "in Gwynedd."

"They can have it all."

"There are other assets," Dr. Wellbelove says. "His savings."

"The Mage had money?"

"He had his stipend as headmaster and very few expenses."

"His cousins can have all that, too."

"No," Dr. Wellbelove says firmly. "They can't. Son—" Dr. Wellbelove calls me "son" sometimes, but he doesn't mean it like a father would. (Well, maybe he means it like *a* father, but not like he's mine.) "Listen to me. I know how unorthodox this is—"

"It's not unorthodox, it's demented! I can't take money for killing him!"

"You'll take the money because it's yours, Simon. Legally. And—" Dr. Wellbelove's face is getting red. "*Justly*. The man misused you. We all know that now."

"He never *misused* me, sir—are people saying that?"

"No, I mean—Well, what I mean to say, Simon, is that we still don't understand the scope of the Mage's corruption, but we do know he was trying to steal your power. Possibly he *did* steal it."

"He didn't, I gave it away!"

"The bottom line is, he *owes* you, Simon. He owes you more than *this*. There's no way that he—that anyone—can make up for the way he manipulated you, the years you spent furthering his interests."

"He didn't have to manipulate me. I wanted to help."

"You were a child—"

"No, I was the Chosen One!"

Dr. Wellbelove looks down. And I look away. Both of us, embarrassed and ashamed. I was never the Chosen One. That was just another of the Mage's lies. And Dr. Wellbelove and I were both fools to go along with it.

"It's been decided by the Coven," Dr. Wellbelove says. "The estate is yours, Simon."

I lift up my chin. "I'm not the Coven's concern anymore. I'm not a magician."

Dr. Wellbelove sighs forcefully. "For Merlin's sake, lad, just take the money."

3

SHEPARD

I have known Penelope Bunce about a week.

In that week, I've tangled with a were-skunk, incited a vampire gang war, and been spelled stupid at least twice.

I'm having the time of my life.

We're in London now. She insisted on bringing me home with her, with all of them, as soon as she realized I was cursed.

What kind of girl brings you home *because* you're cursed? I mean, that's something *I* would do, but I'm pretty foolish about these things—which is how I got cursed in the first place.

She faked my passport. She faked my plane tickets. She and Baz will both cast spells in front of me now like it's nothing. I never thought I'd be this *in* with a group of magicians. Nobody gets in with magicians!

I mean, I think my heart will burst if I betray them . . . Literally. There was a magical handshake, and I crossed my heart and hoped to die. But I was glad to do it. I'm seeing things no Talker ever gets to see—no "Normal," that's what the magicians call us here. That's what Penelope calls me half the time. "The Normal." Like she's only ever met one.

"Well," she says now, letting me into her apartment. "Here we are."

It's just the two of us. We all got out of San Diego in a hurry. I guess Baz's aunt has been arrested or something? Something about their old school. He took off as soon as we landed at Heathrow. And Simon and Agatha went straight to Agatha's house; she was pretty shook up.

We're all pretty shook up. I get the feeling that last week was intense, even by magician and vampire and dragon-boy standards. "I could sleep for a month," I say, sitting on Penelope's couch.

"You can sleep tomorrow," she says. "We're going to see my parents as soon as I've had a shower."

"Is something wrong?"

"Yes. Shepard. You've lost your soul to a demon."

I shrug. "Right. But that's not . . . *urgent.*"

"How is your spending eternity in demonic service not urgent?"

"It's eternity," I say. "Not tomorrow."

"Unless you get hit by a bus tomorrow."

"Are you going to throw me in front of a bus?"

"No, but on that note: Remember to look *right* when you cross the street. Americans are always walking into traffic . . ."

"Penelope. I've already been living like this for two years."

"Which is why we're going directly to my parents' house. Then you'll have your soul back, and you can die whenever you want."

"Your parents are going to unbind me from a demon over dinner?"

"Well"—she's looking through a stack of mail, twirling the end of her long, brown ponytail in her fingers—"there probably won't be dinner unless we bring it. No one in my house likes to cook. But otherwise, yes. My mother is the smartest and possibly the most powerful mage in all the World of Mages."

"Is she some sort of queen?"

"What? No." Penelope looks up at me, disgusted. "Mages don't have queens."

"Oh, right, pardon me for making that assumption in a country that actually has a monarchy."

"My mother is a magickal historian, and a headmistress, and an elected official."

"And she's really the most powerful magician in the world?"

"In the World of Mages."

"Which is . . . the world?"

"Which is the United Kingdom. And Ireland. And various islands." She drops the mail back on the table. I kind of hoped Penelope and Simon's apartment would be full of magical devices and artifacts. Like crystal balls and mystery boxes. But so far it looks like any other college student's apartment. They've got the same Ikea couch my sister has.

"Let me call and make sure Mum's home . . ." Penelope kicks off her chunky black Mary Janes. Doc Martens. I like them. She's wearing argyle knee socks. I like those, too. I like her whole *Velma from Scooby Doo, but make it lazy* look. Her plaid skirt and baggy purple T-shirt. The tortoiseshell eyeglasses.

"Are you sure your mom will want to help me?" I ask.

"Of course she'll want to help you."

"In my experience, Speakers don't go around helping Talkers out of traps . . ."

Penelope folds her arms and frowns at me. "Your experience with magicians is extremely limited and doesn't include my mother. It just *barely* includes me."

I return her frown with my warmest smile. (Which is *very* warm.) "Let's do it," I say. "I'm up for anything."

She frowns more deeply at me. "That *is* the problem, you know."

"I do know that. Yes. Indeed."

4

BAZ

"You here to bust me out, Basil?"

My aunt is sitting on a velvet-upholstered chair in the corner of a stone cell. The Coven summoned a tower to lock her up. The guard outside had to wait till dusk before he could cast the spell to open the door.

"I'm here to bail you out," I say. "For snake's sake, Fiona, what were you thinking?"

"Bail? Pitches don't pay bail. Or ransom."

"Well, that's fine," I say. "My father paid it, and he's a Grimm."

She leans back and rests her boots on a writing table. "Come back when you're ready to break me out properly."

"This isn't a joke. They're only letting you out because Dr. Wellbelove and Headmistress Bunce vouched for you." I only found out Fiona had been arrested because Penelope decided to call her mother before we left San Diego. When Penny came running down the beach yesterday afternoon, I thought someone had died.

"Wellbelove?" Fiona sneers. "And *Bunce*? Why on earth or below would they vouch for me?"

"They're vouching for *me*. I promised that you wouldn't do a runner."

She huffs. "That was foolish of you."

"Fiona. Can we *please* go?"

She sighs and takes her time standing up, then kicks over the chair. "Fine."

Fiona's wand and car were impounded. I had to sign for those, too. If she fucks up before her trial, they'll put me in a tower with her. I hold out her wand and keys.

"Back seat," she says, taking them.

"I'm not sitting in the back seat."

She opens her door. "I think you are. Because the front seat is for people who haven't been kidnapped by—"

"Ha ha," I say.

"Ha ha," she says, tossing her handbag onto the passenger seat.

I climb into the practically nonexistent back seat of her MG (1967, Grampian Grey—classic), which Fiona treats as carelessly as everything else in her life. (You should see our flat; there are mice living in the sofa, it's *shambolic*.) I have to sit sideways to fit. I wrench my knees past the seat in front of me. "Are you going to tell me what you were doing at Watford?"

Fiona starts the car. "I needed to pick something up."

"In Headmistress Bunce's rooms?"

She glares at me in the rearview mirror. "Those are your mother's rooms, Basil."

"No. Not anymore."

"Always."

"*Fiona.* The Mage is dead. The war is over."

"That's what they'd have you think."

"That's what I *do* think."

"The war isn't over until we get back what's ours!"

"*What's* ours, Fiona?"

"Our power, Baz! Watford! The Coven!"

"The Coven has already rolled back most of the Mage's reforms. What more do you want?"

"They were never reforms!" She points at me in the mirror. "They were a campaign against the Old Families!"

"Well, they're mostly gone now, is my point."

"It's too little, too late."

"Fine then," I say, "maybe you should run for the Coven and change things." (This is a terrible idea, I'd never vote for Fiona. And I *can* vote now—the injunction against my family was dropped. All the Mage's laws targeting specific families were overturned. We've got Bunce's mother to thank for that.)

"In the old days," Fiona pouts, "Pitches didn't *have* to run. We were guaranteed three spots on the Coven."

How am I supposed to reply to that? The woman is ridiculous. I roll my eyes and try to change the subject. "What were you trying to find at Watford?" I ask again, more gently this time.

She shakes her head. "Something of your mother's."

"Headmistress Bunce said there's nothing of my mother's left at Watford. She already gave me all of her books."

"Then why are they still on the shelves in Bunce's office?"

"That was my decision. I thought Mum would want them to stay at Watford."

"How do you know what she'd want?" Fiona scoffs. "You never even knew her."

I sit back. Away from my aunt.

Her eyes jump up to the mirror. "Fuck. Basil. I'm sorry. I didn't mean that. I'm just—I haven't had a cigarette in three days."

And she isn't having one now. Fiona isn't allowed to smoke in the car with me; I don't trust her with fire in close quarters. I look out the window, ignoring her.

"Basil. Don't pout."

"What were you looking for?" I ask again. Less gently.

"Nothing." She's holding the steering wheel too tight. "Something I need. Something I know Natasha would give me."

"You need to leave it be. If they catch you at Watford again, they'll lock you up without a trial."

"I'll go back to Watford when I please—I'm an alumnus! The observatory is named after me!"

"The observatory is named after your grandfather."

"So were you, boyo. It's Pitch blood in both our veins."

It's rat blood in my veins. Currently. I ducked into an alley and fuelled up as soon as I got back into town.

"Stay out of trouble, Fiona. You'll drag me down with you. And that's the last thing my mother would want—I know enough to know that."

5

PENELOPE

My mother didn't seem too upset when I called her from America. She was so happy to hear that I'd broken up with Micah—and so eager to complain to me about Fiona Pitch—that there wasn't really time to tell her the whole story . . .

All right, I swear I'm going to tell her about the vampires and Las Vegas and *definitely* the NowNext. I just need to figure out a way to do it that won't get us all dragged before the Coven.

I can't overstate how many laws we've broken in the last week.

Theft, more theft, counterfeiting. Flagrant misuse of magic. Criminal indiscretion. Manipulating Normals, exploiting Normals, exposing Normals to magickal secrets.

Exposing one *particular* Normal to all of the above.

Maybe I shouldn't have brought Shepard to England; he'd be the most valuable witness in a case against us.

But I couldn't just leave him as he was. He risked his life to help us in America, knowing that he'd go straight to hell if the risk didn't pay off. I wouldn't abandon *anyone* who was trapped by a demon.

And Shepard, much that I regret meeting him, isn't just anyone. He saved my life in the desert. And Agatha's, too. We were about ten seconds away from Joan-of-Arc territory when he intervened.

We take the Tube to my parents' house. Shepard talks too loud and points at everything. "Londoners don't talk on the Underground," I tell him.

"But I'm not from London," he replies.

I haven't asked him much about his demon problem yet. I want Mum and Dad to hear the whole story. I know for certain that Mum's done a course in demonology, and Dad knows a lot about magickal law; it was part of his linguistics training.

I've only got the usual demon training: Don't talk to them. Don't take sweets from them. Never, ever get in their vans.

It's not usually a danger. Demons don't just show up—they have to be summoned.

"All right," I say, when we're off the Tube and walking down my street, "we're almost there. Remember, you promised not to ask impertinent questions."

"I remember."

"Maybe just don't ask *any* questions—I don't trust you to judge what's pertinent."

"Do you have to cast a spell to reveal it?" he asks.

"To reveal pertinence?"

"No, your house—is it magickally hidden?"

I can feel the disdain on my face. "How would we get our

mail if our house was magickally hidden?"

"So, you just . . . walk in?"

"Well"—I turn up the path to our house—"I have to use a key."

Shepard frowns up at the brick two-storey. It's painted light blue, and my dad's planted hydrangeas out front.

"Magicians don't all live in caves and castles," I say. "Sorry to disappoint you."

"Do *any* magicians live in caves and castles?"

"This is what I mean about impertinent questions."

I open the door and let him in. The house is a mess; it's always a mess. Too many people live here, too many people with too many things, and nobody cares overly much about cleaning. Both my parents work long hours—though that's shifted some recently. With the Mage gone, Mum took over the headmaster's post at Watford. And with the Humdrum gone, my dad's work on magickal dead spots is less critical. He's spending less time in his lab and more time managing my siblings.

I have three brothers and one sister, and they're all home for the summer. Premal, the oldest, moved back home a year and a half ago, when the Mage's Men were disbanded. Premal still doesn't have a job, and he hasn't started university, but Mum won't let anyone mention it.

After the news broke—that the Mage was a power-mad murderer—one of the other Mage's Men, a boy from Premal's year, tried to kill himself. No one in our house is allowed to mention that either.

I give Shepard a hard once-over before we walk into the living room, as if some last-minute adjustment will make him less Normal. Shepard looks like he's looked every other day since we met: tall and lanky, long face, bright eyes. He's Black, with hair that's two inches tall on top but shaved close over his ears. He wears John Lennon glasses and corduroy trousers. (We picked up extra clothes for him at the airport, and somehow he managed to find *more* corduroy trousers.)

I've only seen Shepard without his denim jacket once, the day he showed me his curse tattoos. The jacket's unbelievably naff, covered in badges that say things like THE TRUTH IS OUT THERE and SOMEWHERE, SOMETHING INCREDIBLE IS WAITING TO BE KNOWN. Honestly, he looks like a complete nerd, but that, at least, won't be a problem in my house.

"What?" he whispers.

"What," I whisper back.

"You look like you're trying to find something wrong with me."

"I am."

"Parents like me," he says. (Smug.)

"My mum won't."

"Is she racist?"

"What? No! I'm biracial."

Shepard shrugs.

"She's not racist," I say. "She just doesn't like people. Fortunately, you're interesting."

He grins. "I mean, I think so. But it's nice to hear you say it."

I roll my eyes, turning away from him. "Mum!" I shout. "Dad!"

"In here!" Mum shouts back. It sounds like she's in the kitchen.

I lead Shepard through the living room. Pacey and Priya are playing Nintendo. "Hey," I say flatly. "This is Shepard."

Shepard's ready to launch his usual charm attack, but my siblings just nod and say, "Hey" without looking away from the screen.

Mum's in the kitchen, standing right under the light, holding Pip's hand. Pip's 10, he's the youngest. He'll start at Watford in the autumn.

"Penelope," Mum says. "How's that reversal spell you're working on?"

"It's promising," I say.

"Pip's got a splinter. I thought I'd try reversing an 'Under my skin.'"

"You're not casting experimental spells on my hand," Pip says.

"I'm good with splinters," Shepard says. "Can I help?"

"What spell do you use?" Mum asks.

"I usually use tweezers," he says.

She looks up at him for the first time. "You're Penny's friend with the urgent problem."

"Mum," I say, "this is Shepard."

He holds out his hand, but she's already looking back at Pip, holding her wand over his palm.

"No experiments," Pip says. "I play piano!"

"You never practice," she says.

"I will!" he swears.

She hitches her wand up in a plucking motion. ***"No trespassing!"***

Pip yelps. A bit of something flies out his hand.

"I can't believe that worked," Mum says.

Pip yanks his hand back—"Mum, you're the worst"—

and stomps out of the room.

Mum finally gives Shepard and me her full attention.

Simon says my mother and I are two peas in a pod. *"She's you in twenty-five years, when you give even fewer fucks."* I don't see it. Mum's much tougher than I am. And much smarter. And *much* more confident about her hair.

"I don't think we've met before," she says to Shepard. "What year were you at Watford?"

"Shepard's a—an American," I say, before he can say anything.

Mum's mouth twitches downward. She'd been so pleased to hear that Micah and I were done. *"Martin!"* she yelled at my dad. *"Penelope has finally grown out of the American!"* She must think I immediately replaced him.

"Where's Dad?" I ask. "I want his opinion, too."

"He had to run out," Mum says. "You're stuck with me. Are you two hungry?" She opens the refrigerator. "There are fish fingers, I think. Is Simon hungry, as well? I probably don't have *that* many fish fingers."

"Simon isn't here."

Mum looks over her shoulder. "Isn't he? Did you have him surgically detached?"

Shepard laughs.

I frown at him, but Mum finally smiles. "I just assumed, when you said 'urgent, interesting problem,' that Simon was involved."

"It isn't urgent," Shepard says, like he doesn't want anyone to fuss.

I huff. "I respectfully disagree!"

"Out with it," Mum says, leaning back against the counter. She's rubbing her forehead, like she's already heard and been exhausted by our problem. This is how it's been since Mum took charge of Watford—like she's always down to her last nerve.

"Well," I say, "Shepard is cursed."

"What kind of cursed?"

"He made an unfortunate—"

"Does the curse keep him from speaking for himself?"

I *just* stop myself from answering her.

"No," Shepard says, looking directly in Mum's eyes and squaring his shoulders. I can see he'd like to make this light, the way he makes everything light. But there's no light way to say it. He's smiling, and then he isn't. "I lost my soul to a demon."

"Oh, Shepard," Mum says, already disappointed in him. "You didn't take their sweets."

"Ah, no," he says, smiling again. "Only because I wasn't offered any."

"Who summoned a demon? Do people just leave the gates open in America? Have you all found a way to frak the Netherworlds?"

"I . . ." I've never seen Shepard at a loss for words. He tips his head down. "*I* summoned one."

She looks appalled. "*Why?*"

He winces. "To see if I could?"

"Oh, *Shepard*. Penelope, where do you find these tragic morons?"

"Mum!"

"Honestly!" She waves at Shepard. "Go on, take off your jacket. Let's see them. I do wish Dad was here. We've only ever *read* about demon entrapment. There hasn't been a documented case since the 1800s. An ounce of prevention goes a long way—it's like cholera."

Shepard takes off his jacket and looks down at the floor. He's wearing a T-shirt underneath. The tattoos start at his wrists and wrap around his arms. They're incredibly intricate, and it's hard for your eyes to focus on them. Sometimes they look like vines, and sometimes they look like writing— writing in an alphabet that uses all the letters we know and about a dozen we don't.

"Hell's spells . . ." Mum says, whistling. "You are well and truly fucked, young man."

"Mum! You're being rude, even for you."

"I'm sorry, Shepard. I don't mean to be rude. But this is a . . . *breathtaking* hole you've dug for yourself. Do your parents know?"

"No. They don't."

"Where's my phone, we're going to need photos. And a team of occultists and a demonic Rosetta Stone. *Morgana*, what a mess." She's warming to the problem now, and I can't help but be relieved. For a moment I thought she was going to let Shepard go to hell just because she was in a bad mood.

"There's no recent scholarship," she says, lifting Shepard's shirtsleeve with her fingertips, "but there is precedence. The last outbreak was at Watford. A secret society . . . Never join a secret society, either of you. How bored do you have to be to do terrible things for the sake of having a secret? Wealthy people can't even earn their secrets with any integrity."

Shepard is keeping wisely—and shockingly—quiet.

Mum has her phone out. She's focusing the camera on his elbow. "Do you remember when it happened? How old were you?"

"I do. I was twenty—it was two years ago."

"Well old enough to know better."

"Yes."

"Did someone put you up to it? Were you tricked?"

"No. I was just . . . curious."

"About *demons*, Shepard?"

"I'm curious about *everything*, Mrs. Bunce."

"Dr. Bunce. And I'm curious to hear how you think you're getting out of this predicament?"

"I don't think I am."

"What?" She's pulled away, and she's looking down her nose at him.

"I think I'm well and truly fucked. Just like you said."

She glares up at him. "I was only *insulting* you, Shepard. I was trying to make you feel so bad about your actions that you won't repeat them; it's a common parental tactic. You *are* well and truly fucked, but I don't intend to *leave* you this way." She smiles at him, just a little.

He's so grateful for it that he smiles back widely. "Thank you, Dr. Bunce."

Mum tucks her phone in her pocket. "Now, let's see your wand. Is it compromised, as well?"

"I don't have a wand, I'm not a magician."

She jerks her head up at him and then at me. "You're not a magician? What are you? You don't smell like a pixie. No offence."

He laughs. "I'm a Talker. I mean—a Normal. I figured that was obvious."

Mum's got her wand pointed at him before her chin has finished dropping. ***"Let bygones be bygones!"***

Shepard lurches back like he's been shoved.

"Rock-a-bye, baby!" Mum shouts.

Shepard slumps forward. Mum and I catch him.

"Mum! What are you—"

"Penelope Leigh Bunce, have you lost your mind?"

"Have *you*?"

"You brought a Normal into our house?!"

"Mum, he needs help!"

"All Normals need help!"

"Mum—"

"You told him about *magic*? About our *family*?"

"If you'd just *listen*! Shepard is my friend. He helped me through—Well, I found myself in a very dicey situation . . ."

"Imagine my surprise."

"Mum, that's not fair."

"Penelope, you're so addicted to danger that you manufacture it as soon as things get quiet!"

"I've manufactured nothing! I wasn't responsible for the Mage!"

"No, but you were one of three children in five hundred who couldn't steer clear of him. You are *recklessly* bent on finding trouble."

"That is an extreme and unfair mischaracterization."

"Is it? So there's *not* a demon-cursed, American *Normal* in my kitchen?"

Shepard is slipping out of our arms. We lower him to the floor. "Mum, he's my friend."

"I'm sure he is! I'm sure you befriended him the moment you realized what a hopeless disaster he is!"

"I didn't know, actually." I'm making sure Shepard doesn't hit his head on the tile.

"It's a sixth sense, then."

"Your disapproval is well noted, Mother. I feel bad about my actions, and I won't repeat them. Can you just help him now? He really is in trouble."

"Penelope . . . *no.*" She's standing up, looking down at Shepard with her hands on her hips. "There's no way to help him without compromising ourselves."

"He won't tell anyone about us."

"*Now* he won't. He won't remember you or me or any of it. He'll spend the rest of his life wondering how drunk he must have been to have forgotten getting such elaborate tattoos. Get him on the next plane home."

"You want me to abandon him?"

"Yes!"

"He's my friend."

"No. Penelope. He's a *Normal.* Whom you've known for how long—a few days? A week?"

I don't reply.

We both hear the front door open. My dad's home, he's calling up to Premal.

Mum's face falls even farther, like someone has heaped another trouble on her back. "Wait here," she says. "I've got to deal with this, then I'll help you send Shepard on his way."

She walks out of the kitchen.

I lay my right hand on Shepard's forehead and whisper: ***"Rise and shine!"***

He opens his eyes, then blinks at me. "Penelope?"

Amazing. He really is resistant to memory spells.

"Come on," I say, quietly. "Can you walk?"

"Yeah, I'm fine."

I pull him up and towards the kitchen door. We run through the back garden and out into the street. I wave down the first taxi we see and shove Shepard in.

He isn't smiling when he looks at me. "You were right. Your mom *really* didn't like me."

6

BAZ

Simon Snow is terrible at texting. To no one's surprise.

I message him from the train station—*"I called in every favour to bail out my aunt. She didn't thank me, and I still don't know what she was after. How's Wellbelove Manor?"*

"fine," he texts back. *"agatha's mum made chicken, you in trouble?"*

"With my aunt?"

"for america"

"Goodness, no. I don't think anyone noticed we were gone. Fiona's an excellent distraction."

I wait for him to text back, but Simon never feels obligated to keep a conversation going.

"I'm heading to Oxford," I send. *"I want to talk to my father about Fiona."*

"kk"

"I'll tell him you said hello."

"really?"

"*No, I was joking. He's still pretending you don't exist.*"

"*right*"

"*It wasn't a good joke,*" I send.

"*not your worst,*" Simon sends back.

I laugh, desperate for anything that passes for banter, then quickly type out, "*You wouldn't want to come along with me, would you?*"

Simon doesn't text back immediately. Then—"*is that another joke?*"

I sigh. "*Yeah.*"

The last and only time Simon came to my house, the Christmas before last, he inadvertently drained the entire countryside of magic. He's the reason my parents had to relocate to Oxford. They live in a hunting lodge now. My younger sister had to change schools.

My father disliked Simon Snow long before he ruined our ancestral home. Simon was the Mage's protégé, and the Mage spent the last fifteen years undermining families like mine. Old families. Powerful families. Wealthy families.

(You might think that *all* magickal families would be wealthy, but that's not true. Look at the Bunces. And the Pettys. My father says magic is a tool just like any other, and some people don't like to work. Bunce would argue with that assessment. But Bunce isn't here right now, so I don't have to suffer through her dissent.)

So Simon was already persona non grata in our house. And then he came over for Christmas and made our land unliveable. And *then* my father figured out—I'm not sure who told him, Fiona wouldn't have—that Simon and I were being extremely homosexual together.

If I even mention Simon's name in front of my father, the

temperature in the room drops ten degrees.

I usually *don't* mention him. My father and I are still firmly pretending that I'm going to make an honest woman out of someone someday. When I went home for my step-mother's birthday, they'd invited some poor magickal girl from the next town over to sit next to me at dinner. She'd been a couple years ahead of me at Watford, and apparently hadn't heard the news that Simon Snow showed up at my Leavers' Ball and snogged me stupid.

I wish he'd show up and snog me stupid right now . . .

Un-bloody-likely. It's only been twenty-four hours since Snow tried to talk me into dumping him so I could take up with a 300-year-old vampire. (Imagine bringing Lamb the Vampire King home for dinner . . .) I'm hoping we don't have to talk about that again—that coming back to London has brought Simon back to his senses. Or at least back to himself.

"I'll be home tomorrow," I text him.

He doesn't reply.

As soon as I open the front door, I can hear the television, and my first thought is that I'm in the wrong house. Then I hear my father shouting, and I'm *certain* I'm in the wrong house—I've never heard him raise his voice.

"I won't ask you again, Sophronia! Put that down this minute! *Sophronia!*"

One of the twins runs past me, holding a doll over her head. I snatch it.

"Basil!" she shouts, grabbing my waist. Sophie and Petra are 5. This is Sophie, I think, but I'll be honest, it's hard for me to tell the twins apart unless they're smiling.

I pick her up. "Goodness, you're all grown up. It's like holding a baby rhinoceros."

"Basil," she grins, "hide me." Definitely Sophie.

"You are well over the line, Sophronia!" Father yells. (Actually *yells*.)

I carry Sophie into the family room, where Petra's sobbing on the sofa. I hand her the doll. I always thought that twins were supposed to be best friends, but these two fight like rats. The baby's crying, too. My father—or possibly his unhinged doppelgänger?—is pacing with him. He stops when he sees me. "Basilton?"

"Father?"

Malcolm Grimm has two looks: gentleman farmer and gentleman's gentleman. This is decidedly neither. His white hair is sticking up, his shirt is untucked. He looks like he's just been roughed up in an alley—no, I've seen my father get roughed up in an alley, and he stayed much more pulled together than *this*.

"Is everything all right?" I ask.

"Tip-top," he says, automatically. "Basil, would you be so kind?" He hands me the baby and takes Sophie. He scoops up Petra, too. "You pair are going to bed. And if you don't stay there, I'll—well, I'll be very disappointed."

The baby—Swithin's nearly 2, I should stop calling him "the baby"—is screaming in my ear.

I pat his back, swaying. "What's wrong, little puff? Bad night?" I check his nappy, then his forehead. "You're allowed a bad night. Should we sing a song? Your sisters always liked my singing . . . Even Mordelia."

I bounce him around the family room, singing songs from the White Album. The whole room is a mess, strewn with toys and clothes. It looks like my father let the girls eat dinner out here—frozen *pizza*?—and there are two dirty nappies shoved under the coffee table. Is this what happens when my stepmother goes out for the night? Poor Daphne.

Swithin stops crying during "Martha My Dear" and finally falls asleep the second time through "I Will." I ease myself down onto the sofa, trying not to disturb him.

"Oh, Basilton. Thank magic." My father's standing in the doorway, looking a hundred years old. He drops into a leather club chair and groans.

If he had asked me at the time, I would have told him that 46 was too bloody old to start a second family. The man was already past his prime when he had me! But Daphne was young and had baby fever, and he was in love.

That was eight years and four children ago. Magic knows whether Daphne wants to have more; she's still in her 30s and doesn't seem to have any other interests.

"Is Daphne at book club?"

Swithin makes a fussy noise, but settles back on my chest when I pat him. I look up at my father to see if he heard me.

He's starting to cry.

7

SHEPARD

"Hey. Penelope. It's all right."

She's been pacing for an hour. "I know it's all right," she snaps.

"Okay, good," I say. "That's good. Maybe you could sit down?"

"I don't feel like sitting down. I feel like pacing. It helps me think. I need a blackboard, why doesn't this flat have a blackboard!"

Her phone pings. It's been going off every ten minutes or so since we left her parents' house.

"Is that your mom again?"

"Yes." Penelope has paused her pacing to furiously thumb out a reply.

"What are you telling her?"

"Lies."

"You don't have to lie to your mother for my sake."

"I think I do, Shepard, unless you'd like me to magically

concuss you and leave you in Piccadilly Circus."

"I told you—I can just go home."

"You don't even have a real passport!"

"Cast a few spells my way, and I'll get on a plane. It'll be fine."

She stops raging at her phone to rage at me directly. "You. Will. Not. Be. *Fine.* There's nothing *fine* about being cursed by a demon!"

"We all die someday, right?"

"Yes, but most of us aren't obligated to go to hell afterwards."

"I don't think it's hell exactly. I've done some reading . . ."

"For snake's sake, Shepard—"

"My point is—" I say.

She takes a deep breath, like she's about to shout at me.

I keep talking, holding up both hands. "My *point*, Penelope, is that it's not your problem to fix."

"Of course it is!"

"Why?"

"Be-because—" she sputters. "Because it's a problem that—that *exists*."

"You're responsible for all existing problems?"

She buries her hands in her hair. "No! But *yes*. What sort of person would be if I didn't help you?"

I try to look reassuring. "A normal one."

"I'm not Nor—"

"You know what I mean. If I had cancer, would you feel like it was your job to cure me?"

"Possibly."

"Penelope, listen—"

"No, Shepard, *you* listen! I understand I can't fix everything. But it's like, you can't pick up every piece of litter, right? You can't stop and pick up every napkin or piece of paper you see on the street. But my mum used to say that once we touched something, we were responsible for it. So if we picked up a can or a sweet wrapper, we had to deal with it—throw it away or recycle it or whatever—because we'd made it our business."

"Okay." I nod. "I think I get what you're saying . . . I'm like a piece of trash that you picked up."

"Exactly! I can't just drop you now. Then *I'd* be the one littering."

"What if I give you permission to throw me back?"

"It doesn't work like that. You've penetrated my sphere of accountability."

"*Penelope* . . ." I smile. "Does that mean we're friends?"

She rolls her eyes—like she thinks I'm worth helping, but not talking to—and starts with the pacing again. "I can't believe Mum was so dismissive. She's the one who *taught* me the sphere of accountability."

"Maybe it doesn't apply to Normals."

"Normals are still people, Shepard!"

"I'm surprised to hear you say so."

She doesn't look up. "On top of everything else, I owe you a life debt. We might *all* owe you a life debt. I can't just—"

The front door bangs open, and Simon walks in, shuffling off his raincoat. His wings spring out.

"Simon, thank Morgana!" Penelope says. "You won't believe what Mum did tonight—"

Simon walks past her. "We can talk about it tomorrow, yeah?"

"Simon, it's urgent, I—"

He walks into one of the bedrooms and shuts the door behind him.

8

SIMON

Dr. Wellbelove told me to sleep on it. So I did.

And I woke up thinking he was right. I'm taking the money.

I don't deserve it. Nobody owes me. But I could use it—I could really use it right now.

I've been trying to hang on to the World of Mages because I didn't have anywhere else to go. Because I couldn't find a way forward. I thought I'd find my way at the bottom of a cider can. I thought I'd find it, or something, driving across America. And for a few hours—a few hours in the back of a truck, somewhere in Utah—I fooled myself into thinking that I had.

But the only way forward is out.

This money is my way out.

There's enough to get a flat. I won't have to worry about rent for a year, at least. And I'll have a job by then. I made an appointment with Dr. Wellbelove to finally deal with the wings. It's going to have to be surgical, he says; magic won't touch them. That's fine. I'm ready.

I'm ready to let go—to be me again. The me I thought I was before the Mage ever showed up.

9

BAZ

"I just tried to call you. I'm going to stay down here for another day. Things are a bit of a mess. I think my father and Daphne had a fight. Text me when you wake up."

"Are you around?"

"Are you sleeping? You shouldn't sleep in the middle of the day when you're jet-lagged."

"I don't have a room here. I slept on the sofa. Mordelia woke me up this morning, playing video games."

"Daphne still isn't home. She hasn't returned my texts. There's a lot of that going around . . ."

"I'm staying another day, maybe two, I'm not sure. I still haven't cornered my father.

I don't know how to corner my father.
Anyway . . .
I can't leave yet."

"I'll just pretend you've replied with a thumbs-up emoji."

"Good night, Snow."

"Good morning."

"Daphne has left my father.
As far as I can tell.
He hasn't *told* me so—magic forbid my father tell me anything other than 'Tea's ready' or 'The night mares are nearly ready for brooding.'
(He's into heritage livestock now—the barns are full of rare magickal creatures. Battering rams and Judas goats. 'The only lllama herd outside of South America.')
But my stepmother isn't here—and hasn't been here in days, maybe weeks. A Normal woman from the village comes up on weekday mornings to take care of the children—who all have mobile phones and iPads glued to their faces. Even Swithin! He watches the same YouTube videos over and over, and cries if you take the thing away. These Grimm children are being raised by algorithms."

"Bunce says you're awake and running a lot of errands. I leave the city for three days, and suddenly you have errands."

"Sorry."

"That was rude."

"I'm still camping out in the family room. I think you'd like this house better than the one in Hampshire. It isn't haunted, for one. And the lighting is better.

You could come sleep on the sofa with me, if you like. My father is in such a state, I don't think he'd notice.

There's not actually *room* for you on the sofa, but there's no room for me either. I wouldn't be any less comfortable with you here. And I think you'd like the twins. All they do is eat jam and butter sandwiches and throw things at each other. It takes me back to our first year at Watford.

I wish I'd brought a change of clothes with me, but I never expected to stay this long. I'm still not certain how long I should stay. I'd thought 'until Daphne comes home.' But what if Daphne isn't coming home?

I'm not raising my father's ill-advised second family.

(If I *were* raising them, we'd have a stern talk about screen time.)

I'm half asleep, can you tell?

You could come down, if you like. You don't even have to text. Just show up on my door, caked with mud. Coat open. Snow in your hair.

It's June, isn't it?

Good night, Snow."

"Mordelia walks from room to room, video-chatting with Normals. She says her mother is in London, taking classes, which seems unlikely. I've never known Daphne to be studious. Or to have any interest in a career.

Maybe she's having a midlife crisis? (I'd be in constant

crisis if I were married to someone like my father. He refuses to have a conversation about anything that's actually happening!)

Anyway, I can hardly interrogate Mordelia. She's 8."

"Is this about America, Snow?"

"It's going to be all right."

"I change nappies now. And by that, I don't mean that I know how to change nappies; I already knew how. What I mean is, it's all I do. Daphne could have at least house-trained this child before she abandoned him."

"This isn't like Daphne."

"All right, I've interrogated Mordelia."

"I think I need your help with this, Simon."

"Good morning."

"Good night."

"Good morning."

"I miss you."

"I don't need a phone to talk to myself.
I'll tell you more when I get back to London."

10

PENELOPE

I used to think I was always right.

I was wrong . . .

About that.

Which really makes me wonder what *else* I was wrong about. I mean, if you're wrong about almost always being right, anything is possible. Maybe you're almost always *wrong*. Maybe I am, I mean.

It's like I'm a detective who's been solving cases for nineteen years with flawed methodology, and now I've had to reopen every one.

How am I supposed to *operate* like this? How do wrong people do it? (*I* am a wrong person now. I'm one of them!) How am I supposed to make even *basic* decisions now that I know how little I know?

I mean—I believed I was in a healthy relationship with a person who had already dumped me; that is a *staggering* thing to be wrong about.

What other false things do I believe in?

Am I delusional? Am I hearing voices?

"You are definitely not getting your security deposit back."

"Be quiet, Shepard, I'm trying to think."

Talk about a giant mistake—this Normal, sitting in my living room. Still completely cursed. And now an illegal immigrant, to boot. Throw another bad decision on the bonfire. I should make a list of them . . .

It took me sixteen spells, but I've finally magicked our living room wall into a giant blackboard.

"You know, there's a paint," Shepard says, still not being quiet, "that turns any wall into a chalkboard."

"Sorry I don't know where to buy magic paint." *Ah, there's my chalk. Excellent.*

"No, it's a regular paint . . ."

I write *What we know* in big letters on one side of the wall and *What we don't know* on the other.

"Penelope, this might not be my place to say—"

"Then perhaps you shouldn't say it."

He does, of course: "Maybe you should consider getting some sleep."

I shake my head. "Every time I fall asleep, Simon slips past me."

"He said he had an appointment."

"You don't understand—Simon never has appointments! He never even leaves the flat!"

"I did meet him *in America* . . ."

I rub my eyes. They won't stop watering. "You don't know anything, Shepard."

"Better add that to your chalkboard."

"Oh, I'm planning to."

He takes the chalk from my hand and writes *The human body requires sleep* on the left side of the wall.

"I'm fine," I snap. "I've cast the appropriate spells."

I told Mum that I spelled Shepard stupid and left him at the American embassy. I think she believed me.

It's more plausible than the truth—that I smuggled a Normal into the country and have been letting him sleep on my sofa for days. I never planned on this. I really thought I'd have Shepard fixed up and headed home within a few hours. But Mum sent me packing, and I can't even approach my dad—he'll go straight to my mum.

I stare at the blank blackboard and groan. "Where is *Simon*? I can't do this without him."

"Do you need Simon because he knows about demons?"

"Morgana, no. I need him here to listen to me think."

"Maybe Baz knows where Simon went?"

"Baz is in the middle of a 'family crisis,' apparently."

"Oh—does he need our help?"

"I don't know. He's being cagey."

Shepard still has my chalk. He writes *Where is Simon?* and *Does Baz need our help?* on the right side of the blackboard.

I turn to face him. "You're really extremely infuriating, do you know that?"

He smiles. Almost like he's being patient with me. It's infuriating. "Penelope, you're honestly the first person to ever say so."

I rub my eyes again and groan.

It's dark when I wake up. I must have fallen asleep on the sofa. If I'm sleeping on the sofa, where is Shepard sleeping?

There's someone sitting near my feet. Something with horns and wings. It's a demon, *it's the demon*—

"Hey," Simon says, grabbing me by the shoulders. "Hey. Penny. It's just me. It's me."

I've sat up. My heart is racing. "Nicks and Slick, Simon!"

"I'm sorry."

"I thought you were . . ."

"Shepard was sleeping on the floor," Simon says. "I told him he could use my bed."

I fumble around for my glasses. "Why aren't *you* using your bed? Where have you even *been*, Simon?" My glasses are on the floor. "You won't believe what happened with my mum. Also, you need to text Baz. I think he's worried about you. He's been stuck in Oxford all week . . ."

"Penny, I need to talk to you."

Simon is sitting sideways at the end of the sofa. His wings are spread out behind the arm, so he doesn't have to lean on them. It would drive me round the twist to have to sit on those wings all the time. I don't know how he sleeps.

My gem is tucked into my bra. I fish it out and hold my hand out to him. "I've got a new spell to try, to take care of your wings around the house. I think it will only shrink them, but it takes less magic than the others—"

Simon closes a hand over my fist. "Penelope, no. I need you to listen."

11

BAZ

Penelope Bunce isn't making any sense.

I've come back to London, put on some decent clothes, finally, and headed straight to Penny and Simon's flat. I've decided not to punish Snow for ignoring my texts. (Well, I'm going to evaluate the situation: If he's a little sorry, then I'm going to punish him a little. But if he's very sorry, I'm just going to pretend like it didn't happen. I've got bigger problems than him being a terrible boyfriend.) (I've got more *pressing* problems, at least.)

But now I'm here, and Bunce is telling me that Snow *isn't* here—that he's *left*—and that we aren't supposed to look for him.

"Have you been bewitched?" I turn to Shepard, standing in the kitchen doorway. "Has she been bewitched?"

Shepard shakes his head. He looks uncomfortable. Shepard *should* look uncomfortable—why is he still here? Snow told me that Shepard was only staying for a few days;

Penelope owes him a favour of some sort. I assumed he'd be off breaking bread with dragons by now.

"I don't have time for this, Bunce. Just tell me where Simon is."

"He left you this note," she says, proffering a yellow envelope.

I open it, and take out a matching card. Where did Simon get *stationery*? Did he purchase stationery for the purpose of writing me this confounding note? It hardly counts as a note, anyway. All it says is, *Baz, I'm sorry*.

"He's sorry?" I hold the note up to Penelope. "What does that mean?"

She won't look at me. "He doesn't want to see us right now."

She isn't making sense. This doesn't make sense.

"*What?*"

I think Bunce has been crying. Her eyes are red, and she looks haggard. "He says he needs time," she says.

"Time isn't something a person needs, Penelope. Time is a constant."

"You know what I mean—"

"*No. I don't.* I don't know what any of this means! Are you telling me that Snow moved out?"

Her chin is wobbling. "I think he's lost, Baz."

"Because you lost him, Bunce!" I'm charging into Simon's bedroom. "I left him with you for a week, and you lost him!"

She's right—Snow's things are gone. He didn't have much, but it's all gone. His duffel bag, his books, all of his grotty T-shirts with the slits cut down the back.

Penelope has followed me as far as the doorway. "I didn't lose him—he decided to leave. Simon is an *adult*."

"Oh, for snake's sake. He is *not*. He's a walking catastrophe!" I turn to her, my palms held out in frustration. "You know that! You *taught* me that! The only thing for it is to never let him out of your sight. Come on." I point past her. "Put on your shoes. Let's find Snow."

"No." Bunce's arms are folded. She's crying.

I'm not crying. This is all too ludicrous to cry about. "What do you mean 'no'? Why aren't you making any *sense* tonight?"

Bunce looks like she hasn't slept or brushed her hair since the last time I saw her. She shakes her head, and her bedraggled ponytail swings from side to side. "No, I'm not going to chase him. No, I'm not going to make him come back. No, I'm not going to *make* him do anything. If Simon wants space, I'm going to give it to him."

"Space, is it? Did he say he needs space?"

"Yes."

"People don't need space, Penelope!" I'm shouting. "They need *people*! Simon needs *us*!"

"That's what I always say, Baz!" She's swinging that ponytail again. She's shouting, too. "'*Simon needs me*'—that was always my excuse!"

"Your excuse for what?"

"For doing whatever I wanted! For making him do what I thought best. I was more like a commanding officer than a friend."

"You kept him alive."

"Barely! I kept him alive after goading him into danger."

"I wouldn't say you goaded him," I mutter. "Snow never needed goading." I hate how little sense she's making. I hate this note. I hate Snow's messy handwriting; it looks like a child's. I hate the view I have of his empty wardrobe.

"Baz, I'm not going after him. I promised him I wouldn't."

"Bunce . . ." I hate this.

"No."

I hate it. "Bunce, please."

"I know it's different for you," she says. "Maybe it's worse."

I hate—

I don't—

We landed at Heathrow, and I went off to get Fiona. Simon offered to help, but I said I didn't need it. I kissed him good-bye. That felt like a risk, saying good-bye; I wasn't sure where we were with each other at the moment. But it seemed fine. I said I'd text him. He said . . . What did he say? *"See ya,"* I think. Nothing was any different than it's been. Nothing was any better, but nothing was any *worse.*

He'd said those awful things in America. On the beach. But that was in *America.* And that was about me, not him, about whether *I* was happy. (I'm not happy, but I'm smart enough to realize that losing Simon would only make it worse.)

And there were other moments in America. Better moments. Before the beach. In the desert. In the back of Shepard's truck.

I don't believe Snow would just *leave* without telling me. That he would leave *me* without telling me.

"He left me a note, Penelope. After everything we've . . . We're . . . He's my . . . And I'm supposed to just . . . *'I'm sorry'?* What am I supposed to *do* with this?"

Penelope is crying, fat tears running down her red cheeks. "I don't know, Basil. Maybe it's true what they say—if you love someone, set them free."

"That isn't a *truth,* it's just a spell! When I was six, my shoelace got caught in an escalator, and my Aunt Fiona cast it to get me clear. Simon *needs* us, Penelope." I take her by the shoulder. "We have to find him. Let's go."

She steps away from me. She shakes her head. "No. He needs me to let him make his own decisions."

I let my hand fall.

I nod.

I look at Bunce the way I used to look at her—when she was my worst enemy's best friend.

"Fine then. Perhaps he just needs me."

12

SIMON

There's a goblin in my stairwell. Not even in disguise. Just sitting there, picking his teeth with a dagger. He better not have eaten my landlady.

I've only had this flat for a day. It's a house that's been split in two. The landlady's got the main floor, and I've got the upstairs. I convinced her that I'd be a quiet tenant. No drugs. No parties. (Goblins are worse than parties.)

"Hello, Mage Prince," the goblin says. He's red-lipped and green-skinned. Dead handsome, like every goblin.

"I've tried to tell you lot that I'm nobody's prince . . ."

"Word on the street is, you've lost your blade."

I shrug. There's a price on my head—the goblin who brings it back to their council or whatever gets to be king.

This one thinks he's got a fair shot at it. He gets to his feet, almost lazily, and points his dagger at me.

I shoot my right hand out to the side and grab a broom that's leaning against the wall.

"You *have* lost your blade!" the goblin cries, absolutely delighted.

He runs at me, and I wallop him in the gut so hard that the broom handle cracks. He doubles over—but comes up quickly, swinging his dagger at me.

My wings are strapped down under my shirt, and my tail is tucked away. (I've just been to see Dr. Wellbelove at his practice.) It sort of feels like fighting with one hand tied behind my back.

I've still got the end of the broom handle, so I use it to bat the goblin's hand away from me.

He keeps coming.

I decide to let him. The Mage taught me this—that sometimes the best way to get under someone's guard is to let them get close.

The goblin runs at me, and I grab the wrist of his dagger hand, spinning around behind him, so I can crush him against the wall, my chest to his back. I hold the splintered broom handle in my other hand, an inch from his eye. When he tries to turn away from it, I use my face to grind his head into the wall. I bang his wrist against the wall until he drops the dagger, then I step on it.

His eyes are open, staring at the splintered broom handle.

"If you leave now," I say, right into his ear, "I'll let you keep your eye."

He bares his teeth. "Another gob'll be right behind me. All of London knows you've lost your blade."

I nudge the broom handle closer to his eye. "Yeah, but you're going to tell them I don't *need* my blade—cuz now I've got yours."

He closes his eyes, still trying to wrench himself away

from me. Fortunately goblins aren't any stronger than people; you just have to stay away from their teeth.

"Do you understand?" I say, slamming his body hard against the wall.

He starts to nod his head—which is a terrible idea.

I move the broom away. "*Watch yourself.* Just say it out loud."

"Yeah," he pants. "I understand."

"If I see you again, I'll kill you."

"Why aren't you killing me *now*?" he asks. A bit narky for someone in his position. "Wouldn't that send the same message?"

I huff into his ear.

Because I'm tired, I think. *And because for all I know, you've got a goblin wife and goblin kids, or a goblin boyfriend, and I'd like a life—I'd like a* week*—with a lower body count.*

"Because I'm tired of washing goblin blood out my jeans," I say.

I heave him back by the collar and shove him towards the door.

He glances over his shoulder at me, like he still can't believe I'm letting him go.

"Seriously," I say. "If I see you again, I'll kill you. Even if I just accidentally run into you at Tesco."

The goblin runs away.

I lean over and pick up his dagger. (Too bad I can't keep it. Goblin gear is *always* cursed.)

Does this mean I have to find a new flat?

I bolt and chain my front door. I don't have any furniture to shove against it, so I decide to use the broom handle like a wedge—that should slow someone down, at least. Then I call and order myself some pad thai from the place down the street.

I take off my trench coat. There's nowhere to hang it, so I toss it on the floor. And then my shirt. I go into the bathroom to unstrap my wings. I've been using two belts. The leather chafes, and the buckles bite into my chest, and if I pull them too tight, I can't breathe. But if I *don't* hitch them tight, my wings work themselves loose and push out the back of my coat—which is too fucking hot to wear in the middle of summer. Honestly, it's not worth leaving the flat.

I won't have to deal with this after tomorrow.

I get the belts off and drop them on the floor, then try to crane my head around to see the spot where my wings actually attach to my shoulders. I can't quite manage it. But I can feel the joints there, the two knots where my skin goes from soft to leathery.

I can't see my tail either. But I can touch the place on my back where it comes out of me. I pull the tail out of my jeans and wrap my fingers around the base, feeling the bones inside shifting. Dr. Wellbelove says the tail's connected to my spine. He doesn't want to remove it outright—he's afraid of nerve damage—so he's leaving an inch or two. I'm going to look like a docked terrier when he's done with me, but at least I'll be able to wear normal jeans again.

The wings will be gone completely. (His intern wants to dissect them, and I said that's fine.) I'll have long scars down my back when it's over. Dr. Wellbelove was sorry about that, but I don't care—I'm already covered in scars. I've been magickally patched up too many times to count, and most healing spells aren't cosmetic.

Tomorrow.

My wings will be gone tomorrow.

I face the mirror and try to imagine myself without them. It's not the same as imagining myself before I had them. Before I created them.

I square my shoulders. My arms are tanned from the sun— all that American sunshine—but my chest is pale. Soft. I look soft. I look like someone who's spent the last year on the sofa, which is exactly who I am.

Or was. I don't know who I am. Fuck, I'm nothing at the moment. I'm between Simons. I don't even *have* a sofa.

I don't have anything. I've burned it all down, and tomorrow I'm going to burn some more.

There's a knock at my front door. That was fast.

I head into the living room and shout at the door. "Just leave it outside, mate! Thanks!"

They knock again.

"Christ," I mutter. "No one is going to steal my pad thai." I grab my T-shirt on the way to the door, but I'm not going to hassle with putting it on over my wings unless I have to. "Just leave it!" I shout, kicking the broom handle away. "Thank you!"

More knocking. If this is that goblin again, I'm gutting him.

The dagger is in my back pocket. I get it out and crack the door. "Just leave—"

It isn't Deliveroo.

Or a goblin.

It's Baz.

13

BAZ

It took me an hour to find him, and most of that was just the cab ride. Simon's living in Hackney Wick.

He's got the door chained. He's standing on the other side, shirtless, his eyes cold and his jaw set. "How did you find me?" he asks. Like he doesn't know there are a hundred spells just for this. It's hard to hide from someone who loves you.

"Magic," I say.

"I asked you not to."

"No, you asked *Penelope* not to. Me, you left a note."

He unchains the door but doesn't open it. He's looking at the floor. "I can't do this with you," he whispers.

"Too fucking bad, Snow. Let me in."

He turns away from me, flinging the door open with his tail. I try to follow, but the threshold pushes me back.

"You know I need an invitation," I hiss.

Snow glances over his shoulder, like maybe this is his reprieve. But he flicks his tail at me, motioning me in.

It's enough. The pressure in the doorway eases, and I storm in, slamming the door behind me. I told myself I'd be calm when I found him. Warm. Understanding. But all I am is angry—I'm *livid*—with him, with Bunce, with myself.

I turned my back for *five minutes,* and literally everything fell apart. This is why I haven't turned my back on him in a year! This is why I've been rushing home from class to sit next to him on the sofa. Because I couldn't *trust* him. I could never trust him . . .

The room is empty. Snow is standing at a window, looking at the closed curtains. His jeans are riding low, and his tail is tucked between his legs. His wings are hitched up around his ears. For some reason, there's a dagger tucked in his back pocket. "All right," he says, "so you found me. I can't hide from you."

"You bloody well can't."

"So what do you want me to say?"

I come up behind him. "I want you to explain what's going on!"

He doesn't turn around. He doesn't even raise his voice. "You know what's going on, Baz. I've already told you."

"You haven't even answered my texts, Simon!"

"I told you, I keep telling you . . ." He sounds so flat, like none of this affects him—like I don't affect him.

No. Unacceptable. Untenable. I *always* affect him.

I grab his bare shoulder. "You never tell me anything!"

Snow whips around, nearly clipping me with his wing. "I told you I'm *done*!"

"Done what?" Done with me, he means. I know that's what he means.

"Done!" he shouts, his wings spread wide. "I already *told*

you. Christ I—I *tried* to tell you! Done . . . *pretending*!"

"Pretending *what*?" I shout. Like I don't know. Like it isn't already killing me.

"Pretending . . . *this*, Baz. *Us*. Pretending I can . . ."

I'm dying.

I'm dying, this is death.

Simon's in my stomach, he's in my heart, and he's punching.

"Use your words, Snow. For fuck's sake."

SIMON

I can't *do* this with him.

I can't *say* this. It will slit my throat to say it, it will slice its way out, and then he'll cut me down—I won't survive it. (I was never going to survive this. Everything I am is nearly gone. Finish me off, Baz.)

"Use your words," he sneers. (That's right, that's my boy.)

He's wearing jeans and a navy shirt. I think that's his favourite colour—a blue that's almost purple. It makes his skin glow like a pearl. His top two buttons are unbuttoned, he never bothers with them anymore. His throat is bright. His throat is mine. There are scars beneath his hairline. I've fit my teeth over them.

"You know," I say again. "I've already told you."

He steps into my space. Taller than me. His hand comes up, and I think he'd grab my shirt if I was wearing one. He's grabbed me like this before. He's shoved me against a wall. He's loomed over me, his breath cold on my face.

"What have you told me?" He curls his lip. "What have you actually ever told me, Snow?"

"That this isn't working! I'm not a magician!"

"And I told you, I don't care!"

"Well, I do—I care! Do you think I like being a charity case?"

Baz is rolling his eyes. "No one treats you like a charity case."

"I can't even leave the house without your help. Without Penny's."

"We don't *mind* helping!"

I throw my hands up. "You're not listening—you never listen!"

"I *always* listen!" He jabs a finger at me. "*You* never talk!"

"I'm talking now, all right? I'm *telling* you. I'm done with magic! I'm done with mages! I can't—You're both—I can't *live* with you!"

"We don't have to live together, Simon. We *don't* live together."

"I can't even *be* with you! I hate it."

"You hate *being* with me?"

"Yes, all right?" I'm screaming. "Are you happy? I hate being with you! I hate your fucking wand! I hate how easy it all is for you! I hate *looking* at you!"

"You hate looking at me."

God, yes, I do. I do. I hate the sight of him.

All I see is what I've lost—who I was. His match. Someone who might someday deserve him.

My hands are in my hair, pulling. I'm shaking my head. "What are we even *doing,* Baz? Where did you think this was all *going*?"

He steps back. "I thought . . ."

BAZ

I thought I was being patient.

I thought he was getting better.

I thought we were in love . . .

. . . though he's never said so.

"I like you," he said once. *"I like this."* But that was before. When he still had magic.

And then he told me I was all he had left to lose. I thought that meant that he wouldn't let me go. But maybe Snow was trying to tell me his plans: *You're all I have left to lose, and eventually I will.*

I take another step away from him. I'd been reaching for him. His broad shoulders, his freckled chest. It isn't fair of him to say these things with his heart so naked. It makes them seem true.

I thought we had the sort of love that you can't set down or walk away from. An undying fire. The love you hear about in the old stories.

No one told Simon Snow the old stories.

(Fuck, he's already saved the princess and walked away from her. Maybe I'm one more unwanted prize.)

I take another step back. And another. Snow's wings drop a bit. He's looking down at the floor, rubbing the back of his neck. His chest is pale—cream and gold and pink—but his arms are still sun-kissed from those days in the back of Shepard's truck. It's only been a week.

No.

I step forward. His head jerks up.

"You can't just decide that you're done with me," I say. "That's not what we are."

Snow looks even more confused, even angrier, than before.

"I can't decide I'm done? I have to pretend that I'm happy like this—sitting at home waiting for you to spell my wings away?"

"Shut up about the wings! You don't have to keep the wings!"

"I'm not! I'm having them off tomorrow!"

"Wait, *tomorrow*?" His wings . . .

Snow lurches towards me. He points at my face. "I'm done, Baz—I'm done playing dungeons and dragons with you lot. I'm done with, fucking, *spells*. And prophecies. Werewolves and vampires. I'm just a person. An ordinary bloke."

"How can you say that? You were the most powerful magi—"

His wings flare out. "Was! I *was* all that. Not anymore. It's like I've been living in a museum—'*Here's Simon Snow. We thought he was the Chosen One for a few years. Gave himself a tail. Look at the state of him.*' I've got to let all that go, I have to figure out what comes next!"

"That's what we've been doing! We're figuring it out together."

He rolls his eyes and shrugs his wings. It's all one gesture. "I know what's next for you and Penny—magic! It's always more magic."

"You keep talking about magic," I say. "I'm talking about *us*."

"It's all the same thing!"

"I don't care about magic!" I do care, I care passionately. But I'd give my magic to the Humdrum to fix this.

"That's a lie," Simon says.

I pull my wand out of my sleeve and hold both ends. "I'll break it, Snow. I don't care. I don't need it. Not like I—"

"You're not *breaking* your *wand*." He tries to yank the thing out of my hands, but he ends up pulling me closer.

My face hangs over his. I've been yelling. I've been angry. But now I'm just . . . "Please," I say, so quietly. "Please, Simon. Don't do this."

SIMON

His hair is brushing against my forehead. We're both holding on to his ivory wand. The fight's gone out of him, and that's no good, because fighting is all I can manage right now.

"*Baz* . . ." I whisper.

He presses his forehead to mine. "Don't do this. Don't do this to me, love."

"I have to."

His head is rocking against mine, from side to side. "No, Simon. No. We can't come apart like this. We're not made of pieces that come apart."

"Baz—"

"You can't just *give up* on this. On me. Don't you know what we have? It's the sort of thing people dream about. They make potions to steal it." He pulls his wand against his chest. He pulls me with it.

"I know," I say.

And I do. I *know.*

I know I'll never love anyone like I love Baz. I know he's the love of my life. Of all my lives. The Mage believed in reincarnation. Of a thousand lives stacked on top of each other. "*Some lives we squander,*" he said. "*And some we seize.*"

This was my life to find love. The truest love. The biggest. But it isn't my life to have it.

I'm too . . . broken. I don't know how to be close to people. I don't know how to be quiet. When Baz gets like this with me . . . When he hands me his heart, I don't know how to hold it. I want to scream. I want to run. Maybe it's part of what the Mage did to me. He said he got me wrong, that I was a cracked vessel. I can't hold on to anything good.

"Baz . . ." I'm still whispering. "I can't be with you."

"Because of magic?" His voice breaks on the last word.

"Because of me. I was never going to make this work."

"*Fuck.*" He shudders. "You're killing me, Snow."

I'm killing me, too. There won't be anything left of me after they take off the wings. "I'm sorry."

BAZ

"I'm sorry," Snow says. Like that's a *thing* . . . Like that's a thing that matters.

I push him away with my wand, then pull it back, out of his hand. He lets go.

His cheeks are red, and his chest is flushed and blotchy. The arrow end of his tail is lying on the ground. His wings have fallen.

There's nothing left for me to say. How can I convince him that we're a good thing if he doesn't believe in good things?

It makes me so angry. I'm. So. *Angry.* I've never hated him more. I want to break my knuckles on his chin, I want to cast off his tongue, I want to shove him down a thousand flights of stairs—and then I want to catch him.

"I love you," I say. (And I know it's a not a thing. I know it doesn't matter.)

I turn away from him then, and tuck my wand in my pocket. It's only anger making my legs move. I can't believe he's doing this, I can't believe I'm leaving. I can't believe this is it—that *this* is how we're ending.

It wasn't the Mage. It wasn't the War. It wasn't the Humdrum.

I stop at the door. I look back at Simon one more time.

"I never thought *I'd* be the first thing you ever gave up on."

14

AGATHA

For the first few days I was home, my parents let me hole up in my room without bothering me.

I didn't tell them what happened with Braden and the NowNext. I'm not telling anyone. Penelope can fill out the proper paperwork if she wants; her mother is practically running the World of Mages these days.

I keep expecting a summons. Or for someone to show up and take my official testimony about the incident. The American Incident. I don't *think* I'll be arrested. I didn't intentionally break any rule—it's legal to kill vampires—and Penelope's the one who counterfeited our plane tickets. If anyone deserves to be arrested, it's her. As per usual.

My parents *are* starting to worry about me now . . . My father keeps stopping by my room to talk about his day or to see if I'd like to come down for dinner. My mother keeps asking if I'd like to go shopping.

I would not.

I'm doing exactly what I'd like to do: I'm lying in bed, watching cat videos and ignoring Ginger's text messages, while I twirl my wand first in one hand and then the other.

I dug it out of my top drawer as soon as I got home, and I haven't set it down since. It's teak with a red Bakelite handle. It belonged to my grandfather, my mother's father. He died before I was born, which is why his wand was available. He wasn't much of a magician. Neither am I.

That's all right. I don't need to be. I just need to keep this wand on me, and I need one spell at the tip of my tongue.

I'm not letting it happen again.

By "it," I mean "kidnapped by megalomaniacal vampires." And I also mean "hidden at the bottom of a well because someone was mad at my boyfriend." And: "chased by werewolves." As well as: "treed by a direhog."

Never. Not again. Not one more time.

The next person who touches me is ash. The next thing to look at me funny . . .

There's a stuffed bear sitting on my dresser. One of its eyes is hanging by a thread. Simon gave it to me. He won it for me at a funfair.

I point my wand at it—*"Ashes to ashes, dust to dust!"*

The bear dissolves in a satisfying puff, coating my dresser in soot. Good. Now it matches my duvet and the rug. I may have to leave my room soon; I'm running out of things to point my wand at.

"Agga, darling . . ." My dad has opened my door and is standing there with his arms folded. I don't snap at him. He probably knocked. "Why don't you get dressed," he says cheerfully.

"I am dressed."

"Why don't you get changed, then. I need your help with something."

Well.

This is a dreary scenario. My parents apparently have limits. They've taken charge.

I have a job now.

I'm to go to work every morning with my father, and then hang about his surgery, taking orders from literally everyone. So far today, I've hoovered the waiting area, kept an eye on two toddlers whose mother might have shingles, and learned how to empty the bins. Now I'm answering the phone while the receptionist monitors me to make sure I'm doing it correctly. I've hardly seen my father at all. His waiting room has been full all day.

My dad's the only magickal doctor in this part of England. He went to Normal medical school, too, so magicians come to see him for every sort of ailment.

There isn't a magickal veterinarian in the World of Mages (the only one died a few years ago), so Dad also sees a lot of farm animals and pets. He's got an intern now who's studying to be a magickal vet. A hulking Irish girl with a face like a battleship. She made me clean Exam Four *three times* before she was satisfied.

"Miss Wellbelove." Crowley, there she is again—*Niamh*— looming in the doorway to summon me for some grim new task.

"I can't right now," I say. "I'm covering the phones."

"She's covering the phones," the receptionist agrees, as if she's my new supervisor.

Niamh frowns at me. "Quickly, Miss Wellbelove. Now."

I reluctantly get up to follow her. She's three inches taller than me, and twice as broad, and she wears her hair in a large, dark knot at the back of her head. She's headed for an exam room. The light over the door means a patient is inside.

"I don't have any medical training," I say.

"I'm well aware." She opens the door.

Simon Snow is standing there. Shirtless. Shaking. His devil wings clenched against his back. He's holding a scalpel.

"*Simon?*"

"*Agatha?*" There are more knives on the floor. And broken glass. Cotton swabs. The exam room looks like it's been ransacked. Simon's eyes are wild. "I'm sorry!"

"It's no trouble," Niamh says. "We'll just try again. Wash your hands, Miss Wellbelove."

"I—"

She gives me a pointed look, so I close my mouth and go to wash my hands in the sink.

Simon hands Niamh the scalpel and crouches to pick something else up from the floor—a large saw.

"I've got this," she says, taking it from him. "Sit down, Mr. Snow." She mumbles a spell, and the room rights itself, all the sharp tools flying up onto a tray.

Simon sits at the end of the exam table, looking numb and exhausted. It's the look that used to mean he'd just blown all his magic at once—the look he'd get right after he came to, a burned-out husk. I can practically smell the ozone. (Merlin, Simon used to stink of magic. It turned my stomach.)

Niamh joins me at the sink, pulling another face at me and nodding her head towards Simon. I still have no idea what my role is here, but when she nods his way again, I walk over to him.

Simon glances up at me, then folds his arms over his chest—as if I haven't seen him like this before. I mean, I suppose I *haven't*. Not with the wings. And Simon's thicker now than he used to be. I can't see his ribs.

But I know all this golden skin . . . I've counted these moles.

It's a strange feeling to look at someone's chest and know it's nothing to do with you anymore, but still to remember kissing every inch.

"I didn't expect to see you here," he says.

"Sorry," I say. "I can go."

"No," he says. "Please."

Just as Niamh says, "No. I need your help."

"Sorry," Simon says again, to Niamh. He swallows, and his Adam's apple bobs miserably in his neck.

"Nonsense," she says. "I startled you. We're going to start fresh . . ."

He nods. I stand there uselessly—I don't know what we're starting.

"Now I'm going to extend just the left side," Niamh says, gingerly touching Simon's wing.

Simon flinches—and nearly stabs her in the throat with one of the stony spikes that poke out at the peak of each wing. Niamh frowns at me. She has a fantastic face for frowning: long and wide, with a nose that looks like a prosthetic an actress would wear to win an Oscar. "Miss *Wellbelove*," she says.

Simon's face is pale. His jaw muscles are popping out of his cheeks, and his hands are knotted in fists on his thighs. Niamh tugs at his wing again, and he squeezes his eyes shut.

I touch his hand. "Can I—"

His eyes jerk up to mine, and he nods, clamping my hand

in his. I take his other hand, too, and he squeezes it.

"Does it hurt?" I ask.

He shakes his head. "No. It just"—he shakes his head again—"feels wrong to be touched there."

Niamh has his left wing spread out. It takes up most of the small exam room. She's got a bottle of iodine and a cloth. Has Simon been *injured*? I mean, recently? Penelope and Baz healed all his bullet holes in the desert. Simon and I haven't really talked since . . .

Well, ever. We didn't talk after the Mage died. And we didn't talk much in San Diego. And we haven't talked at all since we got home. I didn't even ask him what my father wanted the other night.

Niamh swabs the back of his wing with her cloth, and his whole body clenches. "All right?" she asks.

"I'm fine," Simon says, white-knuckling my hands. "Niamh's a vet student," he tells me.

I nod. "I know."

"Lucky for me." He's trying to smile. His face is so pale that his skin looks yellow, and there are purple circles under his eyes.

"Lucky for me," Niamh says flatly. "I'd never get a chance to dissect an actual dragon's wings."

Dissect?

Simon's still trying to smile at me. "Don't worry. She's going to take them off first."

Oh. He's having the wings removed. Finally. That makes sense. If I woke up with dragon wings—and a bloody tail— I'd have them taken off before breakfast. Simon's had wings for more than a year, and he doesn't even have magic to hide them. Still . . .

I remember him flying towards me, over the sand. That look on his face, like he wouldn't leave without me. The way he lifted Baz up and away from the fire. Even with no magic.

"Where's Baz?" I ask him. "And Penelope?"

Simon shakes his head, jaw rigid, then turns to speak to Niamh. "I guess I *am* a rare opportunity," he puffs out. "It's not like a dragon will ever show up at A&E with an injured wing . . ."

"If a dragon loses the use of a wing," she says, scrubbing him with the disinfectant, "the other dragons kill it."

Simon flinches.

"Out of mercy," she says, pulling his wing taut again.

"Right," he says.

"That's savage," I say.

She rolls her eyes. "They *are* dragons."

Simon swallows. "I met a dragon once."

"I'm not surprised," Niamh says. "Look here—I'm already done with the back of this one. I told you it'd be quick. I'm moving to the front now." She manoeuvres herself around his wing and starts on the paler leather there.

Simon jumps again. He yanks my hands against his chest—sweet Circe, he's chilled through. I can't remember Simon's skin ever being cold. He used to be a furnace. When I'd sit next to him to watch a film, he'd sweat through his shirt and mine, and his arm would stick to my neck.

He may not be in pain, but he is suffering.

I lift my chin at Niamh. "Why do you have to disinfect his wings if you're just going to cut them off?"

"Surgical procedure," she says.

"But you wouldn't be able to disinfect an animal this way. In the field."

She narrows her already narrow eyes at me. "I would try."

Simon squeezes my hands. "It's all right, Agatha."

It isn't all right. He's trembling. Simon doesn't tremble. "He's clearly uncomfortable."

"Well, it *is* an amputation," she says. "Uncomfortable is rather our best-case scenario."

I lift my chin higher. "Your bedside manner leaves something to be desired, Miss—Niamh."

"No one has ever complained, Miss Wellbelove."

"Have you worked on any *talking* animals?"

"I'm not complaining!" Simon says.

"*Look . . .*" Niamh releases Simon's wing, and it snaps closed so tight, it's practically flat against his back. She frowns at the wing, then frowns at me. "Look," she says again, more calmly. "I'm going to take good care of your boyfriend, I promise. Your father never would have asked me to do this if he didn't trust me."

I let go of Simon's hands—just as he's letting go of mine.

I step away from him. "I—"

"It's *all right.*" Simon has sat up straight. He's squared his shoulders. He still looks badly shaken, but he's spreading his left wing out again and holding it mostly steady. "I trust you, Niamh. I can get through this." He looks at me. "It's all right, Agatha."

"Of course," I say to him, my voice mild again. "I'm sorry."

"No . . ." Simon shakes his head. His shoulders fall a bit. "You shouldn't be. I mean—Agatha. *I'm* sorry. You know?"

Oh.

No.

Not now. Not . . .

Now *I'm* shaking *my* head. And I'm crying. For heaven's

snakes and hell's, too—I told myself I was done crying over Simon Snow.

He holds a hand out to me, and what am I supposed to do, not take it? He reels me in close. "I'm sorry," he says.

"Stop." I'm still crying.

"Agatha, I—"

"Simon, I beg you, please don't choose *now* to start talking about your feelings."

The door to the exam room opens. We both look up—Niamh is stepping out.

"Niamh!" Simon says. "Don't go. Please."

"I can give you a moment." She frowns at us. (That might just be her face; she's trying to be kind, I think.)

"No," he says. "I don't want to lose my nerve."

"Fat chance of that," Niamh says. "I've seen you in action."

"Oh?" Simon looks like he's trying to place her.

"I was at Watford, a few years ahead of you." She glances at me, as if to say, *You, too.* "You saved my life once."

"That's everyone at Watford," I say. "And in the whole World of Mages."

"True enough," she agrees. She smiles tightly at Simon.

"Please," he says. "I'm all right."

Niamh frowns at us more intently, then steps back into the room. She motions towards his wing. "Shall I?"

"Yeah. Just ignore my jumping around, I can't help it."

She picks up the iodine and starts again on the inside of his wing. He shudders, but doesn't pull away. I hold his hand steady.

"Fascinating," Niamh says—to herself, I think. "It's like the inside of a lamb's ear. Covered in fine hair."

"You look like hell," I whisper to Simon.

He smiles. "Thanks."

"When was the last time you slept?"

"I don't know. Utah?"

"Are you caught up in some new trouble?"

"No," he says. "I mean, nothing new."

"Simon . . ."

"Nearly done," Niamh says. She must be rushing it. (Which won't matter at all—she's just cutting them off. I can't believe she doesn't have a spell for this.) She moves to the joint of Simon's wing, the place where it juts out of his back.

He looks like he wants to crawl out of his skin.

"You're *sure* this doesn't hurt?" I ask.

"It's more like someone is sticking their finger down my throat," he says. "Or shoving something wet into my ear. Every instinct I have is screaming, *No!*"

"I wonder if you'll have phantom pains when the wings are gone," Niamh says.

Could she be *less* helpful?

"What did Simon save you from?" I ask her, hoping for a better topic.

"Paindeer," she says.

He nods, still wincing. "Oh, right . . . On the Great Lawn?"

"No, but I was there for that one, too. This was on the lacrosse field. During a practice."

I remember both those attacks. The Humdrum rarely repeated himself, but he fucking loved paindeer.

"They cornered us, against the fence," she says. "Some of us were casting spells, but we were too scared to do much good—" Simon is hunching forward over his knees again. Niamh lifts her cloth from his wing. "Is it better if I'm gentle or firm?"

He clears his throat. "Firm, I think."

She goes back to it, scrubbing harder. The whole room smells like iodine. "You came out of nowhere," she says. "I don't think you used any magic at all. You had that sword . . ."

Simon nods. "I remember that day. Agatha was playing."

I was. It was my first year on the team . . . Did I play lacrosse with *Niamh*?

"The whole herd of them went after you," she says. "We thought you were gone from this world, Mr. Snow. We were all screaming for you to run."

"I don't remember that part," he says. Why *should* he remember that part? Why should one near-death experience stand out from all the others?

"I've never seen anyone fight like that," Niamh goes on. "You didn't stop swinging till they were gone." She stands up straight, holding his wing out to check her work. "It was the most foolhardy thing I've ever witnessed."

Simon is looking down, past our joined hands. Maybe he's trying to remember.

"Right," Niamh says. "Let's do the other wing now. I'll make quick work of it."

Simon pulls his left wing in, and Niamh helps him extend the right. She frowns at it—maybe that's just her thinking face—running her hand along the bony ridge. "You did save our lives, though. Thanks for that."

15

BAZ

"Hello, Basil, you look wretched." My aunt sails past me into the kitchen.

She didn't come home last night. Which means there was no one here to tell me to get up and wash my face and stop listening to the same James Blake song again and again. (I think the neighbours tried—they were banging on the ceiling around 2 A.M., I ignored it.)

I've been lying here on the sofa, uselessly, in a little tribute to Simon Snow. This is apparently what you do when you feel terrible, and you never want to feel better.

I'd say that I've been reliving everything Snow said to me last night—but he didn't say much, did he? It doesn't take long to relive: *"We're done, this is over, I hate the sight of you."*

So I've been reliving all of it, our whole story. Every night I stayed awake to watch him fall asleep, every time I threw a punch just to touch his face . . .

I always knew Snow would ruin me. I thought he'd do it with his hands. That he'd run me through with that bloody sword. (*Ha.* Like Simon Snow would ever settle for a flesh wound.) He had to get me close to finish me off. Our *relationship* was the killing blow.

Did Simon ever love me? I'm not sure.

Would it be worse if he never loved me—or if he loves me still, but doesn't want to be with me?

As soon as I decide which is worse, I'll know which is true.

Fuck, this is bad. It's so bad. It hasn't been bearable for even a breath.

I thought I was ready for it—losing him. I thought I'd been bracing for it, for months. But I couldn't know how awful it would be. And I have a feeling it's just starting, that I'm still in the slow-motion part of it—that scene in a film where someone takes a bullet, then it takes ten seconds for their face to fall and another eternity before they clutch their chest. I'm in that scene, and my hand hasn't even reached my heart yet. I'm still opening my mouth to scream.

"Turn off that music!" Fiona shouts from the next room. "No emo shit in my flat."

I *am* emo shit. "This is electronic soul," I mutter.

"It's crap!"

I sit up and rub my face with my shirt. I should corner Fiona while I have a chance. I should make sure she doesn't get arrested again. I should talk to her about Daphne. The world hasn't stopped turning just because I'm dead and slowly dying. It could still get worse.

I stand up, and the blood drains from my head. I give myself a second, then walk into the kitchen. The kettle's on, and Fiona's reaching into the fridge.

"Where have you been?" I ask.

"Working. I do have a job." My aunt is a vampire hunter

now. The Coven gave her a warrant card. At some point, I should probably talk to her—I should probably talk to *someone*—about what I've learned about vampires. (The fact that they may not all be murderers. That some of them are more like sexy bedbugs.) If I thought Fiona was any good at vampire hunting, I'd make it a higher priority.

I lean heavily on the open refrigerator door, resting my elbows on it. "That's why you've ignored my texts all week? Too busy working?"

She stands up, holding milk in one hand and ham in the other. She's got a plum in her mouth. She shrugs.

I relieve her of the milk. "Fiona."

She spits out the plum. "Is this about your stepmother? Christ, is that what's got you all cut up?"

"What do you know about Daphne? Have you spoken to her?"

Fiona drops the ham onto the counter and starts slapping together a sandwich. "What I *know* is that your father's marriage isn't any of your business."

"I've been talking to Mordelia—"

"Who is *not* my blood relative."

"Well, she's mine, and she hasn't seen her mother in weeks. From what I can tell, Daphne's either joined a cult or run off with another man."

"Neither would surprise me." Fiona gets out two mugs and goes for the kettle. "You know, under the old laws, your father is still married to your mother; those children aren't even legitimate . . ."

I drop into a chair at the kitchen table, rubbing my forehead. "Curses, you're impossible. Daphne is a lovely person."

Fiona "pffft"s and sits across from me with her sandwich.

She shoves a mug of tea in my direction. "Doesn't make her your business. You can't interfere in a marriage, Baz, legitimate or otherwise. If Daphne and your father are having troubles, that's for them to work out."

I press my fingers into my eyes.

"You really do look frightful," she says, still chewing. "Do you need to, you know . . ."

I need to replace every single person in my life with someone more functional, is what I need. "Do I need to what?"

"You *know* . . ." she says.

Is my aunt asking me if I need to get *laid*?

She pushes her eye teeth over her bottom lip. "*You* know."

"Oh, for fuck's sake."

She holds up both her hands, in surrender. One is holding a ham sandwich. "Just looking out for you. No need to get chippy."

"No, I don't need to *you know*." I do, actually, but this isn't something we just *talk about*. "I need you to focus. What if Daphne's got herself into real trouble?"

Fiona rolls her eyes and takes another bite. "Your stepmum's fine. She isn't the first person to have their head turned by the latest Chosen One. You know plenty about that."

I sit up. "Wait. What do you mean."

Fiona stops chewing. "Nothing. It was just a figure of speech."

"Figure of bollocks. What do you know, Fiona?"

She sits back, sighing, and working her tongue at her teeth like something is stuck there. "It really isn't our business, Basil."

"Tell me anyway."

She sighs again. "All right . . . Well . . ." She sighs one more time. "I've heard your stepmother might be caught up in one of those Chosen One groups."

"*What* Chosen One groups?"

"Is this actually news to you?"

"I don't even know enough to know what you're talking about!"

Fiona leans over the table. "The whole World of Mages thought your boyfriend had come to save them from a bad end, that he fulfilled thousands of years of prophecy . . ."

He isn't my boyfriend, I think. "He isn't the Chosen One," I say—though I still half believe that he was.

She waves a hand in the air. "Well, we all know that now, don't we? But thousands of years of prophecy don't just go away. This is an excellent time to get into the Chosen One business. Everybody's got a pet theory or a pet candidate."

"So Daphne . . . what? Ran off with some new golden boy?"

Fiona shrugs. "I've heard whispers. There's a lot of this going around. The Coven sent me to talk to Lady Salisbury last week—her son's missing. It looked like vampires, but old Ruth is sure he's joined one of these cults. They do prey on the daft and the gormless . . ."

"Daphne's hardly gormless."

Fiona raises her eyebrows like she's refusing to comment.

"And you really don't care?" I ask. "That she's abandoned her marriage to chase some charlatan?"

"Who says he—or perhaps *she*—is a charlatan? Someone has to be the Chosen One. Maybe your stepmum's got it right." Fiona pushes the rest of her sandwich into her mouth. "All I'm saying is, when someone runs off like this, they're usually running *from* something as much as they're running *to.* I'm not telling Daphne Grimm how to live her life, even if she is as thickheaded as she is thin-blooded." Fiona washes her last bite down with tea, then stands, brushing her hands on her jeans. "Right then, I'm off."

"But you just got here."

"I came by to check on you, and now I have. You look a mess."

"Where are you going?"

She's walking away. "Work."

"Vampire hunting? On a Monday afternoon?"

"Something like that. Drink your tea, and mind your business." She turns back to me. "And—"

"Don't say it."

"Eat something." She winks.

16

BAZ

The good thing about my aunt's terrible flat is that I can do some light hunting without even leaving the building. I just have to dispose of the empty rodents when I'm done.

Fiona let me move in here after I left Watford. Simon and I didn't want to live together; that seemed premature—even though we'd shared a single room for eight years. Maybe that's *why* it seemed like a bad idea. Some distance seemed prudent.

Still . . . I didn't expect to be sleeping in my aunt's flat *every* night. I didn't expect to become so accustomed to the night bus back to Chelsea.

Simon needed time. He needed care. He still startled at bright lights and sudden noises. And prolonged eye contact. He'd get jumpy when we were alone together. He'd actually shudder if I touched him too softly—and not a good shudder. (My kingdom for a good shudder.)

On the worst days, on the even worse nights, I used

to think about all the bad things that have happened to Simon—just the ones I know about. And then I'd wonder about all the terrible things that have happened to him that I *don't* know about. Twenty years of bad things. How long would it take for those painful memories to die back? Or, at least, to wither?

I'd wait.

I was going to wait.

The neighbours are tired of my music again. They've come to the door this time. Well, they can push right off—James Blake is a Mercury Prize winner, and this song was written by Joni Mitchell, surely Canada's finest. They think they're tired of this song? Once I figure out the magic, I'm going to loop the same two lines again and again:

"You're in my blood, you're my holy wine. You taste so bitter and so sweet."

That's the part that hurts the most, and I've decided that it *helps* to hurt the most. It sort of maxes out my nerve endings.

They're knocking on the door. *Fuck off.*

More knocking. *Seriously, fuck off.*

I turn up the music. I have to use a spell to do it, because the speakers are already at their limit. ***"These go to eleven!"***

The neighbours are really banging on the door now. I should spell off their hands. I'm not even going to answer the door—I'll just spell their hands off from here.

Wait . . . They've stopped.

Have they stopped?

There's no knocking . . .

No knocking . . .

I think they've given up. Good. Go back to your flat, and

get used to this. This is our soundtrack now. Oh—my favourite part is coming around again. Sing it, James.

"You're in my blood, you're my holy—"

Knocking! Fucking *pounding* on the door!

I jump off the couch. My head spins. I give myself a moment. More bloody knocking. I plow over to the door and yank it open. My fangs might be out, I can't be held responsible.

Simon Snow is standing there.

About to knock again.

His hand drops.

"Baz," he says. He looks down at me. "You haven't changed."

SIMON

Baz is still wearing the clothes he had on yesterday. He's wrinkled looking, and his hair is stringy. "What?" he says. I think that's what he says. It's so loud inside his flat, I can't hear him.

"What?" I shout.

I can't make out his next sentence.

"*What?*" I say again. "Why is it so loud in there?"

Baz walks away from me, into the living room. He turns down the music. His arms are folded when he comes back, and he's sneering. "Oh. Snow. You're still here. I expected you to run and hide as soon as my back was turned."

I lift my chin. "I deserve that."

"You deserve worse. Why are you here?"

I try to sound more steady than I feel. "I came to tell you something."

He huffs. "You've already told me enough."

"Baz—"

"Unless you've thought of another way to say that you don't want to be with me."

"Baz, I—"

Baz keeps talking. His top lip is curled so sharply, it looks like someone snagged it with a fishhook. "Because that would be unnecessary, Snow. Message received!"

"I'm sorry!"

"Also unnecessary!"

"Baz!"

He shouts at me: "I don't care that you're sorry! Do you understand that, Simon? It makes no difference to me whether you feel regret or not! You're sorry? What do I care? What can I *do* with that? You came here to tell me you're *sorry*?"

"No!" I really didn't. "Listen—"

"Listen? I have been listening. I've spent the last year listening, and you didn't have anything to say to me. You couldn't assemble a complete sentence until you'd already left me. And now you're back to say you're sorry? Guess what? You already put that in your note. It didn't matter then either!"

"*No*," I growl. I know it's a growl because that's what Baz calls it when I sound like this. I grab him by the front of his shirt. "I didn't come here to say I'm sorry—I came to tell you that you were right!"

He didn't even flinch when I grabbed him. He's sneering down at me like I'm miles beneath him.

"Of course I was," he says.

He shoves me back and slams the door in my face.

BAZ

I let my forehead fall against the door. I'm panting. Maybe I'm hyperventilating. I haven't had enough food, water, or blood for this. I can't get enough air.

Simon came to see me.

After saying he hated the sight of me.

Simon came to say he was *sorry*.

(Which really is worthless. And more about making him feel better than making me feel anything. And *fuck him* if he thinks—)

He came to tell me I was *right* . . .

I open the door again. He's still standing there.

"What was I right about?" I demand. "And you better make this clear and to the point, for once in your magic-forsaken life."

Simon looks tired. He's wearing baggy jeans and a Watford hoodie and someone has spelled his wings invisible—or maybe they're already gone.

He pushes his shoulders back and points that square chin at me. "You were right, Baz. I never tried."

SIMON

Baz doesn't say anything.

I meet his grey eyes. As hard as it is. As hard as they are. As much as I feel like I don't have the right.

"I've just been waiting for you to get tired of me," I say. "Since the day I lost my magic. Before that, even. I never thought—" I shake my head. "I never really thought this would work."

Baz is shaking his head, too, just slightly, like he's quietly rejecting every word. "I thought you'd go down fighting if you believed in something . . ."

He's right, he's always right. I look him in the eye. "I never believed in us."

BAZ

I didn't think there was anything left that Simon could say to hurt me . . .

I was wrong.

I laugh and wipe my eyes. "Seven snakes," I say. "What a thing to hear. Fuck, Snow . . ." I bring my arm up and laugh into my elbow, sobbing.

Simon's mouth is hanging open. "No," he says. "I mean . . ." He reaches out a hand but doesn't touch me. "What I mean is, as soon as I turned against the Mage, I left *the map*. It was like I walked right out of the story everyone had been telling about me. I started losing, and I didn't stop. You felt like something I grabbed on my way down—but I never believed I'd get to *keep* you. I didn't get to keep anything . . . What did I get to *keep*, Baz?"

Simon is crying, too, but he doesn't wipe his tears. Just licks away the ones that hit his lips.

"I didn't try," he says, "because I thought it would be worse if I tried. I told myself to enjoy it—*you*—while I could. But that didn't work. It felt like eighth year again, waiting for the Humdrum to attack. The waiting . . . I'm not good at waiting."

I rub my nose against my sleeve. I nod. I know.

"I just wanted to, like, *make it happen*," he says. "To like, charge into it and get it over with. Whenever we were together, I just wanted to get it all over with."

I laugh again. The hits keep coming.

Simon shoves his hand up into the front of his hair and pulls. "*Stop*," he says. "I know how that sounds. That's not how I mean it!"

"No." I shake my head. "I know. I know how you mean it. It still hurts."

He looks in my eyes. He's hardly looked away. "Baz"—his voice is small—"do you think it would have been different if I'd *tried*?"

SIMON

He doesn't answer me. I shouldn't have come here. Nothing I've said *changes* anything, I was a berk to think it would—

But I haven't been able to get it out of my head, what he said. That he was the first thing I ever gave up on. *He's right.* I didn't give up on Agatha—I waited until she gave up on me. I fought whatever the Humdrum threw at me. I did whatever the Mage asked of me. I gave myself wings because I couldn't stop fighting.

Why haven't I ever fought for Baz?

What would happen if I did?

Baz takes a step back, into the living room. His hand is on the door. And he's looking at me the way he did in my flat last night, like I've got a knife in his heart, and I'm holding it there.

Then his head falls forward a bit, and he tilts it away from me. "Come on," he says softly. "Come in."

BAZ

Snow doesn't move.

I back out of his way. "Come on. We don't have to do this in the hall."

He steps over the threshold and seems to wait for me to change my mind. I close the door behind him, so he has to come all the way in. (I still might change my mind, I don't know.) Then I sit at one end of the sofa and wave my hand at the other end.

He hesitates some more, still standing with his feet apart and his shoulders back. Battle mode.

When I clear my throat, he finally moves—taking the spot on the far end of the sofa and leaning forward with his elbows on his knees. (He's moving stiffly. I wonder if he's sore. I wonder if Dr. Wellbelove took his tail as well.) He scrubs at the caramel-coloured curls at the top of his head. They already look thoroughly scrubbed.

"I could make tea," I say.

"No," he says. "Just"—he makes a fist in his hair—"say it."

"Say what?"

"That it wouldn't have mattered. That it doesn't matter."

I turn more fully towards him. My voice is getting haughty again, I can't help it. "The question on the table is whether it would have *mattered*, to our relationship, if you had *tried*?"

He looks over at me, infernal chin raised. "Yeah."

"Of fucking course it would have mattered!" I say. "What kind of question is that?"

He's nodding, too quickly, looking at my aunt's rug. "Right. Right. Of course." He scrapes his fingers up the back of his hair to the top of his head. "Right."

I want to grab his wrists. I want to shake him. (I want to cast spells over his shoulders and make every pain in his body go away.)

"*I* was trying," I say. "Every minute."

Simon nods. "I know. I'm sorry."

"Don't."

"All right. Sorry. I mean. Just—"

Use your words, Snow.

He turns on the sofa, pulling one leg up, to face me. His fists have dropped to his thighs. "How?"

"How what?"

He looks in my eyes. He looks like a dog trapped in a snare. Like he's begging me to set him free from something. "*How* would it have been different if I'd tried?"

I huff out a breath. "I can't answer that. How would I know that?"

"Baz . . ."

"What do you *want* from me, Snow?"

He's breathing through his teeth. "I just—"

"You just."

"I mean—"

"You mean." I wonder if I sound cruel. I wonder if I mean to be.

"*I want to try!*"

SIMON

That came out wrong. Like a threat. Like an armed robbery.

Baz is looking down at his lap. He pushes a lock of black hair behind his ear.

"It's okay," I spit out, trying to reel things back. "I don't expect—You don't owe me—"

"Shut *up*, Snow."

I shut up.

I think Baz is still crying.

I'm so bad at this. At people. At him. I shouldn't have come here. I stand up—

His hand latches on to my wrist. "Don't you dare."

I sit down again. "Okay. Sorry."

Baz doesn't let go. His hand is cold. He's still looking at his lap. "What does that mean?" He sounds careful. "That you want to try?"

"Just what I said. That I want—That I wish I could—That I would like to—" I clench my jaw for a second. "*Try*. With you. To *see* . . . if it could be different."

"Why?"

"Because I don't want to give up."

Baz scowls up at me. "Am I a video game you're trying to beat?"

"No!"

He pulls on my arm, but doesn't pull me close. "Then why?"

"Because you were right! I didn't try. I gave up on us. And I can't—I can't live with myself—"

"I don't care!"

I take Baz's other hand. By the wrist. He's holding me back, and I'm holding on to him. "I can't go on, Baz, knowing that it could have been different!"

"That sounds like another apology."

I look in his cold, grey eyes. I beg him to understand. I'm growling again, I know it. "I want to . . . *try*. Because—Because *I love you, Baz.* I love you, and I didn't think that I could *keep* you. But if there's a chance . . . If there's any chance at all . . . I *can't*—I *want*—I *need*—"

Baz's hand goes slack on my arm.

I let go of him.

I push my palms into my eyes. They're wet—how long have I been crying? Baz isn't saying anything, and I'm not sure what I'm supposed to do now. I drop my hands and look up at him, desperate for a clue.

Baz's mouth is slightly open, and his eyebrows have pulled up in the middle. "You . . . *love* me?"

BAZ

Snow nods. "Yeah," he says, "of course."

Like it's obvious.

It isn't obvious. It has not been obvious.

"You never said," I say.

"Haven't I?"

"No."

He frowns. "I thought—I mean . . . I've killed *so many* things for you."

I laugh. It might be another sob, but maybe it's just a laugh. "What are you, a house cat? Am I supposed to know how you feel because you brought me a mouse?"

The corner of Snow's mouth twitches. "I brought you a cow once, remember? And I killed that chimera for you in fifth year."

"You killed it *near* me. There's a difference."

He reaches a hand up towards my face, then hesitates.

I hesitate, too—I feel torn in every direction—then I slowly close the distance.

Snow's thumb connects with my chin. He tucks his knuckles under my jaw. He swallows, and it's a whole show. "I do," he says. "Love you."

I close my eyes for a moment. Like I'm trying to trap his words in my head. Then I open them again. "What about . . . everything else?"

"What else?"

"Everything you said last night. About magic."

"Oh. Well, I meant all of that. I still mean it."

I shake my head. "Fucking hell, Snow."

He holds on to my chin. "I don't want to live in the World of Mages, Baz—I want a Normal life. But maybe we could, like, meet in between?"

"In between."

"Like, you do your thing. Magic. And I'll do mine. And we don't have to talk about it all the time."

"You said it makes you miserable, that I remind you of everything you've lost."

"Well, I can work on that."

"Can you?"

"Yeah . . ." He reaches his fingers up my cheek and sucks one side of his bottom lip into his mouth. (It's an entire Joni Mitchell song. It's a Mercury Prize.) "*Yeah*," he says, letting his lip go. "Maybe when I feel that way, I'll turn it into being glad that I didn't lose you, as well."

I raise an eyebrow at him. "This is you trying, isn't it?"

"I suppose." There's a lightness in his expression that I haven't seen for so long. I want more of it. Even if I can't trust it.

"If we do this"—my chin hits his palm with every sylla-ble—"I want the full Simon Snow treatment."

"What does that mean?"

"I want the locked jaw. The squinty eyes. The shoulders."

He wrinkles his forehead. "The shoulders?"

"I want you to slay a dragon before you give up on me, do you understand?"

"I thought you didn't like it when I slew dragons . . ."

I press my hands into Snow's chest and clutch them in his jumper. "I want you to try *everything* before you give up on us again."

He rubs his thumb below my lip. "I won't give up, Baz. Unless you tell me to. Unless you're, like, *really clear* that you want me to. And even then, I won't give up. I'll just persist from a distance."

"You can't put me through this again, Simon. I don't want to spend my whole life, losing you. Watching you slip away. I never want to come home to another note."

"You won't." He shakes his head. "I promise. I won't."

I wish I could believe him—what would it take for me

to believe him? And what do I need in the meantime, what am I willing to withstand? (How would someone with *pride* answer these questions . . .)

I close my eyes. My voice is low. "I'm not saying you have to stay with me forever. But you can't just give up without a fight."

"I'm so sorry, Baz."

I push and pull on his jumper. His forehead thunks against mine. I nod. "Okay," I whisper.

"Okay?" he whispers back.

"Okay, Snow. We'll try. We'll try this with you trying."

"Yeah?"

I nod against him. "Yeah."

"*Okay.*" He exhales roughly against my lips, then takes another shuddering breath. "Christ, I'm so scared."

"Already? Don't we get a day of clinging to each other before things fall apart again?"

Simon laughs over my mouth. He's been drinking orange juice. He needs a shower. He smells like a locker room and a back alley and something bleachy.

"I don't—" he says, looking down. "I—"

His hair is in my eyes. I brush my nose against his.

He starts again: "I don't know how not to be afraid that you'll leave me."

I scoff. "*I* won't leave *you*. When have I ever left?"

"You can't know how it will be," he says, head hanging. "Over time. You might not want me once you don't have to worry about me leaving."

Who even knew Simon was capable of such mental gymnastics? "You have a real genius for catastrophizing, Snow."

"Is that the same as having a genius for catastrophes? Because, obviously. How many times has Penny's mum said so?"

I pull back so he can see me. "I'm not going to get *tired* of you."

"You can't *know* that," he says, bumping my nose with his forehead.

"I *can*. Look at me." I catch his chin. I wait for his blue eyes to settle on mine. "This thing between us didn't start with us dating. It didn't even start when you kissed me. You're in me so deep, I wouldn't know how to dig you out. I may get fed up with you . . . But, Simon, I'll never get *tired* of you."

His hand is still on my face. He traces his thumb under my eye. "Penelope always says that the best predictor of future behaviour is past behaviour."

"Penelope didn't say that. Everyone says that."

"I *literally* destroy *literally* everything I touch."

"That's an overstatement."

"I fuck it up, Baz, with everyone. Look what I did to Agatha. And the Mage. Merlin, who knows what happened with my own parents . . ."

"There is so much to unpack in that sentence."

He laughs, but he looks miserable again.

I tug at his jumper. "Stop feeling sorry for yourself, Snow. You're not allowed to feel sorry for yourself as long as you get to have me."

I mean it. I'm thinking about kissing him, to drive the point home, but I'm gun-shy and unsure of my permissions. Maybe we have to build back up to kissing. Maybe Snow needs a high-speed chase to get him in the mood.

I'm thinking about it. About what I'm allowed. And what I deserve. And what I can stand—

And then *he* kisses *me*.

I kiss him back.

And back.

And back.

17

SIMON

I was worried that Baz wouldn't want to kiss me—but it turns out, that wasn't an issue.

He held my face with both hands, and I held his, and we kissed until my chin hurt from pushing into him. Baz can probably kiss for days without getting sore. With his superhuman vampire chin. His lips don't even get puffed up.

We've stopped kissing now, but we're still holding on to each other. I think we're both afraid to pull away.

Baz smells terrible. Like day-old sweat, but also like day-old raw meat. I'm trying to remember if he's *ever* smelled bad before. I don't mind it, really. More proof that he isn't dead.

He's rubbing the corner of my mouth. "You're bleeding," he says, looking worried. "Did I cut you?"

I shake my head. "I think that's from you. You've got a little . . ." I rub at the blood lingering near his chin.

"Oh, fuck!" he says, turning away from me and covering his mouth. "That's rat blood. I got *rat blood* in your mouth."

I try to pull him back by the shoulders. "Hey, I don't mind."

"You don't mind *rat blood*?"

I shrug. "I'll brush my teeth."

"Fat lot of good that'll do against the plague." He's still pulling away.

"Don't go," I say. "Not yet."

Baz's shoulders soften in my hands. He lets me turn him back. He lets me touch his chin, his cheeks. His hand is still over his mouth—I kiss it. I'm so relieved to still be here, I can feel it rolling off me in waves. I'm surprised it's not visible.

"I need a shower," Baz says. "I haven't cleaned up since Oxford."

"I'm kind of enjoying it." I grin. "I didn't know you *could* get rank."

He rolls his eyes, and shoves at me. "You need a shower, too. You smell like—actually I don't know what you smell like. Something corrosive."

"It's my wings," I say.

His face falls. And so does his hand. I lick my thumb and scrape the rest of the rat blood from his mouth.

"Does it hurt?" he asks. He's looking at my shoulder.

I shake my head. "Oh, uh—*no*. I mean, I didn't have it done yet. I chickened out."

It wasn't quite like that. I didn't chicken out. It was more like I got overwhelmed. I couldn't stop thinking about what Baz had said and how I needed to talk to him. Immediately. It felt like some window was closing. It was probably already closed, and I'd need to break it open. And what if I needed my wings somehow? To get to him?

I told Niamh I was sorry, said good-bye to Agatha, and left.

Baz sits up tall and reaches around my shoulder to where my wings are flattened against my back. He hasn't touched me there since I walked in. "I thought these were bandages," he says, patting them.

"No. Just my wings. They, like, pulled in super tight when the doctor was trying to clean them. Some sort of panic response, I think."

"Could you do this on purpose?" He's probing my back with his fingers, one eyebrow cocked. "If you could, you wouldn't even need a spell to hide them—they're hardly noticeable like this."

"Pfft, I look like that Disney character with the droopy eye."

He stares at me for a second. "*Quasimodo?*"

"Yeah, him."

He rolls his eyes again. "All right, maybe, but you don't look like a dragon."

"They're so bunched up, I'm afraid to move them. It hurts a bit." I pull my hoodie and T-shirt up over my head and turn, so Baz can see my bare back.

"Circe . . ." he says.

He touches me there, and I wince.

"They're folded up like origami, Snow. How is that possible?"

"How is any of it possible? Dragons are magic, I reckon."

Baz runs his hand up one wing to the bony black talon that's curled against my shoulder. "Is this where it hurts?"

"No, it's more like a muscle cramp, in the wings themselves."

"Maybe from clenching them so tight?"

"Yeah, maybe."

"You're sticky," he says. "There's this orange film . . ."

"That's the Betadine. The disinfectant."

"So you *did* go in for the surgery?"

I glance at him over my shoulder. "Yeah. I went. And then . . . Well. I needed to come here. I'm still going to do it, have them off, but I—I needed to talk to you."

I feel something against my wings and crank my head back. Baz is kissing me. Well, he's kissing the wings. Down one side. Slowly. And . . . Up . . . The other.

It feels like he's kissing the inside of my ear. Or the back of my throat.

I shudder.

Baz puts his arms around my waist, and holds me there.

"You'll get Betadine on your mouth," I say.

His voice is low: "Probably needs it."

It's too much. My skin is crawling, and my wings are flinching. I'm worried they're going to fly out, like someone opening a spiked umbrella in his face. I pull his hands apart at my stomach and turn around. His lips really are orange; it makes me laugh.

"We should take a shower," I say.

Baz raises an eyebrow.

My cheeks get hot. "I mean, we should both take showers. Like you said. Can I—I mean, this is your aunt's place, right? Does she have a shower? Would she mind?"

18

BAZ

Snow has never been to my flat, not in all the time we've been together—too far from his beloved sofa, I assumed. Also, I suppose there was the risk of my aunt trying to kill him if she found him here. (Fiona still hasn't forgiven Simon for being the Mage's No. 1 henchman and for helping to arrest some of my second cousins.) (I mean, fair enough.)

He's standing in my bedroom door now, probably thinking about how little there is to take in: A couple of racks of clothes. My violin. The down duvet and pillows from my room in Hampshire.

Since I left Watford and moved to London, I've spent most of my free time at Simon and Penny's place—I even studied there. All I really needed here was a bed.

I dig out some clean clothes for Simon to borrow and point him towards the bathroom connecting my room and Fiona's. He can have the first shower.

While he's in there, I make him a plate of ham sandwiches.

I should eat, too—and I should probably hunt again. More substantially. But I don't want to walk away from Simon right now. What if he's not here when I return?

I hear it from the kitchen when the shower stops. It takes me back to Watford. To lying in my bed, knowing Snow had just finished his shower. Bracing for him to come out, all damp and surly. Telling myself that I wasn't going to *look* at him. That I wasn't going to *care*. And always doing both.

When I walk back to my bedroom, Simon is dressed and sitting tentatively at the edge of my mattress. Damp. Nervous. He looks like a dog who knows he isn't supposed to be on the bed.

He's wearing one of my old football shirts. (Have I manipulated this whole scenario just to see Snow in my Watford shirt? Perhaps. Take it up with the courts.) He must have pulled his wings in tight again, because he's got the shirt stretched over them. They're hanging out below the hem. It doesn't look comfortable.

I motion at his back, walking closer. "I can fix that shirt for you—"

"I don't want to ruin it."

"I don't mind." I don't. Then it would be *his* shirt, and he might wear it again. My name on his back, my number. I've already got my wand out and pointed at him.

Simon lifts up his hands, suddenly distressed. "Baz, *no*."

"Oh," I say, looking down at my wand. "Is this bad? Do you not want me to . . . *magic*? Around you?"

His hands drop. "No, I mean—Yeah, of course you can, you know, magic. I just—" He shakes his head, like he's clearing it. "You know what? Go ahead. Do it. I'd like to spread my wings out a bit anyway."

"If you're certain."

Simon takes my wrist and points my wand at his chest, so I cast the spell—*"Like a glove!"*—and the shirt refits itself around his wings. It looks very tidy. I can reverse the spell, too, but even when Penelope and I help Simon like this, he ends up cutting himself out of his clothes later; he won't ask for our help getting undressed. (I should have just cut vents in the shirt for his wings, to make it easier for him. I could do that with magic, too.)

He arches his back and sighs. His wings unfurl behind him.

I remember thinking at first that it was too bad Simon gave himself *dragon* wings. He could have gone with something far more elegant. Pegasus wings—soft, white feathers tipped with sky blue. Or green fairy wings that shimmer in the moonlight.

But in the moment that he needed to fly, Simon summoned brute force and sharp edges. Red leather and bony black spikes. Now it's ridiculous to think of him with anything else. Simon Snow with white feathers—absurd. He'd look like a cartoon angel. Or a Victoria's Secret model . . .

"Is it all right that I'm sitting here?"

I shake my head. Then switch to nodding it. "Of course," I say. "Make yourself at home. There are sandwiches in the kitchen. The kettle's on."

"Right," Simon says. "Thanks."

I nod again, backing towards the bathroom door. "I'll just be a minute."

The bathroom is still steamed up from Simon's shower, and I swoon a little, thinking about him in here, even though it smells like he used my aunt's shampoo. (Smoke and mirrors, how did I survive sharing a room with Simon Snow through my entire adolescence?) (Oh, yes, I remember: furious wanking. Furious everything.) I wash up more thoroughly than usual. Paranoid about the rat blood. And the fact that Simon said I smelled "rank." I'm rather less thorough than usual with my hair, just towel drying it and combing it off my face. Chomsky, I used to spend so much time on my hair every morning when Snow and I shared a room . . . Carefully parting it and slicking it back. I thought it looked dramatic.

When I walk out of the bathroom, Simon is on my bed again. He's got the plate of sandwiches, and there's a pot of tea on the side table (sitting right on top of a stack of books, for pity's sake). I clear my throat. "You didn't have to bring them in—"

"Oh." He stands up. "I thought that's what you . . ." He picks up the plate and motions towards the door. "Should I?"

"No, it's fine. This is fine. Better to stay out of Fiona's path, anyway. Aren't you hungry?"

"I was waiting for you."

"Oh." Why is this so strange? Why am *I* being so strange? "Thank you." I take the plate from him and sit down against my pillows, crossing my legs and setting the sandwiches beside me.

Simon sits next to me, careful not to upset the plate. He's pushed down the waist of his trousers to free his tail—and pulled down his shirt to hide how low his trousers are riding. It must wear him out, the constant adjusting and manoeuvring and tucking. He's got his wings held close to his body to keep from knocking everything off the bedside table as he pours me a mug of tea.

Our fingers touch when he hands it to me. I'd be blushing if I had enough blood in me. Why am I being so *weird*. Is it just relief? Is it the novelty of having Simon here? In my room? Or is it because we're starting over, so everything feels new?

I pick up half a ham sandwich, and take a second to control my fangs before taking a bite. (I'm getting better at this.) Simon takes a sandwich as soon as I do, and shoves most of it into his mouth. He bites down, and his face lights up. He's kissing my cheek now, holding his tea out to the side, so it won't spill.

"What's that about?" I ask.

He noses at my ear. Softly: "There's butter on these ham sandwiches."

"I thought you liked them that way."

He nips at me. "I do."

Then he pulls back, still smiling. What a ridiculous creature. Happy that I put butter on his sandwich. As if I wouldn't make the world spin backwards if I thought he'd like it better that way.

"I haven't eaten since last night," he says, taking another sandwich.

"I haven't eaten since the train yesterday."

"That's not true, you had rats."

"I didn't *eat* them," I say.

"Maybe you should. There'd be less waste."

"Maybe *you* should eat them. Then it could be something we do together."

Snow laughs. He's curling towards me as he eats. His legs are tucked up, and he's leaning on me, his left wing pushing behind my shoulder. I move forward a bit, and he spreads it out, wrapping it around my back. The inside of his wings is softer than the outside. It's rather like being wrapped in a suede blanket.

I can feel myself tensing up. Moments like this with Simon are so few and far between, and I never know what will startle him out of one. Or when he'll collapse entirely. It's like trying to be in a relationship with one of those fields Princess Diana was always drawing worthy attention to—the war is over, the armies have gone home, but no one knows where the mines are buried.

What does it even *mean* that Simon's going to try now?

How does a minefield *try*?

He picks up the last sandwich and offers me half. I take it, and he moves the plate away, pulling his legs up closer. Then he says, "This is what people are talking about when they talk about make-up sex, isn't it?"

I choke on my tea. "Not exactly."

He laughs at me. "No, I mean . . . It's like when you think you're going to die—like, you're *sure* you're about to lose your head—and then, at the last minute, you don't. The other guy bites it instead. And it feels like you cheated somehow—"

"Knowing you, you probably *did* cheat somehow."

"—but you're still *alive,* and everything feels so amazing and, like, *urgent*. Like, you can't believe how lucky you are to breathe, and you just want to breathe all the air at once."

"Most people," I muse, "have more experience with make-up sex than with near beheadings."

He laughs. "Well, I get it now. The whole concept."

He's holding his mug with both hands. I am, too.

I lean against his shoulder, looking down at my tea, attempting to appear casual. "It could always be like this."

"I don't think so," Snow says. "This is '*I nearly lost my head and then I didn't*' euphoria."

"Nah." I brush the outside of my knuckles against his. "I can promise you 'this' on a regular basis. A hot shower and luke-warm tea? Ham sandwiches in bed? This is table stakes, Snow."

He catches my fingers in his. "Baz . . ." His voice drops to a near whisper. "I don't know what happens next."

I shake my head. "Me neither."

He pulls at my fingers. His eyebrows are down. Like he's thinking hard, or trying not to. "I guess," he says after a moment, "we just go along until I feel like running away.

And then I stay and fight instead."

"Who are you fighting in this scenario?"

"Myself, I suppose."

I nod, in part to hide how discouraged I feel all of a sudden. It won't help to say so.

"Baz?" Simon says eventually.

"Yeah."

"Can we take a nap?"

"Oh." I sit up, away from him. "I mean, yeah."

"It's just"—he looks apologetic—"I haven't slept since . . . I don't know, really."

"Yeah, me neither." I take his cup and reach for the plate. "You take the bed. Fiona won't be surprised to see me on the sofa—"

"No. *Baz.*" He grabs my arm. "Stay."

"But your wings . . ." Simon almost never lets me sleep next to him. He says it's because he thrashes around. "I thought you didn't want to impale me."

He's making an effort to smile. "I won't toss much during a nap. Besides, you're pretty hard to kill."

I take a breath to think about it, but I don't get much thinking or breathing done. "All right," I say out loud. Then I say it a few more times to myself. *Right. All right.*

I set down our dishes and look around. I don't have to close the shades—I keep them closed all day—but I turn off the lamp next to my bed, then stand up and pull back the duvet. Simon catches on and pushes it down, tucking his feet under. I slide in next to him, and tug it up over us. It's strange to be under the covers like this. Him in joggers, me in jeans. It's strange because we don't *do* this. We never quite got to this stage. The boyfriends-being-boyfriends stage. Naps and cuddles and wearing each other's clothes. Simon lies on his side, with his wings behind him, and pulls the duvet up under them as far as it will go.

"You need a special blanket with wing slots," I say.

"Like a Snuggie for demons."

"Or angels. Do your shoulders get cold?"

He shakes his head and stretches his right wing out, wrapping it snugly around us. It reminds me of Utah, of the back of Shepard's truck.

"It's only a few more days," he says. "Then I can pull the covers up all the way. I'll be able to wear normal clothes again—I'm gonna buy myself a leather jacket to celebrate."

"Very cool," I say. "You'll look like Danny Zuko. Or a bad boy celebrity chef."

"I know you're making fun of me, but I *am* going to look really cool . . ." He shifts his wing back behind him and wraps his arm around me instead. I find a way to slide one arm under his neck. We're breathing each other's air. It's a little claustrophobic.

"Are you comfortable?" he asks softly.

"No," I whisper.

"Me neither."

"But don't move," I say. "Not yet."

He shakes his head. "Not yet."

I wake up, and my right arm is dead. No blood in it at all. I pull it out from under Simon, and roll over, shaking it out. My throat is on fire, I ignore it.

I wake up, and the room is blood red.

The sun is shining, and Simon's wing is spread over my head.

I wake up, and the room is pink. The sun is setting. Simon's wings are behind him, his arm is around me. He's pulled me in tight, my back to his chest, our hips nested together. He's breathing heavily on my neck. I can't remember ever being this warm.

Sleep finger-walks up the back of my skull and pulls me under again.

I wake up, and it's dark. Simon's arm is around me. My back is against his chest. His breath is harsh and uneven on my neck. He's awake.

"Simon?"

"Yeah." His voice is rough.

"What time is it?"

"Don't know," he says into my hair. "Didn't want to move."

"Maybe we shouldn't have fallen asleep in the middle of the day."

"Maybe not." He tucks his hand under my ribs and pulls me even more snugly against him. He's rubbing his face into the back of my head. "You smell so good, Baz . . ."

I close my eyes. I let him move me.

"So good," he says, pushing my head forward. "I can't get enough of it. I can't swallow it. And it . . . it doesn't help to hold my breath . . ."

He inhales again. Unsteadily. Then he's biting my scalp, his mouth wide and wet in the hair above my neck. "So good . . ." I think he says. "So good."

He bites right at my hairline. He's found the scar there before, stretched and faded. "If it were me," he rasps, "if I were you . . ."

He bites and bites.

"I'd drain you fuckin' dry, Baz, and it still wouldn't be enough."

My fangs break though my gums—that happens, it's all right, I try to suck them back. I try to turn, but Simon holds me fast against him.

I let him.

I lay my arm atop the arm he has wrapped around my stomach. He's champing at my neck now, sucking. He knows he can suck hard; there isn't enough blood in me to leave a mark. "I can't get enough," he says, hot behind my ear. "Baz, help me. *Help me.* I can't get enough."

"I'm right here," I say.

"I know." He bites hard on my ear, pulls at it. "It's not enough."

"Simon . . ." I press my head back into his face. He grinds his nose in my hair. "Simon, are you saying I'm not enough?"

"*No.*" He practically shouts it into my skull.

I push his arm away, forcing him to let me turn. I push him back onto his back, onto his wings; I push his head down with my chin. I hold his wrists above his shoulders. He's still trying to bite at me.

"I'm right here," I say.

"I know . . ." He's growling.

"Tell me what you want."

"I don't know." His tail coils like a steel cord around my leg.

I'm careful with my hips. Even as he's mauling me. (Land mines. Permissions. Boyfriends being boyfriends, etc.)

"You smell so good," he says, burrowing his face into the neck of my T-shirt. "I don't know how to get enough, Baz—I don't know how I'm supposed to get enough."

I'm holding myself over him, my hands on his wrists, my knees bracketing his hips. He works his wings around us, pulling me closer. Then he latches on to my collarbone, right through my shirt. "*You smell so good*," he says, his mouth full of me.

Simon Snow smells like my aunt's shampoo. He smells like iodine still. Like ham. And butter. Like PG Tips.

He smells like sleep—sour breath and too-warm skin.

He smells like blood, always. His blood. Salt and milk and something burnt. (It used to be fire, now it's ashes.)

He smells like sex.

I can't help knowing this. Any of it. It's in the air I'm somehow still breathing. But I don't know what to *do* with it. What he wants me to do with it, what I'm allowed to do with it, what will help . . . What will lead to something strong enough *to lean on* between us.

I let him bite me. I let myself feel his teeth. I rub my face in the chaos of curls at the top of his head. "I'm right here, love, I'm yours."

He growls, miserably, letting go of my collarbone, mashing his face into my chest again. "I don't know how, Baz."

"What, Simon."

"To get enough."

"You don't have to get enough." I push his wrists down. I pin his arms with my elbows. "I'm not going anywhere."

His head falls back onto the pillow. I think he might be crying again. Maybe he wasn't awake. Maybe this is all a bad dream for him.

My hair hangs in his eyes. "I'm not going anywhere, Snow."

"Come here," he says. His wings are winding tighter around me. I can see the spikes curling over my shoulders. My knees give out, and my hips fall on him.

"Are you awake?" I ask.

"I think so."

"Are you crying?"

"Yeah. Baz . . . come here."

"I'm here."

"Come closer."

"All right." My elbows give out, too. I let go of his wrists, and he wraps his arms around my waist. Arms. Wings. Legs. Tail.

"Closer," he says.

"I can't."

"Can." He's kissing my mouth with his teeth now, lips and tongue almost an afterthought.

I try to retract my fangs, but it's hopeless, so I turn away and let him bite my face.

"Baz." He's biting my fangs through my cheek. "Baz . . ."

I'm awake. I'm thirsty. I'm dizzy. All the blood I have left has gone to my cock, and I'm running on fumes. On good manners and bad memories. "*Simon,*" I say, with my last measure of caution.

He's all around me now. His heels are in my calves. His tail is around my ankle. I can feel the bones in his wings, like long fingers along my spine.

It isn't enough.

"*Simon,*" I say, taking his head in my hands.

His skin is hot. So is mine. Under the blankets with him like this for hours, I could be mistaken for a living thing.

"*Simon, Simon.*"

He's biting my neck, and I'm not biting his—but I am kissing him. I'm kissing his hair, his ear. I'm pulling up his shirt. "I love you," I say. "I'm here."

"Baz, I need—"

"Yes."

"I can't—" He's pushing too hard to kiss. He's holding too hard to touch.

I wrench my head back. "Simon, let me—"

He won't let me pull away. His head is still in my neck. He's panting. "Baz, I can't—I need you."

I'm kissing his cheek. My fangs are out, I can't care. "Simon," I slur, "my darling, my love . . ."

"I can't . . . *breathe,*" he says. "It isn't enough—It's too much—I can't—"

He's crying. And clinging to me. Arms. Legs. Wings. Tail. All of him trembling.

I'm breathless, too, but in the wrong way now—the wind has changed. Hopefully it only just happened. Hopefully I didn't misinterpret every moment of this moment.

"Simon," I say, my hands in the back of his hair. "My darling. My love. It's all right."

"I can't," he sobs.

"I know," I say, stroking him. "It's all right. I'm here."

"I can't."

"I'm here."

"Baz . . ."

"I'm here, love."

19

SIMON

It's been a while since either of us said anything.

It's been a while since I stopped blubbering.

As soon as I loosened my panic-hold on Baz, he pulled away from me a bit. But he's still here. Lying quietly on one of my wings. Probably thinking about how much sex he could be having if he were with literally anyone other than me.

I mean, have a look at him—he's the most fuckable person alive. Or otherwise.

I'm the problem. As is always true, in literally every situation. It's me.

I've been here before. Wanting to crawl out of my skin and leave myself for dead after a miserable attempt to do more than kiss. What I'd normally do now is stand up and walk out of the room. Then Baz would leave the flat, not wanting to embarrass me further, nor to dwell on the fact that he's stuck with me.

But he can't leave—this is his flat. And if I leave, it would be in direct violation of the promise I made *not* to leave. Or not to give up. Or whatever.

Baz sighs. I know all his sighs; I lived with them for eight years. This one means: *Simon Snow is a chronic pain in my neck.*

"Do you want me to leave?" I ask. I'm on my back with my arms up, my elbows folded over my face.

"No." Baz's voice is quiet. "Are you going to?"

"No. I don't think so."

"That's something."

I breathe out hard. "I want to, though. I kinda want to die when I think of having to face you again."

Baz pulls my arms away from my face. "Here." He's hovering over me. "Get it over with."

My eyes slide away from him. "I'm sorry."

"Don't," he says.

"Because apologies don't matter?"

"No—because you don't have anything to be sorry for. Come on, Snow, *look* at me."

I try. He looks tired. And sad. And embarrassed.

"I don't mind this," he says. "Any of it."

"Oh my God, Baz—don't lie to me! This isn't what anyone wants to happen in bed." I try to cover my face again, but his hand is on my cheek. He's too close.

"I'm not lying! I don't mind *comforting* you, Simon. Or holding you. I don't mind giving you what you need, whatever it is you need. I prefer it to you pushing me away. Or ignoring me."

I look up at him. "But you could date anyone you want. You could date *everyone* you want. And none of them would start bloody crying during foreplay."

Baz shrugs. "You don't always cry . . . Sometimes you go glassy-eyed and nonresponsive."

My hands are twisted in my hair. "Fuck-ing *a*, I can't

believe you're *joking* about this." I try to roll away from him, but he's all steel bands when he wants to be. He pins me down by the shoulders.

"Wait," he says. "Listen to me. Are you listening?"

I close my eyes but stop trying to push him off.

"I want to be with you," he says. "And this is where we are right now. And I truly don't *mind*, Simon."

I open my eyes. Baz is looking right down at me.

"You don't want more?" I ask.

He shoves at my shoulders. "Of course I do. But not with just anyone. I want more with you, you twit."

I try to sit up, away from him, and this time he lets me. "What if I can't give you more?" I say. "What if this is my best-case scenario?"

Baz is dismissive. "I don't believe that." Then he goes still. He turns to me with one eyebrow raised. "Are you saying you don't *want* more?"

"Are you barking? Of course I want more!"

He relaxes again. "Then I'm confident we'll get there . . . someday, I don't know, *eventually*. Honestly, Simon, this isn't even our biggest problem."

He shocks a laugh out of me with that. "What's bigger?"

"The vampire thing, for one." Baz looks so twisted up and peeved and, like, unimpressed with me. It makes me want to start inhaling his carbon dioxide again.

I can feel myself smiling at him. "That's not a real problem . . ."

"It's about to be." He's rubbing his jaw. He sighs. "If I leave to hunt, will you be here when I get back?"

I'm still smiling. "I'll do you one better: I'll come along."

Baz frowns at his lap, picking at the knee of his jeans. His hair has dried fluffier than usual, and it's falling over his eyes. "Simon . . ." he says, like I've said something unkind and tiresome.

I take his hand. "Baz, if you really don't want me to be ashamed of what a complete and utter shambles I am, you can't be ashamed of your thing either. You already know I don't care—I've known you were a vampire since we were fifteen!"

He lifts his chin. "Yeah, and you tried to fucking Van Helsing me, Snow!"

"I never *properly* tried . . ."

He frowns. "Have you *ever* made an effort with me?"

I tug on his hand. "The takeaway here is—I truly don't care that you're a vampire."

"Well, I care. It's humiliating."

"Baz, I hate to say this, but . . ." I'm grinning at him, and I can hardly believe it. Like, I really expected to be miserable *for days* after breaking down so completely. But somehow I'm still here, and he's still here, and even though I still feel like a hopeless case, this thing between us doesn't feel hopeless at all.

Plus, as soon as Baz is unhappy, that's all I can think about. I'm crazy about all his little fretful faces, and I also want to be the thing that chases them away. I think I might be willing to make him miserable just for the thrill of making it better. That's fucked up, isn't it?

I dip my head to find his eyes.

"I just want to be with you," I say. "And this is where we are now. I'm a broken-down mess, and you're a rat-drinking monster."

We walk down an alleyway near Baz's flat. We won't have to go far, he says; London has rats everywhere, some of them the size of cats.

"Does it have to be rats?" I ask. "They're so gross."

Baz is pulling on a pair of tan leather gloves. "What else does the city provide for me? House pets? Pigeons?"

"You could breed mice. Clean ones, like in a laboratory."

"Oh, that's good, Snow. I'll have a flat full of pink-eyed mice in glass enclosures. That won't be creepy." He leans over and snatches a rat by its tail, then brains it against a brick wall.

"Christ," I say. "It's already well creepy."

Baz sneers at me. "You're the one who wanted to come. I told you it was disgusting."

I grin at him. "I'm happy you let me come. We could do this together. On the regular. I could help you hunt."

"I don't need your help." He starts walking again.

"Aren't you gonna drink that one?"

"I wait and drink them all at once. It's neater." He frowns at me. "You don't get to watch me drink."

"You already said that." Back at the flat, when he agreed to this.

"I can hear you getting ideas." Baz crouches, darting his hand into the gutter to grab another rat.

"Merlin, you're good at this." He catches another one while I'm saying it.

"Practice," he says.

"Must have been nice in the country. Proper hunting. Deer."

He kills the rats and moves on. "It did feel more wholesome."

I trail after him. "Will you live in the country after uni?"

"Will you?"

"I don't know why you haven't given up on animals altogether."

"What do you mean?"

"Well, the American vampires just drink people, don't they?"

He scowls at me over his shoulder. "I'm not a murderer, Snow."

"Lamb said you don't have to murder people. You can just drink."

"Well, I'm not a parasite either." Baz stops, crouches. "Or a thief."

"You wouldn't have to steal it."

"Good idea, I'll find a blood bank and open an account."

"Come on, don't be thick—you know I'd give it to you."

He stands up abruptly, facing me. "Don't say that, Simon."

I shrug. "But I would." I would.

Baz looks fierce. "Don't be idiotic! We don't even know how it works—I might drink too much."

"You wouldn't." He wouldn't.

"I could accidentally Turn you."

"We'll do research," I say. "I'll get Penny on it."

"Don't you *dare* mention this to Bunce. Just stop, all right? I don't even want to think about this."

"You'd rather drink London rats than me?"

Baz's eyes are wide. He's shaking his head. "*Fuck you*, Snow."

"Someday, perhaps. I've been told there's hope." I see something scurrying past me, and stomp on it. "Hey, look—I got one!"

BAZ

Simon Snow is grinning at me, holding out a live rat like a single-stemmed rose.

I stare at him.

He shakes the screeching rat. "Finish him off," he says, "before he starts to grow on me."

I take the rat and put it out of its misery.

Who will put me out of mine? I used to think it would be this fool. "You're not even wearing gloves," I say, still dumbfounded.

"Just 'Clean as a whistle' me."

"That'll only get you—"

"Clean as a whistle, I know. But right now, I'm clean as a rat."

I wave my wand over his hands, casting the spell, then start walking again.

He's unbelievable! He wants me to drink his *blood*? As if *not drinking his blood* hasn't been my primary concern since my fangs grew in!

He'd actually let me *drink* him . . .

Never mind the pain. Or the scars. Or the blood loss.

Or the risk of becoming a monster.

I thought maybe Snow didn't want to share a bed with me because he was afraid I'd bite him in my sleep. But apparently that's fine! Bloodletting is fine—intimacy is the real taboo!

"Don't people notice you?" he asks, still unbothered. "Strolling around with a bunch of dead rats?"

"Not usually. I cast a spell if they do."

"How many rats do you need to get full?"

"Depends on the size. Four to six."

Simon giggles. "Four to six."

I shake my head. "I still can't believe you're doing this with me."

"I've kind of already done it with you. I used to follow you around the Catacombs every night."

I laugh. "Those weren't dates, Snow."

He grins. "Is this a date, then?"

I go back to scanning the alley for rats. "You really were obsessed with me, weren't you? I can't believe you didn't know you were gay."

"I'm not gay," Simon says. Immediately.

I stop and turn back to him. "Oh. I'm sorry. I suppose, I mean—" We've never really talked about this. I've just assumed . . . I don't know what I've assumed. "Are you bi, then?"

"What?" He looks put off. "*No.*"

"Well . . ." I look around the alley, like I might find something helpful there. I hold up my hands. I forget I'm carrying rats. "What does that *leave*, Simon? Do you still think you're straight?"

"Christ, Baz, I never thought I was straight. I never thought about it at all." He's walking down the alley, away from me.

I follow after him. "Haven't you thought about it a little? Since *us*?"

"What's there to think about? I'm with you. And you're a . . ." He trails off.

"Man," I say flatly.

Simon shrugs. "I was going to say 'boy.'"

"I'm twenty years old. I could go to war."

"I'd rather you didn't."

"So, you do know you're dating a man. That's a start."

He turns to wink at me. "A-ha, this *is* a date."

"Simon, I'm being serious." I've stopped walking.

He stops, too. "Yeah, but *why* are you being serious? Is this important? Is this, like, our *second*-biggest problem? Me not knowing what colour flag to hold at the Pride Parade?"

"I didn't think it *was* a problem," I say. "But you're being a real twat about it. So maybe it is."

Simon sighs and rubs his forehead. I'm glad I spelled his hands clean. "I just . . . don't know. All right? I know I'm not straight. And obviously I was whatever I am now back when I was going to all your football matches and hiding outside your violin lessons."

"I thought you were trying to figure out whether I was a vampire," I say. I really did.

He's exasperated: "I already knew you were a vampire!"

I want to put my hands on my hips, but I'm still holding four dead rats. "Are you saying you *liked* me? In fifth year?"

"Baz, I was obsessed with you."

"I knew that. But you *liked* me?"

Simon sighs again. Really put out now. "I didn't *like* you. I still don't really like you . . ." That's a lie, and he knows it.

"But you wanted to kiss me?"

"I wanted to jump on you. I didn't really think past that."

"Plus ça change . . ."

"Fuuuck you," he says, extravagantly. "I know that's French for something smug."

I laugh. Snow makes me laugh. He makes me lose track of why I'm irritated with him. I see a rat scuttling past us in my peripheral vision and crouch, catching its neck in my fist. It's small enough to kill with one hand. "I liked *you,*" I say.

"You hated me," Snow says, above me.

I stand. "That, too."

I'm nearly done hunting. I should probably grab one more, so that I don't have to do this again later. Snow walks beside me. I clear my throat. "But you liked Agatha then, right? In fifth year?"

"Yeah. I suppose."

I get ahead of him a bit. "You were *attracted* to Agatha," I say over my shoulder, like it's nothing to me, "right?"

"You've seen Agatha," he says. "Inanimate objects are attracted to her. Trees bend her way."

"Yes, but did you—" I ask. I try to ask. "I mean, you've—"

Simon double-steps to catch up with me. "I've what?"

"You and Agatha. You, um . . ."

"Dated? Yes. Though she never took me midnight rat hunting. She wouldn't even go to the cinema with me. She said—"

I interrupt him. "You had sex, right?"

Simon stops. "Jesus, Baz, what a question."

He's right. I can't believe I asked it. "It's a normal question," I say.

"Is it?" He sounds genuinely surprised.

"Yes. People talk about previous partners."

"You've never mentioned any."

I lash out: "I don't have any, you halfwit! Don't you think you'd have uncovered them when you stalked me for three years?"

"I don't know how you spent your summers!"

"Reading!" I say. "Violin! Playing *Mario Kart* with my sister!"

We've both stopped walking. Simon wrinkles his nose. "Were you *never* actually plotting against me?"

"I plotted *a bit*. I was over it by sixth year." I sound flustered. Because I am. And it's all my own fault. Give me a little bit of honest communication, and I open the floodgates. Next I'll be asking him if he wants children. "Look, I'm just going to drink these now."

Simon seems confused. "Right," he says. "What do you need me to do?"

"Turn away."

He does.

I would like to pinch the bridge of my nose and sulk. Instead I get out my knife.

"Do you actually put your fangs in them?" Simon asks, facing a brick wall. His wings are bunched up under his jumper.

"Not if can help it. I slit their throats."

"I'd like to see that."

"You're a pervert."

"I just appreciate a job well done."

I untangle one of the rats. "Does Wellbelove?"

"Hey—" Simon turns around. He looks angry. Finally.

I decide to be angry, too. "I knew you couldn't keep your word!"

"*What?*"

"You promised you wouldn't watch."

"I—" Simon's face is red. He whips around, facing the wall again.

"I shouldn't have said that," I say tightly. "I'm sorry. I won't mention Agatha again."

"It's all right," he says, rubbing the back of his neck, unexpectedly subdued.

"Don't turn around," I say. "I really am going to do this. I can't let them get cold."

I slit the first rat's throat and hold it to my mouth. This truly is disgusting. What sort of diseases would I have if I were a person?

I drop the empty rat on the street and open the next one.

Simon kicks the wall. "We had sex," he says. "We dated a really long time."

I startle, splashing blood on my white shirt. I throw the rat to the ground. "That's good," I say, strained.

Simon sounds frustrated. "*Is* it?"

"*Wasn't* it?"

"It was fine, it was sex. Are you done?"

"No. I have three more."

"Right," he says, kicking the wall again.

I start drinking another rat.

"I don't know if I was *attracted* to her . . ." Simon says.

"You had *sex*," I gurgle.

"Yeah, but what does that mean?"

I make a disbelieving noise in my throat. I'm trying to swallow.

"It was just going through the motions," he says.

I drop the rat; it isn't even half empty. "But surely that means you were attracted to her."

"I thought I was!" He's got a hand fisted in the hair at his crown. "I thought I was going to *marry* her. But everything with Agatha was just going through the motions, wasn't it? I didn't have to think. I didn't have to sort out my feelings—or what did my therapist used to call it, 'process.'" He kicks the wall hard. "There was no *processing* with Agatha. That's what I liked about her! She felt like the opposite of dealing with my shit. I never looked at Agatha and thought, *How will I ever be big enough to hold my feelings for this person?* I felt plenty big enough! My feelings felt extremely manageable. I'm not sure I even had any!"

I wipe my hands on my jeans. "Turn around, Snow."

"Are you done?"

"No." It comes out soft. "Turn around."

He does. His hand drops from his hair. "Hell and horrors—you look like a butcher. Are you always this messy?"

"Only with you."

"I had sex with Agatha," he says. Like it's an apology. "I thought you knew."

"I did know. Mostly."

He shakes his head. "I still don't know if that makes me bi."

"It doesn't matter."

He knots his hand in his hair again. "Well, it makes me feel like a bloody idiot! Like, I was with a girl for three years, and I still don't know if I like girls! What the fuck?"

"You don't have to know."

"But it seems like I should, right? It seems like I should have a large enough sample size. You didn't need to sample anything to sort yourself out!"

"Please, Simon. I'm sorry I brought this up."

He drops his hand. "All I really know is that nothing I've experienced so far compares to you. Maybe that makes me gay." He swallows. "Or maybe that just makes me yours."

We're standing a foot away from each other. I'm covered in blood, and I'm holding two medium-sized dead rats and a very sharp knife. "I want to kiss you," I say.

"I always want to kiss you, Baz." He steps closer. "I always have."

"Don't."

"I don't care if I get the plague. You can Turn me into a vampire to cure me."

"Don't test me, Snow."

He takes another step towards me. I take a step back.

"I'm going to finish these rats," I say. "And then we're going back to the flat, and I'm going to brush my teeth."

Simon looks down at the rats, then back at my mouth. "Can I watch you finish 'em?"

I close my eyes. "Fine."

"Ha! I knew you'd say yes in the end."

As if I could ever deny him.

20

SIMON

I can't believe I'm sitting in Baz's bed.

I can't believe he let me hunt with him.

I can't believe I'm still here.

I've said at least a dozen things in the last ten hours that I thought would kill me—that I would have rather died than try to put into words. Yet here I am. And there he is. Well, he's in the shower again. But he's coming out. He gave me clean clothes to sleep in. He told me to make myself another sandwich.

I found Bourbon biscuits in the kitchen. I'm dipping them directly into a bottle of milk.

"My aunt really is going to kill you now," Baz says.

I look up. He's standing in the bathroom door, wearing cotton pyjama bottoms and a fresh T-shirt. His hair is wet, he must have washed it again. I'd never seen him as bloody as he was tonight; his gloves were still sticky, even after he cast a cleaning spell on them. He said he isn't going to take me hunting anymore, but I know he was just saying it. I want to go with him every night. Maybe I like hunting. I've always wanted my own longbow. "Should I not be eating these biscuits?" I ask. There are two in my mouth.

"Too late now. I'll buy more tomorrow." He arches an eyebrow at me. "Do you want my help with the shirt?" Baz gave me a clean T-shirt, but I left it on the dresser.

"If it's all the same to you"—I shrug one shoulder and twitch my wing—"it's easier to sleep without one."

Baz nods and licks his bottom lip. "Yeah, it's . . . all the same to me."

He shuts the bathroom door and comes to the bed, getting in next to me. I make room for him. His skin has pinkened up again. Still pale and grey—but a pinker grey. Rat blood looks good on him.

"Are you getting crumbs in my bed, Snow?"

"I'm the worst," I say. "I don't even notice them. You don't mind sleeping some more?"

"No," Baz says, reaching for the milk bottle. "I'm knackered." He takes a drink. I watch him swallow. I like it. I like him. His everything.

I dig out the last biscuit, then hold it out to him. He smiles softly, taking it.

I put my arm around him. "This okay?"

"Yeah," he says. "Pretty much always."

"Yeah?"

"Yeah, Snow. There's no use denying it."

"That's . . ." I tighten my arm around him. I get my wing around him, too. I like having four arms to hold him. "It's good. It's better already, isn't it?"

"Better than what?" he asks. (I think he knows the answers

to half the questions he asks me. He just likes to make me talk.)

"Yesterday," I say.

"Everything is better than yesterday," he says. "Yesterday was the nadir."

"It feels so long ago."

Baz sets down the milk. He brushes some crumbs off the duvet. I slink back in his bed, leaving my arm and wing open. His pillows are so fluffy. They probably cost a fortune. He glances at me, then away. I bring my other wing around to herd him in—he lets me. I pull him down to me, and he lays his head on my shoulder. I like this. It makes him seem shorter than me.

Baz sets his hand on my chest. I don't think he's ever touched me here, bare, when we weren't fooling around, or trying to. Maybe he's trying to . . .

"I like your chest," he says.

"That's because you remember what I looked like before I got fat."

"Nonsense, Snow. You're not fat."

I bloody well am. But, as Baz would say, it's not my biggest problem.

"You used to get so thin over the summers . . ." He traces his fingertips over my heart.

I shiver and cover his hand with mine, stopping him. "I could never keep up with the magic."

He looks up at me.

I try to explain: "I think the magic took a lot out of me. It was always there, even when I wasn't using it. They didn't starve me in the care homes, but it wasn't pot roast and all the scones you could eat. I'd come back to Watford so hungry, I could hardly think. One year, I went straight to the dining hall, and sat there eating from lunch to dinner."

Baz turns his face to kiss my chest. "You're not fat. I like you like this."

"Is there a way you don't like me?" I say it like it's a joke. But I bite my lip.

He looks up through his eyelashes and shakes his head. Christ, he makes me feel warmed through. It's so good, I can hardly stand it. It makes me want to bash my head into a wall, just for the distraction. Maybe he can tell. He doesn't kiss me again, and his hand stays motionless.

"Is your aunt still in jail?" I ask.

"No, I bailed her out—didn't you get my texts?"

"Yeah, sorry, I—"

"Was ghosting me, your boyfriend of eighteen months, hoping I'd get the message and silently fade away?"

I sigh. "It's like you don't want me to forget even for a second that you're merciless."

Baz tweaks my nipple. "I don't want you to think this is all a dream."

"Hey!" I squirm and squeeze his hand. "*Hey* . . . I'm sorry. About the texts, specifically."

"I bailed Fiona out," he says. "She was trying to steal something from Watford, I still don't know what."

"So she could come back to the flat at any minute?"

"Not likely. I think she has a boyfriend."

"I did read the texts about your stepmum. I'm sorry. How's your dad holding up?"

Baz rolls his face into my shoulder.

I let go of his hand, so I can touch his hair. It's dark and thick, and it falls past his shoulders when it's wet. "That bad? Is there another man?"

He pushes himself up onto an elbow. I shift my wing out of the way.

"You're not going to like this," he says.

"Why *would* I like it?"

Baz pinches the bridge of his nose.

Then he tells me the whole story.

21

PENELOPE

I got a series of texts from Simon in the middle of the night:

"pen, call me"

"something weird going on, a magickal thing—you'll prolly think it's interesting, could use yr brain. + prolly yr wand"

"call me"

"or baz."

I saw them when I woke up at nine.

"*Simon*," I texted back. "*This is exactly what you said you didn't want to do anymore. And I think you were probably right. Who are we to investigate 'interesting' magickal problems? If you really think something is amiss, you should tell my mother.*"

Then I shoved my phone off my bed and went back to sleep.

When I wake up again, my room smells like a Greggs. Shepard is sitting next to my bed. He's hauled in a chair from the kitchen.

"I brought you breakfast," he says, "even though it's technically lunchtime. And even though I'm pretty sure you didn't eat dinner last night. Did you know there's a place down the street that sells every sandwich you could imagine? I literally couldn't choose. An entire wall of sandwiches."

"Are you talking about Pret?"

"So I brought you this instead. It looks bad, I know. But trust me, it's delicious—and vegan. I've already eaten three."

I sit up to see what he's set on my lap. "That's a sausage roll."

"It's like a very mushy pig in a blanket."

I glare at him. "I've eaten a sausage roll before."

"Oh, good, then you know the drill. I brought you orange juice, too. If I'm going to be bringing all of your meals to you, you should probably give me a heads-up about your allergies, dietary preferences, and religious beliefs."

I rub my eyes. I still feel just as terrible as I did when I fell asleep. And just as clueless about my life. But significantly hungrier . . . I can't believe I'm going to give Shepard the satisfaction of eating this sausage roll he brought me. I take a bite. "Have you been wandering around London again?"

"I considered sitting alone in your living room for another day, but—"

"You can't just walk around. You're an illegal immigrant."

"I really don't plan on immigrating . . ."

"You didn't talk to anyone, did you?"

He tilts his head at me.

Right, that's a stupid question. I need to get him out of here. I've been licking my wounds since Simon left, ignoring Shepard completely. I can only confront a limited number of my mistakes at once—there are too many for me to cope with concurrently. But this has got out of hand.

"Thank you for breakfast, Shepard."

"Don't thank me," he says. "I took money from the kitchen table. I hope that wasn't your rent. It was either that or steal your gem and try to Bibbidi-Bobbidi-Boo us some breakfast. I'll pay you back. Unless it was more fake money."

"It's fine," I say.

"This is such a great neighbourhood. There's a family of either/orcs living downstairs, have you met them?"

"In this building?"

"Yeah, the young couple? With the schnauzer? I'll introduce you later."

"You talked to my *neighbours*?"

He tilts his head in the other direction.

Right. Completely out of hand.

I haven't even been *trying* to help Shepard. I erased the blackboard. I've been watching Norwegian soap operas and reading fanfiction and occasionally heating up Cup Noodles. Meanwhile Shepard's been doing magic-knows-what with magic-knows-who.

I can't let Shepard set up shop in my living room. What will *he* bring home?

"Shepard, I've been thinking."

"So have I."

"When I brought you here—"

"Penelope, I have been so ungrateful."

"What? No, you haven't."

He nods, emphatically. "I have. To be honest, I didn't really think you could fix my whole demon situation."

My head is hanging forward. "Shepard, you *were* honest. You *told* me you didn't think I could fix it."

"But I still came home with you," he says. "Just to see what would happen. You and your friends are the most interesting people I've ever met—and that's saying something. I came along because I wanted to see what would happen next."

"Shepard—"

"But the other day, after Simon left, and you broke all your chalk, it got me thinking . . ." He pushes up his wire-framed glasses. "I have met *so many* magickal creatures. And none of them have ever offered to help me before."

"I'm not a *creature*—"

"I showed my tattoos to a genie once—"

What? "Where did you find a genie?"

Shepard grins. "In a lamp."

"You found a genie trapped in a lamp?"

"I found a genie who *lived* in a lamp. In South Sioux City. The point is, he didn't offer to help me. He said, *'I've got two rules: You can't wish for more wishes, and I don't fuck with demons.'*"

"Morgana preserve us."

Shepard's grin goes warm. "But *you* didn't say that, Penelope."

"That's true," I groan. I put my face in my hands. My fingers are greasy from the sausage roll.

"You immediately offered to help."

"I did."

"You *insisted* I accept your help."

"Yeah . . ."

"Because you are a good person. A heroic person. You're, like, who I'm out here trying to be in the world."

"*What?*" My head jerks up. How can he say that with a straight face? With a *sincere* face?

"I accept your help, Penelope."

I groan again, loudly. "Shepard, nooooo. You were right all along."

"No. *You* were right. I should trust you. I do trust you!" He's gesturing broadly with an unopened bottle of orange juice. "You're a wise and powerful witch, and I'm grateful for your help."

"No! No, no, no. I'm none of those things. I'm an idiot!"

"Are you kidding? I've known you for two weeks, and I've seen you make one daring escape after another. I watched you kill *three* vampires, Penelope. Single-handedly!"

"Shepard, you only saw me get out of terrible situations because I had put myself—and my friends—*into* those situations. I *only* make bad decisions. It's even worse than you realize! The day before we met, I got dumped by someone who had apparently already dumped me multiple times. I was just too thick to figure it out! *I'm* the reason we were on that disastrous road trip. And it wasn't *wise* of me to kill those vampires. It's probably on YouTube!"

"Oh, it's definitely on YouTube. I've watched it."

"I'll probably lose my ring over it!"

"Penelope—" he says, as if I'm *just now* getting out of hand.

I keep getting there: "And what happened after that? I got captured by a skunk! And a dragon! And more vampires! And I did nothing to get myself or anyone else out of it. Nothing!"

"You saved Agatha."

"*Agatha* saved Agatha! I was along for the ride!"

"Penelope, I watched you—"

"That's a problem, too, Shepard. Magicians aren't supposed to do magic in front of Normals. Our entire culture depends on secrecy. I should have wiped your memory a dozen times over."

He smiles again. "To be fair, you did try."

"Argghhhhhhhh." I fall back against the headboard.

Shepard leans closer. "I know you're a good witch," he says gently. "Your friends treat you like a Jedi Master."

"My *friends*?" I know Shepard doesn't mean to be cruel, but that was a low blow. My voice drops away from me. "You mean, Simon? He broke up with me, too. Because I kept getting him in trouble. You heard my mother: I make problems." I shake my head. "I don't solve them."

Shepard finally stops arguing.

I can't face him. I stare at my lap instead.

After a few minutes, I hear him sigh. "So, that's it? You're going to send me home?"

I look back up. He's got his lips twisted to one side. Like he can't quite fathom that his powers of persuasion have failed.

"Yes," I say. "I can send you to Las Vegas if you want. And give you money to get your truck back."

"Would it be counterfeit money?"

"Yes."

"You can just send me back to Omaha."

"All right."

His shoulders are slumped, and he (finally) looks sad. Maybe he isn't thinking about how his charm failed him; maybe he's thinking about how *I* did.

"I am sorry that I dragged you here," I say.

He lifts up his chin. "It's okay, Penelope. It was fun. I got to see a little bit of London. And a little bit of magic." He smiles. "I met some either/orcs."

"Let me get cleaned up," I say. "Then I'll figure out your ticket."

Shepard hands me the orange juice he's been holding. "I'm sorry you got dumped," he says. "I didn't know."

"Me neither, apparently."

He gathers the sausage roll trash and stands up. "Anyone who would break up with you multiple times isn't playing with a full deck."

"That's not true, but thanks."

Shepard walks away. His hair nearly brushes the top of my doorway.

"I do wish I could have helped you," I say.

He pauses and shrugs. "It's okay." Then he walks out of the room and turns back to me. "You really were the first person to ever give me any hope of getting my soul back. I'm still grateful for that."

22

AGATHA

Someone puked in Exam Three. Dad says I don't have to clean it up, but I'm keeping a low profile anyway, restocking the paper towels in all the other exam rooms and wiping down the counters. I'm just finishing Exam Five when Niamh barges in.

"Oh. Miss Wellbelove," she says. "There you are."

I keep wiping the counter. "Dad says he'll take care of it. My cleaning spells are pants."

"What?"

"Exam Three."

Niamh frowns at me for a moment. "I wanted to talk to you about yesterday."

"Yesterday?"

"Your . . . friend."

"Oh." I throw my paper towel in the bin and click my tongue. "Of course. You want to talk about Simon."

"Yes, I—Well, I wanted to apologize. You were—Well,

you *are* correct. My bedside manner isn't ideal. I'm better with things that can't talk back or . . . walk away. I think it's my fault that Mr. Snow spooked."

She's standing there, with her head down, looking surprisingly pitiful. Part of me appreciates it very much. Niamh is awful and should feel awful. But another part of me . . .

"Niamh. It isn't your fault."

"It is," she tells the ground. "If your father had been presiding, the wings would have come right off, and everyone would be happy."

"Ha!"

She lifts her head. To frown at me.

"Honestly. Niamh. You can't blame yourself for anything Simon Snow does. You can't try to influence him at all. It's like trying to influence a mad dog."

She's still frowning—I think this one indicates confusion. What a *spectrum* of frowns this woman is capable of. Fifty shades.

"Don't feel bad about this," I say. "Simon will have his wings off when he wants them off. Or he'll saw them off himself with a dull blade. Or lose them in a run-in with a harpy."

She looks truly appalled with me. Which is fine. Let her spend eight years of her life with Simon Snow, and then she can judge.

"My point is," I say, "this isn't on you. Or me. We're just bystanders."

The door to Exam Three opens again. It's my dad. Niamh frowns at him.

"Oh, Niamh," he says. "And Agatha. Niamh, are you still heading out to Watford this afternoon?"

"Yes, Doctor. But I can stay if you need me."

"No, no, go ahead. Nice day for it." My dad glances over at me. "Say, you should take Agatha with you. I'm sure you could use an extra wand."

"No," I say, before I've thought it through. Niamh and my father look at me, waiting to hear why not. "I . . . I told Janice I'd cover the phones for her while she goes on break."

"Pish," Dad says. "She'll manage somehow without you. Niamh, Agatha had planned to study veterinary care herself." He looks back at me, and I can hear him thinking, *But who knows what she's planning now?*

Niamh is looking at me, too, trying very hard to smile like a normal person. (Close but no cigar, Niamh!) "Of course," she says. "I'd be glad of the help."

"Grand," my dad says. "Have a good time, Agatha. Say hello to Mitali if you see her." The door closes behind him.

Niamh is still grimacing at me. "I'll come find you when I'm ready."

"Great." I nod.

Grand.

23

PENELOPE

I try to pull myself together in the shower. It helps to have a plan. Next step: Get Shepard home.

I buy him a plane ticket for this evening. Don't tell my mother, but I can pay for almost anything online with "A penny for your thoughts." (I think it works so well for me because of my name.) I'm not going to worry about getting caught for this. If anyone figures out I've been kiting plane tickets, *this* won't be the one that seals my fate.

The only real risk is that the magic will fail somehow before Shepard gets home. I don't want him to get into any more trouble. (Though I've never met anyone with such a nose for it, not even Simon.) (I'm trying not to wonder about the "interesting" thing Simon was texting about. I am *not* falling back into this routine with him. Not if he hates me for it.) (Evidently Baz was less easily dismissed than I was. Fine. Let Baz be the one who gets repeatedly dumped.)

When I walk out into the living room, Shepard is pulling

on a fresh T-shirt. His denim jacket is lying on the back of the sofa. It's rare to see his arms—he wears that jacket even indoors, even in June. The tattoos trail out from his shirt sleeves, all the way down to his wrists. They're so ornate, they almost seem to move.

No. They *are* moving.

I think they're really moving!

I walk over to Shepard and grab his arm, staring down at the symbols.

"They do that sometimes," he says softly.

"What does it mean?" I ask.

"Don't know," he says. "Can't read Demon."

"Does it hurt?"

"No. Sometimes it sort of flashes—like, tingles—before things start to change."

I watch the symbols shift and turn, winding around his arm. There must be some rhyme, some reason . . .

"It's kind of cool-looking, huh?"

I look up at him. "No. Shepard. It isn't cool. It's horrid. I lament your inability to tell the difference."

He flashes a smile at me, pulling his arm away and sliding it into his jacket. "I'm going to miss your lamenting, Penelope Bunce. And your derision. And the way you occasionally threaten to turn me into a frog. Will you threaten me by text every once in a while? So I know you're doing okay?"

I fold my arms and watch him shove the T-shirt he was wearing into his backpack. His watch has three dials on it, and there are crystal bracelets on his wrists. I'm not sure I can let him walk out of here, knowing everything he knows.

He adjusts the collar of his jacket and cocks an eyebrow at me. "You're not thinking of rebooting my memory, are you?"

"I'm thinking about it, but I won't follow through."

"I'm already sworn to keep your secrets." He smiles at me. "And I would anyway."

Look, I'm not blind. Shepard's got a lovely smile—warm and wide, full brown lips, a hint of dimples—but he uses it on absolutely *everyone* for every occasion. I refuse to be affected by it.

I remain stern. "I thought our secrets were valuable currency on the magickal dark web, or wherever it is you hang out."

"I wouldn't have so many unusual friends if I couldn't keep their secrets," he says.

"How could you possibly be keeping *any* magickal creature's secrets? You never shut up about them!"

"I only tell you about the not-secret ones, Penelope!"

"You told me you met a *river phoenix*. Those are the rarest of the rare. Are you saying that wasn't supposed to be a secret?"

"I didn't tell you any identifying details!"

I'm rolling my eyes. I should just stare at the ceiling until Shepard leaves, to conserve my energy. "I'm not going to spell your memory," I say.

When I look back at him, he's smiling wider than ever. "Thanks, Penelope . . . I didn't want to forget you."

I pull out my phone and hand it to him. "Here, type in your phone number. I'll send you your boarding pass. You've got your passport, right?"

"Yeah, it's not going to turn into, like, a leaf or something when I get out of range of you, is it?"

"Why would it turn into a leaf?"

"I don't know. Magickal reasons."

"No. You'll be fine. I mean, call me if you have any problems, but you'll be fine."

He laughs.

"What's so funny?" I ask.

"The idea of me calling you with my problems." He puts his backpack on.

"You don't have to leave yet—your flight isn't for hours."

"I think I want to kick around London for a while. Who knows when I'll get back?" He's smiling at me again. With his eyes, as well. I decide to be slightly affected. This is sort of a special occasion.

"Shepard," I say, "I'm sorry I brought you here—"

"Hey. Stop. We've been through this. It was an adventure, and you know how I feel about those." He puts his hands in his jacket pockets. "Oh, I almost forgot." He pulls two pieces of yellow chalk out of his pocket and holds them out to me. "I saved these from Chalkmageddon. Seemed like you might want them later."

I look down at the chalk.

Then back at up at Shepard.

I grab his hand.

"Wow," he says, "you really want to break this chalk."

"Shepard—*wait*."

He looks down at me, his tongue on his bottom lip, like he's trying to figure out what's wrong with me. I could try to tell him, but it would take a while.

"You don't have to leave yet," I say. "So, we, um—Well, we may as well see if we can make some progress."

"Progress," he repeats.

"On your . . . situation."

His voice is kind: "Penelope, you already tried."

"No," I insist. "I *didn't*. I asked my mum. And then I waited for Simon and Baz. Look, I can't fix this by myself, but I can maybe help you sort a few things out—maybe something that will come of use later."

Shepard nods. Carefully. "I mean, I'll take any help I can get . . ."

"Right." I close my fingers around the chalk in his palm, then pull my hand away. "Go on then. Sit. And take off your jacket—it's hot in here." I look at my blank blackboard. "Right," I say again. "Let's start at the beginning. You still haven't actually told me what happened."

Shepard is sitting on my sofa, taking off his jacket. "I told you I was cursed by a demon."

I turn back to him. "You haven't told me in any detail."

He pushes up his glasses. "That's because I feel like you're going to be very critical and judgmental."

"Shepard, it's impossible to *think* without being critical and judgmental. That's literally the process."

"The way you do it, yes."

"Come on," I say, rolling my eyes. "I know you're dying to tell me. Where did it happen? Dubuque, Iowa? Topeka, Kansas? The banks of the Colorado River?"

He smiles. More sadly than usual. "It happened in Omaha, as a matter of fact."

"Excellent," I say, turning to my blackboard. "That's something we know. Omaha, Nebraska."

24

AGATHA

Niamh's shitty Ford Fiesta doesn't have air-con, so we have to drive all the way to Watford with the windows rolled down. My hair is a mess, and it's too loud to talk, which would be fine, but now I'm going to have to scream, *Turn this car around!* for her to hear me.

Back at the surgery, all I could think about was how much I didn't want to spend the afternoon with Niamh. But now I'm thinking about how much I don't want to go back to Watford. I haven't *been* back to Watford. And maybe I *can't* go back. Maybe I actually can't manage it.

We've left London behind us, and most of the suburbs, and we're in the countryside now. We'll see them soon. The Watford gates.

"Niamh," I say.

She doesn't hear me.

"Niamh!"

Her head jerks my way.

"Could you pull over?!"

"Why?!"

"I think I'm going to be sick!"

That does it, and it isn't even a lie. Niamh pulls over to the side of the road. I lean forward, trying to get my head between my knees. My door opens, and Niamh is reaching over my lap to unlatch my seat belt. "You're all right," she says.

"I'm really not, thanks."

"Sorry. Here. Have some water."

I ignore her. There are waves of anxiety washing over me. I'm trying to figure out if they start in my stomach or my head.

"Agatha . . . have some water."

I look up at Niamh and take the water bottle from her hand. I drink some.

"Do you want some fresh air?" she asks.

As if that's what's been lacking. I climb out of the car anyway. Perhaps Niamh will leave me here and pick me up on her way back to London.

"Look," she says, "there's even some shade."

I follow her to a tree, a little bit away from the road. She's holding her hands out, like she might have to catch me if I faint. I'm sure Niamh could carry me if she had to. She's built like a lumberjack.

I lean against the tree trunk, sliding down to the ground.

"All right?" she asks.

"Still no."

Niamh stands there for a minute with her hands on her hips, watching me. "Has this happened before?"

"No," I say. Then, "I don't know." (I fainted once when I was abducted by a troll. Does that count?)

"Should I call your dad?"

"*No.* No, I'm just carsick. I just need a minute."

Niamh sits down near me. "Drink some more water."

"I'm carsick, not dehydrated."

"You look rattled."

I take another drink. "I'll be fine."

She's watching me, red-faced and unhappy.

"What time is your appointment at Watford?" I ask. I could stay here under this tree. I have my phone. And Niamh's water. And my wand, I suppose.

"It's not an appointment," she says. "I'm just checking in on the goats."

I set down the water. "The goats?"

Niamh nods.

"*Ebb's* goats?"

"Ebb Petty is dead," she says, and wow, this is exactly what I mean about her terrible bedside manner. What if I was a loved one? Or a friend of Ebb's who hadn't heard? Or what if I was *anyone* who found this news upsetting in some way?

"I know," I snap. "But you're checking on her goats?"

"They're the Watford goats," she says. "The school herd."

"Whatever," I mumble, looking down again.

"I come out once a week to check on them. There's a pregnant doe I'm keeping an eye on. Or trying to."

"Oh." Now I feel bad for snapping.

I look up at Niamh again. She's sitting in the grass with her legs bent in front of her, and her arms resting on her knees. She left her white doctor's jacket in the car, and she's got on heavy tan trousers and a dark green T-shirt. Plus tortoise-framed, green-tinted sunglasses that are very nearly fashionable. She's staring out in the direction of Watford. Maybe she can see it.

"It's always strange coming back here," she says. "It makes me feel like I'm going back to school."

"Yeah . . ."

"You must miss it," she says.

I bark out a laugh. "*No.* Do you?"

"No. But I wasn't . . ." She glances over at me.

I scowl back at her. "You weren't what?"

"You know . . ."

"I don't."

Niamh shrugs and looks away. "Agatha Wellbelove."

"What does *that* mean?"

"Oh, come on." She shifts her sunglasses to the top of her head. "You must know . . ."

"Enlighten me."

"It *means*," she says disdainfully, "that the whole school revolved around you and your friends."

I lean towards her. "It did *not.* And how would you even know? We weren't in school together."

"I'm only three years older than you, Agatha."

Is that true? Could Niamh have already made that many bad skin-care choices? I lean back against the tree, folding my arms, and staring at her. "Did we really play lacrosse together?"

"You don't remember?"

"I remember playing *lacrosse* . . ." I say sharply.

"Well, I was on the team, three years ahead of you." She frowns at me. "Why are *you* acting offended? You're the one who doesn't remember *me.*"

"I didn't pay attention to the upper years."

Niamh tips up her chin and laughs unpleasantly. "Did you pay attention to *anyone*?"

That's when I see it. "Nicks and Slick, I do know you!"

She puts her sunglasses back on. "I've been telling you that you do."

"Snakes *alive*. What happened to you?"

"What?" She looks surprised and offended, and this time, I can't blame her.

I try to backtrack—"I mean . . ."

Niamh . . . Niamh is *Brody*. I didn't even know Brody had a first name. (I mean, *of course* Brody had a first name.) The girls my age were afraid to speak to her. She was our best attacker. Six foot one, built like a brick wall. Crowley, her thighs were a wonder—you could serve *tea* on them. And she had this short, platinum-blond hair, all quiffed up like Niall Horan.

"I mean . . ." I say again, "your hair."

Niamh touches her dark brown bun. "Oh. Well. I got tired of bleaching it. And getting it razored every three weeks. Vet school is a grind."

Brody. Niamh is *Brody*. She was absolutely merciless on the field. She plowed into me once. I had time to get out of the way, but I was paralyzed with fear when she came bearing down on me. Her face was all red. White hair, black eyebrows. That monstrous nose. I should have recognized that nose!

"You shoved me once," I say.

Niamh shrugs. "I shoved everyone."

"Like, *really* shoved me."

She brushes some grass off her boots. "It was lacrosse."

"A noncontact sport."

"Yeah, the way you played it."

"Hey," I object, "I was good at lacrosse!"

Niamh looks at me again. Gimlet-eyed, even in sunglasses. "Were you really?"

"Not in fifth year, but eventually."

"Huh." Niamh doesn't look like she believes me. It's a very Brody look.

"Our team went to Nationals my last year!" I insist.

"That's nice," she says. "The closest I got to Nationals was seventh year. We had to cancel our qualifying match because your boyfriend brought home a werewolf, and the whole school was quarantined."

"He didn't bring it home; he fought it in the dining hall." I keep leaning towards her to make my arguments, but none of them are landing. "He fought four!"

Niamh shrugs. "The match was cancelled."

"You're lucky you didn't get the lupine virus."

"I was vaccinated. The whole team was vaccinated!"

"Well, don't take it out on me," I say. "I didn't cancel your precious lacrosse match."

"You were part of the goings-on."

My mouth drops open. "I. Was. Kidnapped."

Niamh rolls her eyes, *very* meaningfully, like what I've just said is both irrelevant *and* ludicrous.

I lean towards her again. "What was that? Do you not believe I was kidnapped?"

"We all believed you were kidnapped . . . the first time."

"The first—Are you serious?"

Niamh is holding her hands up. "It doesn't matter, Agatha. It's ancient history."

"As the person who was actually kidnapped, multiple times, it doesn't feel like it was all that long ago."

"Look, I'm sorry I mentioned it. I'm sure it was very dramatic for your whole . . . circle."

"There was no *circle*," I say, my voice getting high, but Niamh isn't listening. She's on her feet.

"Hell's spells," she mutters, jogging away from me.

I stand up to see what she's after—

There's a goat nosing around in the field, a hundred feet away.

Niamh is running towards it, her wand held out in front of her. "Come on, billy. Come on . . ."

I run after her. The goat is watching Niamh now. It's a big white one, with long horns and a beard. Niamh is twenty feet away from it. She stops running, like she's afraid to startle it. She slowly raises her wand. ***"Get your goat!"***

The goat just stares at her. Chewing.

Niamh looks like she's trying to decide whether to make a run for it. The goat looks like it's making the same decision. It breaks first—scampering deeper into the field. Niamh runs after it. I run after Niamh.

"You'll never catch it!" I yell.

"I have to!" she yells back.

After a few minutes, I'm too spent to keep up. Niamh keeps running. (Thighs still competitive, it seems.) "Niamh," I shout, "you'll never catch it!"

"I have to!"

The goat pauses to look back at her. Niamh powers towards it. The goat runs again. Oh, there's a fence; Niamh's going to corner it against the fence. Clever girl, but then what? The goat's horns are a foot long. I get out my wand and try to think of a few first-aid spells. (My first-aid spells are pants, too.)

The goat sees the fence and turns abruptly. Suddenly it's headed towards *me*. Sweet Circe, it's headed towards me! So is Niamh. "Agatha!" she shouts. "Catch it!"

"Catch it?" I scoff to myself. "With my giant goat net?"

The huge, horny goat is barrelling towards me, and I start to move out of its way, but Niamh is screaming my name. "Agatha! Don't let it go!"

"Oh, for fuck's sake," I say, holding my wand out to the goat. Honestly, the only spell I have at the ready is "Ashes to ashes." The goat stops running just as I'm about to cast it.

It cocks its head at me.

My wand is already pointed, so I decide to try something. It won't work. I'm an anaemic magician, even on a good day. (Iron pills didn't help.) But I go ahead with it anyway:

"Mary had a little lamb!" I sing softly at the goat.

It watches me tap my wand in the air, then looks at me like, *Not a lamb, sister.*

I keep going. *"Little lamb, little lamb!"*

The goat's still watching. I can hear Niamh pounding closer to us.

"Mary had a little lamb, its fleece was white as snow!"

Niamh has slowed to a stop behind the goat. I'm waiting for her to tackle it, but she turns to me instead, motioning for me to go on.

"Everywhere that Mary went! Mary went, Mary went!"

The goat takes a few nimble steps towards me. I look at Niamh and point urgently at it. She points back at me and mouths, *"Keep going!"*

I give her what I hope is a furious look, but I tap my wand in the air again. *"Everywhere that Mary went, the lamb was sure to go!"*

The goat is nosing at my trainers now, its horns rubbing up against my shins. I take a step backwards. It looks up at me and steps forward.

"It followed her to school one day," Niamh whispers.

I swallow. ***"It followed her to school one day!"***

Niamh has my arm. She's urging me backwards.

I keep singing—***"School one day, school one day!"***— then whisper to Niamh, "What are we doing?"

"Leading it back to Watford."

"You take over."

"Why would I do that, Agatha? It's under your spell."

I keep walking backwards. The billy goat follows, not a care in the world now, like I have it on a leash.

"It followed her to school one day, which was against the rules!"

When we get to the Watford gates, there's no one guarding them. Niamh opens the latch and holds one side open. I step through. The billy goat looks around. It glances up at me, then trots through and away, out onto the Great Lawn.

Niamh is frowning at me in a very pleased way. "Good show, Agatha."

"Won't it just get out again?" There's a wall around the Watford grounds, but it's mostly just for show. There are spells to keep out Normals and intruders, but not wildlife. (That's probably why the Humdrum sent so many creatures after Simon.) If the goat got out once, it will get out again.

"I'm not worried about them escaping," she says. "I'm worried about them leaving."

"Isn't that the same thing?"

"We can't exactly keep the goats of Watford in a pen. They're supposed to *know* they belong here. They shouldn't just be wandering away."

"That sounds like exactly the reason people keep animals in a pen."

Niamh's looking down at my wand. "That was some tidy spellwork. I've never seen anyone cast a nursery rhyme before."

I've never even *considered* casting one before. "You just have to commit to it," I say, tucking my wand into my pocket.

"Well, I never would have tried it," she says. "The rhyme's about lambs, not goats. Your dad's always telling me I'm too literal . . ."

I look up over the Lawn, at the drawbridge and the ramparts. And the peak of the White Chapel. "I'll wait here for you," I say. "I'm still feeling a bit off."

"Oh," Niamh says. "Well, if you feel better in a while, I really could use your help finding the rest of the herd. Sometimes it takes hours."

"Hours?"

"They're crafty."

The goat we caught is already heading out to the fields behind the school, where Ebb used to take them to graze. "I suppose I could help," I say. "Do we have to cross the moat?"

"No. The goats stay in the hills, usually. They hate the merwolves."

"So do I."

"Yeah," Niamh says, "they're horrible. They killed all the fish in the moat, and the school has to feed them horse meat. I talked the headmistress into euthanizing them, but some students led a protest."

"Ebb used to bring them in every night," I say.

"The merwolves?"

"No. The goats. They slept in the barn with her."

Niamh frowns at me. "Ebb Petty is dead."

25

PENELOPE

Well, one way of looking at this is—there's a lot more written on my blackboard.

WHAT WE KNOW:

- Omaha, Nebraska
- Two years ago (Normal, age 20)
- Midnight ritual
- Curse victim was alone
- Victim does not wish to be called "victim"
- Where did curse victim (hereafter called "C.V.") acquire ritual?
- "Some guy I met" (!)
- Where is ritual now? In C.V.'s pocket (!!)
- C.V. was told ritual would help him "meet a demon" (!!!)
- C.V. thought that sounded like a <u>corking</u> idea
- C.V. possibly already cursed? "Conked on the head with

the stupid stick," as my grandmother used to say? Worth investigating . . .

MY NAME IS SHEPARD

- Demon was successfully summoned

WHAT WE DON'T KNOW:

- Name of demon
- Type of demon
- What the ritual says
- What the ritual does
- How to reverse it
- What Shepard was thinking
- What Shepard is EVER thinking

"Right now I'm thinking that you'd make an excellent prosecuting attorney." Shepard's sprawled out on the sofa, all long legs and orange corduroy.

"That sounds like a compliment," I say, surveying my lists. "Thank you." I turn back to him—and to the demonic ritual which he's taken from his pocket and *spread out on my coffee table*.

At least it isn't the actual ritual. This is just a phonetic transcription, written in purple ink on a piece of notebook paper. I start to read it out loud, and Shepard jumps off the sofa to cover my mouth. "Don't do that," he says softly, hand still pressed over my lips.

I nod. I suppose he's right.

He slowly takes his hand away, and we both exhale.

"Is that it how it happened?" I ask. "You just read it out loud?"

He sits back down. "No, there was more. I drew a doorway on the floor."

"Not a pentagram?"

"No, it was a door—there was a diagram for how to draw it. I think the door worked like a metaphor. Like it was the *idea* of a door, and then it became a door."

I flop down on the sofa, wiping chalk on my skirt. "So it was only a *metaphorical* summoning."

"Why not?" He's still smiling. (One nice thing about talking to Shepard is that I don't even have to pretend not to be patronizing. It rolls right off of him.) "After all," he says, "*your* magic is based on clichés . . ."

I wince. "I think you mean that we use the power of language to harness the world's magic in a way that you can only contemplate. But go on, you drew a door . . . Where?"

"In my bedroom." Shepard cracks open another boxed sandwich. Coronation chicken this time.

After an hour of list-making, I let him take a break to get dinner. With all the sandwiches on the coffee table right now, it's like Simon never left. (It's *very much* like Simon left. I can hear him—and Baz—not saying anything, not here, not wanting to be here. It's like giant gongs of silence. Shepard's constant chatter does nothing to crowd it out.)

I'm crushing the end of my chalk with my nail. "So, you created a door to *hell,* in the room where you *sleep* . . ."

He finishes his bite. "Oh," he says. "It's curry. I wasn't expecting that. The queen was coronated with curry chicken salad?"

"Shepard. *Focus.*"

He tilts his head. "I'm focusing, focusing . . . I like the raisins."

I groan, and wipe some chalk on his leg. He pulls his thigh away, laughing.

"What's your surname?" I ask.

"Is it that hard calling me 'Shepard'?"

"It's awfully familiar," I grouse.

He laughs some more. He's very good at smiling and laughing while he eats. It isn't even a little disgusting. "It's Love."

I frown and pull away from him. "It's not—"

"My last name. It's Love."

"You're joking."

He takes another bite, still smiling. "I am not. Feel free to call me that if it feels less familiar."

"Ugh, you're *inherently* impossible."

"Untrue, I'm *Normal*. I'm utterly possible."

"Tell me more about the door," I say. "Why'd you do this in your bedroom?"

Shepard's smile falls a notch. He looks down at his lap. "Well, I didn't want to do it in anyone else's space—and I don't think demons live in hell, by the way. I think they're more like beings from other dimensions."

"What did you use to draw the door?"

He sets down the sandwich, wiping his mouth with a napkin. "Blood, soil, water, ash, and milk."

"Your own blood?"

He licks his bottom lip. "It had to be my own blood. The guy who sold me the ritual was very clear."

"How much did the ritual cost?"

He raises an eyebrow. "Nothing?"

"Is that an answer or a question?"

He shrugs and looks back at his lap, brushing off some

crumbs. "It's one of those 'we don't get paid unless you get paid' situations . . ."

I have a bad feeling about this. I almost don't want to push him for a real answer. "What did it cost?"

"Nothing. Yet." He closes his eyes, like he's bracing himself. "My thirdborn child."

I slap his shoulder. "*Shepard.*"

He peeks over at me.

"How *could* you," I say.

"I talked him down from my firstborn—they always want the firstborn—he was cutting me a deal!"

"So there's some shady character out there waiting for you to start a family?"

"Aw. Ken's not shady. He's a stand-up guy with a big heart." He smiles. "That's a joke—he's a giant."

I smack him again. "Shepard!" I'm shaking my head, dumbfounded. "You know that giants *eat* babies . . ."

"Penelope, it's fine. I'm not having three kids. I may not have any kids. I'm a child of divorce."

I stand up, still shaking my head, and add *GIANT!* to my *What We Know* list. "So you met this giant . . . *somehow* . . ."

"I met him the usual way."

"You chased him off the road?"

"No. I noticed him and said hello. We've been friends for a while."

I lean back against a blank spot on the blackboard. "I guess I'm impressed he hasn't eaten you."

"I think he only eats babies . . ."

"Merlin and Morgana and bloody Anne Boleyn," I say. "So this baby-eating giant you've befriended collects demonic rituals?"

"It was in a book he had."

"He collects old books?"

Shepard holds a finger up as if he's about to say something interesting and not something outrageous. "He collects *miniatures*."

"Of course he does."

"Magickal miniatures," he adds.

"Naturally," I say.

"I was helping him organize his collection. He tends to break things . . ."

"I mean." I'm just nodding my head now, like this all stands to reason.

"He liked having someone else around who really appreciated his collection."

"Which includes a book of demon-summoning rituals."

"It was a book about demon culture! That's what Ken told me, anyway. He could read some of it, but only with a magnifying glass, and kind of the way you or I could read Spanish out loud, phonetically, even if we didn't understand it. Ken knew I'd always wanted to meet a demon."

"*Why* have you always wanted to meet a demon?"

"Who wouldn't? Can't you think of a thousand questions you'd ask a demon?"

"I'd ask him to let go of your soul. That's all. Then I'd close the door."

Shepard's back to eating his sandwich. "They're not all 'he's, you know. I'm not sure any of them are 'he's. What's gender to a demon?"

"Did you get a chance to ask him that?"

Shepard looks sheepish. "I did not."

"Okay . . ." I look back at my board. I write in *Ken*.

"If Ken is such a good friend, why didn't he just give you the ritual?"

"A guy's got to eat. Plus, it was a lot of work for him. He had to write the whole thing out phonetically."

"And he didn't tell you what it actually said?"

"He didn't know! Like I said, he knew the letters, but only a few words here and there."

"What did Ken say afterwards, when you told him what happened with the demon?"

Shepard's face falls—like he pities *Ken,* of all people. "He felt terrible."

"He's going to feel a lot worse when I talk to him about this thirdborn situation. Did he try to help you at all?"

"He said he was afraid of making it worse."

"What's worse than losing your soul to a demon?"

"Dying, I guess. Getting cursed along with me."

"Let's call him," I say. "This Ken. Right now."

"We can't call him. He's asleep."

"Nonsense, it's ten A.M. in Chicago." This is math I'm used to doing.

"No, I mean he's hibernating. He'll be asleep for years."

"Giants *hibernate*?"

Shepard shakes his head at me. "If you ever gave me a chance, I could teach you so much about magic . . ."

"Oh my goodness, Shepard, *stop.* I'm going to roll my eyes so hard, they'll get stuck." I sit back down on the arm of the couch, tapping my lip. "Let's stick a pin in Ken and come back to him. All right, so it was midnight . . . You drew the door, you read the ritual . . ."

"And it worked. The demon showed up. The marks appeared on my arms. It left." Shepard is looking at his lap, scratching the back of his head. He isn't smiling at all.

"Tell me about *it*."

He sighs. "It was a demon."

"What did it look like?"

"Does that matter?"

"I guess not. What did it say?"

"Not much. Small talk . . . *'Who calls me?' 'Did you call me of your own free will?'* Yada, yada."

"Yada, yada?"

"It really was just small talk, Penelope. I thought we were having a nice time."

"And then?"

"And then tattoos."

"And it didn't explain?"

"It said . . . I don't remember exactly what it said."

SHEPARD

"Who calls me?" the demon said, pushing open the door in the floor.

"Hi," I said. "My name is Shepard Love. I'm from Omaha, Nebraska. I'm studying journalism." I was still in school then.

It climbed into the room with me, like it was walking up stairs—I wasn't expecting it to do that. It sat on my bed. I offered it a can of Coke, and it took it. *This is going so well,* I remember thinking.

The demon spoke English with no accent. Or maybe with my accent. (When I was a little kid, I thought my accent was the true neutral. Because everyone on TV sort of sounds like they're from Omaha, Nebraska.)

It seemed a bit hassled at first, like I'd interrupted it in the middle of something. But then it was polite. I told it a lot about myself. That's something one of my journalism professors taught me. You can soften up a source by sharing things about yourself. It's like saying, *This is a safe place for intimacy.* This has always come naturally to me. I like telling people about myself. I like listening when it's their turn to talk. I like being such a good listener that they sort of forget about me. Most people really like to talk about themselves; it doesn't take much encouragement.

The demon was less forthcoming than most people. It didn't forget itself.

It sat on my bed—Penelope would be horrified—and drank my Coke and got right to the point.

"Did you call me of your own free will?" it asked.

"Yes," I told it. "Of course. I was excited to meet you."

It nodded at me. My room was full of sulphurous smoke by then. *"All right, Shepard Love from Omaha, Nebraska— you've got yourself a deal."*

PENELOPE

I'm running out of space on my blackboard wall. I cast the spell on a second wall and push the TV out of the way. Simon would complain about this if he were here, but Simon isn't here.

NEXT STEPS, I write in big block letters, as high as I can reach. "I still think we should wake the giant. I'm putting that on the list. And also, if the giant could read this demon language, maybe someone else can. Maybe it's not totally dead or obscure—maybe there's even another copy of that book. Was it handwritten?"

Language! I write.

The book. More copies? Check at Watford. Pitch Library?

"You know, the Mage actually seized a bunch of old magickal books. Wonder where those ended up . . ." I tap my chin.

Ask Premal about the Mage's book stash.

"Was the book handwritten?" I ask again.

When Shepard doesn't answer, I turn away from the wall.

His head is down, and he's running his fingertips up and down the raised stripes of his trousers.

"The book," I say, "was it handwritten? Could there be more copies?"

Shepard looks up at me, with one eye closed, like he's thinking. "Penelope. I have to go now, if I'm going to make my flight."

"What? No—you've still got time."

He shakes his head. "I don't think so."

I pick up my phone . . . Oh. He doesn't have time. He's already going to be cutting it close. I look back at the blackboard. "But . . ."

Shepard stands up, pulling his backpack straps over his shoulders. "This helped."

"It didn't help," I say. "We were just getting started—"

Then he reaches for my face, and for a completely absurd moment, I think he might be trying to kiss me good-bye—but he's just rubbing chalk from my chin. "It helped," he says. "You have a way of making things seem manageable. I like it."

"But we didn't manage anything."

He hooks his thumbs on his backpack straps. "You have my number now. Remember, you're going to send me derisive texts."

I'm examining my blackboard again, like it might give me something useful to send home with him. "About what?"

"Ah, just assume I'm doing *something* you wouldn't approve of."

I look back at him. "That is a safe bet."

He winks at me. "I know."

Shepard is walking to the door now, and I'm walking with him. He's going back to America. Where he doesn't have a truck anymore. I mean, he'll be fine. He'll bounce back. He's very bouncy. Unsinkable. Cursed, but unsinkable. Still totally cursed. And foolish. Too trusting. Will he even make it to Heathrow with both kidneys?

I would help him if I could.

If it were my responsibility . . .

No—if it were in my *power.* I would help him if I were a better mage.

But a better mage *wouldn't* help him . . .

There's a patch sewn to his backpack that says, BE SOFT.

"Shepard!" I say.

He stops in the doorway.

"Stay."

He smiles, but it's sad. "Penelope . . ."

"Stay," I say again. "We just got started."

"We've been through this already. Twice."

"I know, I'm sorry!" I hold my palms up to him. "I'm sorry I keep jerking you around. I've had a *really* rough couple of weeks, and I don't know which way is up. I still don't know if I can help you by myself—honestly, I wouldn't bet my thirdborn on it—but just . . ." I take hold of his denim sleeve. "*Stay.* Let me try. What have you got to lose?"

Shepard looks down at me. "You know you don't have to do this by yourself."

"No, it's okay. I want to do what I can. I'm not *completely* useless. In *every* situation. Usually. I think."

"No. I mean—Penelope, I'm here, too. We can work on this together."

Oh . . .

Right.

I suppose we can.

26

BAZ

Simon didn't take it well.

"There's a *new* Chosen One?"

This was last night. After we went hunting. (I still can't believe that he came *hunting* with me. That he watched me drink rat blood and still wanted to kiss me. *Repeatedly*.) We'd eaten my aunt's Bourbons, and we were headed back to sleep. My head was resting on his chest. It was bliss.

Simon sat up forcefully, pushing me off.

I sat up, too, sighing. "More than one, apparently."

"But *I* was the Chosen One!" He turned to face me, his wings flared out behind him. "I mean, I was a fraud, but—"

"Disagree."

"*Baz . . .*" he groaned, hiding his face.

"Simon, you know how I feel about this. You fulfilled every prophecy."

"The Greatest Mage was supposed to *defeat* the greatest threat to the World of Mages; I *was* the greatest threat to the World of Mages."

I shrugged. "Why not both?"

Simon shook his head, still trying to make sense of it all. "So, like, new people are calling themselves the Greatest Mage now?"

I leaned back against my headboard, elbows up, crossing my wrists on my head. "That's how it seems. Fiona didn't give me many details—just that, with you and the Mage out of the picture, a few charlatans are taking advantage."

He still looked dumbfounded. "So your stepmother is following around a new *Chosen One*?"

"I'm not sure. Aunt Fiona thinks so."

"Well"—Simon squared his shoulders—"we have to rescue her."

I could have hugged him in that moment. And then I realized that I *could* hug him. That nothing was stopping me. I wrapped my arms around him, under his wings, and held tight.

"Baz?" Simon's arms fell more gently around me. "Are you okay?"

"I'm just very glad that you're here."

He held me more confidently then. "Why would anyone even *want* to be the Chosen One?"

I huffed a laugh into his neck. "Power, obviously."

He shook his head against mine. "There's no power," he said, his voice low.

I didn't know what to say to that. Simon could have *ruled* the World of Mages with his magic. He could have ruled the *world*.

"I'll text Penelope," he said, pulling away from me to find his phone. "She must not know about all this. She would have mentioned it—to you, if not to me."

"Simon . . . Are you certain you want to get involved in this? It is *magic*."

He looked back at me, like I was being silly. "It's your *stepmum*."

I smiled. I watched him send his texts. "I can make a few calls tomorrow morning," I said. "Ask around. See if anyone knows anything."

"Shouldn't we get started now?" He was sitting on the edge of the bed, ready to go.

I held my hand out to him. "No. Nothing will change overnight. Let's just sleep."

He looked surprised. "Are you sure?"

"I'm sure, Snow."

He bit his lip for a moment, then took my hand and folded his wings. "All right. We'll rescue Daphne tomorrow."

I pulled him down beside me, and laid my head on his chest again. "Tomorrow."

The next morning—this morning—while Simon made toast, I sat at the kitchen table and called someone I could trust to be honest with me.

"Hello, Dev."

"Well, if it isn't Basilton Pitch. Did you take a break from getting your cock sucked and remember that you have friends and family?"

"Took a break from sucking cock, actually."

Simon's head spun around. I shrugged, apologetically, and turned away from him in my chair.

Dev sighed. "You don't call, you don't write."

"I've been busy studying. Haven't you?"

"Yeah, yeah," he said. "Uni is a ball-ache. As it turns out, pledging allegiance to the Mage twice a week and working on my *diction* did nothing to prepare me for higher education."

I snorted. "I've heard the new headmistress is making people do maths."

"Unacceptable! Cares she not for tradition?"

"What's next," I said, "geography?"

Dev's voice dropped, confidentially. "Niall's brother says it's worlds better down at Wats these days. They can have mobile phones. And they brought back the admissions test. Old Bunce has *some* standards."

I decided to push on while Dev was being sincere; it only happens biannually. "Say, have you been hearing this twaddle about a new Greatest Mage?"

"Aw. Poor Baz. Threw it all away for the Chosen One, and now you have to start over."

"So you have heard about it."

"Crowley," Dev swore, "it's all my grandmother talks about. She follows one of them on Facebook."

"On Facebook? What do they call themselves?"

Dev sounded amused: "Baz, are you *actually* interested? Have you found religion?"

"Nah. I have a friend who's all caught up in it. I want to make sure they're not in any trouble."

"A friend, eh? Well, it's not me, and it's not Niall. Has Simon Snow joined a saviour cult? That's rich."

"You don't think there's anything to all this, do you?"

"Do I think the Greatest Mage has been hiding out in Swansea, and my grandmother was the first to know? No, dear cousin, I do not. I think some greedy tosser wants to make sure I don't inherit her Aston Martin."

"Your poor grandmother," I said.

"My poor car," he replied.

"So, it's all a financial scam?"

"Grandmum's Facebook saviour? Assuredly. But better him than the Chosen wanker Máire Clark is following around."

"Máire Clark, is that someone I know?"

"Year ahead of us at Watford. Dark hair. Good legs. The Mage arrested her dad for insider dealing."

"Oh right." Máire. Scottish. Sat near me in Magic Words.

"She's obsessed with some 'miracle worker.' Volunteers at his compound. The guy bleeds from his palms, spits doves, the whole bit."

"What's the difference between miracles," I asked, "and good old-fashioned magic?"

"Don't ask Máire," Dev groaned. "She'll gnaw your bloody ear off—and her legs won't even be a distraction for you."

"So, what's that one called? Máire's miracle worker?"

"You're actually invested in this, aren't you?" This was a real treat for my cousin, I could tell. "Which of your friends has gone off the deep? Is it Wellbelove? Because I could find religion with Wellbelove. I could bleed from the palms, if you catch my meaning."

I pretended that I didn't. Once Dev starts on Agatha, he never stops. "Will you send me the name of your grandmother's guy?" I asked. "And Máire's, too. Could you find out?"

"Yeah, yeah. Will you come out to the pub with us? Before term starts? You can even bring Snow. I heard he's slowly turning into a dragon; can he still have a drink? Can he still take it up the—"

I cut him off. "Who told you that, the dragon thing?"

"My grandmother. She saw it on Facebook. Is it true?"

At the moment, Simon was sitting across from me, eating toast. There was melted butter running down his wrist. I held out a napkin.

"He can still have a drink," I said.

Simon took the napkin, then licked the butter off his arm.

"Excellent," Dev said. "I'll call you next week. Cheers."

"Cheers," I said, hanging up.

"Who was *that*?" Simon asked, sucking on his thumb.

"One of my cousins," I said, taking a piece of his toast. "Dev."

"Dev from school? Your little minion?"

"If you like."

Simon hadn't made any tea. I got up to start it.

"So Dev is your cousin . . ." he asked. "Huh. He doesn't look Egyptian."

"Because he's not."

"Aren't you?"

I was standing at the sink, filling the kettle, but I glanced Snow's way. "You understand how cousins work, right?"

I turned off the tap, careful not to drop my toast. "I think our great-grandparents were siblings . . . Mine became headmaster at Watford—Tyrannus Pitch, I'm named after him. Tyrannus grew up in Hampshire and married a woman from Egypt—Karima Pitch—famously powerful. Like, *legendary*."

I flipped on the kettle, and reached for two mugs, setting them on the counter. "They had a few kids. Two of them of them moved to Egypt. One stayed and became another Watford headmaster—you've seen his picture in the Weeping Tower, Balthazar. My grandmother was his second wife. *She* moved here from Sicily. Adolorata, another staggering witch. I can sort of remember her, she died the year before my mother was killed—"

I stopped myself. This was probably too much information. Literally no one is as interested in Pitch family history as I am.

But when I looked back at Simon, he was rapt.

"Anyway," I said, winding it up. "Dev's line goes off in the other direction. They're mostly from Cornwall, I think. My ancestors married for power. His were all about dosh." I took another bite of my toast.

Simon looked like I'd just given him huge news. "Baz . . . I didn't know you were *Italian*."

I laughed. "I was so busy trying to hide my vampirism from you that I didn't disclose my family tree. I'm only giving you the Pitch highlights, by the by, but that's because the Grimms don't really have highlights. They're all middling farmers, a few of them from Scotland. My mother, it seems, married for love."

The kettle clicked off, and Simon hopped up to fetch it. "So you have cousins all over?"

"Indeed," I said, getting the milk. "The Grimm-Pitch network is vast. Though I seem to be a dead end."

Simon frowned over our mugs as he poured. "I don't have any cousins."

"Well, you might . . . yeah?" I sat back down at the table, watching him poke at one of the tea bags. "You could always do that thing the Normals do. Genetic testing." Simon might find cousins. He might find *parents*.

He pushed out his chin, rueful. "Best not. Who knows what they'd see in my DNA . . . Dragon parts, Humdrum holes." He brought the mugs to the table and set one down in front of me. "Was Dev helpful? I always thought he was a ponce."

I pulled out my tea bag. "You thought that because he hung out with me."

Simon shrugged.

"Well . . ." I reached for the sugar. "He *was* a ponce. *And* he was helpful. His grandmother's entangled in a Greatest Mage scam on Facebook. And he's heard of another rotter who's out there performing miracles."

Simon looked personally offended. "Chosen One miracles?"

"I gather."

"Is he, like, *going off*?"

"Circe," I say. I'm trying to stop saying "Crowley"—Bunce says he's problematic. (Which seems obvious, but whatever.) Half the time, I forget. "I hope not. Maybe going off isn't necessarily a Chosen One thing."

"Yeah." Simon poked at his tea bag again. "Maybe that was just me."

"But Dev's going to get some names for me, and I already have one name—my aunt told me about someone whose son may have run off with this circus. A friend of the family. We could go talk to her. I suppose it's the closest thing we have to a lead at the moment."

"Yeah, may as well start somewhere. What's her name?"

"Lady Ruth Salisbury. She lives in Mayfair."

27

SIMON

Baz makes me borrow more of his clothes.

"I don't see why I have to be dressed up to talk to an old lady."

"We're strangers showing up at her door out of nowhere. We need to look presentable."

For Baz, that means a full-on suit. Three pieces! It's the colour of toffee sauce, and he's got a bright blue shirt on underneath—blue like butterfly wings and unbuttoned a *bit* low for visiting an elderly person. (If you want to know the truth, he looks good enough to eat. He's looked good all day. You should see Baz when he first wakes up: His eyes always look sleepy, but when he's actually sleepy, he looks like somebody trying to seduce you in a silent movie. One of those black-and-white fellows with the heavy eyeliner. I feel like I'm following him around with my heart in my hand. It's even more terrifying than it used to be—because before, I was telling myself that this thing with him would either fall apart before it killed me, or that I'd die before I had to deal with it. But now . . . What now?)

I get off relatively easy—dark jeans and a pale-green knit, button-down shirt. Baz casts a spell to tailor it around my wings and another to magickally shorten the sleeves. "So you won't be too hot in this coat," he says, holding up a grey mackintosh.

I groan.

"Or," he says, "you could let me spell your wings away?"

I take the coat. And his jeans, the shirt, the whole thing. Though I refuse a giant watch—and shake him off when he tries to arrange my hair. "For fuck's sake."

When we get to Lady Salisbury's neighbourhood, I'm half glad Baz made me dress up. I should have guessed from the "Lady" that it would be posh. We stop at a red-brick terraced house with big bay windows that sort of push out from the front, almost like turrets. The windows are framed in white plaster and decorated with unicorns and mermaids and little otters with wings. (Are wealthy magicians *never* subtle?)

Baz uses the door knocker. It's shaped like a smiling cyclops.

"Maybe we should have called first," I say.

"Then she could have said no."

"She could *still* say no . . ."

"Who says no to the Chosen One?"

I start to argue some more, but there's someone in the window, pulling back the curtain. Baz steps neatly behind me. After a second, the door opens an inch, and a woman peeks out. "Is that . . . It is!" she says, opening the door. "Simon Snow, on my very own doorstep!"

It's an older woman, I'm not sure how old—I don't know

many old people. She's heavyset with lots of blondish hair and a giant purple sweater. She's looking at me the way no one has looked at me for a while, like I'm all that. Her eyes are wide, and her face is awed. "You *are* him, aren't you?"

Baz pokes me in the back.

"Y-yes," I say. "I am."

The woman stands tall. She's only a couple inches shorter than me. Her hands are in fists at her side. "Is it true you killed the Mage?"

"I—" I haven't had to talk about this since the inquiry. And I've never really had to face anyone outside of the Coven. I mean, of course everyone in the World of Mages knows I killed the Mage. Of course they'd be angry. The woman's jaw is clenched. Her lips are pursed. I look down at my feet. "Yes. I did."

And then, suddenly—she's *hugging* me.

Like, *really* tight.

"Thank you," she says, and it sounds like she might be crying. She's sort of rocking me back and forth. "You're a hero, Simon Snow. Thank you."

I'm too stunned to hug her back. *Should* I hug her back? I'm glad she's not angry, but I'm a little worried that she's so happy. Did all rich people hate the Mage as much as Baz's family did?

She's pulling away now, wiping her eyes. She sniffs. "Come in, come in. Get out of the—Well, it's lovely out, isn't it? Come in, anyway. Your friend, too. And tell me what brings Simon Snow to my door on a Tuesday afternoon?"

Baz has stepped up beside me, smooth as silk. "Lady Salisbury?"

"Yes?" she says, looking a bit concerned again.

"My name is Basilton Grimm-Pitch."

"Grimm-Pitch . . . Natasha's son?"

"Yes."

"*Oh!*" She holds her hand over her heart. "Well, you're a grown man, aren't you! When did that happen? And so handsome! Snakes alive. Natasha Pitch's son." She takes his arm and squeezes it. "I knew your mother. She was a dear friend once. And your grandmother! *Basilton Grimm-Pitch.* Tyrannus, isn't it? As I live and breathe. You know, your aunt was just here—Oh." Her face falls. She clutches both hands to her chest. "You're here about my Jamie, aren't you? Do you have news of him?"

"No," Baz says. "No, we don't have any news, I'm sorry. But we were hoping you could tell us more about his disappearance."

Lady Salisbury looks confused, maybe a little wary. "You were?"

"My stepmother is missing, too."

BAZ

Lady Salisbury shows us into her drawing room—a big, airy room, crowded with antique coffee tables and richly upholstered furniture. "Here," she says, still sounding rattled. "Sit. I'll get some cake. Would you like some cake? It's homemade."

"Oh, no, we couldn't," I say.

"Sure, we could," Simon says.

She laughs. "Good answer. I was going to make you have some anyway. Should we have tea? I prefer milk with cake, myself."

"Milk is great," Simon says.

"You boys sit. I'll be right back."

We look around the room. There are plenty of seats to choose from. I sit down in an antique bergère chair, embroidered with peacocks. It wobbles, but holds. Simon sits on a rose-coloured sofa and sinks to the springs. I stifle a laugh. His blue eyes meet mine, and it's good. For just a moment. It's unexpectedly *good*. He looks too handsome in my clothes. He looks too handsome in his own terrible clothes; he's bloody unbearable in mine.

Lady Salisbury is back soon enough with a tray. She still seems tearful. "I hope you like chocolate," she says, serving Simon a mountainous wedge of cake.

"Who doesn't like chocolate," he replies, earning another smile.

She hands me a slightly smaller slice—fair enough, I didn't kill the Mage—and sits down next to Simon to pour the milk.

Lady Salisbury is a large woman. Tall and sturdy look-ing, even at her age. She must be about 70—a full gen-eration older than my mother. I wonder how they became friends . . . She's wearing a long mauve sweater, loose grey yoga pants, and patent leather Dansko clogs. Her hair is a yellow grey, and she wears it in a large, loose bun, with bluntly cut bangs that make her look like a Scandinavian tourist. I don't know if she's a "Lady" in the British sense or the magickal sense—I suppose she could be both. I think her husband may have been active in the magickal community before he died . . . Perhaps that's how she knew my mum.

Clearly, Lady Salisbury wasn't a fan of the Mage. Which could mean she's sensible and progressive—or could mean she's petty and corrupt. (For my own family, it's a bit "all of the above.") She might just miss the old days, when families like mine and hers ran things. Whatever else, her cake is very good. Snow is inhaling his.

"So," Lady Salisbury says, sitting back in the sofa, "did Malcolm send you to talk to me? Is he frustrated with the Coven as well?"

"Oh," I say. "Well. No. My father—"

"We took this on ourselves," Simon cuts in. (If ever someone was emboldened by baked goods.) He takes a moment to swallow. "When I heard that there were people claiming to be the Greatest Mage, you know, you can see why I'd be concerned."

Lady Salisbury is smiling sadly at him again. "Many still believe that title belongs to you, Mr. Snow."

Simon's face is wide open. "No. That was never me."

"But you're the most powerful mage—"

"No. Not anymore."

I know that Simon is a hopeless liar, but I wish he wouldn't tell people the truth so easily. There's no harm in letting them *believe* he's still powerful.

"Probably I was never a magician," he goes on. "The Mage was just using me."

"But they say you gave yourself flaming dragon wings . . ."

"Pfft," he says. "They don't flame."

"So you *do* have wings." There's a light in her eyes. She leans over her plate. "May I see them?"

I try to object. "I don't think—"

But Simon is already shuffling off my grey mac. He's handed Lady Salisbury his plate. "Sure. I'd love an excuse to take off this coat."

You look very smart in that coat, I think.

"You look very smart in that coat," Lady Salisbury says. "But you must get tired of hiding them—" She sets both plates on the table to cover her mouth. "Oh!"

Simon's wings are free. He spreads them some, careful not to stab Lady Salisbury, who looks genuinely dazzled.

"They're *splendid*," she says. "*Much* bigger than I was expecting. And the loveliest shade of red. May I touch them?" She's already touching the wing closest to her. Simon flinches, and she pulls her hand back. "Oh, I see, I'm so sorry." She smiles again. "I understand why you keep them hidden from the Normals, but these are tremendous. Can you fly with them?"

"Yeah," he says.

"Oh, that's remarkable. Did you teach yourself?"

"I must have."

"Imagine!" She holds a hand to her chest. "I've always wanted to fly." She turns to me. "Haven't you always wanted to fly, Basilton?"

I have flown. With Simon. "Yes," I say.

"There are no good spells for it," she says with real disappointment. "The most you can do is float around like a week-old party balloon."

"That's true," I agree.

She looks down at Simon's mostly eaten cake. "Here, let me cut you another slice. You, too, Basilton, hand me your plate."

"I have plenty."

"Rubbish. Look at you. You could use some shoring up at the foundation." She serves herself some, too.

"You can call him Baz," Simon says.

"Is that so?" She smiles at me.

"Yes," I say.

"All right." She nods. "So, Simon and Baz, you've taken it on yourself to investigate this Chosen One conspiracy."

"I know we look like children," I say, "but we have good

heads on our shoulders, and Simon has spent his whole life defending the World of Mages."

"You don't look like children to me. You look like veterans. And I'm grateful to have someone who's willing to listen. The Coven laughed at me. They sent your aunt to convince me it was vampires who took my son. There hasn't been a vampire attack since—" She looks at me, dismayed. "Oh, darling, I'm sorry."

"No, it's fine. Please go on."

"I know Jamie is alive," she says. "He's in danger—but he's still out there."

"You have a feeling?" Simon asks. "Mother's intuition?"

"No. I cast a spell."

SIMON

I feel like a creeper, walking into a strange woman's bedroom—but that's where Lady Salisbury takes us. On the second floor of her house. It's darker up here. Cooler. Her room is huge, with a little sitting area and kind of a shrine by the lace-curtained window. There's a table with two lit candles—one burning brightly and one sputtering like it's about to go out. Each candle is surrounded by photographs: a fair-haired boy on the side that burns bright; a girl on the side that gutters.

"You 'Lit a candle' for him," Baz says, awed. "That's an enormous spell."

"I've cast it twice," Lady Salisbury says. "A mother whose child is in danger can lift a car."

"I'm so sorry."

"Don't be. Look . . ." She leads us to the table. "Both candles still burn. It's a comfort to me." She lifts a picture of a thickly built man wearing a Queen T-shirt. "That's Jamie," she says. "I took this photo last year, on his thirty-eighth birthday."

I was expecting him to be younger, I don't know why.

Baz pulls a notebook from his pocket, and it gives me a pang. Penny should be here. She still hasn't texted me back. I don't blame her—I know I owe her a proper apology, but I still don't know what *else* I owe her. Everything I said was true. I'm done with the World of Mages.

"How long has your son been missing?" Baz asks.

"A month." Lady Salisbury seems like a different person in this flickering light. Downstairs, she was warm and cheerful, if a bit sad. Now she's woebegone and mournful. This room feels too full of people who aren't here anymore. Her son, her daughter—apparently lost before the girl had a chance to get old—and a curly-haired man in an Air Force uniform looking down from a large photograph over the bed. "My husband," she says. She's caught me staring at the portrait. "Gone ten years now."

I nod, not sure whether I should offer condolences.

"Did Jamie tell you he was leaving?" Baz's pen is poised over the notepad.

"No . . . But there were signs." She lays her hand on his wrist, stopping his pen. "Let's go back downstairs. The light is better."

We follow her back down to the sitting room, past more family photos. There's one hanging over the staircase—the same blond girl as a teenager. I stop. "She looks familiar," I say. "I think I've seen a painting of her."

"At Watford," Baz says, over my shoulder. "In the Catacombs."

Neither of us mention that it weeps.

Lady Salisbury doesn't smile. "Yes," she says. "Lucy was a student there." She walks ahead of us down the stairs. "I think I will make tea after all."

"It's been hard for Jamie," Lady Salisbury says. She insisted that Baz sit next to me on the sofa. *That chair won't wobble for me; it knows better.* And she's given me a third slice of cake. (I can't believe she made this herself. It's four layers deep.) "He's never quite fit into magickal society."

"Why's that?" I ask.

"Well, Jamie was a different sort of learner . . . He didn't learn to read until quite late, and he's never been fond of reading aloud. His tongue would tie itself in knots."

I can sympathize. "So he did badly at Watford?"

"In those days," she says, "a reading disorder would keep you out of Watford."

I sit up straight, jamming my wings against the sofa. "Even if you were a magician? With your own wand?"

"Even then," she says.

I look at Baz for confirmation. His face is grim but unsurprised.

Lady Salisbury goes on: "Jamie's older sister went to Watford and learned magic, while Jamie stayed home with us and went to Normal schools. He learned a bit of magic, some household spells—but it was embarrassing for him, and eventually he stopped trying to get better at it."

She's turning her cup in her hands, looking down at her

tea. "We thought he'd made peace with it. He never had many magickal friends, and after his sister . . . well, ran away, there was no one to compare himself to. Jamie went to Normal schools, he married a Normal girl. I thought he'd let it go, magic."

She's quiet again. Baz and I don't try to fill the silence. What could I say—*"That's easier said than done"*? *"Even when you're terrible with words"*?

"But since his divorce," she says, "I don't know . . . He spends too much time online. He's got a cousin, a magician, who sends him conspiracy theories. Speciesist claptrap, most of it. I thought Jamie knew it was a lot of balls—" She looks up, abruptly. "Oh, excuse my language, boys. Anyway, I thought Jamie was repeating all of this nonsense just to get a rise out of me at the dinner table."

"What sort of conspiracy theories?" Baz asks.

"Siegfried and Roy, it's hardly worth saying out loud. *'Did you know the government is manufacturing gryphons?' 'Did you know that Silicon Valley is controlled by vampires?'"*

Baz freezes, rattling his teacup on its saucer. Lady Salisbury keeps talking.

"A few months ago," she says, "he started to fixate more and more on these Chosen One prophecies—you know how it is, everyone's a Greatest Mage expert these days."

"It seems we've been left out of those conversations," Baz says, fully recovered.

"Oh." Lady Salisbury looks from him to me, and chuckles. "I suppose you *would* be. Well"—she waves her hand—"you're not missing much."

I'm scrubbing at my hair; it's probably driving Baz mental, but I can't seem to stop. "Is this, like, something that most magicians believe now? That's there's a new Greatest Mage?"

"I think it's more a thing that most magicians like to gossip about," she says. "The various candidates, the evidence for and against, who's having a cocktail party where you can meet one of them . . . Plenty of mages are still loyal to you, Simon."

"To me?"

"Oh, yes"—she smiles—" 'Snowvians.' "

"No," I say. "That's not a thing."

"They think you'll get your powers back and rise higher than ever."

"Hmm," Baz says, looking down his nose at me. "I think *I* might be a Snowvian."

"I'm a bit of a Snowvian myself." Lady Salisbury smiles at him.

"No . . ." I say. "Just, no."

"Well," she goes on, "there's another school of thought that says the time hasn't come yet for the Greatest Mage, and that when that person *does* come, it will be obvious."

I huff. "Doesn't anyone think that maybe all of this is bollocks?"

Baz elbows me.

"Excuse my language," I tack on. "But maybe there *is* no Chosen One. Maybe the prophecies were made by people like the Mage who just wanted to take advantage of everyone."

Lady Salisbury doesn't look convinced.

Baz looks even less convinced. "We can't just stop believing in prophecies. Our whole culture is built on them. Watford itself was prophesied."

"How do we know that?" I ask.

"They taught us about it at Watford," he says.

"Penny would call that circular reasoning. I'm guilty of it all the time."

At the mention of Penelope, Baz looks back at his notebook. "So . . . Jamie was interested in the Chosen One theories?"

"Yes," Lady Salisbury says, "I think in a way he was *especially* interested because he'd been so removed from the World of Mages. This was something he could participate in, just like everyone else. As I said, I didn't think Jamie was taking any of it seriously, but maybe you can't spend so much time engaging with nonsense *without* taking it seriously . . ." Lady Salisbury presses her fingers to her forehead, like she has a headache coming on. "One name started to come up more and more . . . Smith Smith-Richards."

"That's a hell of a name," I say.

"I have cousins who are Smiths," Baz says, "but I've never heard of a Smith-Richards."

"No one seems to have heard of him until recently," she says. "Born in Yorkshire apparently."

"I see." Baz is writing that down. "And what made Smith-Richards stand out? To your son?"

Lady Salisbury looks so genuinely troubled, I think she might start to cry. Properly this time. She looks away from us. "Smith Smith-Richards is promising people magic."

BAZ

"Magic?" Snow and I both say at once.

Lady Salisbury pulls a tissue from her cardigan pocket and wipes her eyes. "Yes."

"He's *giving* them magic?" Simon asks, and I know he's

thinking of those days when he pushed his magic into me—it shouldn't have been possible. Or perhaps he's thinking of the Mage's last moments, when the man tried to drain Simon's magic into himself. Would it have worked?

"Not exactly," she says. "Smith-Richards claims to be *healing* their magic. Helping them realize their true potential."

"And your son believed this?" I ask.

"He didn't at first," she says, "or he acted like he didn't. But Smith-Richards's name kept coming up. Jamie started to get very agitated talking about the other Greatest Mage contenders. He'd say they were swindlers, obvious frauds— that only Smith Smith-Richards was saying anything interesting . . ."

She wipes her eyes again. "Jamie started going out more," she says, "in the evenings. Before all this, he'd spend every night upstairs, on his computer. I tried to tell myself that it was a good thing, him getting out a bit, meeting new people—but it made my blood run cold . . .

"Finally," she says, "I confronted him. Oh, we had such a row!" She smiles ruefully at us, blinking away tears. "Me asking him if he was getting too involved in all this Chosen One hullabaloo, and him telling me he's an adult who can do what he likes. Me saying I was worried, and him saying . . ."

Lady Salisbury looks down at her teacup again and slowly shakes her head. "Well. He said I didn't want him to be a success. That I *liked* him being a failure because it kept him here with me.

" '*Mum,*' he said, '*what if Smith can fix my magic?*'

" '*Your magic isn't broken!*' I told him, and I meant it! Jamie isn't *broken.*" She looks at Simon and me, like she's pleading for someone to believe her. "It's always been more nuanced than that. Magic didn't come easily to him, and then he wasn't trained, and then he built up all of these behavioural ways to cope with it . . . Maybe he just didn't have much access to magic in the first place! Call it genetics or call it circumstance. It happens. Sometimes it's a trickle, and sometimes it's a stream."

"Sometimes it's a spark," I say, "and sometimes it's a fire."

"Exactly!" she says fiercely. Then her gaze falls to her lap. "Well, he didn't want to hear that. He stormed up to his room. A few days later, he left for one of his meetings and didn't come back."

"No note?" I ask.

"No note," Lady Salisbury says. "I've tried every spell I can think of to find him. It's like he's being hidden behind a curtain. His candle burns, I know he's out there . . ." She reaches a hand towards us. "But I can't see him or feel him." She closes her fist. "It's like summoning air."

"Have you talked to Smith-Richards?"

She scoffs. "It was easy enough to find his meetings, but I was turned away. The magician at the door said they're trying to maintain an 'atmosphere of support and optimism.' That's when I went to the Coven. Now, *there's* an organization that doesn't know its arse from its elbow. All of the Mage's cronies are out, which means no one has five minutes of institutional memory. They're still plumbing the depths of his corruption; who knows when they'll hit bottom!"

She looks at us again, like she's remembering herself. "I apologize. I must sound like an old coot. The Coven thought so. Even my friends think so. They think Jamie was always a lost cause, and that he finally met a bad end. They feel sorry for me, but they don't take me seriously."

"We're taking you seriously," Simon says.

And it's true, we are.

Lady Salisbury may be an old coot. But there's something shady happening here, and I have a feeling my stepmother is caught up in it.

Didn't Mordelia say Daphne was away working on her magic?

My stepmother is the limpest mage I know. She doesn't use magic for anything. When she wants to cast a spell, she has to go and get her wand out of a drawer, the same drawer where we keep extra batteries and rubber bands.

When the Humdrum sucked all the magic out of our house in Hampshire, Daphne joked about staying there anyway.

I know she just barely made it through Watford. She told me she only got the grades she did because she was good at written tests and diligent about homework.

She's even talked about sending Mordelia to Normal school—"because they're more academically competitive." I thought she was kidding, but maybe she doesn't want to put Mordelia through it. Mordelia's a bright girl. She could be a star at some Normal school. At Watford, she'll be known for what she can't do.

I thought Daphne was at peace with herself. That she accepted her place in the world. It could be worse: She's married to a wealthy farmer who worships the ground she walks on. She has a big house and a bunch of noisy friends. She has healthy kids.

I didn't think she cared about magic.

Maybe I was wrong.

"We want to help," I say to Lady Salisbury. "Tell us everything you know about Smith Smith-Richards."

28

LADY RUTH

I watch them from the window after we say good-bye.

They aren't halfway down the walk before the Pitch boy is taking the Chosen One's hand. Ah, I'd heard as much. Now that I've met them, I'm glad to know it's true. They could both use a fierce ally, I think.

Did the Mage hurt anyone worse than that boy?

Even my Lucy got away.

But Simon Snow was snatched off the streets and turned into a puppet of war. There's no official account of what happened, but we all know that Simon defeated the Humdrum and then the Mage—and that the Coven, packed as it was with Davy's friends, was still unanimous in acquitting the boy.

What could Davy have done to turn his most loyal disciple against him?

And what did it cost Simon Snow to make that turn? To bite the only hand that ever fed him?

I'm glad he's not alone in this.

That he has someone to take his hand when they think old women like me aren't looking.

Can two boys do what the rest of the World of Mages won't?

Perhaps. They've done it before, haven't they?

29

SIMON

Baz made us take the Underground to get to Lady Salisbury's.

I hadn't been on the Tube for more than a year. Not since I got my wings. But Baz insisted they're hardly noticeable now that I've got them folded up so tight.

"*I look strange*," I said to him on the ride to Mayfair. "*People are staring.*"

"*Yeah, but they don't think you have* wings."

"*They think I have a* hump."

"*They'll get over it. Bodies come in different shapes.*"

I suppose he was right—no one jumped me or threw holy water on me. So now we're taking the train back to my flat, standing side by side, holding on to a bar.

It was relatively easy to talk Baz into coming back to mine—I don't think he wants to deal with his aunt yet—but he's still whinging about it.

"You don't have a sofa," he says.

"We can sit on the floor."

"You don't have food. I'll bet you don't have cutlery. Or bath towels. You don't even have a bed."

"I have a bed. A mattress is a bed."

He looks away from me. I think he might be blushing. With Baz, that's more of an expression than a change in colour. I knock my shoulder into his, and he smiles at the floor.

"So, what do you think?" I ask him.

"About what?"

"Lady Salisbury, Smith-Richards—the whole thing."

Baz glances around us. Nobody's paying any real attention. There are a few girls checking him out, but there's never any getting away from that.

"I think Daphne might be caught up in it," he says. "What do you think?"

"I liked her," I say. "Lady Salisbury."

"You like anyone who feeds you."

"I don't think she's barmy . . ."

"No." Baz shakes his head. "Me neither. What do you want to do about it?"

"Well, we're going to have to meet the new Chosen One, aren't we?"

He looks at me for a moment, then nods. "I suppose we are."

30

PENELOPE

The sign over the door says THE WHISTLING OGRE.

"Right in plain sight," I say.

Shepard just grins at me. I swear, he's *excited*. I thought it would take days of detective work to find a place like this, but Shepard assured me it wouldn't take long. *"I'll sniff one out. Just wait until it gets dark. The sort of Maybes we're looking for don't truck with daylight."*

"Maybes." As in magickal beings.

I wasn't sure what to wear. None of my clothes scream "dark creature pub night." I don't even like *ordinary* pubs. I don't drink, and I don't smoke. And I don't play darts. So going to the pub means watching other people drink and smoke and play darts. Secondhand darts—what an abject waste of time.

"I don't think I can do this," I say. "I'm going to stand out like a sore thumb."

"Trust me," Shepard says, "everyone in there will be minding their own business."

"Not you. You never mind your own business."

"That's one of my unique charms, Penelope."

I roll my eyes and let his "unique charms" go without comment. "They're going to see that we're not creatures," I say instead.

Shepard has done nothing to alter his appearance. He's really walking into a dark creature hangout with a NEVER SASS A SASQUATCH badge on his jacket and smelling like patchouli. "I told you," he says, standing close to me and talking under his breath, "they'll assume we're something else in disguise."

"All right," I say, "what am I, then, what's my backstory?"

He laughs. "Do you need to get into *character*?"

"*Shepard.*"

"Okay, okay, um . . ." He raises his narrow shoulders and bites his lip for a second, like he's thinking. "You're a muskrat maiden."

"What the hell is a *muskrat maiden*? Did you just make them up?"

"No! Muskrat maidens trick human beings into trapping them, and then they trade skins."

"Do people trap muskrats?"

"Well, not so much anymore. These are lean times for muskrat maidens."

"We don't even have muskrats in England."

"See," he smiles, "that's good, that means no one will see the holes in your story."

"Shepard."

"Penelope, it'll be fine. Just stay behind me and stay quiet."

"Oh, is that a woman's place?"

He points at me. "Nice. Muskrat maidens are notoriously thin-skinned."

"Very funny."

"It's because they only steal the human epidermis," he explains. "It's really very intere—"

The door to the pub opens, and a squat woman leans out. "If you're not coming in, you need to move along. I don't like a commotion."

I duck behind Shepard.

"We're coming in," he says, "thank you. I'm Shepard."

"I don't need to know your name," she grumbles, waving us into a small, dark room. She's wearing black leather trousers and a leather coat (unseasonable), and standing in front of a second door. "This is a private club. Are you a member?"

"I am a friend of the establishment," he says.

"Are you now?"

"I've walked the hills."

She folds her arms. "Have you."

"And crossed the rivers." There's a gleam in his brown eyes. She grunts.

"I've sat in the dark and never asked for a light," Shepard continues. "I carry no weapon, though I may not come in peace. And there's enough in my purse to cover the night."

Her mouth is flat. "I suppose that'll do," she says, opening the door behind her.

"Thank you"—Shepard pulls me inside by the elbow— "have a great night!"

"Americans," I hear her mutter behind us.

Inside, the place looks like every other dirty old pub. A bit darker than usual. They've got Imagine Dragons playing too loud. Shepard still has my elbow. "I forgot to mention," he says softly, "don't stare."

"I'm not going to—" Nicks and Slick! The barman is an actual *tree person*. In full leaf! Is that an *Ent*? Are Ents *real*?

Why would an Ent work in a pub? Don't they require sunlight?

Shepard takes a seat at the bar and hauls me up beside him. The tree turns our way and sort of rustles. It's a rowan tree, I think. Immune to magic. That's probably useful.

"I'll have a Coke," Shepard says.

"Pepsi all right?" the tree asks. It has a man's voice. A very resonant man's voice. Like someone is knocking on wood right in the middle of it.

"No," Shepard says, "do you have ginger ale?"

The tree nods its leaves and starts to fill a glass with one branch. It's wiping the bar in front of us with another.

"I'll have the same," I tell it.

"My name is Shepard," Shepard says. Like someone pulled the ring on his back. "And this is my friend—" I frown at him. "—Debbie."

The barman gives us our ginger ales.

"We're not from around here." Shepard smiles.

"You don't say . . ." the barman says. I can't see its mouth. Does it have a mouth? Is it just emitting words from its leaves? Like pollen?

"We're looking for someone with a special skill."

"My special skill is serving alcohol," the barman says. "Are you going to order any?"

"Definitely," Shepard says. "Please, pour yourself a drink."

I get the feeling the tree is giving Shepard a flat look, but I can't be sure. After a second, it pulls itself a pint of dark ale, then tips the pint up to a crack in its bark. "What sort of skill?" it asks—*while* it's drinking. Which is either a trick or proof that it doesn't have a mouth. Unless it has more than one . . .

"Translation," Shepard says. "We've found some old papers—some really old papers. Found a giant who recognized the letters, but not the language."

"No giants in here," the tree says. "We're not zoned for it."

"I don't think it's a giant language," Shepard says. "Just an old one."

"This look like a library to you?"

Shepard smiles again. "No."

"Some sort of centre for ancient languages?"

"It does not, no."

"Did you just walk into the first underground pub you found after you got off the plane, figuring it'd be full of ye old-ey tim-ey linguists?"

"I can see why it would seem that way."

The tree leans a large branch on the bar in front of Shepard. "Look, you seem like a good guy . . ." (*Does* he? Based on *what*?) "And if the special skill you were looking for involved making a bet or engulfing a corpse in bark, I could steer you in the right direction. But this isn't *The Da Vinci Code* starring Tom Hanks. Or *National Treasure* starring Nicolas Cage. I can't just point you to the back of the pub, where we keep our wizened old *keeper of the sacred texts*."

"Well, there is Old Kipper . . ."

The three of us turn towards the voice. There's some sort of gnome standing on the barstool next to me. I didn't even see him when I came in. He's dressed like a builder. What do gnomes build? And is he wearing doll's clothes? Is there mass-produced gnome clothing?

"They didn't say they needed a passport," the tree snaps. (We *could* use a passport, actually; the magic on Shepard's is temporary.) "They want some ancient treasure map translated."

"It isn't a map," Shepard unnecessarily offers. "It's a curse."

The tree backs up. "You didn't mention any curse."

"We think it's more of a treatise about curses," I improvise.

"Is that so, Debbie," the tree says, somehow conveying a sneer.

"Kipper's a dab forger," the gnome says. "But she knows a bit about languages, as well. Don't want to go copying something you can't read. Could end up summoning something ugly—or, worse, too pretty."

"We'd love to talk to Kipper," Shepard says. "Is she here?"

"Kipper doesn't come down here," the tree says. "She works at the coffeehouse up the street."

"A magickal coffeehouse?" Shepard is thrilled.

"Yeah," the tree says. "Costa."

There is indeed a Costa up the street. I think Shepard is disappointed by how banal it all is. I'm relieved; I could use a muffin.

When we ask for "Old Kipper," we're directed to the 30-something manager, a tired-looking woman with bobbed purple hair. "I'm Kipper," she says pleasantly. "Do you need some help?"

"Hi, Kipper," Shepard says. "Someone at the Whistling Ogre suggested we talk to you—"

"Oh," she says, brightening up a bit, "are you here for a commission?"

"Yes!" he says. "A commission."

"I can take my break in a few minutes. Just have a seat."

I get my lemon muffin, and we park ourselves in the corner of the shop. "I wonder if there *are* magickal coffeehouses . . ." Shepard says. "Do magicians have their own coffeehouses?"

"We don't need magickal coffeehouses," I say. "We're magickal wherever we go."

"Yeah, but you're so put off by Normals, I'd think you'd

want a place to escape from them."

"Magicians don't mind Normals, in general." I break my muffin in half and offer him some. "It's just *me* who finds you off-putting."

He takes the muffin. "So magicians make friends with Normals."

"All the time."

"And tell them about being magicians."

"Never."

"There must be exceptions."

"There really mustn't." I think of Micah and his new probably-Normal girlfriend. Does she know what he really is? I always thought Micah liked me (in part, at least) *because* I was a good magician. We practised our spellwork together. We talked about the magickal life we were going to share.

Kipper sits down at our table, taking off her apron. "Hi again, thanks for waiting. Unfortunately I only have a few minutes before I have to go back to the register."

"We'll get right to it, then," I say.

"I'm Shepard," he says. "And this is Debbie."

Kipper smiles at me. "That's my mother's name."

I have no reply to that, so I cut to the chase: "We're looking for someone who knows about languages, a translator."

"Oh." Kipper looks disappointed.

"We're sorry," Shepard says. "Is that not your area?"

"No," she says, "it is. I just thought you wanted an actual commission. I've been doing more watercolours. Portraits, mostly. Sometimes I do pets."

"Really?" he asks, sincerely interested. "They didn't tell us that. I'd love to see some of your paintings."

Kipper already has her phone out, opening her photo folder.

"I have a shop online, but sometimes people see my prints down at the Ogre and ask about me."

Shepard is looking delighted by something on her phone. I lean over to see. It's a watercolour of a cat wearing a bow tie.

"Oh my God," he says. "Adorable. And really reasonable pricing."

"People like to get their pets done after they die," she says. "After the pets die, I mean. To remember them."

"That's a cool idea," he says.

She smiles. "I kind of happened into it."

"So you don't know languages?" I ask.

Kipper looks like she forgot I was sitting here. "No, I do. A little. It's sort of a family specialty. My mother can speak in thirty-nine tongues."

"That's impressive," Shepard says.

"Yeah, especially for someone who only has four."

(Four what? Four *tongues*?)

"Wow," he says.

I elbow him. "Get out the thing," I say. "The . . . writing."

"Right, right." He pulls the folded-up ritual from his inside pocket and hands it to Kipper.

When she spreads it out onto the table, two extra fingers unfurl from each of her hands. "Oh shit," she says, sitting back, away from it.

"What," I say, "what's shit?"

"That's, like, really obscure."

"Yeah?" Shepard asks.

"That's not even, like, from this dimension, you know? Like, this is not from Earth-616. You shouldn't translate this. I *can't* translate it, but you shouldn't anyway—you could end up slicing a trapdoor into another dimension."

Shepard gives her a sad smile. "Kipper, I think I already did."

31

AGATHA

I am *flattened* by the time we get back to Niamh's Fiesta. My legs feel like jelly, and I'm hungry besides. Niamh pops the back of her hatchback open and gets out two bottles of water. Her face is flushed and sweaty, and her dark hair is coming out of her bun and sticking to her cheeks.

She tosses me a water—it's warm—and tips her own bottle up, emptying it one swallow.

I gulp some water down, then wipe my mouth on my wrist. "Hell's spells, I won't be able to walk tomorrow."

"What happened to that championship lacrosse athlete?"

"Oh, ha ha."

She's undoing her bun. Her hair falls down past her shoulders in shiny, dark brown waves. It's incongruous. Niamh's face is too hard to be framed by something so soft. She's already pulling it back up with her fingers and twisting it back into place.

"All that work," I say, "for nothing."

"It wasn't for nothing," she says, getting into the car.

I get in, too. "We spent *hours* herding those goats—and then we just left them in the hills."

"What were we supposed to do with them?"

"I don't know, you tell me. Shouldn't we have taken them down to the barn?"

"I already told you, you can't pen up the goats of Watford. The best you can do is invite them in."

"*Invite* them? Are they vampire goats?"

Niamh was about to start the car, but now she's turned in her seat to frown at me. "You're just like everyone else, aren't you."

"Oh, lay off." I roll down the window. "I tried to help."

"I suppose that's true," she mutters, starting the car. "You were extremely helpful for someone who doesn't care at all about anything outside of herself."

My head whips back to her. "Hey. You don't even know me."

Niamh scoffs, backing the car out onto the road. "*Everyone* knows you, Agatha. You're Simon Snow's girlfriend. You're the Chosen One's chosen one. You so much as break a nail, and he burns down the Wavering Wood."

"I feel like you're once again referring to a time when I was *kidnapped* . . ."

She looks over at me, actually angry now. "Maybe it doesn't matter to *you* whether Watford falls—but it's the heart of who we are, as magicians. It's our only institution, the only thing we've ever managed to get done and make work."

"*Niamh.* I went to Watford, too. I'm not *anti*-Watford." I'm leaning over the gear shift to make my point.

She's trying to watch the road and argue with me at the same time. "Then I'd think you'd be concerned about the goats!"

I shrug my shoulders with my palms in the air. "I mean,

I'm more concerned than I was yesterday. I've bonded with a few of them now."

"The goats of Watford are wandering away," she says, hunching over the steering wheel, "and no one cares! Not you, not even the headmistress—she has too many other problems. *The whole World of Mages* has too many other problems! Or too many other distractions. Most of them care more about who's going to replace your boyfriend than—"

I cut her off. "If you call him my boyfriend one more time, I'll scream."

"Why? Are you engaged now? Are you Simon Snow's *fiancée*?"

"No! We broke up ages ago! Everyone knows this!"

"What?" Niamh sits back in her seat, chastened. "I didn't know that."

"You must live under a rock." I fold my arms and look out my window. "It's all anyone talked about for months."

"I don't really pay attention to gossip . . ." she says.

"Well, we broke up our last year at Watford, and now he's with Baz Pitch. It was like boy–*Romeo and Juliet*."

"Romeo was already a boy."

"You know what I meant."

"Simon Snow dumped you for a Pitch?" Niamh sounds thoughtful. "Which one, again?"

"He didn't dump me, actually, but—you know, *Baz*. He was at school with us."

"What did he look like?"

I turn back to her. Is she kidding? "Basilton Grimm-Pitch? The headmistress's son?"

"Oh, right . . ." She still looks uncertain. "Pale? Crooked nose?"

"I mean, yes. But I've never heard him described that way."

Niamh shrugs. "Like I said, I didn't really follow your whole soap opera."

"You are so *exceedingly* unpleasant," I say. "I almost forgot that for a few hours. You're so much easier to be around when you're yelling at goats."

"Yeah, well, we have that in common." We're at a stop sign, and Niamh is redoing her bun again, making it even tighter. I'm *this* close to telling her how bad it looks that way. But she doesn't deserve constructive advice. I huff instead.

She ignores me.

I try to ignore her back, but it only lasts a minute. "I don't want Watford to fall, by the way. I've helped save Watford *multiple* times. Tangentially."

"Well," she says, "all your efforts will be in vain if the goats leave."

"Oh good, back to the goats again."

"I know that you believe the Goats of Watford are just a myth. But a myth is just another word for a story, and what do we have if we don't have stories!"

"Niamh! I've never even heard of the Goats of Watford— *should* I have?"

She rolls her eyes. "I mean, *I* think so. I think the heritage and care of magickal animals matter, that these are things we should study and share and—"

"Wait, they're *magickal* goats?"

Niamh puffs out a frustrated breath. "Why doesn't anyone know this? The goats are part of Watford history! They're in the coat of arms!"

"I thought those were pegasus . . . ses."

"No, they're goats."

"But they have wings," I say.

"So do the goats."

"*What?*"

"How do you think the goats are getting out over the wall, Agatha?"

"I thought they were jumping. They're magickal, *flying* goats?"

"Obviously."

"Obviously *not* obviously. Do people know this?"

"They *should!*" she half shouts, then looks embarrassed to have raised her voice. Her shoulders fall. "The story's so old that it seems like an old wives' tale now," she mutters. "And it's hard to find any scholarly accounts. The Mage hoarded books on magickal history but didn't let anyone else read them— and he was notoriously dismissive of animals and creatures. He's the reason we haven't had a vet in years—"

"Tell me the story."

"Agatha, I'm *trying*—"

"No, tell me the old wives' tale. About the goats."

"Oh." She glances over at me like she's trying to make sure I'm being sincere. "Well." She looks at me again. "The story goes that the same herd has been watching over Watford as long as it's existed. If they ever choose to leave, it would mean the school is truly lost. The goats would take all of their protection with them."

"Wait, *really?*"

"Well, really according to the story."

"That doesn't sound any less legitimate than half the stuff they taught us in Magickal History," I say. "Professor Bunce honestly doesn't care?"

Niamh sighs. "I shouldn't have said she doesn't care. She

just has a lot on her mind. And this feels very . . . *theoretical* to her. There isn't any hard proof that the goats protect the school, and Headmistress Bunce likes proof."

"Indeed . . ."

"I found out the goats were leaving a few months ago. I got called out to Watford to look at Miss Possibelf's Greater Dane, and I noticed that the goats weren't in the barn. The headmistress said they hadn't come back to the school since Ebb Petty died, and that she'd given up worrying about it— that they seemed fine in the fields."

"They did seem fine," I say. "They certainly weren't starving."

"Their numbers are way down," Niamh says gloomily. "Half the herd is gone, and only one of the does is with child this year."

"Well . . ." I'm feeling frustrated and helpless—and like we shouldn't drive away from the goats now that I know they might fly away. "Well, what actually happens if they leave?"

"According to the legends? Watford becomes mundane."

"Like, you couldn't do magic there?"

"Like the Normals could see it on Google Maps."

"*Niamh.* That can't happen!"

"It probably won't happen," she grumbles. "It probably *is* just an old wives' tale." She looks utterly defeated. "I think your father and the headmistress indulge my visits because I'm not hurting anything. It's my job to take care of the goats whether they're magic or not."

I watch the fields roll by us. It doesn't take long before we're in the outskirts of Watford, the city, which is really just the outskirts of London.

"Niamh . . ." I turn my head to look at her. She's got the

silhouette of a cartoon character. Heavy brow, long nose, sharp chin. I still can't believe I didn't recognize her from school. "I'm sorry. I genuinely didn't know why you cared so much."

"It's all right," she says. "You really were a help . . . I'm sorry I didn't know you broke up with Simon."

"Oh, Merlin, that's all right." I wave my hand. "It's kind of nice to think there were people at Watford who weren't paying attention to us."

The corner of her mouth twitches. "Well, if it makes you feel better, I *truly* didn't give a shit about you."

I roll my eyes back to the window. "Yeah, all right. I get it."

32

BAZ

Snow is on my last nerve.

"I can't just walk into a Chosen One rally as the defunct Chosen One!"

"Then let me change your face," I say for the tenth time.

"I'm not letting you fuck with my face," he mutters. "Though I'm starting to feel like you really want to . . ."

I'm sitting on his empty living room floor. Simon is pacing in front of me, wings spread, tail whipping around. Every time he stomps past me, he nearly smacks me with it.

"I could just spell your face back to normal when I'm done," I say, also for the tenth time.

"*No,* " he says. "No more spells on my wings, no more spells"—he waves his hands from his head to his stomach—"anywhere on my body."

"Then I'll go to the Smith-Richards meeting by myself."

"You're *not* going by yourself!" He marches past me again, tail snapping like an angry cat's.

"I'll be *fine*, Snow. You can listen in on my cellphone."

He throws his hands in the air. "Oh, because that worked so well last time!"

"It really did, if you'll remember. I'm not the one who blew our cover." It was Simon himself who blew our cover in Las Vegas, by breaking the plan, and then by breaking one of the Vampire King's chairs.

"Yeah, well," Snow says, "I'm not sitting here and listening while you get yourself killed—or end up going on another date."

"For Chomsky's sake," I say. "It wasn't a *date*." It wasn't.

"You went out for *ice cream*."

"So what? Lamb wasn't even interested in me in that way." He *really* wasn't.

Simon stops pacing to roll his eyes at me. His tail is still lashing from side to side.

"He was trying to mentor me," I say. "He could see I was clueless."

Simon huffs. "He could see that you're hot."

I huff, too. "Well, *I* was actually there, and I didn't get that vibe from him."

"You didn't get that vibe from *me* either, Baz. You've got no vibe . . . *check*."

Simon starts pacing again. His tail swings towards my face, and I snatch it.

He spins around, grabbing his tail at the base. "Hey!"

I don't let go. In fact, I give it a deliberate tug.

"Fuck," he spits out. "You know that's attached to my spinal cord."

"Then you better come here," I say, coiling his tail once around my wrist and tugging again.

He narrows his blue eyes and steps towards me slowly, like he's doing it on his own time. I draw my fist back to my shoulder, steadily pulling him closer, until he's kneeling between my legs, resting back on his heels.

He's taller than me like this. I hook my free arm around his waist and sit up straight, so I can knock my forehead against his. "Do you want me to take you out for ice cream? Is that what this is about?"

He cuts his eyes away. "I don't need ice cream."

"That's not what I asked . . ." I squeeze his tail. I'm holding the very end, near the spade. It doesn't seem to hurt him, so I do it again, rubbing it between my thumb and forefinger. It's warmer than you'd expect—maybe dragons are warm-blooded. And there's a nap to it, like the texture of kid gloves.

I unloop his tail from around my arm, then slowly work my hand up the length of it, partly massaging it and partly just feeling it. Normally Snow would have pulled it away by now.

He isn't pulling away. His cheeks are flushed, and he's looking at the floor beside us.

"I want you to know," I say, "that I didn't consider staying in America. With Lamb. Not for a single second." I loosen my grip and draw my arm out, so that his tail slides through my fist.

Simon shivers. His wings spread out—reflexively, I think. "You should have considered it," he says.

"Well, I didn't, I haven't . . . *I won't.*" I work my hand back up his tail, towards the base of his spine. "I'm sorry I put you through it that night."

He's still making a miserable face at the floor. "I would have understood, Baz—"

"Crowley, Snow, I need you to promise that you won't keep

bringing this up." I let his tail slide through my palm again, more gently this time, lightly dragging my nails down it.

Simon flinches, and whips his tail out of my hand. "*Stop.*"

"Sorry," I say quickly. "Did that hurt?"

"No, it . . ." He looks uncomfortable. "I just don't like that feeling. That, like, feathery feeling. Like, touch me or don't— but don't, like, *whisper* on me."

I take hold of his tail again, firmly. "Is this better?"

He licks his bottom lip. He's embarrassed. "Yeah. I mean, I don't need you to do it at all."

"That's not what I asked." I rub his tail again, pressing hard with my thumb.

"Yeah," he says, blushing fiercely. "It's better." He brings his arms up around my neck, still looking reluctant, still not looking in my eyes. "Lamb was well fit."

I shrug, working at his tail. It's so warm. And it's always moving. Like holding a current in a stream. If you'd asked me ahead of time, I would have said I wasn't into tails. But I guess I'm into anything attached to Simon.

"Oh," he says, finally looking up at me, "you didn't notice he was fit?"

"I didn't care," I say. "A lot of people are fit."

"Not like him."

"Fuck, Snow, maybe *I'm* the one who should be jealous."

Simon rolls his eyes.

I tighten my arm around his waist. "You're all I want," I say. It comes out softer than I mean it to, like my lungs are more insecure than my head.

Simon closes his eyes and drops his forehead against mine. He's breathing hard through his nose. I keep rubbing his tail, reminding myself not to be gentle.

"Okay," he says, "fine, I'll stop bringing him up. It up. America."

"It's all right," I say. "If you need me to keep saying all this out loud, I will."

He shakes his head, like he's irritated—possibly with me, possibly with himself. "You keep telling me *everything* is all right, that *whatever* I need is fine . . ."

I nod. "That's correct. I'm glad you're finally hearing me."

He twists up his face and throws his head back, so that his throat is a mile long. "I just don't think it's *true.*"

"Simon—" I pull him in closer, I wish he'd open his eyes. "—*of course* it's true. All you've asked of me so far is kindness."

He groans and buries his grimace in my shoulder. His arms are still around my neck. His tail is still undulating through my fingers. Is it wrong that I like him like this? Afraid, insecure, worried—but turning to me for comfort? Letting me hold on?

I rub my nose into the hair at his nape, still short from that haircut in Las Vegas.

His voice is muffled: "What if I asked you to be less kind to me?"

"What?" I draw my head back. "*Why?*"

He's slumped into me, his forehead on my shoulder, whispering harshly into the space between our chests: "Because it makes me feel *mental.* It's like being touched too lightly. Makes me feel like I'm being turned inside out. Like I need to get away."

I pull his tail through my hand, firmly. I press my other hand into his back. I push my nose hard into his ear. "No," I say. "I won't do that."

Simon shrinks from me. His hands fall to his lap. He looks anguished.

I loop his tail around my hand again and hold him everywhere tight. "No," I repeat. "I can touch you less gently, but I won't love you less kindly."

He exhales roughly, and his head sinks onto my shoulder again, his back still tense, his hands still clenched on his thighs.

I brace myself for whatever he's going to say next . . .

I'm more used to *guessing* what Simon is thinking—what he's feeling, what he wants. Bracing myself against his silence, wave after wave of it. That's how our relationship has worked so far.

But the last thirty-six hours have been different. He promised to try, and he *is* trying, and he keeps taking me off guard. First I don't know what's coming, and then I don't know what's hit me . . . *And I can't believe how much better it is.* Bracing for *something* instead of more nothing.

I wait for it . . .

After a few minutes, Simon's body relaxes against mine. His wings settle on his back. His breathing slows. He turns his head away from me, laying his cheek on my shoulder. "I can't believe you pulled my tail . . ." he says, wearily, and like he genuinely can't believe it.

I relax, too. "Oh, like you wouldn't be yanking me around by the tail if I had one."

Simon laughs, just with his breath. "If you'd had a tail back at Watford, you'd have woken up every morning with it tied to your bed."

I'm still massaging his tail, inch by inch. My hand is at the base now, and I let it slide through my palm all the way to its spaded tip. "I've got to pull your tail while you still have one."

Simon lifts his head to face me. He looks in my eyes for a second. It's measuring, observant. Possibly resigned. Then his gaze drops to my mouth.

He moves towards me slowly, and I part my lips to get ready for him.

He kisses me.

I kiss him back, squarely. Firmly. Matter-of-factly. *You're all I want,* I think. *And you can have everything you need.*

I'm not sure what he's telling me with this kiss. I pretend it's *Yes* and *Yes* and *Be kind to me.*

SIMON

Fine, you fucker. Have me. Just have me.
  Do your worst, you stubborn twat.
  Be the death of me.

  You'll be the death of me.

33

SIMON

Baz pulls away first.

He almost never pulls away first.

He sits back against the wall. "Hey," he says, like he's just thought of something. He has my tail twined around his arm again from wrist to elbow. He lets go, and it slithers away. (I can control the tail if I think about it, but it mostly moves of its own accord.)

I rest on my heels. We should sit like this more often—I like the way Baz looks, looking up at me.

He wipes his mouth with his butterfly-blue cuff. "Everyone at the meeting tonight will know who you are," he says.

"Right. That's the problem."

"And everyone knows you've lost your magic."

"Apparently they don't believe it," I say, thinking of Lady Salisbury.

"So we lean into that."

"Lean into what?" My knees are killing me. Maybe we

shouldn't make a habit of this. I try to shift onto the floor, but there's nowhere to put my legs.

"Here." Baz pulls my left leg over his and then does the same with my right. As soon as he has them settled, he puts his arms around my waist again. It's fuckin' cosy is what it is. "Lean into your whole thing," he says. "*'I was never the Chosen One, I've lost my magic, I've heard that you can help . . .'*"

"Oh," I say. And then, *"Oh."*

"Right?" Baz says, squeezing me. *"Right?"*

"Pretend I'm looking for a saviour."

"Because why wouldn't you be! You'd be such a score for this Smith-Richards. If the old Chosen One thinks *he's* the Chosen One . . ."

"Yeah," I say, nodding, "all right. I can do that. Lean into it. I mean, it sounds kind of humiliating . . ."

"You're used to humiliating," he says.

"Am I."

"I want to go hunting first." Baz is already moving on. "You can come," he adds.

"I always get to come along now, remember?"

He tips his head back and cocks a thick eyebrow. "I don't think I said *always.*"

"Yeah," I say, "always. Every time. Every night for the rest of my life."

"Not for the rest of *my* life?"

"Pfft." I move closer to him, holding on to his sides. "You're going to be young and pretty forever."

Baz pulls me even closer, by the small of my back. "Don't say that," he says, soft. "You don't know that."

"I don't mind."

He shakes his head, like he doesn't want to think about it.

"Snow . . . we've got a few minutes"—he pulls on me again—"before we have to leave."

"All right, I'm ready."

"No, I mean . . ." Baz moves his head from side to side like he's trying to find words for something. It's a rare look on him. "No matter what happens right now," he says, his eyes on my chin, "we have to stop in a few minutes. So you don't have to—you don't have to worry about it going too far. Or being too much."

Oh.

Baz glances up at my eyes. His pupils are wide and shiny. I've got us both shadowed by my wings. I nod, sucking nervously on my bottom lip.

"Lean into it," he whispers.

My shirt is untucked. He slides one cool hand under it, just above my tail.

I lean forward to kiss him.

"Just for a few minutes," he says, before I reach his mouth. "I'll tell you when."

The Smith Smith-Richards meeting is in the back room of a trendy pub, the kind of place that hosts acoustic concerts and stand-up comedy. There's an older man with a clipboard outside, managing the door.

Baz and I watch from the patio of a Costa across the street. We've been watching for fifteen minutes. I bought us both muffins.

"All you've eaten today is cake," Baz says.

"I had toast for breakfast. Toast isn't cake."

Smith-Richards's meeting was supposed to start five minutes ago. The man at the door gives one last look up and down the street, then goes inside.

"Now?" Baz asks.

"Not yet," I say.

A couple is walking quickly towards the door, like they're late.

I yank on Baz's arm. "*Now.*"

We jog across the street and slip in behind them. I remember to wave Baz through the door.

It's crowded inside. The room probably holds a hundred people. Baz and I take two of the last empty chairs, in the back. There's a handsome man already standing onstage, wearing jeans and a worn blue jumper. He looks like he's in a band. Maybe there *is* a band playing tonight . . .

"Hey," the man says into a microphone. "So, this is cool." He spreads his arms wide. "Look at us . . ."

The crowd around us claps. These must all be magicians, right? I see a boy who was a few years ahead of us at Watford. I wonder if there's anyone else I know.

"Yeah, no more meeting in living rooms for us," the man onstage says, smiling. "No more manky pubs."

A few people laugh.

"Only the finest pubs for us!" he cheers.

They applaud for him again.

"And now we have our new residential centre . . . That's because of you, all of you. You're making things happen!"

Baz is sitting tall, scanning the crowd. He's got his toffee-coloured jacket back on, and he did something before we left my flat to make his hair look perfect. It hangs around his face in shiny black waves. Baz didn't get even a little mussed up tonight when we went hunting. (Apparently he works more cleanly when

I'm not talking about my previous sexual partners.) (Partner.)

I wonder which of these people is the Chosen One . . . Maybe they've got him stashed in the wings, waiting for his big entrance.

Baz elbows me. I turn, and he points discreetly towards the front of the room. Daphne is sitting there, gazing up at the guy in the jumper. Shit, maybe *that's* who she left Baz's dad for. She's got stars in her eyes.

I mean . . . he is fit. Tall and broad-shouldered. Curly, golden-blond hair. Lead-singer face.

"Thanks for giving me a chance to recuperate," he says. "Our last meeting was pretty intense. More intense for you than anyone, eh, Beth?" He's smiling at someone in the audience. I can't see their reaction. "Why don't you come up here, and share with us?" He holds out his hand.

A woman is standing up and making her way to the stage. She takes the man's hand and stands beside him for a moment, smiling at him. She's pretty. Chubby. In her late 20s. The man seems older, 30 maybe. I'm not a good judge.

"How're you feeling?" he asks her gently.

She laughs, wiping her eyes. "Good," she says.

He takes the microphone off its stand and hands it to her. "Good," she says again, into the mic.

"Good," he says, putting his arm around her. "Why don't you tell us about the last week."

She laughs tearfully again. "I don't know where to start!"

He just motions for her to go on.

"I'm not used to using magic," she says. "So, at first nothing changed. Then I wrote myself a note, and I stuck it to my desk, and I made myself cast a spell every time I looked at it. It was hard, I kept hearing the Mage. You know how he was—'*Conserve your magic.*'"

I nod. A lot of people nod.

"But then I'd think of you." She smiles at the man, and he smiles back at her.

"*Magic is infinite*," they say together.

The woman smiles wider, blushing and looking away.

Wait. Is *that* the Chosen One? That guy in the jumper? *Him?* I don't know what I was expecting. Someone more intimidating. Or someone more obviously shamming, maybe even twirling a moustache. Not a hot young guy in jeans.

The woman keeps talking. "But every time," she says, "my magic came to me when I called for it. There's been no reaching. No scraping. One morning, I just stood in my kitchen, casting spells. I cast a 'Full English.' I cast a 'Primrose path.'" The crowd is murmuring, impressed. "I cast a 'Bread and roses'!"

The crowd gasps. A few people start clapping.

"I've been using magic every day," the woman says. She wipes her eyes, but she's crying too much for it to matter. "Even when I don't have to. I've been casting spells just for the pleasure of it. And I keep thinking . . . *This is what it's been like for everyone else, all along.* My parents, my boyfriend. It's always been this easy for them."

The man—it must be Smith-Richards—pulls a handkerchief from his pocket and actually wipes the woman's cheeks for her, like she's a child. She just keeps smiling and blushing. He takes the microphone back.

"This is what you deserve," he says, still dabbing at her cheeks. "This is what you've always deserved. You're a mage, Beth."

Merlin, he's just making her cry more. He's crying, too.

"You're a mage!" he says, laughing through his tears. "This was always yours, this was always inside you."

He stops wiping her face, and they embrace. When they finally pull away from each other, the woman starts talking to him again. He quickly holds the microphone back up to her.

"When Jamie told us how it felt—" Baz and I look at each other. That's gotta be Jamie Salisbury; has his magic been fixed already? "—it's not that I didn't believe him. I did! But I thought . . . Well, I thought he must have something that I don't. That he was from an older family. Or that he must have more latent magic than I have. But I was *wrong*."

Smith-Richards wraps his arm around her, and she leans against him. "You're a mage," he says into the microphone. "That's all that matters, Beth. Magic is your birthright." He looks around the room. "It's all of our birthright."

People at the front of the room are clapping, but everyone in the back seems distracted by something. Baz clears his throat and shifts in his seat.

Bloody hell . . . they're distracted by *me*. I slouch down, as much as my folded-up wings will let me.

Smith-Richards is looking out into the audience, trying to figure out what everyone is looking at.

"Snakes alive," Beth says, still standing close to the microphone, "it's the Chosen One!"

Smith-Richards looks down at her, confused. But then he looks out into the audience again and makes eye contact with me. His eyes get wide. "Simon Snow," he says into the mic.

Everyone who wasn't already staring turns to gawk at me now. I sit up in my chair, smiling uncomfortably. Time to lean in, I suppose. Smith-Richards is walking towards me, down the centre aisle.

"If he touches you," Baz murmurs, "I'm eviscerating him."

Smith-Richards stops at our row. He's even better looking this close. High cheekbones, square chin. He looks like a Burberry model. "It's such an honour to have you here," he says. He looks around, and everyone starts clapping, like they agree with him.

I smile tightly, sort of nodding at the rest of the room. If there's one thing I can thank the Mage for, it's that he never sent me out on dog and pony shows. Most of these magicians have never seen me in person before.

"We all owe you such a debt," Smith-Richards says gravely, "for serving the World of Mages to the best of your ability."

That seems like an insult, but I smile anyway and mutter, "Yeah, thanks, mate."

"Is this your first meeting?" he asks. "Is there anything I can tell you about myself and our work?"

"Nope," I say. "I'm good. Just came to check it out. Go ahead and, um, carry on. Thanks."

"If you have any questions, please ask. We're all happy to talk." He runs a hand through his hair, like he's embarrassed about something. The curls pop through his fingers one by one. "I'm glad you came *tonight*," he says, looking out at the room again, "because this is a special night."

A few people clap, but most of them just seem to be holding their breath, like he's about to start giving out cars or something.

Smith-Richards walks back up the aisle. "Tonight we're going to help another mage live up to their potential." He's looking from side to side, smiling. "So many of you have waited for so long . . ." He stops next to Daphne, and takes her hand. "And been so loyal."

Baz takes a deep breath. He's slid his wand from his sleeve into his palm.

Daphne's looking up at Smith-Richards like he's some sort of angel. He squeezes her hand and lets go, stepping back onto the stage.

He smiles out at the audience—you could hear a pin drop—and slowly reaches out his hand. "Alan."

An older man stands up, whooping. Everyone around him laughs. Some people clap come more.

Smith-Richards waves him up. "Come on, Alan! Come on up!"

Alan walks to the front of the room, people patting him on the back as he goes. He climbs up onto the stage.

"You've waited so long for this," Smith-Richards says, then points the microphone at Alan.

"I have at that," Alan says, chuckling. "I didn't realize I was waiting for you, Smith. But I was—I was."

"Well, let's not make you wait anymore," Smith-Richards says. "Let's give you the life you've deserved all along!"

He puts the microphone on its stand and pulls a wand out of his back pocket. He holds his other hand out to Alan.

I lean into Baz and whisper, "What should we do?"

"I don't know," Baz says. "I don't think we can stop him . . ."

"We could stop him if we *had* to," I counter.

"Whatever spell he cast didn't kill Beth. It probably won't kill Alan either."

Everyone around us is leaning forward, eyes wide. (No one is gawking at me at the moment or checking out Baz.)

"Let it all out!" Smith-Richards casts.

There's no noise, no sparks. I don't know why I was expecting some; magic doesn't work that way. Smith-Richards shuffles back a bit away from Alan, like the spell took great effort.

Alan looks up at him.

"Go on," Smith-Richards says softly, reaching for the microphone again, "get out your wand."

"It's a fountain pen," Alan says.

Smith-Richards laughs, but less exuberantly than before. "Get it out, man."

Alan reaches into his jacket, takes out an antique fountain pen, and removes the cap.

"That's inconvenient," Baz says under his breath. "Though I suppose it could be worse, remember Gareth?"

I don't answer. I'm too sucked in to what's happening on-stage.

Alan looks down at his pen, like he isn't sure what to do with it.

"What's a spell you've always wanted to do?" Smith-Richards asks.

Alan's eyes are shining. "'Death by chocolate.'"

"Do it, Alan. I know you have it in you."

Alan holds up his pen. I don't think anyone in the room is breathing. Maybe Baz.

"Death by chocolate!" Alan cries.

A giant Toblerone—the size of a rifle, it must weigh ten pounds—appears above them. Smith-Richards just barely catches it. Everyone laughs and applauds. Some people are crying. Baz is making a face like, *Hmm. Not bad.*

Alan has turned away from the crowd, his hands pressed to his face.

"Alan?" Smith-Richards says. "It's all right, brother." He pulls Alan into his arms, nearly dropping the chocolate bar. "It's all right," he says. "You're healed now. You're healed."

After a minute, Alan pulls away, wiping his eyes with his sleeves.

"I don't have another handkerchief," Smith-Richards says. Everyone laughs. "Come on," he says to Alan, "share this Toblerone with me."

"I was going to bring it home to my wife."

"Oh, Alan," Smith-Richards says, opening the box, "you can just cast the spell again. As often as you like."

Baz has his arms folded. He tilts his head back sceptically. "No one can cast that spell more than once a day."

The chocolate bar is enormous. The audience applauds when Smith-Richards manages to break off a chunk. "That's all I've got for tonight!" Smith-Richards says to the crowd. "But I'll see you soon. Until we meet again, keep the faith. Keep encouraging each other. Don't listen to anyone who tries to discourage you. Remember—they're used to you as you are. They're used to feeling more powerful than you. You're challenging the world as they know it, and they don't like it. They don't like it, friends."

He looks a little peaky, like the spell took something out of him. The man from the door—an older guy with longish grey hair and an earring—has stepped onto the stage to offer Smith-Richards an arm.

"You're mages," Smith-Richards says, looking out at the crowd. And then, I'd swear, he looks right at me. "Every one of you. Magic is your birthright."

He gets one more round of applause as he walks offstage, letting the older man support him.

People are standing up. Some of them are turning to me, curious again. Some older lady hands me a leaflet. I should probably be leaning into this, trying to find out more about Jamie Salisbury. But I really just want to leave now.

Baz pulls me by the elbow. "Come on, let's catch Daphne."

I follow his lead, trying to find Daphne in the crowd. I don't see her. But I do see someone else I recognize, walking quickly with his head down, at the edge of the room—Professor Bunce.

34

BAZ

I know Daphne saw me. She looked directly at me when that charlatan was fawning all over Simon. (That worked exactly as planned—Snow pretending to be interested. It was a Bunce-worthy idea.) As soon as said charlatan slinks offstage, I grab Simon and rush towards the front of the room, where my stepmother was sitting, hoping she won't try to sneak away.

I recognize a few other people in the crowd, people I'd never even thought of as weak magicians. There was a girl sitting across from me who looked so familiar, but I couldn't place her. I don't think she went to Watford . . .

Smith-Richards seems to draw more women than men, which isn't surprising, given his glossy appearance. His look is very—*The Greatest Mage, a new fragrance from Ralph Lauren.* He looks like Simon, frankly. But more Simony than Simon. He looks like the guy who would get cast to play Simon in the Netflix series.

No bloody thank you.

Daphne isn't trying to get away from me. She's standing just where I saw her earlier, her arms open. "Basil!" she says, sweeping me into a hug. "I'm so happy you're here. That you've even heard about Smith. This means his message is getting out."

"Mum"—I'm holding her by her shoulders—"I came to see *you*, not him. I've tried to call you so many times . . ."

"Oh, Baz," she says, pulling away from me and frowning. "I was hoping you hadn't come to fetch me."

"That's exactly what I've come to do. The girls miss you—they need their mother."

Daphne looks around. There are people watching us, staring at Simon mostly. She pulls me farther out of the crowd. I pull Simon along with us.

"They need their mother to be strong," Daphne says. "I'm doing the absolute best thing I can do for them by staying with Smith."

"How can you think that?"

"You don't understand, Basil; you've always been powerful. You've always lived up to your parents' standards—to the world's standards."

"I think you know that's not true," I say meaningfully. Daphne knows I'm a vampire, even though she'd never say it out loud. And further, she knows I'm queer as a clockwork orange, and that we're not allowed to say that out loud either.

She takes my hand. "I don't want my children to live half a life. I don't want to go on living half a life myself."

"But you have a *great* life," I say, and then immediately wish that I hadn't, because who I am to say so?

Daphne smiles sadly at me.

"You have great kids," I try again. "And they miss you."

"I miss them, too," she says. "And I'll be home soon. Or I'll bring them to stay with me. Smith hasn't cast the spell on any children yet, but he's considering it."

I don't even want to think about what that means. Surely, my father won't let his children move onto a *compound*.

"You could call home," I say. "Even the babies have mobile phones."

Daphne shakes her head. "It's too confusing for them. They just want to know when I'm coming home, and it's too hard to explain. Better to wait until I have some clear answers."

"Mum . . . they *miss* you."

"Basil." She puts her hand on my arm. "They're so young, they won't even remember that I was gone for a few weeks. They won't remember missing me. Soon I'll be home, and I'll be strong, and *that's* what they'll remember."

I can't think of what else to say.

Simon clears his throat—to remind us he's here, I think. "Hello, Mrs. Grimm."

Daphne looks at him, and her face cools. (Fair. He did destroy her house.) "Hello, Mr. Snow. Did you enjoy the meeting?"

"Yeah," he says. "Wow. Does he do this every week?"

"He tries," she says, immediately warming again. Apparently one mention of Smith-Richards is all it takes to make Daphne forget her motherless children and her ruined estate. "It's an enormous spell," she goes on, "so he can't always manage it. But he's helped six of us so far."

"And those people can all do magic now?"

"Well," she says, "they could always do magic. But, yes,

they're all very powerful now. Not even just middling powerful," she says to me. "They're all at the top of the game."

"Wow," Simon says again, looking genuinely impressed. "Can anyone cast that spell?"

"Crowley, no," Daphne says. "I mean"—she's sheepish—"I think we've all tried. But it's Smith's gift. It's part of what makes him special."

"What else makes him special?" I ask.

She's still sheepish. "You've seen him. He's here to lift us all up. To bring equality to the World of Mages."

"But that doesn't make him the Greatest Mage," I say. "The Greatest Mage is supposed to conquer the greatest threat to magic."

Her eyes are wide and shining. "What if the greatest threat to magic is the thing that holds each of us back? What if the threat to magic was inside of us, all along?"

Well, that's crap, and it takes every ounce of my self-control not to tell her so.

"Who's that Jamie?" Simon asks. "The one they mentioned?"

Daphne practically beams. "Oh, Jamie Salisbury. He was one of Smith's first believers—Jamie is his first miracle."

"So Jamie can do powerful magic now?" Snow is doing a poor job pretending he doesn't know who Jamie is. He seems far too happy for him.

"Yes," Daphne says, "and he was the least among us. He couldn't even cast a 'Light of day.'"

"That's so cool," Simon says. "Is he here?"

"No," she says, "Jamie hasn't come to meetings lately. I think the attention was getting to be too much for him. Plus, people were jealous that Smith chose him first. Politics." She rolls her eyes. "You can't get away from it, I suppose."

I touch her arm. "Will you at least answer my texts? So that I can reach you in an emergency?"

Daphne sighs. "I'll unblock *you*, Baz. But you can't tell your father. I can't let myself get distracted right now."

"Distracted from what, Mum? Aren't you just here waiting your turn?"

"Your father hasn't exactly been supportive . . ."

"Can you blame him?"

"Yes, Basil, I do blame him! If there was a way for you to heal yourself, I would support you, even if the means were unorthodox."

(Genuinely not sure whether she means the vampire thing or the gay thing.)

"When you love someone," she says, "you support them!" She closes her eyes and takes a deep breath. She's patting the air with both hands, like she's trying to gather herself. "Right now I just need to stay focused on Smith and Smith's message."

"What *is* Smith's message?" I ask.

She looks up at me again, like she's hoping I'm really listening. "That he's the Greatest Mage, and that if we follow him, he can make us *all* great."

"Well, that was bollocks," I say, as soon as we're on the street again.

"Wait till we're home," Simon says quietly, glancing back at the door.

"Are we . . ." I don't quite know how to ask what I'm asking. Are we going home together? Whose home? For how long?

Simon arches his back. Like his wings are bothering him under his coat. "We could get Nando's and take it to my flat?"

"Yeah," I say. "Good."

"Yeah," he says, smiling at me. "Good."

35

SMITH

Simon Snow . . .

Here. To see *me.*

It's a sign. Another sign—Evander was thrilled.

It's happening this time! It's right! Everything is lining up for me. Planets. People. I know that if I harvested seven duck hearts and threw them, they'd land right in a row.

Simon fucking Snow . . .

Here.

To see *me.*

The Chosen One.

36

PENELOPE

"Why are you being so quiet?"

Shepard looks away from the window and smiles at me. "I thought I was supposed to be quiet on the train."

"You are," I say. "But usually you aren't."

He holds his Cornish pasty out to me. "Are you sure you don't want a bite of this?"

I shake my head.

"I can't believe you can just get these anywhere," he says.

"You don't have pasties in Nebraska?"

"No. We have so much less *pie*, in general. It isn't fair. I guess we have runzas . . ."

"What's a runza?"

"This"—he smiles again, pointing the pasty at me—"but with cabbage." He takes another bite, then looks out the window. I've never seen Shepard like this before; I think he might be *pensive*.

"Are you afraid?" I ask.

His face jerks back to me. "Afraid? No. What would I be afraid of?"

"Well, we *are* going to meet some shady dark creatures in their lair . . ."

"Why do you assume every magickal being is dark?"

"Asks the man who thought he should befriend a demon." Shepard sighs.

"Is that it?" I ask. "Are you afraid to see the demon again?"

"No," he says. "Should I be?" He looks thoughtful. "Maybe I should be . . . but it's not like I can get *more* cursed . . ." He shakes his head. "Anyway, no, I'm not afraid. We aren't even summoning it today." He looks at me and suddenly seems very afraid indeed. "You weren't planning on summoning it *today*, were you?"

"Morgana, no," I say. "I'm not cold-calling a demon. Let's figure out the details of the curse first. Hopefully Kipper's mother can read your arms—and hopefully they say something useful. What if, after all this, the tattoos are just decorative?"

I keep saying "hopefully," but I'm not feeling especially hopeful about this trip. Kipper didn't give us any reason to be optimistic last night. Once she got over the shock of seeing Shepard's arms, she basically told him what he already knew: that he's up the River Styx without a paddle.

But she clearly *liked* him. (Everyone likes him.) She invited him, a perfect and obviously cursed stranger, to come to her family home in Croydon this morning, so her mum can take a look. Apparently forging and translation is a family business, and Kipper's mother is more fluent in Demonic languages than she is.

I think Kipper just wanted to see Shepard again.

(Merlin, am I *jealous*? Because some rando and her mother

might help Shepard when my own mother wouldn't? Or is it because Kipper has cool purple hair and a beautiful delphinium tattoo on her wrist that she probably drew herself . . .) (I could have purple hair. It's a simple enough spell.)

I hope Shepard isn't planning on adding Kipper's family to his collection of interesting magickal friends. Not with me involved. I don't need new friends. Like, ever. But especially not amongst strange magickal creatures who live in Croydon. I don't want to end this day with more problems than we started with.

"When we get there . . ." Shepard says carefully.

Could we actually be on the same track for once? "We'll be in information-gathering mode," I say, "not information-*sharing* mode."

"Right, but—"

"No 'but's, Shepard. No extraneous words at all. The fact that you're cursed is already too much information. They don't need to know your life story—or mine."

"It doesn't hurt to be sociable, Penelope."

I grab his tattooed forearm. "It literally does."

"I just don't think Kipper's mother is going to be dangerous . . ."

"Do you ever?"

"All right. Fine." He's not smiling. He rubs one eye, under his glasses. "Ten-four, Debbie."

"'Ten four.' What's that?"

"It means—I've got it. Copy. Roger that. Message received. No being sociable."

"'Impenetrable,' that's just what my friend Ken said. Ken's a giant. There aren't too many giants in the Midwest. I've never met any in Omaha. That's where I'm from—Nebraska, right in the heart of America."

We're sitting in a kitchen with Old Kipper and her mother, who is indeed named Debbie, and Debbie's boyfriend, who is literally a fox. (Maybe a fox spirit? Maybe something disguised as a fox? I'm waiting for Shepard to ask an impertinent question that will shed some more light on the subject.)

At the moment, Shepard's sitting on a stool with his jacket off and his T-shirt sleeves pushed up, while Debbie and Jeremey (the fox) shake their heads over his tattoos. Debbie has her reading glasses on. She has eight eyes when she wants, but she only wears glasses over one set of them. (*Eight* eyes. And at least thirty fingers! Shepard didn't even flinch when she unveiled an extra hand to poke at him.)

"Bloody impenetrable," Debbie says again.

"So it's *not* a Demonic language?" Kipper asks, craning her head over her mother's shoulder.

"No, it is," Debbie says. "But it's legalese. You don't need a translator—you need a lawyer."

"A lawyer?" I'm on Shepard's other side, at the table. "For a curse?"

"For a contract," Debbie says. "It's as bad as he told Kipper—"

"Where did you learn Demonic languages, Debbie?" Shepard cuts in. "Did you go to school for it?" He's sitting there, perfectly at home, drinking a cup of Yorkshire tea. He's already eaten half a packet of biscuits—it's no wonder he's been trapped by so many fairies.

"Live long enough," she says, "and you pick up all sorts of things."

"She's being modest," Jeremey says. With his voice. Because he is a *talking* fox. A talking fox wearing a *tracksuit.* "Deb has a real head for languages. And she's a whiz with song lyrics. She can hear something once on the radio and sing the whole thing."

She swats him. "He's exaggerating."

"Maybe you could just give us your best guess," I suggest, "even if you're not sure of the precise translation."

"I *could* . . ." Debbie says, standing up straight again and taking off her glasses. I would have described Debbie as a white woman in her 50s with a brassy blond ponytail—if not for the extra limbs and things. Now I don't know how to sort her . . . Is she human? *Was* she human? Why doesn't a magickal forger live in a nicer house? I keep thinking about what my mother would say about all this, but I don't get past, *"Get out of there, Penelope! Right now!"*

"The thing is"—Debbie shifts her attention to Shepard's other arm—"I don't want to accidentally summon the demon. I wouldn't read any of this out loud."

"Surely, the demon won't show up without a *proper* summoning," I say. "Ashes, blood, et cetera."

"I wouldn't want to risk it." Debbie pokes Shepard in the shoulder. "What got into your head, lad? There are easier ways to live forever."

"It was a misunderstanding," he says. "I just wanted to talk."

"You'll have plenty of time to talk in hell," she says, more sympathetically than he deserves.

"Talk about some trouble and strife." Jeremey shakes his head.

"I don't think it is *hell,* so to speak," Shepard says.

"Well, you'll be an expert," Debbie says, "won't you."

Kipper has sat down next to me at the table. She's leaning

on one hand, staring at Shepard. (Staring at his surprisingly fit arms, I suspect.) "I think you should help him, Mum. Translate what you can."

Debbie rests two hands on her hips. Another appears holding a Coke Zero. She takes a sip. "How will having his bad end explicitly spelled out for him make it any better?"

"If we knew the terms of the contract," I say, "we might find a loophole."

"Demons don't leave loopholes." Another of Debbie's arms emerges to point at me. "Sometimes they leave things that *look* like loopholes that are actually ways to further fuck yourself."

"We could do the translation inside a protective circle," Kipper says. "And we could leave out any words that make you nervous . . ."

Her mum snorts. "This whole thing makes me nervous."

"I could lend some extra protection," I offer.

Debbie narrows all eight of her eyes at me. "Could you now . . . Debbie."

Jeremey gets his car keys out of his pocket. "Well, I'm hooking it. *I'm* not trying to get engaged to a demon today." He pats Shepard on the back. "Best of British, mate!"

Engaged . . .

Engaged?

I look over at Shepard. He's rubbing his eyes beneath his glasses.

I cast some protection spells. Who knows whether they work.

Debbie wouldn't do the translation in her house. (More credit to her.) She took Shepard out to a shed in the back garden and made space for him to stand in the middle of the floor. Then Kipper drew an extremely artful protection circle around them both. The plan was to write the translation out on notebook paper, apparently leaving out the most dangerous words—like the demon's name and address, I suppose, and "with this tattoo, I thee wed."

Shepard tried to talk to me before we left the house. I wouldn't let him. I wouldn't even look at him. I followed Debbie out to the shed, waited for Kipper to draw the circle, cast my spells as quickly and quietly as possible, then went to sit on Debbie's front steps. At the moment, I don't much care if all three of them end up cursed.

I can't believe I put myself out like this for a *Normal* . . .

That I cast spells in front of strangers . . . That I spent the morning with dark creatures and criminals, all because I thought I *owed* him something. Because I thought, *at the very least,* that he had been honest with me.

Why am I even sitting here, waiting for him? I should hook it, too! I'm sure Old Kipper could help Shepard find his way back to my flat. Or back to hers. Or back to Omaha, for all I care.

"Hey," he says, coming out the door behind me.

I stand up and start walking. He can follow me if he wants.

"Hey. Penelope."

I walk a little faster.

"Penelope, are you angry with me?"

I walk even faster. I'm not having this conversation with him right now. I might not have it at all.

"Penelope . . ."

I don't actually *have* to speak to Shepard again. I shouldn't have spoken to him in the first place. I should have trusted *everything I've ever been taught* and *every bone in my body.*

Smart mages don't befriend Normals. Even witless mages don't tell Normals their secrets.

"You can't ignore me all the way back to Camberwell," he says.

I laugh out loud, like this—"Ha!" I can ignore him for the rest of my *life*. I can make *everyone* ignore him! I can make him forget he *exists*.

Just because I haven't spelled Shepard silly yet doesn't mean it's impossible. I just have to put my back into it. I'll get the job done.

"Penelope . . ."

We turn a corner. I whip around and stick my finger in his face. I've got my gem clutched in my fist in case I decide to cast a spell. "When were you going to tell me that you were engaged to a demon?"

Shepard looks pitiful. Fortunately, I'm pitiless.

"I can explain," he says.

"Apparently you can't! Because I asked you to explain, multiple times, and you didn't!"

"I was going to, Penelope!"

"Really? When!"

"When it was relevant!"

"Shepard, we were investigating your curse, which was *apparently* a marriage contract, which you *apparently* already knew. It was relevant the whole time!"

"I was going to tell you, I swear." His tone is very sincere. "I tried."

"No. *Close*. Rhymes with 'tried' . . ."

"Penelope."

"You *lied* to me, Shepard!"

"I didn't! I just hadn't explained yet!"

"We have literally been making lists of things that we know and things that we don't, and not once did you say, *'Here's something I know: I have a fiancé in hell.'*"

"She's not my fiancée!"

"Wait, is it a 'she' or a 'he'?"

"I really don't know whether demons have gender."

"But you said 'he' before. Is this another lie?"

"No! I mean—maybe. I just . . . I didn't want you to think . . ."

"Think what?"

"That I'd been seduced by some she-devil!"

"Well, now I can assume that's exactly what happened!"

"No, it wasn't like that!"

"I don't know what it was like, do I, Shepard? Because you didn't tell me! Apparently you told Kipper the truth as soon as you met her, but to me? You *lied*."

"Penelope, when I first told you, I didn't know that I was going to see you again, that we were going to be friends. 'Cursed' covers a lot of bases."

"It doesn't cover 'engaged'!"

"This isn't a real engagement!"

"It's legally binding!"

Shepard rolls his eyes at me, which he has no right to do, now or ever.

I start walking away from him. Then I realize I'm headed away from the train station and spin around and march past him.

"Penelope!" he shouts after me.

I keep walking.

He keeps shouting. "I didn't tell you, because I didn't want you to think I was in a relationship!"

37

BAZ

We're eating at the kitchen table this time. Lady Salisbury has made another cake and given us each a far-too-generous slice.

She's got a fork raised halfway to her face, and her mouth's gone slack with shock. "Jamie . . ." she says eventually, "has been *healed*?"

"That's what Daphne—Baz's stepmum—said. She said he was Smith-Richards's first miracle."

"His first . . . *miracle*?" Lady Salisbury glances at her fork and seems to remember she's holding it. She sets it down on her plate, then immediately picks it up again, and takes the bite. Then she starts to cry. Curling over the table, her shoulders hitching.

Simon looks at me, his mouth full and his eyes something like panicked. I scoot my chair closer to her and touch her shoulder. "Lady Salisbury . . ."

"Healed," she says after a moment. She wipes her mouth

with a cloth napkin and then wipes her eyes. She takes another bite of cake, then sobs again, covering her mouth. "Healed," she says, coughing on crumbs.

I rub her back, fairly uselessly. She smells like buttercream icing and lavender.

"We don't know what it means," I say. "But Daphne says all the magicians Smith-Richards has . . . *affected* can do powerful magic now."

"It's just so hard to fathom." She wipes her eyes again, smearing chocolate on her cheek.

I point at my own cheek, and she wipes most of the chocolate away, smiling to thank me.

"My Jamie . . ." she says, still looking shocked, "doing *magic*."

Simon has pulled his chair closer, too. "It's good news," he says carefully. "Isn't it?"

Lady Salisbury laughs, more tears streaming down her chocolate-smudged cheeks. "I genuinely don't know, Simon." She takes another bite of her cake. Simon takes a bite of his, too. "On the one hand," she says, "it *is* a miracle. It's what Jamie's always wanted. It's what we expected for him, once a upon a time."

Simon smiles at her, hopefully. He wants this to be good news. I think he wants to believe that walking cologne ad is offering something real.

"*As far as we know,*" Simon kept saying last night, "*Smith-Richards is the Chosen One.*"

"*By what logic?*" I scoffed. We were sitting on his living room floor, eating peri-peri chicken.

"*Well, we don't know that he* isn't," Simon said.

"*We don't know that* anyone *isn't.*"

"*We know it isn't me.*"

"*All right, Snow, so everyone who isn't you could be the Chosen One?*"

He shrugged. "*We watched Smith-Richards fix that guy's magic. I never fixed anyone's magic.*"

"*One*"—I counted on my fingers—"*you fixed the entire magickal firmament. Two, how do we know that Alan person was actually changed? It could have been a trick. Or a delusion. Maybe there's some sort of placebo effect.*"

Simon stuck out his chin. "*Your stepmum believes it.*"

"*She* wants *to believe it.*"

Simon just shrugged again.

We kept arguing about it for an hour, even after we climbed into his bed. (It isn't a bed; it's a mattress. I had to magic him up some sheets and pillows.)

"On the other hand?" Simon says now, still looking hopefully at Lady Salisbury.

"On the other hand . . ." She taps her empty fork on her plate. "Things that seem too good to be true usually are."

"In my experience," Simon says, "things that seem too good to be true are usually magic."

Lady Salisbury smiles at him. She hasn't stopped crying; she's smiling through tears. She picks up the cake knife and cuts Simon a second piece.

I thought we'd brief Lady Salisbury, then head back to Simon's flat to plan our next move. (And maybe to kiss. There was more arguing than kissing last night.) (Though it was all in the realm of *good* arguing: lying side by side, Simon almost lazily pushing my hair out of my face while he disagreed with me.) But Simon doesn't seem to pick up on any of my hints about leaving.

We stay at Lady Salisbury's table for hours, eating cake and re-examining the whole scenario. I miss Bunce's blackboard. Lady Salisbury—she says we should call her "Ruth," but I don't think I can—isn't an orderly thinker. She jumps from thought to thought and back again. But at least she stays mostly on my side. Even after hearing the whole story twice, she still frowns every time we mention Smith-Richards.

"I think you'd trust him more if you saw him," Simon says to her.

I snort. It would have been a scoff, but I was drinking tea. "He just means he's handsome."

"That isn't what I meant," Simon argues.

"We need to talk to Jamie," Lady Salisbury says. "We need to see him."

"Agreed," I agree.

Simon nods. "Why hasn't he called you, do you think? I mean, you could hardly talk him out of following Smith-Richards now."

"Why doesn't anyone call their mothers," she says with a sigh.

Simon looks like the orphan he is for a moment, and I must look like a similarly kicked puppy, because Lady Salisbury's face falls. "Oh, boys," she says, "I'm so sorry! I've spent my whole life with my foot in my mouth. What I meant is . . . If Jamie suddenly has magic, I'm sure 'calling his mother' is fairly low on his list of priorities. He probably doesn't want me to rain on his parade, if he's feeling good about things."

"He could always call to say, 'I told you so,'" Simon says.

She frowns again, shaking her head. "Smith-Richards doesn't like his followers to engage with doubters. Jamie used to call all my questions 'counterproductive to the cause.'"

"Daphne mentioned something like that, too," I say.

Lady Salisbury leans forward, thumping the table. "*That's* why I don't trust this Smith-Richards. Anything worth believing in should stand up to some interrogation!" She hits the table again. "Truth doesn't burn in the sunlight!"

Simon glances at me, apologetic. (Perhaps because I burn in the sunlight?)

"I completely agree," I tell Lady Salisbury.

Simon looks thoughtful. "Then I suppose Baz and I will have to go to Smith-Richards's clubhouse and see if we can find Jamie there."

"Agreed," I say again.

Lady Salisbury looks between us, like she isn't quite sure.

We don't end up leaving until after lunch. Lady Salisbury stops us at the door, making us promise to be careful and to watch out for each other. I feel like she's saying this more to me than to Simon; she's only known him for a day, and she can already sense his gobsmacking lack of self-preservation.

He and I walk to the Tube station together, lost in our own thoughts, then stop at the stairs. Are we still going the same way?

"I should probably go home and change," I say. I'm still wearing my suit from yesterday. (Camel, wool, unlined. Lady Salisbury pretended not to notice.)

"Oh," Simon says, looking first at my suit and then at the ground, and scratching the back of his head. "Right."

"I can check in with you later?"

"Yeah," he says. "Or maybe . . ."

"Maybe?"

He looks up at me. "Maybe we both go to your flat, and

instead of changing, you pick up some clothes?"

"And then I . . ." I'm afraid to say it even though *he's* the one saying it. ". . . stay with you?"

He nods quickly, licking his bottom lip. "Yeah."

"Like, for a few days, or . . ." I have my hands pressed so deep into my jacket pockets that my collar is pulling on my neck. "For a while?"

Simon's whole body shrugs. "I don't know."

"You don't know." I nod.

He tilts his head forward and pulls at the top of his hair. "Do I have to know?" His eyebrows are up. His forehead is wrinkled. He's squinting at me like he's about to place a bet.

"No," I say. "You don't have to know."

Simon lurches forward and grabs me by the elbow. "I don't know how people do this," he says, his voice low and urgent. "I'm much better at pushing you away than pulling you close. Are we allowed to be together all the time? Or is that too much? Just tell me if it's too much."

That'll be the day.

I put my hand on his forearm. "Come back to Fiona's with me," I say. "I'll pick up some clothes."

His eyes are scrabbling on mine. I try to give him whatever it is he's digging for.

"Yeah?" he says.

"It isn't too much, Snow."

He licks his lip and nods.

I pull him towards the stairs.

38

SIMON

In the early days after the Mage was gone, when I was still having video calls with that American therapist, she used to tell me to break life into bites you can swallow.

Like, don't think about the fact that you don't have magic and you killed your mentor and you have a fucking tail now . . . (I'm the "you," obviously.) Just think about the next few hours. Are you going to have lunch? Are you going to see your friends? Will you take a walk?

There were days when even that was too much for me to swallow.

There were days that I broke up into minutes. And days that I could only live one second at a time. *Now I'm going to sit up. Now I'm going to piss. Now I'm going to plug in my phone.*

I'm doing it again now.

Not because the future is too terrible to reckon with—because it's too terrifying. Too uncertain. There are parts of it that are too bright.

Is this what people do when they're in love? Do they just keep touching and talking? And *then* what? Like what is it all leading to? I don't mean sex, I mean . . .

If I knew what I meant, it wouldn't be so frightening.

I'm living second by second. All of this with Baz is petrifying. All of this *without* Baz is intolerable. I'm just making whatever decision I have to make in the moment to keep him in the picture, even though I can't look at the whole picture without shitting myself.

I just told him to come home with me.

A few days ago, I broke up with him.

I just told him to come home with me, and he said *yes*. We're on the Tube to his flat, and he's sitting next to me. I've got my arm slung around his shoulder. There's at least one guy giving us a dirty look, and I kinda hope he speaks up, because I would dearly love to punch something right now. That's a decision I could wrap my brain around.

Second by second.

Now I'm holding on to Baz.

Now I'm standing up.

Now I'm going to follow him.

39

BAZ

"Is your aunt home?" Snow asks, hiding behind me while I unlock the door.

"I don't think so," I say. "I don't hear Joe Strummer, so probably not."

"Is that her boyfriend?"

"She wishes." I step into the flat—there's a blur of movement and a noise like a door slamming.

Fiona *is* home. She's standing in front of her bedroom door. Awkwardly. Her legs planted too far apart. "Basil!" she says. "You weren't here."

"I was not," I say slowly. "Now I am."

"Okay, fine," she says. She leans against the wall. I've never seen her stand in that spot before. She puts her hands in her trouser pockets.

"Fiona . . . Did you just hide *a man* from me?"

"No," she says.

"You did."

"Big talk from someone hiding a man at this very moment."

I glance over my shoulder. "Stop cowering, Snow."

"I'm not cowering," he mutters, stepping out from behind my back. I have my hand on my wand, just in case Fiona tries something.

"Hello, Simon Snow," she says, trying to look dangerous.

"Hi," he replies, barely audible.

Fiona puts something into her mouth. It looks like a whistle. Or a recorder.

"Fuck me," I say. "Are you *vaping*?"

She immediately pulls it away and hides it behind her back—then realizes she's hiding it and lets her hand hang at her side. "It's better for your lungs than smoking."

"*Is* it?"

She curls her lip at me. "I thought you objected to the open flame."

"I also object to you looking like a yob."

"Don't be classist, Basil."

I look at her bedroom door. "Is that it?" I whisper. "Are you hiding a Normal in there? I already know you date Normals, Fiona."

"Oh, and you don't?"

"I'll just—" Simon is backing out the front door.

I snatch his wrist and drag him towards my room. Fiona watches us, smiling like she's won. I shut the door behind us.

"Maybe I should wait outside?" Snow is still cowering.

"You're safer where I can see you," I say, walking over to a clothes rack.

"She wouldn't *really* do anything to hurt me . . . All that's over . . . Right?"

"My aunt is a lunatic." I flip through my shirts. I'm not sure what to bring to Simon's flat. Enough for a few days? For a week? I wish there was a spell that would shrink my whole wardrobe down, so that it would fit in my pocket. (There *is* a spell like that, but the reversal is a bitch.) (Reversals are always a bitch. Bunce could make herself famous if that Missy Elliott song sticks.) I have a garment bag somewhere—would that make this arrangement too formal? Too real? Would Simon feel better if I just threw a few things into a duffel and called it good?

Whatever. I pull my garment bag out from under my bed.

Simon has wandered over to my violin case. "Do you need this?"

I lay the bag on my bed. "'Need' is a strong word. Would you like me to bring it?"

"I didn't know if you still played."

"I still play."

He looks uncomfortable. Embarrassed, maybe.

"Grab it," I say. "Perhaps we'll encounter a violin emergency."

"Have you encountered one of those before?"

"Any and all emergencies are possible with you around." Fuck it, I'm bringing a dozen shirts, a few jackets. Another summer-weight suit. I'll need two bags. And I'll keep both of them by Simon's front door, just in case he throws me out.

"Can I help?" he asks.

"I've got it. Just sit down, Snow."

He sits on my bed. Holding the violin in his lap. He looks like an 8-year-old waiting for the bus.

It would be easier if I *were* bringing everything. Then I could just open my suitcase and have the bags pack themselves, Mary Poppins–style.

I lay my shirts and jackets out on the bed, then find my duffel bag and take it to my chest of drawers. I open the top drawer. (Am I really doing this? Taking *pants* to Simon Snow's flat?) I rest my hand on a stack of boxer briefs and clear my throat. "Are you sure about this?"

"Are you?" Simon asks.

I turn around. "I asked you first."

He's looking at the floor. His tongue is in his cheek. Like he's frustrated. Or angry.

I turn back to my pants. Right. Simon isn't sure. Of any of this. I'm putting all of my eggs in his basket, and it's a ramshackle basket—he already warned me.

I close my eyes for a second. *Right.*

I open my eyes and scoop up the entire stack of boxers, then dump them in the duffel. I empty the whole drawer. I grab most of my T-shirts, as well, and half a dozen pairs of jeans and trousers. I'm going to need another bag for shoes.

Simon watches me pack. He's still hugging my violin.

I zip up the duffel and look at him. "I'm sure," I say.

When we come out, Fiona is still guarding her bedroom door. Still puffing on her nicotine whistle like a second-rate Instagram influencer. She looks at my bags. "Going somewhere?"

"I'm going to stay with Simon for a few days."

"A few days or a few months?"

I lower an eyebrow at her. "You're going to get lung fungus. And the worst part will be that everyone will know you got it from vaping."

She sneers over my shoulder. "Take care of my nephew, Simon Snow."

Simon is already sneaking out the door.

"Take care of my aunt, whoever you are!" I shout.

40

SHEPARD

For the first time in two years, I know exactly what the tattoos on my arms say. Debbie translated the incantation that Ken gave me, too—most of it.

Now I know what I said that day, to summon the demon.

I finally see how I ended up like this.

I never thought I'd get this far or understand this much—and it only happened because of Penelope Bunce. Who isn't speaking to me and won't even look at me.

I don't blame her.

I shouldn't have lied. It didn't start as a lie . . . It just happened . . . That day on Agatha's balcony, with Penelope's hand on my collar. I just thought, *I'm probably never going to see this girl again, and I'm never going to meet another girl like her, and the last thing I want her to know about me is that these tattoos are a fucked-up engagement ring.*

I sit across the aisle from Penelope when we get on the train. To give her space. She doesn't say anything, just stares out the window. She's got the end of her ponytail in one hand, and she's twisting it.

Penelope's look today is a giant purple T-shirt with the neck cut out—so it lies wide and open on her shoulders—and a flared denim skirt that just grazes the tops of her knees when she's standing. She's sitting now.

I don't think Penelope thinks about her skin. Or her hair. I don't think she twirls her ponytail around her fingers because she knows I'm watching. I don't think she thinks about me looking at her at all—so I try not to.

I don't think she thinks about me *liking* her . . .

So I try not to do that either.

I should have told her the truth. All of it. As soon as she offered to help me. Definitely before I got on the plane. I should have known that Penelope was smart enough to crack this—that she'd get to the bottom of my mess before I could come up with a good way to break it to her. Because there *is* no good way to break it. There's no version of the truth that doesn't make me seem worse than foolish. Worse than cursed. Worse than taken.

When we get to her stop, I follow her off the train. Then I follow her to her flat. She unlocks the door and holds it open for me.

"I'll just get my backpack," I say.

"Sit down, Shepard."

I'm not sure why she wants me to sit, maybe so that she can chew me out some more. Anyway, I do it.

She stands in front of me and holds out her hand. "Let's see it."

I'm not sure what she means. My arms?

"The translation," she says, snapping her fingers.

"Penelope—"

"I didn't spend all afternoon in some sort of spider-woman's nest, so that I could *not* see the information we came for."

I reach into my pocket and pull out the folded-up translation. It's two pages long. Penelope takes them from me and unfolds them. "Calligraphy," she says. "Why not."

She starts reading.

"Right," she says, nodding. "This is a prenuptial agreement . . ."

She reads a bit more. "Oh, good job, Shepard, it's an *eternal* contract. No divorce in your future. No adultery either, not if you value your eyelashes . . . That's . . . picturesque . . ."

She keeps reading.

She raises an eyebrow and makes a noise like, "Pffft."

She flips to the second page. "What's this? Half the words are missing."

I'm sitting with my knees wide and my elbows on my thighs, my head hanging low. "That's the spell I got from Ken. The summoning spell. Debbie left out everything that made her nervous."

Penelope's quiet. She's reading.

"This is a marriage proposal . . ." she says.

I don't say anything.

"Shepard," she says, "you weren't *forced* into an engagement. You *proposed* to a demon."

I don't say anything. There's nothing to say.

"This is so much more idiotic than I thought."

"All right . . ." I sit up and grab the papers from her hand. "I know! This is why I lied to you—because I didn't want you to know what a fool I am."

Penelope's face is hard. "I prefer fools to liars."

"I'm not *actually* a liar," I say, folding up the papers and shoving them back into my jacket. "I mean, I am *literally*. In this case. But I'm not. *Generally*. As a person. I'll just get my backpack—"

"I believe you."

I look up. Her face is still hard.

"What do you believe?"

"I believe that you didn't mean to lie to me."

My hand is still in my jacket pocket. I take it out. "You do?"

"Yes," she says. "Just . . ." She turns to one of the chalkboard walls. "Don't do it again, okay?"

I nod slowly. Even though she can't see me. "Okay."

She picks up her chalk. "Don't lie to me, and don't leave anything out."

"Okay," I say again.

"Don't *surprise* me."

"I wasn't trying—"

She whips around, with her hands on her hips. "Just assume I want as much information as is possible, in every situation!"

"I can do that." I'm nodding too eagerly. "I want that, too."

Penelope looks up into my eyes, and it feels like a warning. It feels like she's giving me another chance. But only this once.

"Let me see me the translation again," she says.

I hand her the papers. She sticks each page to the chalkboard with a spell—*"Sticking point!"*

"Now that we know the terms," she says, "we can look for a way out."

41

SIMON

My flat looks emptier now that I've asked Baz to stay here. All I've really got is the mattress. "I can get furniture," I say, looking around. "I can get one of those poles."

Baz has dropped his bags just inside the door. He's texting someone. He glances up from his phone. "A pole?"

"For your clothes. For clothes. Mine are just . . ." Mine are just in a heap on the bedroom floor. "I was going to buy furniture anyway."

"Did someone die and leave you their fortune?" Still texting.

"Well . . . actually . . ."

He looks up again. "Did someone *die*, Snow?"

"Who are you texting?" I ask.

"My other boyfriend. The one who texts back."

I grab for his phone. He holds it above me. If I weren't wearing a hoodie, I could fly up and reach it.

"I'm texting *Bunce*," he says. "Like I have time for another boyfriend . . . Your dysfunction is a full-time job."

I shove him back—then think better of it and pull on his shirt, reaching for the phone again. "You're texting Penny? Is she texting you back?"

He puts the phone in his jacket pocket, slapping my hand away. "She texted me back to say that she's trying to respect your needs. I told her you needed a kick in the arse; that I've already delivered it; and now we need her help."

"We *do* need her help," I say.

"I know. I told her to call."

I push my hand through the front of my hair. I hope she does.

Baz bumps me with his elbow. "Who *died*, Snow?"

"Oh." I smooth my hair down again. "The Mage."

"Right," he says. "I was there."

"Right, but . . . Well, he left me his money. In his will."

Baz looks surprised. "Your helping him off this mortal plane didn't affect that?"

"Not according to Dr. Wellbelove."

Baz laughs. "So the Mage paid for this flat?"

"Yeah."

"And the Mage bought that mattress?"

"Indirectly."

Baz grabs me by the waist and starts shoving me backwards towards the bedroom. He kicks off his shoes between shoves.

"Hey!"

"Shut up, Snow, I'm going to have my way with you on the Mage's bed."

He pushes me through the door, and I fall back onto the mattress. Baz grabs one of my legs and takes my trainer off by the heel.

"Is that a turn-on?" I watch him take off my other shoe. "The Mage's bed?"

"Yes," he says, throwing both shoes towards the door. "Because I hate him, and anything that would piss him off is a turn-on." He climbs over me.

I swallow and hook my arms around his neck. "So that's what this is, spite?"

"Hm-mm." Baz kisses my neck. "Spite. Look where the Mage's golden boy is now . . ."

"Depowered," I say. "Deposed. Hackney Wick."

Baz sits up, right on my stomach. I grunt and try to push him off.

"I *meant*"—he smacks my side—"in a homosexual relationship with one of his worst enemies."

"Right," I say, still grunting. He's crushing me. "He'd hate that part, too."

Baz rolls off of me onto his side, propping his head up with one hand. "How much money did he leave you?"

"Enough for rent for a couple years. Less, if I buy furniture. But I'm going to get a job."

"It's all right," he says. "I don't care about furniture."

Baz's dark hair is curling around his neck. It's just long enough to brush his shoulders now. I wonder how long he wants it. I push some of it behind his ear. Not because it looks bad. I just want to touch it. *Is this what people do? They just keep talking and touching?*

"I *want* a job," I say.

"What kind?"

I shrug. "Whatever. Maybe a builder will hire me. I'm a hard worker."

Baz is looking down at me. Frowning slightly. "You don't want to stay at university?"

"I really don't."

"You're not stupid," he says.

I shrug again. Maybe I am. It doesn't matter. The lock of hair has fallen over his ear. I tuck it back—Baz catches my hand. He brings it to his mouth and kisses the inside of my wrist, without looking away from my eyes. It makes me feel . . . I don't know. I pull my hand away and stretch my arms over my head. One of the joints in my wings pops. They're still bunched up under my T-shirt.

"Here," Baz says, pushing up the bottom of my hoodie. I sit up and take off all my layers. He sits up, too, and gives me room to stretch out my wings. He's smiling at me. "You look like a bird, preening."

"I can't help it." I'm still stretching. "They get cramped."

He lies down again, on his back. I take the position he had, propped up on an elbow beside him. I'm still shaking my wings out behind me.

Baz reaches a hand up and pets my chest. I don't have much hair there, not like him—he's got a proper spread across his pecs and a black stripe down his belly. Now that I've got fat, I look like a baby when I'm bare-chested.

"You don't have to wear a shirt on my account," he says, still petting me. "If you're uncomfortable."

"I'll keep that in mind," I say.

"I mean . . . you should feel at ease in your own home." He pinches the chub over my ribs.

I grab his wrist. "*Thanks*," I say, watching him laugh. And then, because I'm holding his wrist, I kiss it—it feels especially cool on my lips. "Are you cold?"

He shakes his head. "You're the one who's half undressed."

"I'm fine, it's warm in here. But you're cold." I kiss his wrist again. Then chafe it with my thumb.

"I don't really *get* cold . . ."

"Like you can't feel the cold?"

"No, I can. It just doesn't usually bother me." Baz looks troubled for a second. "Unless I'm sick."

"When do you get sick?"

"Almost never. But . . . I was sick after the numpties. I was cold then."

I kiss his wrist, harder. Then his palm. I hold his hand over my face, kissing it—it isn't enough. I bring his hand up around my neck and lean over him, rubbing my face in his cheek. "I should have found you," I say. "Your aunt should have told me you'd been kidnapped."

"Snow, you hated me then." He's stroking the back of my hair. "You probably would have sent the numpties a thank-you note."

I pull back. I find his grey eyes. "I would have *slaughtered* them. I was out of my head with worry."

"You hated me," he says again, more softly.

"Yeah . . . but I wouldn't have let anyone hurt you."

"I'm hard to hurt," he whispers. "You said so yourself."

"No." I move closer. Our noses bump when I shake my head. "I said you were hard to kill."

Baz closes his eyes and pulls my forehead down to his. His mouth is open for me when I kiss him. His tongue is cold.

Is this what people do? Do they just keep talking? And touching?

I get lost fast when we're kissing. I want more of it. All of it. I want the lethal dose.

My hands are on Baz's arms. Then they're on his shoulders. Then they're, I don't know where, everywhere. It isn't enough—I need his skin. And then I need more. He doesn't have enough skin for my hands. I don't have enough room in my lungs for the way his hair smells . . .

I'm holding Baz now, tight enough to bruise.

I'm biting him hard enough to break.

It's only okay because he isn't human—he isn't, and I am. And my hands are on his neck now. My hands are on his stomach. He's cold, and it isn't enough. *Where is this going? What's it all for?* I want to kiss him. I want to come on him. But it won't be enough. It won't be enough, *and then what?* My hands are—

My hands are in the air. Baz is holding my wrists.

"*Simon,*" he hisses.

I try to kiss him, I'm lost. (I'm lost, I'm lost, nothing is enough.)

"*Simon,*" he says. "*Stop.*"

I let go—the only way I can manage, by going limp. Baz shoves me off of him, and I fall on my side.

"Sorry," I gasp. I try to cover my eyes, but he's still holding my wrists.

"It's all right," he says. "Just, I don't know, breathe."

I try.

I try.

I'm trying.

All right.

I'm breathing.

I'm trying.

All right.

When I open my eyes again, I see Baz lying on his side next to me. His hair is a mess. He looks worried.

"Sorry," I say. My eyes are burning. Christ, next I'll be crying.

Baz lets go of my wrists and holds my face instead. "It's fine—I'm fine. I mean, if you still had your magic, I think I'd be dead . . ."

I laugh, but only because I feel so pathetic. "You think I'm going off?"

"Yeah . . . I don't think you have gears, Snow. I think you only go full throttle."

I laugh again, miserably, and then the weeping starts—I knew it would. I try to turn my face away. "I'm sorry, Baz. I'm never going to get this right."

"Shut up," he says. "We've only just started trying."

I close my eyes. Now is when I'd leave. Normally. Now is when I *can't* leave. I need to ride this out. I need to keep riding this out.

He rubs my cheeks with his thumbs. "I like your flat," he says.

I laugh. It's ridiculous. He keeps wiping away my tears.

I'm breathing. The pressure is fading in my head. The heat is leaving my eyes. I'm breathing. I'm tired. "What if it never gets better?" I say. "What if I never get better at any of this?"

Baz runs his thumb from the bridge of my nose to my temple and back. "What if every kiss leads us here?"

My eyes burn again. "Yeah."

"Okay," he says.

I open my eyes. "Okay?"

He shrugs. "I'll take it."

"Don't fuck with me."

He wraps one hand around the back of my neck. "I'm not *fucking* with you! I'll take it. I'm a traumatized vampire. I never thought I'd have a normal relationship. I thought I was going to marry some girl, and sneak out at night to sleep with strangers and drink their pets."

I roll my eyes. "When did you think that?"

"I don't know," he says. "Pretty much from age thirteen to . . . however old I was the night you kissed me."

"Fuck, Baz. You deserve better."

He shrugs again, then squeezes my neck. "I'll take it. I'll take you." He kisses my mouth quickly, and I let him shift our bodies closer.

I wind an arm around him.

(I'm breathing. I'm still breathing. And I'm still here. So is he.)

"I never thought I'd have a normal relationship, either," I say.

Baz snorts. "Because you were going to have a royal wedding. There were going to be commemorative tea towels when you and Agatha tied the knot."

His shirt is hitched up to his chest. His jacket is long gone. I rub his stomach with my free hand. "Nah. I mean—I always figured something would get its teeth in me before I'd ever get to settle down."

"Something like the Humdrum?"

"Maybe. Whatever ended up being the Greatest Threat to Magic. That's what the job was—to go down fighting."

"Huh." Baz is playing with the curls at the top of my head. "I wonder if anyone has told Smith-Richards."

He's being too gentle. I shudder and shake my head, pulling away.

Baz lowers an eyebrow, watching. He waits for me to relax next to him again, then puts his hand right back in my hair. He rubs his fingertips into my scalp. It's better. It's good.

I close my eyes and lean into him. "You really don't think he's legit?"

"Smith-Richards? Circe, no."

"But we watched him cure someone."

"We watched him do *something*. I agree with Lady Salisbury—you can't cure someone of weak magic."

"Why not?" I ask. "You can cure other things. Like . . . high blood pressure and gnomeatic fever."

"Weak magic isn't a disease." He combs his hand through my hair, from front to back, then tugs at the crown.

I tilt my head back, eyes still closed. "What is it, then?"

"It's not one thing." He pulls his fingers out of my hair, then combs them through again. "It's aptitude, right? Some people aren't good with words, some people aren't persuasive speakers. Some people can't think on their feet."

He could be talking about me. Maybe he is.

"But it's also ability," he goes on. "Can you speak clearly, does your voice carry . . . And then there's basic *capacity*. Strength, power. How much magic you can control, how much you can channel. Plus, training, education, practice, drive . . ."

"Lucky for you," I say, opening my eyes just enough to see him. "You've got it all."

Baz curls his lip. "Yeah, that's me. Nobody can shut up about my good luck."

I ease closer. "You are lucky though. You and Penny. You're like . . ." I reach my hand up his back, under his shirt. His skin is cool. "Aristocrats. Like, kings and queens compared to everyone else."

"What'd that make you, Snow, a god?"

"I was a fluke."

Baz sighs, frustrated, and gives my hair a sharp pull. "All right," he says, "I'm lucky. What does that prove? Do you think Smith-Richards is changing people's luck?"

"I think he's doing *something*," I say. "Shall we go check it out?"

Baz hums. "Let's wait for Penelope to call. We could use her help."

"You think she'll get back to us?"

"When has Bunce ever ignored a dangerous proposition?"

42

PENELOPE

"Maybe we should just summon the demon and see what happens."

"We are *not* summoning the demon, Penelope."

"Don't want me to meet your girlfriend?"

Shepard is sitting low on my sofa, his shoulders against the back of it and his legs kicked out. He's different now that I know his secret. Less happy-go-lucky. Maybe he can't pretend to be lucky while we're really plumbing the depths of his bad luck. He's got his jacket off, and he's wearing a white Keith Haring T-shirt. And every time I say something that he finds humiliating, like now, he covers his eyes with his forearms and shows me his triceps.

I drop down next to Shepard on the sofa. I'm only half kidding about summoning the demon; maybe she'd be open to negotiation. I elbow him. "Worried she'll get clingy?"

"Penelope . . ." He lets his arms fall. "You can keep making fun of me . . ."

"I shall."

"And insulting me."

"That's the plan."

He turns his head towards me. If I had to describe his face and general mood right now, I'd go with *unhappy-go-unlucky*. "But please," he says, "don't make jokes like that."

"Like what?"

"Don't call her my girlfriend."

"Is 'fiancée' better?"

"Don't, Penelope. It's not funny."

"It's funny to me, I have a lot of jokes lined up."

Shepard frowns at me. It's somehow even more effective than his smiles—more potent for its rarity. "If I were a *woman* being forced to marry a demon," he says, "would it be funny?"

I don't know, would it? I fold my arms. Shepard's *not* a woman. He's a big, goofy man—who got himself into this situation and then hid it from me. "Clearly I understand that this is serious, Shepard—I am trying to help you fix it."

"And I appreciate it! Thank you! Just . . . don't tease me. About that part. Don't call her my fiancée."

"Fine," I say and wish I didn't sound so sulky about it.

"It's not a real engagement," he says, rubbing the stripes in his trousers. He's said it before.

"I get that."

He glances at me, not quite meeting my eyes. "Do you?"

"Yes. I do." (I mean . . . I mostly do.) "Mages used to have arranged marriages," I say, looking back up at my lists. "It made sense from a practical standpoint: We like to marry each other, and powerful mages like to marry other powerful mages—it keeps the bloodlines robust."

Shepard has turned more fully towards me, listening. Of

course he's listening, these are state secrets. I keep going anyway: "There are lots of stories about people trapped in marriage contracts. Beautiful maidens, usually, promised to powerful old men."

He looks down at his lap, embarrassed again.

"Hey . . ." I say, thinking. "That vampire couldn't kill you. Back in the desert. In Nevada."

"I suspect he could have *killed* me," Shepard says, "but he couldn't Turn me—that's where the curse interfered."

"Because if you were immortal," I say, "your soul wouldn't show up for the wedding."

He sighs. "That's my assumption."

I bring my legs up onto the couch to cross them, then push my skirt down in the middle. (Baz is always on me to be more ladylike in skirts.) "Has that come into play before?"

"Once," Shepard says. "I tried to go home with a fairy, but I couldn't get through the mist."

"Why were you going home with a fairy?"

He looks back at his knees, clearing his throat.

"With a *fairy*?" I say. If I sound scandalized, it's because I am.

He peeks up at me, smiling. "Why not with a fairy?"

"I can't even believe you found a proper fairy—but, Shepard, they're evil!"

He smiles at his lap. "She didn't seem evil."

"Morgana below, is this part of your whole . . . *thing*?"

He lifts his chin up and looks at me like I'm the one being strange. "Is what part of my whole thing? Going home with girls?"

"Going home with *creatures*. Are you some sort of collector?"

"No!" He's laughing at me. "No. Not, like, intentionally."

I fall back against the arm of the sofa, covering my eyes. "I can't."

I can still hear him laughing.

"You're lucky the curse saved you from disappearing into the fairy realm," I say.

"Didn't feel lucky at the time."

I shake my head hard, *really* not wanting to imagine what else Shepard has followed home over the years. Then I haul myself back up, smoothing my skirt, and trying to sort out the relevant implications . . . "So you're not allowed to be with anyone else? Romantically? We should write that down."

"Oh no," he says. "That's not the problem. The curse doesn't keep me from hooking up. I don't think the demon cares what I do before I die."

I can feel my cheeks burning. "Then why couldn't you pass through the fairy fog?"

"I think it's because time passes differently with the fairies . . ."

"Oh, sure," I say, getting it, "it's another sort of immortality!"

"Or altered mortality," he agrees.

"Huh." I stand up and find my chalk. I make a note of it on the wall: *C.V. can't be made immortal.* And—*"Engagement" doesn't interfere with sexual congress.*

"Not how I'd put it," Shepard says.

I tap the chalk against my chin.

"What happens in the stories?" he asks.

I turn back to him. "Hmm?"

He looks sheepish again. "To the beautiful maidens?"

"Oh, they get out of it, of course. They find a loophole. Or they trick the old creepy guy. My dad used to love to tell this story about a beautiful magician who secretly married her true love and . . . *Oh!* Oh my words!! Shepard!!! I have an *idea.*"

43

BAZ

I thought we were going to have to do some detective work to find Smith-Richards's residential centre, but apparently someone gave Simon a leaflet at the meeting. (No one offered *me* a leaflet.) (No one ever wants me to join their religion, either.)

Penelope still hasn't called. Or texted. Simon's in a funk about it, but hopefully he'll rally. I sprung for a taxi, so he wouldn't pout about having to take the train or a bus.

"Pull over here," I say to the cabbie.

Simon squints out the window. "Here?"

"Apparently," I say, paying the fare.

We climb out and look across the street. There's a brick building with a tower and a belfry; it might have been a church once. A small, grey-haired man is hurrying away from the door.

"Is that Professor Bunce?" Simon says.

"Penny's mum?"

"The other Professor Bunce, her dad."

"Don't know." I pull Simon's arm. "Come on. And don't forget to invite me in if no one else does."

We jog across the street. Simon looks like he's going to call out to Professor Bunce, but the man is already half a block away.

The building ahead of us has a large, stone doorframe with the words HOME FOR WAIFS engraved in the lintel. "A little on the nose," I mutter.

"Is it an orphanage?" Simon asks.

"Was, maybe." I push the buzzer.

Simon smooths down his hair.

"Don't forget to invite me in," I whisper.

"When do I ever forget?"

"When we tried to have breakfast at Dishoom."

"That was one time."

"I miss America," I say. "All those *'welcome'* mats and *'come in, we're open'* signs . . ."

Simon snorts. "You do *not* miss America—"

The door opens. The girl I recognized at Smith-Richards's meeting is standing there. Chomsky, how *do* I know her? She's got to be around our age . . . Fair skin. Short, brown hair. I know she wasn't at Watford. Are we related somehow, is that how I know her? Her eyes get big when she sees Simon.

"Hi," he says.

The girl's already rushing away from us, down the hall. Talk about starstruck. She's left the front door open. Simon steps in and looks around.

I fold my arms, waiting.

He turns back to me and grins.

"This is a good game," I say flatly. "Can we play this for the rest of our lives?"

Snow reaches out and grabs my elbow, pulling me across the threshold and against him. He's laughing silently and kissing my cheek. (For someone who is afraid of looking gay in public, he sure gets off on public displays of affection.) (That's probably connected.)

"Simon!" We both turn towards the voice. It's Smith-Richards himself. Dressed like a very wealthy folksinger. "I was hoping I'd see you again," he says, clapping a hand on Simon's back.

Simon doesn't know how to respond to that. He looks a bit dazed. (Snow is very easily impressed by Smith-Richards.) (Or maybe he's just worried that Smith-Richards can feel his wings.)

I hold out my hand. "Hello," I say. "Basilton Pitch."

Smith-Richards looks at me for the first time, his hand still on Simon's shoulder. "Pitch . . ." His eyes light up. "Daphne's son!" He reaches out with his free hand. "It's so nice to meet you. Did you come to visit her?"

I shake his hand. "Actually—"

"We came to see you," Simon says.

Smith-Richards drops my hand, turning back to Simon and smiling softly. "Did you? I hoped you would." He wraps his arm around Simon's shoulders—surely he can feel the wings now—and starts walking away with him. "Come on in, both of you. I'm so glad you're here."

Smith-Richards's office isn't an office. It's a tiny sitting room filled with a flat's worth of expensive modern furniture, all of it deceptively simple. He's got a bookshelf that looks like a

shipping crate—I'll bet it cost a thousand pounds. He invites
Simon and me to sit on a leather sofa, and he sits just across
from us in a wooden folding chair that probably cost another
thousand pounds. His chair is so close to us, our knees are
practically knocking.

"Sorry it's so cramped in here," he says. "We needed all
the bigger spaces for bedrooms. We just moved into this
building a few weeks ago, and we've already outgrown it.
I'm not sure what we'll do if more magicians show up." His
face falls. "Did you guys come to stay? Because we can make
room for you—we'll find a way."

"No," I say, worried that Snow will blunder us into joining
this commune. "We just came to talk."

Smith-Richards looks relieved. "Ah, good. Wonderful.
Let's talk. What can I tell you?"

We've already planned this part of the conversation. How
to bring up Jamie. Simon is supposed to start talking about
Smith's miracle spell, and how he'd like to meet someone
who's been cured . . .

Instead, Snow swallows and says in an overawed voice,
"Have you always known you were the Chosen One?"

Smith-Richards's whole posture softens. He smiles directly into Simon's eyes. "No," he says. "Did you?"

Simon wrinkles his nose and presses his lips together,
shaking his head. "The Mage told me. When I was eleven. I
never felt like anything special before that—or after, really."

"But your magic was special," Smith-Richards says. "Your
magic was legendary."

"Nah, I was a shit magician. Talk to anyone who went to
school with me."

"Did *you* go to Watford?" I ask Smith-Richards. "You

must have left just as we were showing up." If he's in his 30s, he would have known my mother and possibly my aunt.

Smith-Richards looks like he'd already forgotten I was there. "Oh . . . no—we travelled too much for that. I went to Normal schools. In Germany, Kenya, Budapest . . . And my godfather tutored me in magic. I *wish* I'd gone to Watford. What an incredible history. And I'd have more friends in the mage community here. More connections."

"But you didn't *know* you were the Chosen One all along?" Simon asks. "When did you figure it out?"

Smith-Richards turns to Simon again, looking a bit dazed and overawed himself. (Fair. Simon is incredibly attractive. Especially when he's being all dogged and earnest like this. With his cheeks pink and his eyebrows drawn low and his throat bobbing every time he fortifies himself to ask a question.)

"I . . ." Smith-Richards says. "Did you want something to drink? I didn't offer. There's cake, too. There might even be dinner."

"No," Simon says, "we're fine. Thanks."

Smith-Richards leans forward. It's like he's giving in. He rests an elbow on one knee and ruffles the back of his golden hair. He wears it long enough to curl, to cover his ears but not his collar. "To be honest," he says, "I didn't think that I might be the Greatest Mage until I heard that you had been . . ."

"Exposed?" Simon says.

Smith-Richards shrugs, like he doesn't want to hurt Simon's feelings. "Explained."

"And then?" Simon pushes.

Smith-Richards is at the back of his hair again. "And then I started thinking about a lot of things . . ."

Simon swallows, waiting.

"About signs."

"Signs," Simon repeats, leaning forward.

Smith-Richard nods. "My mother had a dream about me, before she even knew she was pregnant. Then I was born during an eclipse. And after my parents died—"

"Your parents died?"

"When I was very young."

"I'm sorry."

"Thank you. After they died, my godfather raised me, and he always told me I was special."

I roll my eyes. Every parent says that.

Smith-Richards goes on: "I thought he was just saying it because he loved me, but there was some truth to it. I've always had a way with other magicians . . . even when I was a baby."

Everyone loves babies.

"Their magic was stronger when I was around," he says. "My godfather said he could cast a sonnet with me in the room."

Simon smiles—ruefully. "That's the opposite of me," he says. "I was taking everyone else's magic."

"Not intentionally," Smith-Richards says. "Simon, everyone knows that the Mage used you."

Simon's face is red. I don't think the fact that *everyone knows* he was duped is much of a comfort to him. Especially when there's so much he doesn't know himself. Where *did* Simon's ability come from? And how did the Mage find him? What would have happened if the Mage had been able to take Simon's power on that final, fateful day?

"So you put the pieces together . . ." Simon says. "About yourself."

"I started to think, *perhaps* . . ." Smith-Richards's cheeks are red, too. His eyes are more blue than ever. "Perhaps I was meant to help people."

For fuck's sake—imagine thinking that makes you *special*. Something that's literally true of *all of us*. I hold back a derisive "pfft."

Simon is sitting on the very edge of the sofa. "So no one around you—"

Smith-Richards scoots forward on his chair. Their knees are overlapping now. "When I talked to my godfather, he said he'd always suspected that I might be . . . you know. The one. But that it was the sort of thing I needed to decide for myself. To discover for myself and feel sure of." Smith-Richards runs his fingers through his hair. He's sitting in a shaft of light now. The evening sun catches on each shining curl. "I don't think I could have felt certain of this, as a child. I'm glad I didn't know what I was." He holds his palms out. "I wouldn't have understood what it meant."

Simon is looking down into the man's open hands.

"I'm so grateful for the last ten years," Smith-Richards says. "You gave me that time, and it was a gift."

Simon tilts his head up, and their eyes meet. Simon swallows. Then swallows again.

"How long have you been back in England?" I ask. Crisply.

Smith-Richards is still gazing at Simon.

I clear my throat.

His head turns slowly to me. "A year," he says. "A little more. It felt like it was time to come home."

"To buy an orphanage?"

He laughs. "Well, that's a new development. At first I was just visiting people in their homes. But some of my friends felt I could have a bigger impact if I got organized. That's when the meetings started. Eventually"—he ruffles his hair again, looking around—"this. A foundlings' home, how could I resist? *Orphan makes good.*"

"Have you recovered from last night?" I ask, still very crisp. "The cure seems to really take it out of you."

Smith-Richards sighs. "Yeah, it does. I can sort of help people's magic, just by touching them—" He holds his hand out to me. "You can try it if you want."

"That's all right," I say. "Conserve yourself."

He rests his hand on his thigh. "But the spell makes me feel like I've run a marathon. I'm still getting the hang of it. I've only cast it a few times now. I've been working on a way to *focus* my talents."

"You mentioned the first person you healed," Simon says, somehow miraculously back on track, "Jamie."

"Jamie," Smith-Richards repeats warmly. "He was one of the first people who really believed in me. I mean, he trusted me to cast this totally new, *weird* spell on him."

"And it worked?" Simon asks.

Smith-Richards grins. "It totally worked. Jamie . . . He didn't even have a wand when I met him. Full-blooded magician. Had never cast a 'Clean sweep.' Wasn't even allowed at Watford. And now he's fully fluent."

"That's amazing," Simon says.

Smith-Richards is beaming at him. Literally. The sun has moved behind Smith-Richards's head and is lighting him up like a saint.

"Could we meet Jamie?" I ask.

"I'd love to meet him," Simon says earnestly.

"Yeah"—Smith-Richards looks excited—"I'd love for you to meet him, too."

Simon scoots even farther off the sofa, ready to spring up. (Directly into Smith-Richards's lap.)

"Should we call for him?" I ask.

"Oh . . ." Smith-Richards sits back in his chair. "I'm sorry. Jamie doesn't live here. But I could text him? And arrange something? Maybe at the next meeting?"

"That'd be great," Simon says.

There's a knock at the open door. We all look up. That same girl is standing there, still looking scared of Simon.

"Hey, Pippa," Smith-Richards says. "Is dinner ready?"

She nods.

"Thanks. I'll be right down."

She hurries away.

"You really ought to stay for dinner," Smith-Richards says. "Daphne would be glad to see you."

"Thank you," I say, "but I don't want her to think I'm checking up on her."

"All right." Smith-Richards reaches for my hand again, then claps Simon on the shoulder. "Let's exchange numbers, in case something comes up."

"Sure," Simon says, getting out his phone.

Smith ends up doing the typing. "I'll see you at the next meeting, yeah?"

"Yeah," Simon says, "for sure."

"And Simon—let yourself be comfortable. If you want to keep the wings put away, I get it. But we're all magicians here. You don't have anything to hide."

Simon is blushing. "Okay, um . . . thanks."

Smith-Richards walks us to the door.

44

SMITH

Simon Snow.

Here.

Like someone out of a story.

A fallen angel. A prodigal son. A returning hero, Achilles tendon sliced in the war.

He looks the part.

(Can he *see* how people look at him? Can he see how they *see* him?)

The wings were a genius twist. Scarlet wings, what a visual. He's a stained-glass window waiting to happen—I'm almost jealous.

I mean, I am, a little . . . jealous.

But I'll get there. Who knows what destiny holds for me? Who knows how my legend will build? There will be windows someday and statues. Full-colour plates in gilded books.

One day at a time, Evander always says. One chapter.

My godfather raised me with all the old stories. We travelled the world, but he kept the World of Mages alive in me. What a world! What glory! I hardly recognized it when he brought me home to London . . .

This is how magicians live now? Among the Normals? *Like* the Normals? Afraid of them?

What's the point of being magickal if you have to fill your days with mundanity?

(Can they even *see* themselves? Do they see how they *look*?)

In the stories, there are *castles*. There are feats of power. Dragons!

In the World of Mages, there's almost nothing. A school. A few clubs. Dishwashing spells.

I give them a lifetime's worth of power, and they make chocolate bars. (Maybe I should just hand out chocolate bars . . .)

At least they haven't forgotten all the old stories. They still know who I am. They're still waiting for me.

The Chosen One.

The Greatest Mage.

The Power of Powers.

The one who will come to save them from the greatest threat to the World of Mages.

I *will* save this world.

And Simon Snow will help me.

45

SHEPARD

Penelope doesn't even have to cast a spell to find her dad; she's got a key that will take her right to him. There's a piece of yarn looped through it. "My mum made this," she says. "When I was a kid, they made me wear it around my neck."

She hangs the key over a map of London. "Mum meets with the Coven tonight, so we should be able to catch Dad alone."

"What's the Coven?"

"Not even a little bit your business."

The key twitches. "Not at home . . ." she says. "Not at work . . ."

It settles near the British Museum. I've always wanted to go to the British Museum.

"Come on," she says, "let's try to catch him."

We get into a cab, which I predict she won't pay for. Penelope plays fast and loose with goods and services. I feel so guilty about it that I can't make eye contact with the driver.

She keeps holding the key over the Maps app on her

phone to keep track of her dad.

"Why can't you call him again?"

"I can't risk him telling my mum."

"Won't he tell her anyway? Eventually?"

"I'm going to plead my case in person." She frowns at her phone and mumbles, "Or spell him if I have to."

"You'd do that to your own father?"

She shrugs. "Well, I haven't yet—He's moving again!" She leans forward and raps on the Plexiglas screen between us and the driver. "Here is fine!"

The driver lets us out at the corner. Penny knocks her gem on his credit card reader and says, ***"Fair enough!"***

"Do you *ever* pay for cab rides?" I ask her, as the taxi drives away.

She's scanning the street. "I only take cabs when it's an emergency."

"So, that's a no . . ."

"There he is!" She starts waving.

There's a small, gray-haired white man crossing the street ahead of us. I guess Penelope did say she was biracial. Her mom's Indian, I think.

"Dad!" she calls.

The man looks up. He gets across the street and waits for us.

"Penny," he says. "Your mother's been calling you."

"Dad . . . I need your help."

We end up at a coffee shop, and Penelope's dad buys us scones with jam. (The scones over here are more like biscuits. They sell them everywhere, and it's perfectly acceptable to order them at any time of day. They give you a cup of butter and sometimes your own little bottle of jam. I really don't think English people realize how great it is to live here. The sandwiches alone are on another *level*.)

Mr. Bunce is rubbing his eyes. He's got a tired face. Up close, his hair is more blond than gray. "Penny . . . you know I can't keep secrets from your mother."

"I'm just asking you not to *mention* this," she says. "I'm not asking you to lie about it."

"That sounds like a lie of omission," I point out. "People hate those just as much."

She goggles her eyes at me. "*Shepard.*"

Mr. Bunce is looking at me. One side of his mouth is quirked down, but it still seems like he's smiling. "You're the American, huh? Martin Bunce."

"Shepard," I say, holding out my hand.

He takes it. "Whereabout in America?"

"Omaha," I say. "Nebraska."

"I know where that is. I've done some work in Ohio."

"Nebraska is a lot like Ohio. Similar vibe."

"Well, let's have a look at them," he says, gesturing at my jacket.

I look around the coffee shop. Penelope rolls her eyes and holds out a fist—**"*There's nothing to see here!*"** I take off my jacket.

"May I?" Mr. Bunce asks.

I nod, holding out an arm.

He takes it gently in both hands. "Look at that, that's beautiful . . ." He twists my arm a bit, so he can see the whole thing. "Huh . . . Mitali said this was a curse. This isn't a curse." He looks up at my face. "It's a handfasting."

"Dad"—Penelope looks shocked—"I didn't know you could read Demon!"

"I can't." He traces his hand along one of the swirls. "But I can tell from the patterns. You see these same patterns in a lot of ancient marriage rituals."

"Dad studies marriage and family magic," she tells me.

"It's a hobby," he says.

"We've had the contract translated," she says.

"Have you?" He looks up from my arm.

Penelope elbows me. "Show him."

I reach back into my jacket and get out the papers.

Mr. Bunce puts on his reading glasses and takes a look. "So you found someone who could translate a Demonic ritual . . . Do I want to know who?"

"Nope," she says.

Her dad lowers his eyebrows. "*Penelope*," he says, like he's constantly having to lecture her for this sort of thing. Then his eyes get big, and he looks up at me. "Shepard—*this* is the summoning ritual you used?"

I nod. "We had that translated, too."

"So you . . . *proposed* to a demon?"

"Unintentionally, sir."

Mr. Bunce turns back to the ritual and shakes his head. "Nicks and Slick, what a predicament . . ." I must look miserable, because he pats my hand and says, "Well. Don't beat yourself up about it. You couldn't have known what you were getting into."

"Well, he *did* know he was summoning a demon . . ." Penelope says.

Her dad shoots her another reproving look. "It's remarkable that you have a translation," he says to me. "I've never seen anything like this. Do you mind if I take photos?"

"Go ahead."

He gets out his phone.

"We need to find a way out of this," Penelope says.

"Yes, of course," Mr. Bunce agrees. He's taking very careful photos. "Hold that paper flat for me?" I spread out the papers.

"*Dad.*"

"Hmm?"

"Don't you have any ideas?"

"Well." He blows out a long breath and sits back in his chair. "I mean, there's more legend than actual scholarship. I've read about people promising their souls to demons in exchange for power or wealth or some sort of intervention . . . What did you get out of it, Shepard?"

"Nothing," I say. "I didn't ask for anything."

"Of course you didn't." Penelope is rolling her eyes.

"No, that's good," her dad says. "It would be harder to get out of the contract if you'd spent the money or cured your cancer."

"Could we argue that I didn't know what I was doing?"

"We could," he says, "but it's not like there's a judge and jury to hear the case."

"Then how can I possibly get out of this?"

He rubs his chin. "Well, you could appeal to the demon himself."

"Herself," I say.

"Herself," he amends. "Demons are historically very lawabiding. They love signatures, terms, contracts . . ."

Penelope looks surprised. "They do?"

"Oh yeah," her dad says. "That's how they get you."

"So we have to find a *legal* way out of the engagement?" she asks. "We can't just break the curse? Or dissolve it? Or kill the demon?"

Her dad frowns at her. "Promise me you won't try to fight a demon."

"Is there scholarship on *that*?"

"*No,*" he says.

"What about . . ." She's rubbing her chin, too. "Could we find someone *else* to marry the demon?"

I hold up my hand between them. "I'm not damning someone else."

Penelope cocks her head. "You never know, we might find someone who's into demons . . ."

"*No,*" I say.

"Well," she says, "I'm not ruling it out."

"I don't suppose you'd been married before?" her dad asks me.

"No."

"That's too bad. Any children?"

"No."

Mr. Bunce covers the lower part of his face with his hand, like just holding his chin wouldn't be thoughtful enough. "Hmmm . . ." He shifts his fingers down. "Previously baptized?"

"No. Sorry."

"That's all right. Probably wouldn't have worked anyway." He sighs, then gathers up the papers, folds them, and gives them back to me. "Thank you for sharing these with me, Shepard."

"Dad . . ." Penelope is getting distressed. "Wait. We need a plan."

"Well, I'll keep thinking about it," he says. "I'm going to do some reading."

"What's Shepard supposed to do in the meantime?"

"Nothing dangerous, I hope." Then he smiles at me and nods towards Penelope. "You might want to find different company, Shepard."

"*Dad,*" she says, "I need to fix this."

"And I'll do my best to help," he says. "I'm sorry I don't have any solutions off the top of my head. It'd be easier if I could consult with your mother—"

"You can't!"

"I know. I won't. Just . . . don't do anything to make this worse." He seems to remember something. "Where's Simon? Is he already off fighting the demon?"

"He's . . ." Penelope shrugs. "He got his own flat."

Mr. Bunce's face falls. Like this is worse news than my engagement. "That doesn't sound like Simon. Did you have a row?"

"No," she says, looking down at her scone, "we're fine. It's not like we were going to spend our whole lives in each other's pockets . . ."

"Could have fooled me," her dad says.

46

SIMON

Baz is lying on my bed when I get out of the shower.

He brought pyjamas with him from his flat. I wonder if this is what he always sleeps in—cotton trousers and a T-shirt. I usually sleep in my pants, but I've been wearing joggers while he's here. Baz let me borrow his pyjamas once, on Christmas Eve . . .

This was easier when it started.

This thing with Baz.

We were so caught up—with the Mage and the visitations and finding out who killed Baz's mum. It's always easier to make a decision when your back's against the wall, and there's a knife at your throat. No time to think; just do. Grab the thing you need. Grab the thing you want. Steal the kiss.

I'd live like that all the time if I could.

I'd make all my decisions jumping out of second-storey windows.

You know that phrase, "out of the frying pan, into the fire"?

People say that like it's a bad thing. But what's the alternative—out of the frying pan, onto the counter? Out of the frying pan, onto the sofa.

Baz kept trying to have a normal relationship with me, after I lost my magic. He'd bring me dinner and try to get me to watch films. Maybe that's what he wants now . . . I'm more than a bit worried that I was only able to move forward with him these last few days because the fear of losing him was *like* having a knife to my throat. What happens when the danger fades?

"Are you air-drying?" Baz has sat up. He's frowning at me.

The towel is hanging from my hand. I bring it up to my hair.

"Are the wings hard to clean?" he asks, still frowning.

"Yeah," I say. "They're a pain. I can only spread them out one at a time in the shower."

Baz looks like he's thinking. "I don't have to sleep in the bed every night . . ."

I scrub at my hair. "Well, I'm not going to make you sleep on the floor."

"I could cast a spell to soften it, it'd be fine . . ."

I let the towel drop around my neck. "Do you not *want* to sleep in the bed?"

He shakes his head. "No. I . . . I just don't want to make you uncomfortable."

"For fuck's sake," I sigh. "You've got to stop questioning me. I'm holding on by a thread."

He looks down. "Sorry."

That came out wrong. I throw the towel into the bathroom and climb onto the bed beside him. "Hey, no . . . I'm sorry."

Baz looks up at me, pushing his damp hair back behind his ears. "Simon, are you sure you want me here?"

"Christ, I just told you not to question me."

"Yeah, I know, but you also told me you're holding on by a thread. I don't want to put you in that position."

"I'm *always* holding on by a thread! I thought the important thing was that I'm holding on!"

"Right." He rubs his face. "Right. It is. I'm sorry. I wish I were more confident. I'm not really built for this."

I breathe out a laugh.

He scowls at me. "What?"

"How can you be insecure, Baz? You're the most arrogant person I've ever met."

"They run on different tracks."

I laugh again.

"I'm going to sleep in your bed," he says, like it's a legal declaration.

"All right."

"Until you tell me you don't want me to."

"Or until you don't want to," I say.

"That might be never, Snow."

"All right."

Baz looks down, smiling with one side of his mouth, his eyelashes stark against his cheeks.

I get under the sheets he magicked up for me—they're already going threadbare, I suppose I'll need to buy real ones soon—and lie on my side.

Baz climbs in, too, and lies down facing me. After a second, he's got my tail in hand, and he's twisting it through his fingers. "So we're going to wait for the next revival meeting?"

"Seems like it," I say. "Do you have a better idea?"

"I think that's what Smith-Richards wants—for you to come to another of his meetings."

"You can't *still* think he's up to something nefarious . . ."

Baz lifts his head. "What's the alternative? That's he's *actually* the Greatest Mage?"

"If he's giving people magic, that's pretty great."

"He isn't giving it to them. They were already magicians."

"Baz, we watched him cast the spell."

He drops his head back on the pillow and tugs on my tail. "We should dig up what we can on his family . . . I'll bet he isn't even an orphan."

I hook an arm around Baz's waist. He's solid. I like it. "Why would anyone lie about being an orphan?"

"For sympathy," Baz says, scooting closer to me, "and because orphans are always *marked by destiny,* aren't they? They're never just some poor kid. They're always Luke Skywalker. Or Moses."

"Hey . . ." I squeeze him. "I'm an orphan."

"You're only proving my point, Snow. I'll bet you were born during an eclipse, too, but nobody bothered to write it down."

"Orphans aren't magickal," I say. "We're unfortunate."

"I've spent my half my life saying so," he sighs, "but the world didn't listen." He lowers an eyebrow at me. "I don't know why you of all people would trust this guy, Simon."

"I don't know why you wouldn't."

He hums, his eyebrow still low. "Let's give Lady Salisbury an update."

"You think she'll agree with you," I say.

"I think we could use another opinion, and Penelope is still narked at you."

I shrug and sneak my free hand under Baz's neck. It isn't

really sneaking—he lifts his head up for me, smiles like he might be blushing, and settles his head back down on my arm.

"I don't mind," I say. "I like Lady Ruth. I think she'll be happy if we find out that Smith-Richards actually helped her son."

"I think she'll be happy to find out Smith-Richards didn't bury her son in a shallow grave."

"Oh come on—you can't think that's a possibility?"

"Can't I? He gives me a bad vibe. His teeth are too white. And he's too earnest."

"I'm pretty sure you've said all of that about me."

"That's just it." Baz pokes my chest with the end of my tail. "He's stealing your whole *thing*."

"He's older than I am, so it was his thing first. Maybe I'm the one who stole it. Maybe it was meant to be him all along."

Baz thumps his head against my biceps. "Are we going to argue about Smith Smith-Richards every night in bed?"

I grin. Suddenly I'm smiling so big I can hardly see.

"What are you laughing at, Snow?"

I'm not laughing. I shrug. I squeeze him. He's solid. I like it.

47

AGATHA

Niamh is with a patient when I walk in.

"Your dad's next door." She's got a three-headed dog squirming on her exam table, and she's holding her wand over its heads. **"Stay!"**

All three heads whimper, but the dog stays put.

"I was looking for you," I say, "but I'll come back." Or maybe I won't. This is probably a bad idea . . .

Niamh turns her head. "You were looking for me?"

"Yeah, but I can come back."

She frowns at me. "Say what you need to say. Nigel doesn't care."

"That hellhound's name is Nigel?"

She pets one of the heads. "You're a good dog, aren't you, Nigel?" Nigel jumps when he hears his name, and starts scrabbling off the exam table. Niamh tries to stop him.

I rush over to help. "Where's his owner?"

"I asked her to step out," Niamh says. "She was enabling him."

I've got my arms around the dog's belly. "Enabling?"

She holds her wand up again. ***"Nigel, stay! Please!"***

The dog settles a little, but he's still wriggling in my arms. I pat his—their?—flank. "Good boy, Nigel. That's right."

"He wouldn't calm down at all with her in the room," Niamh says.

"Can you sedate him?"

"I'd rather not for something so simple." She holds one of the heads with both hands. "Hellhounds don't respond predictably to meds."

"Who keeps a hellhound as a pet?"

"You should *see* what people keep as pets," she says. All of Nigel's heads are nuzzling and nipping at her. "Nigel's sweet. He's just excitable. Hold him steady . . ."

I try.

Niamh moves quickly, taking each head in hand, flipping all six of Nigel's ears to look inside. He doesn't like it, but Niamh is deft, and she keeps him in hand.

"Ah, there it is," she says, after a moment. She points her wand in an ear. ***"Just a tick!"*** The dog yelps, and Niamh strokes his face with both hands. "There you go. All gone now, Nigel. Nothing serious." He whines, trying to lick her. His other heads are snuffling in her jacket.

"I really think he deserves three names," I say.

"She's absolutely right, isn't she, Nigel?"

Niamh lifts her wand again. ***"Down, boy!"*** He hops down. ***"Heel!"*** He follows her to the door. She opens it. "Thanks, Agatha. That was perfect timing. Oh—" She looks up. "What were you going to ask me?"

I feel nervous again. "I was just, um . . . wondering if you were going to Watford again this week."

"Yeah, I'm going this afternoon."

"I could come along again." I shrug. "If you'd like. If you could use a hand."

Niamh looks surprised. "I could use two."

"Great," I say. "Just come and get me."

Nigel bolts away from her, and Niamh runs after him. The door swings shut between us.

48

SIMON

"He's an *orphan*?" Lady Ruth says. She was just about to take a bite of an egg and cress sandwich, but now she's frowning. "He's stealing your act, Simon."

"That's what I said, Lady Salisbury!" Baz couldn't be more pleased with himself.

"It's not an act," I say. "I am actually an orphan."

Lady Ruth pats my hand. "Of course you are, dear."

"Yes," Baz says, "but even if you weren't, the Mage still would have told everyone that you were. It's just too perfect. Oh—" He turns back to Lady Ruth. "Smith-Richards also claims he was born under *an eclipse*."

She rolls her eyes. "Was he trying to convert you or get in your trousers?"

"I *mean*," Baz agrees, eating half a finger sandwich.

"But Jamie wasn't there?" she asks.

"No," I say. "Smith seemed excited to introduce us to him, but he wasn't there. Maybe Jamie got his own flat?"

Lady Ruth frowns, like that isn't likely. "I tried to track him down again this morning. All my spells are still hitting dead ends. It's almost like there's a locked door at the end of my wand. Do you think Jamie got magic, and the first spell he cast was to hide from me?"

"I don't think so," I say. "If I got my magic back, I'd be too happy to nurse any grudges."

Baz looks over at me. He's got his lips twisted to the side, like he's thinking. Then he turns to Lady Ruth. "Doesn't it seem like we should have heard of Smith-Richards before? Or his family?"

She's refilling his tea. "They don't have any sort of magickal reputation. He just appeared one day."

"Smith-Richards says he was raised by his godfather . . ."

She shakes her head. "Jamie never mentioned him."

"We're going to Watford this afternoon," I tell her, "to see if we can dig anything up in *The Magickal Record*."

She clicks her tongue, setting down the teapot. "Oh, I wish I hadn't thrown all our old copies away! My husband used to have them bound up in leather volumes, but I cleared them out when he died. Hmm . . ." She taps the table. "Do you have a pair of reading glasses?"

"I don't think either of us needs glasses yet," I say.

Lady Ruth chuckles, patting my hand again. "Give me two shakes . . ." She gets up and bustles out of the dining room.

"Reading glasses are glasses spelled to help you scan books and documents," Baz explains, helping himself to a slice of cake. (Every time we call on Lady Salisbury, she seems to have just finished making a cake. Today it's lemon drizzle. Cracking.)

"Why didn't we use a pair when we were looking for Nico?"

"I don't *have* a pair," he says. "Imagine the magic that would take."

Magickal objects are rare among mages. They have to be spelled the regular way. So first you need a specific spell. And then you need to be powerful enough to cast the spell—to actually channel magic *into* a thing. The Mage could do it, but it always knocked him out. He slept for a full day once, after bewitching a key. I've never met anyone who could charm something powerful, like a sword or a wand.

The Mage hoped *I'd* be able to do it eventually. I had the magic. But I didn't have the magickal dexterity. I destroyed every object he put in front of me, including some expensive-looking jewellery.

I'm probably lucky it didn't work. Imagine how many holes I would have blown in the magickal fabric if he'd turned me into a magic-wand factory.

Lady Ruth is back with an olive-green leather case. She sits down and hands the case to me—even though it'll have to be Baz that uses anything magickal. I flip it open. There are gold wire-framed glasses inside. The arms have springs on the ends that must curl around the back of your ears. Baz is leaning over the table to look.

"Use them with 'Fine-tooth comb,' or any finding spell," she says. "They'll give you a boost."

"Were these your husband's, too?" I ask.

"My mother's. I've never been much of a reader myself. They're a family heirloom, I suppose."

"Lovely," Baz says. "We'll be careful with them."

"I know you will." She squeezes his arm. "Let me pack up some sandwiches for you to take along."

✿

I end up eating the sandwiches on the way to Watford.

Baz frowns at me the whole time.

"Sorry," I say, "am I getting crumbs in the car?" It's his aunt's ancient sports car—we took it from her parking space—and it was already full of crumbs and cigarette butts.

"I don't care about the car," he says. "I care about my shirt."

I look down at the shirt he let me borrow—that he *made* me borrow. (Baz is forcing his clothes on me again; he says none of mine are fit for polite company.) Today's shirt is baby blue knit, with short sleeves and a diamond pattern. I look like the most laddish member of a boy band. I think Baz is only lending me clothes that he'd never wear himself.

He reaches over and brushes some crumbs off my chest.

"Should I have you spell my wings away?" I ask. They're origamied tight on my back at the moment.

"I thought I wasn't allowed to spell your wings."

"Yeah, but . . . people can still see them under this shirt, and I don't really want to put on a raincoat."

"Who'll even be at Watford to see them?" he asks. "The students are on break. And Headmistress Bunce has already seen your wings."

"Yeah . . ."

We tried to get Penelope to come to Watford with us, but she still isn't answering my texts. Baz says I need to apologize to her properly. In person. I'm sure he's right—I just don't know where to start. I've never really apologized to Penny before. I've never had to.

Baz parks in the grass outside the front gates, next to the Bunces' hatchback.

"Wonder why the headmistress is parked out here," I say. "The Mage always parked inside the walls."

"The Mage was a heathen." Baz opens the gate and holds it open for me.

I follow him onto the Great Lawn and take his hand. Baz came back here for school, after everything with the Mage. He finished the term, lived alone in our old room at the top of the tower . . .

I couldn't come back.

And not just because I wasn't a magician anymore and had no use for a school of magic.

I couldn't live with the memories. Every day I'd been at Watford was a lie. Every lesson I learned, every battle. All the magic I had, I stole from the World of Mages. I was draining them dry. And the worst part is . . .

I was happy here.

I was *happy* as a fraud and a magickal incinerator.

"All right?" Baz asks, when we're halfway up the Lawn.

"Yeah, all right."

He holds my hand firmly. "The drawbridge is already down," he says. "That's convenient."

"Ugh, I forgot about the merwolves."

"How could you forget about the merwolves?"

"I tried not to think of them, even when we were here."

"I had a plan to drink them all . . ." Baz looks wistful. "But it took me all night to catch one—and then it tasted like motor oil. Gamy motor oil."

"What'd you do with the body?"

"Threw it back in!"

"Gross."

We walk over the drawbridge and through the fortress

walls, into the empty courtyard. The Mage and his Men never left Watford open and unguarded like this, even on summer break. He and his Men were always here over school breaks, working on secret plans and projects. I used to ask the Mage to let me stay at Watford, too—but he said it was good for me to spend time with Normals.

"I'd send the rest of these children to live with Normals, too, if I could. We get comfortable, complacent, among our own kind. We start behaving like the magic comes from within us—and not from the world around us. Go live in the world, Simon. Stay close to it."

So I spent every summer in care. In group homes. Once or twice, with foster families. At least I got to go home with Agatha most Christmases . . .

The library is to the left, but Baz pulls me to the right. "Best check in with the headmistress first," he says.

I follow him past the fountain, towards the ivy-covered Weeping Tower. "Everything looks the same," I say.

"Did you think the walls would crumble without you?"

"No . . ." But I thought they might crumble without the Mage. This was his place. His domain. And now he's dead, and nothing has changed. Nothing stopped. (Except me, I suppose.) Watford—and the whole World of Mages—just went on without him.

The Weeping Tower is unlocked, too. We take the lift to the top. As soon as the doors open, we can hear Penelope's mum.

"Because we're running a school, not a nursery! Look, Peter, even Normal schools teach Shakespeare, and their kids can't even use it!"

Baz and I stop at the open door to her office. She's on her mobile phone, pacing in front of the Mage's desk—her desk, now. She's wearing an oversized Beatles T-shirt and leggings. The Mage would be appalled.

"Or perhaps!" she half shouts. "I'll hire the new humanities teacher and pay her out of the *football budget* . . . Oh, I think you'll find that I can!"

She spots us and stops pacing, acknowledging us with her free hand. "Peter, I have to go . . . No, I have to go . . . I *am* going to hire her . . . Yes, because I want to, but also because it's the right thing to do . . ." Professor Bunce looks so much like Penelope. Older, of course. With madder hair. "Peter, I'm hanging up now . . . I'm hanging up."

She hangs up, and leans back against her desk with a long sigh. "Well, boys, should I be worried?"

"Worried?" I ask.

"The pair of you don't just show up to say hello, do you? Are you being chased by werewolves? I assume they've already eaten my daughter. Magic forbid she return my texts."

"Nothing's wrong," Baz says. "Hello, Headmistress."

"Hello, Baz." She smiles at him, like she's decided to give him an inch. Are they *friends* now? When did that happen? "Here," she says, "sit down. I don't have anything to offer you. Cook Pritchard has the day off and I don't even know where the kettle is. I'm living off a box of Jaffa Cakes I found in the cupboard. Probably been here since your mum was in charge."

She moves behind her desk, and Baz and I sit in the two wooden chairs across from her. These chairs weren't here when the Mage was headmaster. He didn't usually have people in his office. He didn't talk to students much at all.

The entire office looks like it's got more use since Headmistress Bunce took over. The desk is covered in folders and papers. She's got a big mug of pens, and photos of her family.

And the shelves behind her are even more packed with books than they were before.

"Where *is* Penelope?" she asks. "Is she still angry with me?"

No. She's still angry with *me*. "She's in London," I say. "She didn't feel like coming."

"Hmm." She scratches the back of her head. "Still angry with me, then."

"We're here because we were hoping we could use the library," Baz says.

"Of course you can. It's open to all magicians. What are you looking for?"

"My stepmother has taken an interest in one of the new Chosen Ones," he says. (We've already decided to be up front with Professor Bunce; she might know something useful.) "Smith Smith-Richards."

Professor Bunce rolls her eyes. "Smith-Richards."

"You've heard of him?" Baz asks.

"Unfortunately, yes."

"Do you know him?"

"I assume I know what you know—that he says he's the Chosen One and is promising magickal upgrades."

I lean forward, and my chair creaks. "You don't believe him?"

"Do I believe that there are six new Chosen Ones here to solve all our problems? In a word—no. In two words—hell, no." She frowns at me. "No offence, Simon."

I make a face like, *None taken.*

"At least this Smith-Richards isn't asking for money," she goes on, "though it makes me wonder what else he's after . . ."

I'm not going to tell her that I think Smith-Richards might be the real deal. I understand why she and Baz and Lady Ruth are sceptical. They've all already been fooled once—by me. "Isn't the Coven checking up on these people?" I ask. "Like, can anyone just *say* that they're the Greatest Mage?"

"Woof, the Coven." She leans back in her chair. "We have enough on our hands, trying to clean up the Mage's messes. Half of us are hoping these new COs fizzle out on their own, and half of us are secretly going to their meetings."

Baz is paying keen attention. "You're in the former camp, I gather?"

"I'm so busy out here, I can hardly bother with the rest. My own child could end up doing magic on YouTube, and I wouldn't have the energy to deal with it."

I feel my mouth drop open. Baz doesn't say a word.

Headmistress Bunce pushes up her glasses. "You're all very lucky that no one believes their own eyes anymore."

"Yes, Headmistress," Baz says.

"Yes, Headmistress," I whisper.

Penny's mum walks us down to the library, on the other side of the White Chapel. (Here's something that's changed: All the stained-glass windows in the Chapel broke the night I killed the Mage. Now they've been replaced, but with clear glass. The Chapel looks like all the colour has drained from its face.)

The library is locked, so Penny's mum lets us in. "Don't take anything," she says. "I mean it. Snap a photo if you need a copy of something."

"Of course," Baz says, as if he isn't a library scofflaw.

She flips on the lights in the hallway. "And just . . ." She looks right at me. "Don't make any headaches for me while you're here. I have enough."

"We're just going to look at books," I say.

She frowns at me. "Right. Well, I'll be in my office if you

need me."

We wait for the doors to close behind her.

"Keep up, Snow," Baz says, moving briskly down the hall. "No need to follow from a distance, hiding in shadows. As is your custom."

"Are you going to go hunting rats in the Catacombs before we leave? As is your custom?"

"I probably should. As a public service."

I shouldn't have mentioned it. I don't want to go down into the Catacombs. It's lousy with skulls down there.

Baz is headed towards the long room at the back of the library where *The Magickal Record* is kept. He steps inside and whistles.

"Holy shit," I say, coming in behind him.

Watford's library used to be pretty low on actual books. The Mage wanted us to focus on Normal books and modern languages. He threw out anything that seemed antiquated—or anything that he disagreed with. He'd always say that movies and television were more useful to us than books. (*"Then why won't he let us have the Internet?"* Penelope would rail.)

But this room is *full* of books. "Was it like this when you were here?" I ask Baz.

He's standing with his hands in his pockets and his shoulders back, taking it all in. "No. The headmistress has been busy. I'll bet some of these are the magickal books confiscated by the Mage."

I have Lady Ruth's reading glasses in my pocket. I take out the case and hand it to Baz. He puts on the gold-rimmed glasses, winding the springs carefully behind each ear.

I can't help but laugh once he has them on. His eyes look huge and blinky behind the thick lenses. I slide my arms around his waist. "Look at you, all specky."

He frowns down at me. He's only three inches taller, but I swear he stretches it out to six when he feels like it. He looks like a very handsome, very judgy owl.

"Kiss me," I say. "I've always wanted to kiss someone with glasses."

"Bunce was right there . . ."

"You look like a steampunk vampire."

"That's absurd—"

I kiss him. It is absurd. I can't even see the glasses like this. I pull away just enough that I can.

Baz cocks an eyebrow above the frames. "I don't think this is what Lady Salisbury had in mind when she lent us her heirloom reading glasses."

"I don't think she'd mind. She seems like she likes a good time."

"Really. You think she's up to party."

"You know what I mean . . ." I kiss him again quickly. "I've never kissed you in the library. Think of all the places we could have kissed if we'd figured this out sooner."

He looks up at my forehead, threading one hand into my hair. His grey eyes are enormous. "If *you'd* figured it out sooner . . ."

I could argue with him, tease him, return his serve. But I don't want to. I push him back against a bookshelf and kiss him some more. My hands are on his waist. I can feel his skin, cool through his cotton shirt.

Baz is wearing another long-sleeved button-down. (I don't think the heat ever bothers him, even when the sun does.) This one's got brown and blue stripes, but when you get close, you see that the blue stripes are flowers. His trousers are nice, too—inky blue. He said he dressed up for Lady Ruth, but I think he just likes to dress up. I think he likes to look like he's going somewhere important.

I push my chest against his. The shelf behind him creaks.

How much kissing would there have been? If I'd figured it out sooner? In the library, on the Great Lawn. In our room . . .

Christ. Baz in our room, his hair slicked back, his tie perfectly knotted—hating me. (But not really hating me. Not only hating me.)

He puts his other hand in my hair, too, like he's trying to hold me steady. Every time I push my face forward, the back of his head knocks books off the shelf behind him.

How many walls could I have shoved him up against? How many empty corners could we have found?

This was our place. Watford. Ours like no one else's. Maybe that sounds arrogant, but it's true. His, because his mother died here. Mine, because it was mine to protect.

His mouth opens for me . . .

(I don't understand what this is. Why people do it. Why we stoke fires in each other. What are we burning?)

The shelf creaks again. I rub my cock into his hip.

How many walls? How many hallways?

What else would I have figured out, if I'd got to this sooner?

Baz turns his face away and unhooks Lady Ruth's glasses from his ears.

"I'm sorry," I pant.

He looks confused. The spring on one side is caught in his hair. "For what?"

I shrug. I don't know. I hug him closer. My arms are crossed in the small of his back. "Breaking your nose. In fourth year."

He laughs. "Oh. Well. You *should* be sorry about that."

I lean forward and bite his nose, right at the crooked part.

"Crowley, Snow—don't break it again!"

I let go of his nose. And look in his normal-sized eyes. "I'm sorry . . ." I shake my head. "That I didn't figure it out sooner. I—I would have liked to have had you for a friend here."

He sets the reading glasses on the shelf next to him and puts his hands in my hair again, smoothing my curls down and watching them bounce back.

I think Baz would have liked it, too—to have me, here, on his side—but he says, "It was probably meant to happen like it did."

"Do you believe in that?" I ask. "Fate?"

He shrugs. His back is still against a shelf. My weight is still against him. "Not exactly. But it's hard to argue with the timing. My mother's ghost, the Mage's plan . . . My father says that some things—that some people—are written."

"Like Smith-Richards?"

Baz's eyes go hard, and he shoves at my shoulder. "*Not* like Smith-Richards." He steps forward, pushing me some more. "Make way, Snow. We need to get to the bottom of this nonsense."

I step aside.

Baz puts the glasses back on and gets his wand out. He stands in front of the wall where *The Magickal Record* is shelved. ***"Fine-tooth comb—Smith!"***

The entire wall of bound volumes starts trembling.

"Oh fuck," Baz says. He grabs my arm and pulls me back, just as a hundred books shake themselves off the shelves.

When the dust clears—not a figure of speech—there are less than a dozen volumes still on the wall.

"It *is* a common name . . ." I say.

Baz just sighs.

49

BAZ

We could have used Bunce's input—and her wand—but we're making progress. I'd initially planned to get a broader picture of the Smith family. But narrowing the search to "Smith-Richards" gives us a much smaller stack of books to sort through: just two.

Snow starts re-shelving while I search through the first book. With Lady Salisbury's reading glasses on, I can turn directly to the page I'm looking for—it's a list of announcements.

Announcements constitute the bulk of *The Magickal Record*—births, deaths, and, after the Mage took power, arrests. Only huge magickal news warrants more detailed coverage in *The Record,* something like an attack on Watford. (I wonder whether they'll write up this rash of potential saviours. *Meet the candidates.*)

I scan the page for "Smith-Richards" . . .

"Here it is," I say. "His birth announcement." Simon

comes to look over my shoulder while I read aloud: *"Smith-Richards-comma-Smith. Jemima Smith and Hugh Richards of Skipton are delighted to announce the birth of their son, Smith. The child was named for his paternal grandfather, Smith Alan Richards, who died in June. Young Smith will inherit his grandfather's oaken wand. His mother reports that the child was born during June's solar eclipse. How auspicious!"*

"Huh, look at that," Simon says, "he *was* born under an eclipse."

"Hmm. According to his mother."

Snow pokes my shoulder. "Why would she lie about that?"

"I don't know," I say. "It's a very *boastful* thing to mention in a birth announcement."

"So Smith is thirty . . . He looks good for thirty."

"Does he?" I reach for the second book.

"I expect this'll be his parents' death," Snow says.

He's right. He rests his forearms on my shoulders, and I hold up the book, so we can both read the report:

Jemima Smith and Hugh Richards died January 12th in a car accident near their home in Yorkshire. They are survived by their only son, Smith Smith-Richards, age 1. The child will be cared for by his godfather, Evander Feverfew, most recently of Mexico City.

"Evander Feverfew," Simon says. "What a name. Are you related?"

"Feverfew is an old family," I say. "But I've never heard of Evander."

Simon stands up straight, scratching the back of his head. "So it's just like Smith said. It's all true."

"Well, he does seem to be an orphan named Smith Smith-Richards—"

"Isn't that what we came here to verify?"

"I suppose," I say. "I'd like to see what else we can find on his family."

"We know his parents' names now. We could search for those."

"Indeed."

Jemima Smith and Hugh Richards were two run-of-the-mill magicians. They graduated from Watford together. They got married. They got normal Normal jobs. She was a dentist, and he was some sort of graphic designer. They didn't win any awards. They didn't run for office. They died before the Mage started making mischief.

Evander Feverfew is only slightly more remarkable. He was in the Dramatic Society at Watford, and one of his cousins was on the Coven. There's a Feverfew estate in the North, but it's occupied by a distant relative.

This isn't like researching my mother's death. We don't uncover anything shocking or surprising. After two hours in the library, all we've got is what Smith told us, plus some not-very-interesting backstory.

Simon has put most of the books away, and he's itching to leave.

"All right," I say, giving up. "It doesn't look like there are any skeletons buried here." I push away from the library table. "Would it be all right with you if we stopped in the Catacombs on the way out?"

"To see where the skeletons are actually buried?"

"To visit my mother's tomb, Snow."

"Oh, fuck, Baz, sorry—I wasn't thinking."

"You don't have to come with me." I get up to shelve the last of the books. "I can meet you outside."

"No." His hand is on my arm. "I'll come."

The roses are in bloom, so I don't have to magic up any flowers for my bouquet. (Food and flowers are the hardest things to create with magic. They take it out of you.)

Simon follows me into the White Chapel. He reaches for my hand in the doorway. I don't think he's been inside the Chapel since the Mage died here. "All right, Snow?"

He nods.

We duck behind the altar, behind the sanctuary, through the hidden entrance to the crypt. "How'd you find this door in the first place?" Simon asks.

"I used to come with my father to visit."

"Oh. That makes sense."

The door slides closed behind us. It's dark, but I can still see. "How did you think I found it?"

"I thought it was a creepy vampire thing."

"Well, it was . . . eventually."

"Do you think other Watford kids wander around down here?"

"I only ever saw you."

Simon giggles. "I can't believe we're in the Catacombs together."

Before I can say anything, he's pushing me against a

stone wall and kissing my neck.

"For fuck's sake, Snow, this is hallowed ground!"

"I'm not doing anything to unhallow it." He keeps kissing me.

I rest my arms over his shoulders, letting the roses droop.

"New plan," he says. "We retrace our old steps, and do *this* all of the places we used to fight."

"That's everywhere."

"Everywhere, then."

He's got his arms around my waist, and his chest and hips against mine. This is all my fifth-year fantasies come true: Simon Snow manhandling me in the library, in the Catacombs . . .

"We could go up to the tower," he says.

"That's someone else's room now."

"It will always be our room more than anyone else's."

I close my eyes and drop my head onto his shoulder. The wall behind me is cold and damp. Simon is warm. He's pushing his nose into my collar and biting my throat.

"I can't believe I had you in my room every night," he says, "and I didn't take advantage of it."

"You could have had me in your room every night for the last year."

He groans into my collar. "I'm such a twat."

I lift my head up and get my free hand around his jaw. I can see his eyes, his pupils wide as saucers. Can he see me? "Kiss me in the Catacombs, Snow. Unhallow the ground."

"I'll unhallow your ground," he says, kissing me.

I don't think he *can* see me—his mouth lands halfway onto my chin. I'm laughing, making it worse. "You're absurd," I say.

"Look. I already said I'm a twat."

I hold his jaw in place and kiss him squarely.

Simon's lips are thin. His mouth is wide. We kiss with our teeth.

It's everything I ever wanted.

He's better than I hoped.

Even though he's more fucked up than I could have imagined . . .

I don't want him to lose control down here. I don't want to have to sit in the dirt to comfort him, with all of my ancestors watching. When he starts pulling too hard on my shirt, I ease him back.

"Come on," I say softly. "It isn't much farther."

50

SIMON

Baz lights a fire in his hand, so I can see.

"I hate it when you do that," I say.

"What?"

"You're going to start yourself on fire." I saw how quickly the vampires went up, in the desert.

Baz scoffs. "I'm completely in control."

"Seriously," I say. "Use a torch. There are a thousand of them down here." All along the walls.

"Fine." He waves a hand, and the whole row of them lights up. He shakes the flame out of his hand.

"Look." I stop walking. We're standing right by the portrait I remembered. Of the blond girl. "It's Lady Ruth's daughter, isn't it?"

"It certainly looks like her," Baz agrees.

Someone has painted her right on the wall—and cast a spell to make it look like she's crying. "Do you think she died here?"

"Lady Salisbury says she's still alive."

"Huh."

We both stand there for a moment, watching her cry. Then Baz takes one of his roses and sets it on the ground below the portrait.

"I'll wait here," I say. It didn't occur to me until just now that he might want to be alone with his mum. "You go on."

Baz looks at me, one eyebrow cocked low, then nods. "I won't be long." He kisses my cheek before he walks away. I like that. All the easy kisses he's giving me. All the checking on me and checking in with me. You might think it would be irritating, but it really isn't. It makes me think it would have been nice to have someone looking out for me like this all along.

I lean against the wall across from the portrait and slide to the ground.

I wonder who painted it. I can't really see the paint. Maybe it's more like a photo. Some sort of magickal wall print. You find all sorts of weird shit down here . . . I always thought this portrait must be ancient. But Lady Ruth's daughter would only be in her 40s. Around the same age as Penny's parents.

She's about my age, I think, in this portrait. She's outside, in the sun. Her hair is almost yellow. And even though she's crying, she doesn't look unhappy. More . . . wistful. I used to think she looked like she'd lost something—but maybe I only thought that because I was down here looking for Baz.

It would suck to have to go down into a crypt to visit your mother's grave. I swear his family doesn't even realize how creepy they are.

I get out my phone and take a video of the portrait. I don't know if I want to show it to Lady Ruth—it's kind of disturbing. But maybe it's a clue that could help her find her daughter. Maybe we should help her with that next, after we find Jamie. I hope she's right, that this girl is alive somewhere. All grown up and just fine.

I really don't understand why both of Lady Ruth's kids ran away. She seems grand to me. Laid-back, generous. I like her house. I like the way everything in it feels old. Older than Lady Ruth, even. Like it was built to have multiple lives. I'd like to have a house like that someday.

I wonder what kind of a place Baz wants . . . I think I hear him coming back up the tunnel.

There he is.

He looks dramatic, lit up by torches. He's casting two shadows.

I get up from the ground and walk towards him. He turns his face away when I try to kiss him.

"Did you just drink a rat?" I ask.

He shrugs one shoulder.

"I can't believe you went hunting without me."

51

AGATHA

I'm driving this time. Dad let me take the Volvo. The drive to Watford has been torturous so far, even with air-con. I'm bad at small talk—because I hate it—but Niamh seems to be incapable.

"When do you become a full-fledged magickal vet?" I ask, after twenty minutes of silence.

"It's not like there's a certification," she says. She's got her cool sunglasses on, and she's staring out the window.

"But you'll be done at some point?"

"I just said, there's no programme."

"Right."

After another twenty minutes, I try again—"Will you have an office of your own someday?"

"Look," she snaps, "I know that your dad can't wait to get the thingamapigs out of his waiting area—"

"For snake's sake, Niamh! That's not what I was implying. I was just trying to make conversation."

She looks suspicious. "Why?"

"Because we're in the car together on a long drive?"

"You didn't have to come."

I spread my fingers out over the steering wheel in frustration. "I want to help you with the goats."

"I thought you didn't care about the goats," she mutters.

"I didn't *know* about the goats. Hell's spells, do you want my help or not?"

She glowers out the window. "Yes. I want your help."

When we get to Watford, I park outside the gates. There are a few other cars parked out here. The Mage used to take his Jeep straight through the gates and over the drawbridge. What a dick.

"I suppose it's a good sign that we didn't see any goats on the road," I say.

"Unless they've all fled the county." Niamh has a medical bag slung over her shoulder. She pushes open the gates. As soon as we're through, we see Simon and Baz, walking towards us on the Great Lawn.

Simon breaks into a smile. "Agatha!" He jogs closer. "And . . . Niamh, right?"

"Simon Snow," Niamh says.

"Hey," I say. What are they doing here—*is Watford under attack?* Maybe that's a paranoid way to think, but you're more likely to run into Simon and Baz during an epic battle between good and evil than you are down at the pub.

"This is Baz," Simon says to Niamh. He points his thumb at her and looks at Baz. "This is Niamh. She's going to take my wings off."

Niamh frowns. "He asked me to."

"So I've heard," Baz says, reaching for her hand. "Nice to

meet you." He nods at me. "Wellbelove."

"Baz."

"What are you guys doing here?" Simon asks. He's wearing a very nice collared shirt. Knit. Blue argyle. With short sleeves that hug his biceps. Is Baz shopping for him now?

"Niamh is checking on the goats," I say. "What are you doing here?"

"Research," Baz says.

Simon lowers his eyebrows. "Ebb's goats? Is something wrong with them?"

I glance at Niamh.

"They seem to be wandering away," she says.

"We're going to round them up," I add, "and make sure they're all right. One of the nannies is pregnant."

"Well, we could help with that!" Simon offers.

"You don't have—" Niamh starts to say.

But Simon has already decided. "I could fly up and tell you if I see them. That would help, wouldn't it?"

Niamh frowns. "It would," she admits.

Baz is looking at his shoes. He sighs.

"Great!" Simon says.

So I guess this is happening. Simon and Baz and me, walking across the Great Lawn together. With Niamh, of all people, to bear witness.

Simon ends up taking the lead. I can tell he makes Niamh uncomfortable. Because she failed him, I suppose. She looks like she wants to pin him down and try that amputation again straightaway.

"The goats are wandering off?" he asks. "Who's herding them?"

"No one," Niamh answers.

Simon is surprised. "They haven't hired a new goatherd?"

"Probably not a high priority . . ." Baz says.

"You can't just *hire* a new goatherd," Niamh grumbles.

"Can't you?" Simon asks.

Niamh shakes her head. In dismay, I gather. Especial dismay. "Do *none* of you know about the Goats of Watford?"

"Snow knows all about them," Baz says. "They're practically his siblings."

Niamh scowls at him. She can't begin to understand the dynamic here, but she doesn't like it.

"Niamh says the goats are sacred," I say. (It's unclear why I'm bailing either Niamh or Baz out of this conversation. They both deserve the worst of each other.) "She says they're tied to the spells protecting the school."

"*I* don't say it," she says. "It's oral tradition."

"I've never heard that," Baz says coolly.

Niamh's completely indignant. "They're in the Watford coat of arms!"

"I thought those were pegasus," Simon says. "Pegas-i."

"A-ha!" I say. "See!"

"They're *goats*," Niamh insists. "Magic goats!"

"Magic goats," Baz repeats, distastefully.

"Wait . . ." Simon has gone all earnest and intense. "So you're saying Ebb had a really important job here . . ."

"Obviously," Niamh says. "The goats are vital to the safety of Watford."

"Then we have to find them," he declares. "And make them stay."

Niamh really couldn't be more dismayed with all three of us. "We can't *make* them stay . . ."

Simon's already taking off his shirt. I thought his wings

were spelled invisible, but they were just folded up on his back. He shakes them out and unfurls them.

Baz is reaching out to him. "Let me cast a spell on you, so the Normals won't see."

"I'll be fine," Simon says. "I'll keep a low profile."

"Snow—" Baz looks genuinely concerned. "—please."

"Let him," I say. "Seriously."

Simon rolls his eyes. "Fine, but don't make me invisible."

Baz flicks his wrist, and his wand appears in his hand. *"There's nothing to see here!"*

Simon shudders and shifts mostly out of sight. "I hate that one."

"You hate them all," Baz says. "It'll wear off. I didn't put much oomph into it."

Simon flaps his wings and kicks up into the air. Niamh and I squint up at the sky, trying to keep track of him.

"It's easier if you don't look directly at him," Baz advises.

He's right. I let my eyes drift and watch Simon flying in my peripheral vision.

"I see them!" he shouts down to us. "The goats!"

"Where are they?" Niamh shouts back.

"Kind of . . . everywhere?"

52

BAZ

We spend the rest of the afternoon out in the hills behind Watford. I eventually stop trying to help; the goats don't respond to any of my spells. I thought there might be something wrong with my wand, but the Irish girl—Snow's veterinarian—says it's the goats, not me. "They only respond to magic if they feel like it," she says. "My spells roll right off them, too."

I recognize her from school. Niamh Brody. She used to have fierce blond hair, cut shorter than Simon's. She played lacrosse and rugby, and she wore heavy work boots with her school uniform. Not Doc Martens or something fashionable. The sort of boots you wear to drive a tractor.

She hasn't lost her scowl since those days—nor her flair for brute force. She's bullying the goats around, blocking them like a brick wall. Simon is herding them along from the air; he's got a death-from-above move that gets the goats going—and makes him laugh like a maniac. Wellbelove is the only one the goats seem to actually listen to. I can't tell if she's using magic on them, or if they just like her.

Anyway, the three of them seem to have made some progress—the goats are at least grazing in the same general area now.

I'm sitting in the grass, watching Snow try to keep an old billy goat from wandering away. He gets in front of it and spreads his wings. "Bah!" The goat goes running in the other direction.

Simon sees me watching him and smiles. He still hasn't put his shirt back on—he doesn't seem at all self-conscious about it. I suppose Brody has seen his wings before, and Agatha's seen the rest of him . . .

I scratch the back of my neck, looking down at the grass between my legs.

Snow drops to the ground beside me and lies back in the grass, squinting. The late afternoon sun is picking up every thread of gold in his hair, and throwing every freckle and mole into sharp relief. His cheeks are flushed. He's a bit out of breath.

"Enjoying yourself?" I ask.

He grins at me. "Yeah . . ."

I hold up his shirt. "Any use for this?"

Snow sits up, still smiling, and takes it from me, collapsing his wings, and pulling the shirt up his arms first, then over his head and down his chest and stomach. He's watching Wellbelove try to bring one of the last goats in. "Use your wand!" he shouts.

"I am!"

"Not like that!"

He's up again, reaching for her wand. Wellbelove lets him have it. I wonder for a moment if he's forgotten that he doesn't have magic. But he's not casting a spell . . . He's just flicking the wand—holding it so that she can see.

Since when does Snow understand advanced wandwork?

He gives the wand back to Wellbelove, and she imitates him, hooking her wrist. ***"Join the club!"***

The goat cocks its head at her and scampers closer.

Wellbelove beams up at Snow. "It's working!" She casts the spell again, rolling her wrist more precisely.

The goat goes prancing towards the herd.

Agatha grabs Snow's arm, delighted. "Who taught you that?"

"Ebb," he says. "I can probably remember a few more tricks. Though I think her staff was better suited for this . . ."

The two of them trade the wand back and forth, while Snow teaches her the apparently fine art of magickal goat herding.

They look like a painting, standing there. Or a photograph from the 1940s. Wellbelove is wearing wide-legged blue trousers and a white cotton eyelet shirt. Her hair is down. Straight as a pin and shining. Her colour is high.

Snow stands easily at her side. Comfortable with her in a way he is with almost no one else. He's got on lightweight grey trousers and that blue argyle shirt I lent him—that I bought, hoping to give to him someday. His curls are bouncing in the breeze.

Crowley, they're pretty together.

A goat ambles towards me, nosing at the grass—then seems to catch my scent and startles away. "Good instincts," I say.

Are these goats really magic? Or is Brody having us on?

I look for her on the far side of the meadow. She's been trying to get a closer look at one of the goats—the pregnant one, I assume. But now she's just staring at Simon and Agatha. Simon's holding Agatha's wrist, helping her with a big swooping gesture. It looks like choreography.

I let my head fall farther between my knees. My hair

shades my eyes. I'm getting too much sun.

"Should we bring them in?" Snow shouts. "To the barn?"

"We can try!" Brody calls back.

I decide to help by staying out of their way.

The three of them get on one side of the goats and try to drive them towards the school. The goats aren't having it. They're running through the gaps.

"Enough!" Brody finally says, leaning over to catch her breath. "This'll do. I've never managed to round them all up before. Maybe they'll stay together for a while."

Simon crosses his wrists on his head, frustrated. "I thought they *liked* being together . . ."

"They do, normally."

"Niamh thinks they're grieving," Wellbelove says.

Snow looks stricken. "They miss Ebb?"

Agatha nods.

He looks around him at the goats, newly sympathetic to their terrible behaviour. "So we just leave them here? Alone?"

"They have food and water," Brody says, "and they can go home whenever they want. We can't make them go."

Snow sighs and reaches down to pet the nearest goat. "Don't run off," he says. "You'll regret it."

Wellbelove looks a bit beaten. "It does feel wrong to leave them . . ."

"Well . . ." Brody pulls her bag up over her shoulder. "I have to get back to London, but . . . if you'd like to stay . . ."

Agatha looks up. "I'll take you back."

Brody nods, scowling, and turns to Simon. "Mr. Snow—" she says stiffly.

"Call me Simon," he says. "We're goat-herding pals now."

She nods. "Whenever you're ready . . . I've got a different

plan for your procedure now. I think we should numb the wings at the outset, before we disinfect."

Snow looks taken aback. "Oh . . . Yeah. That's an idea."

"Call the surgery," she says, "and I'll have them put you right into the schedule."

"Thanks. I'll do that."

Wellbelove is looking at me. "See you, then. This was good timing."

I nod.

She puts her hand on Snow's arm and squeezes. "Thank you. That really was brilliant." He lays his hand over hers and smiles at her.

Then she and Brody are heading out towards the Great Lawn.

Snow turns to me. I'm still sitting twenty feet away from him, in the grass. One side of his mouth quirks up. He starts walking my way.

"What about you?" He's standing over me now. "Did you get enough sun?"

I shield my eyes. "Yes, am I getting scorched around the edges?"

"You're looking a bit . . . Iowa."

Snow holds out his hand, and I take it, letting him pull me to my feet. He keeps hold of it. "Can we take the long way back?"

"There's only a long way back," I say.

"Through the Wood? There's a marker there, for Ebb. I've never seen it."

I glance over at the dense line of trees across the meadow. "I might have to drink something . . ."

"Not a goat," Snow says earnestly.

My cheeks twitch. "One of the famous Watford goats? Never."

He looks back over the flock. (Do goats flock? Or do they

only herd?) They're already spreading out. "Could you maybe cast a spell on them before we go?"

"None of my other spells worked, Snow."

He tugs on my hand. "Yeah, but you could try . . ."

"What kind of spell?"

"Something to make them stay together."

I look out at the goats and sigh. I raise my wand. ***"There's safety in numbers!"*** I shout. The goats don't seem to notice.

Simon kisses my cheek. "Thanks." He pulls me towards the Wavering Wood. I really am going to have to hunt soon; that rat in the Catacombs merely took the edge off. "Ebb never mentioned that the goats were magic," Simon says, swinging our hands. "Wouldn't she have mentioned that?"

"Don't ask me. I never heard Ebb say anything useful."

"Your mum gave her that job. I'll bet your mum knew the goats were magic . . ."

I shrug. I don't know what my mother knew. "Wellbelove looked . . . well," I say, changing the subject.

Simon gives me a wary look.

I feel foolish for saying it. I try to clarify: "She looked better than the last time we saw her."

"Huh," he half laughs. "I'm sure she's happy to be well clear of those NowNext vampires."

"Do you think we need to tell anyone about them?" We haven't talked about it yet—the fact that there are vampires trying to steal magic, and vampires running cities. None of us have talked about any of it since we got away from them.

"I'm not sure . . ." We're getting closer to the trees. Simon leans over to pick a stick up off the ground. It's about the size of a sword. He slices it through the air in front of him. "Seems like maybe the Vegas vampires will take care of the NowNext."

"But we should tell someone about . . . Las Vegas, right?"

Simon pulls his chin in. "Should we?"

"I mean, vampires *have* laid siege to an entire American city . . ."

"Baz, the whole world is a mess. Have you watched the news lately?" He swings the stick again, like he's testing its heft.

"I'd think you'd be all over this, Snow. Clearing out a vampire infestation?"

He looks at me like my head is on upside down. "I'm literally sleeping with a vampire."

"Yeah, but we're talking about *proper* vampires," I protest. "They drink blood."

He shrugs. "They don't seem to kill anyone . . ."

"They assault people."

"Again, have you watched the news lately? I don't even think having a vampire city is America's biggest problem . . ." He swings his stick in a circle. "How much of *any* of this are we responsible for?"

"I don't know." We're still holding hands; I hold my other hand up in front of my face, so he doesn't accidentally hit me. "Some of it."

Simon looks apologetic and rests the stick over his shoulder. "Maybe if it were happening here . . ."

"In the UK?"

"In the World of Mages."

"Pfft. Are you still our guardian, Snow?"

"No," he says quickly, "but . . . Oh, I don't know." He swings the stick again like he can't help himself. "I hope your friend Lamb *levels* San Diego. Let's not turn him in until he's done annihilating those bastards."

When I don't say anything, Simon looks over at my face.

Whatever he sees there makes him frown. "You know that you aren't *more* responsible for vampires just because you *are* a vampire . . ."

"Aren't I? They're my kind."

"Baz, you're their *victim*."

"*All* vampires are victims."

"Seems like those NowNext vampires were volunteering for the job."

I roll my eyes. "All right, then—*most* vampires are victims."

"Maybe they start out that way, but then they choose to victimize other people. Whether it's murdering people or Turning them, or just tapping people in alleys and stealing a pint." He's gesturing with his makeshift sword again. I let go of his hand to smack the stick away from me. "That's a choice they're making," he says. "To keep it going. The cycle of abuse."

"Maybe they don't know a different way to survive."

"You figured it out, and you were just a kid!"

I put my hands in my pockets and walk a bit faster. "I'm not special."

Simon takes hold of my shoulder. "You literally are!" He gets in front of me, so that we both have to stop. "You get credit for not being a murderous asshole, you know, especially when *being* a murderous asshole would make your life way easier."

"Well . . . I'm still young."

"*Baz*. I don't think you're going to start draining strangers on the Underground." He takes my other shoulder. He must have dropped his stick. "You won't even drink my blood, and I'm offering it."

"Sto-o-o-op." I roll my whole face up and away from him. "Simon, we agreed."

"What did we agree?"

"That you're not going to talk about this!"

"Fine, but we did not agree that you won't ever drink my blood."

I jerk my head down to look at him. "I'm telling you right now that I won't! And I won't have you bringing it up again."

Snow's jaw is square and there's a line between his eyebrows. "All right. I won't bring it up again . . . unless there's an emergency."

"Hell and horrors." My voice breaks. "There won't be an emergency that requires—"

"What if we're trapped underground?"

"We'd die of *actual* thirst before I'd need blood."

"All right," he says, "what if we're trapped underground with water and food, and—"

"Why would we be in this situation?"

"We're being held captive."

I shove him. "You'll break us out."

"I don't have magic, remember?"

"Then *I'll* break us out."

He steps closer to me, wrapping his arms loosely around my neck. "You can't, you're too weak—you need blood."

"Snow, I've been in many extreme scenarios, and this has *never* transpired . . ."

"It could!"

I cover my eyes and press my fingertips into my forehead. "Why are you doing this? Why are you making me imagine a terrible situation where I lose my humanity and have to do the very worst thing to the person I care about most?"

"*Because* . . ." he whines. "Because it's kinda *hot*."

"For fuck's sake, Snow!" I shout it so loud, some birds go squawking out of the trees. I duck out of his arms.

"Come on. It's sexy. Admit it."

I'm walking away from him. "Cannibalism isn't sexy."

He hums, like I might be wrong.

"*Simon.*"

He jogs to catch up with me. "It's not just me—everyone thinks vampires are sexy! I'm terrible at metaphors, and I still get it. Every vampire movie is about fucking virgins."

I shake my head over and over. "I'm not . . . This is not . . . *You're* not a virgin."

"Well, that part's fictional, right? You don't *have* to drink virgins, do you?"

"I don't have to drink anyone! I'm not drinking anyone! I'm not drinking *you* just because you think it's *kinky.* Also, why do you think you could *handle* anything kinky?"

"Well, not now . . ."

"*Simon.*" I wheel on him. "I'm asking you to stop! This isn't a metaphor for me. It's my *life.* It's my attempt to have a life. Just . . . *stop.* Please."

He's biting his bottom lip. His eyebrows are bunched up. "Yeah," he says, letting go of his lip. "Okay. Of course. I'm sorry." He shakes his head. "I won't mention it again."

"Thank you," I whisper.

He bites the other side of his lip. "Just . . ."

"You said you'd stop."

"No, I am. Just . . ."

"Snow."

He fists his hand in my shirt and yanks me close to him, pressing his cheek into the side of my jaw. His voice is low. "Just know," he says, "that I'd do anything for you. That I'd let you do anything to me. There's nothing about you I don't want."

And then he lets go of my shirt and runs away from me.

I watch him disappear into the Wood.

53

AGATHA

Niamh and I are quiet on the way to the car. But it's a better sort of quiet than before—I think we're both just relieved that no more of the goats have left Watford and that we've managed to round them up, at least.

I suppose I have to make peace with Simon continuing to show up to save my day. Whether or not I've asked him to. Whether or not he has any claim on me.

"Those spells you were using . . ." Niamh says.

"Simon said Ebb taught him. I could teach you—"

"I don't know that you could. You have a way with those goats." Her bun has come loose again. She takes it down and puts the hairgrips in her mouth while she tries to comb her hair back up with her fingers. It's like watching someone give themselves a makeunder.

"Oh, Niamh, don't," I say, pulling on her arm.

"Don't what?" She spits out the pins.

I lean over to find them in the grass. "Don't put your hair

in that awful bun. It makes you look a thousand years old."

"But I can't work with my hair in my face."

I hold the hairpins out to her. "You're not working now."

She takes the pins from me. She looks like she doesn't know what to do with them. Or herself.

"You have perfectly good hair," I say, reaching up to smooth it down. (Penelope says I have too many opinions about other people's hair.) "There's no reason to hide it."

"I don't like myself with long hair."

"Then get it cut. It looked good at school."

"I didn't think you remembered it," she says. "Or me."

"I remember you now."

Niamh is frowning very deeply at me. If I didn't know her face always looked like that, I'd back off. Instead I smooth out the other side of her head. It *is* nice hair. Thick and glossy, with just enough wave to take a style. My hair is too straight to wear any way other than how I wear it.

"I don't want to colour it again," she says. The way someone else might say, *"I don't want to go to prison."*

"Then don't," I reply, arranging her hair around her face. "It's a good colour. Chestnut. With some auburn highlights in the sun. Lots of people dye their hair this colour. You could wear it short and dark . . ." I pull her hair back into a ponytail and hold it so the front poofs out. "You'd look good with a quiff."

Niamh doesn't say anything. Her eyes are hard, and her eyebrows are tense.

She'd look very, very good like this. Her face looks severe with her hair scraped back into the bun. But this makes her look . . . *fierce* instead. Oh, I suppose Niamh looks fierce no matter what. With that nose. That crushed plum of a mouth. That mean chin. But this takes her from fierce to something else . . . Something very nearly intolerable. She looks like Marlon Brando.

I let her hair fall back down around her face. "You should wear it however you like," I say. I start walking again.

When we get to the car, I stand by the passenger side, waiting for Niamh to unlock the doors.

"Agatha," she says, "you drove."

"Oh . . . right. Right." I push the unlock button and go around to my side of the car. "I hope you aren't going to be late."

"Late for what?"

I get in and wait for her to sit down. "For your thing." I start the car. "That you had to get back for. In London."

"Oh . . ."

I look over at her. She looks embarrassed, I think.

"There isn't a thing," she says. "I just didn't want to get stuck hanging out with you and your friends . . . No offence."

"You can't just say 'no offence' after you say something offensive."

"It's nothing against you," she says. "I just didn't want to be the third wheel."

"The third wheel? *I'm* the third wheel. I was possibly the third wheel the entire time Simon and I were dating. If anything, you'd be the fourth wheel, Niamh. You'd balance everything out."

"I didn't want to crash your reunion . . ."

"There was no *reunion*," I say. "We were just . . . herding goats in a friendly manner."

"I was worried we'd, like, end up at a pub."

"Heaven forfend."

Niamh sighs and rubs her forehead. She looks like she's

experiencing a migraine. She hasn't put her hair back up.

"You don't like pubs?" I ask.

"Pubs are fine."

"You don't like my friends?" (*Are* Simon and Baz my friends? Now isn't the time to do the math.)

"I'm sure your friends are fine!" A debilitating migraine. "Look, I'm not trying to offend you, Agatha. I'm just not a . . . people person."

I wasn't ready to laugh so hard at that. It comes up the back of my nose.

Niamh sighs again and rolls her eyes. "Obviously."

"Is that why you became a veterinarian? Because you like animals better than people?" That's why I want to become a veterinarian.

"No," she says.

I wait for her to expand. Of course she doesn't.

"Why, then?" I ask.

She glares at me, but eventually answers. "I like the way bodies work." She takes a second to huff. "And when they're not working, I like to think about why. I like taking things apart and putting them back together."

"Why animals, then, instead of people?"

She shrugs. "Variety."

I laugh up my nose again.

"Stop laughing at me, Agatha."

I don't stop laughing. "Variety?" Still laughing. "Oh my words . . . You're so *strange*, Niamh."

"Fine." She's fed up. "Why did *you* want to become a veterinarian, Agatha?"

"Because I like animals more than people! Like a normal person!"

"I also like animals more than people!" she says. "That just wasn't the deciding factor!"

Still laughing. I can't help it.

"Agatha."

"Yes?"

She's rubbing her forehead. "Do you want to stop and get something to eat?"

"With me, a human being? Won't you feel like the second wheel?"

"Do you want to go to a pub?"

"Yeah," I laugh. "All right."

I really do.

54

SHEPARD

We've spent two days reading about mage marriages. Penelope's dad sent some books over for us. At first she wasn't going to let me read them. Then she reminded me that I've already crossed my heart and hoped to die if I ever tell any of their magical secrets—*"which is a one-way ticket to hell for you, buddy-boy"*—and handed me a book.

I'm not going to tell their secrets.

I'm not going to do anything else to mess things up with Penelope.

I know that she's miserable right now. That she's fighting with her friends, and all broken up over her breakup . . . That she's on the outs with her mom . . . I know that she's only putting up with me because I present an interesting problem.

But I am having the time of my *life* with Penelope Bunce.

And it's not just because she's an endless corridor of magical revelations—and not just because she's excruciatingly cute. I mean . . . That's part of it. I am still human. *Every-*

thing is part of it. Everything is so much fun.

We wake up, I make tea. (I have a feeling that was Simon's job.) Then we spend the whole day reading out loud to each other from books about magic, and telling each other stories. When Penelope gets excited about something, she's much more likely to talk about herself. You wouldn't believe her life—she's fought werewolves, she's invented spells. She has a real crystal ball, but she can't find it. (I would like to help her find it.)

When we get hungry, I run down to the corner to buy dumplings and noodles, or to one of the sandwich shops. (There are *so many* sandwich shops.) (Penelope is partial to cheese and pickle.)

When she's excited, I think she forgets that she's only putting up with me. And I think she forgets what a losing proposition I am. She'll jump off the couch to write something on the wall—*"Aha!"*—or lean into my shoulder to show me something ridiculous, laughing and waving around a piece of strawberry licorice—*"Get a load of this, Shepard"*—and I think maybe she's having fun, too.

This can't go on much longer, can it?

Penelope's filled both walls with notes, and I've learned so much about magical weddings, I could probably officiate one. But I don't think we're any closer to breaking my engagement.

She's going to see that we're not making progress. She's going to give up eventually. She's going to send me home.

The sun is setting now. We had a late lunch, and we'll probably have a late dinner. Penelope is lying on the couch with her legs up and hanging over one end, a book leaning against her thighs and keeping her skirt from falling. She always wears skirts or short dresses, never pants . . .

I've seen so much of Penelope Bunce's knees. Her legs are short and curvy—they're very goddamn cute, if I'm being honest, and her knees are the cutest part. And, okay, maybe I'm more affected by her cuteness than I want to admit, but what am I supposed to do? She's right there, and she doesn't get any less cute. Her cuteness doesn't *abate*. It just gets worse the more I'm around her. The licorice thing is killing me. And she's covered in chalk dust 24-7. It gets on her face and in her hair . . . I've never seen someone with so much hair pay so little attention to it—she's either got the world's messiest ponytail, or a *mop* of thick, dark brown hair, curling every which way, falling halfway down her back. It's cute. It's real cute. I am not unaffected, okay? I am very affected. Very. Very, very aware of Penelope Bunce. And how cute she is.

"This is a dead end," Penelope says. She lets the book she's reading drop on her stomach.

I'm sitting on the floor and leaning against one of her chalkboard walls. I've been reading a book about magical genealogy—when I haven't been distracted by her legs.

"All of these books are about magicians and mage customs," she says. "Not marriage contracts. Maybe Debbie was right, maybe we do need a lawyer."

"Are there magickal lawyers?"

She hums, thinking. "I know of two. But I doubt they'd take your case."

I look down at my book. "I'm sorry I'm not as helpful as Simon and Baz would be."

"Meh." She sits up, and digs a bag of red licorice shoestrings out from between two couch pillows. "Don't sell yourself short. They both get too emotionally invested and attached to their own ideas. You're remarkably clearheaded,

Shepard. It's almost like we're talking about someone *else* who's cursed to marry a demon."

I think that was a compliment . . .

She holds out the bag. "Do you want some?"

"Sure." I go sit next to her on the couch, taking a tangle of candy, even though I never eat this stuff. It tastes like chemical glue.

"Do you think the curse would allow you to get married?" she asks.

"In life?"

"Obviously in life."

"I think so," I say. "I could probably enter another arrangement that's 'till death do us part,' considering my arms say, 'at death do us join.'"

"Hmm." She bites down on a string of licorice, then pulls it until it snaps. "My parents got married when they were my age—nineteen."

"Wow . . ."

"Yeah . . . As soon as they left school. Mages get married young, but that's *really* young. My mum says she knew what she wanted in life and didn't see the sense in waiting."

"My parents were in their late twenties," I say. "My dad might have been thirty."

"When did they get divorced?"

"When I was eight."

She frowns. "I'm sorry."

"It's all right." I rest an elbow on the back of the couch and pull one knee up, so I'm facing her. "You know how they always tell kids, *'This divorce isn't about you, it isn't your fault'*?"

She nods. "Yeah . . ."

"I remember thinking, *Of course, it isn't! Why would you even suggest that? Is someone out there pinning this on me?*"

Penelope laughs, and for once, she doesn't try to hide it. "Did your parents fight a lot?"

"If they did, I don't remember. My dad was gone all the time, for work. And then, he was just gone."

"Did they get remarried?"

"My mom did."

"Do you like your stepdad?"

"He's fine. My mom likes him."

"Do they know . . ." She glances down at my arms.

I laugh. "Have I told my mom that I'm going to *hell*? No. She wouldn't even let me play Dungeons & Dragons when I was a kid because she didn't think Jesus would approve. This would be way too much for her."

"So she doesn't know you hang out with giants and fairies . . ."

"She does not."

Penelope leans one shoulder against the back of the couch and refolds her legs, so she's facing me. "Shepard . . ."

I push up my glasses. "Penelope."

"Did you *really* go home with a fairy?"

"I tried."

"What was her name?"

"Fey."

She rolls her eyes. "That wasn't her real name . . ."

"It's the name she told me."

"Why would a fairy name their kid Fey? That's like a magician naming their kid Warlock!"

"If I ever see her again, I'll ask her."

Penelope gets another piece of red licorice, and spins it

with one hand, watching the end whip around. "So you don't keep in touch?"

"We do not."

"Is there someone else you keep in touch with?"

I clear my throat. I'm looking at Penelope. At her messy ponytail. And her excruciating knees. She isn't looking at me. "Is that you asking if I have a girlfriend?"

"Or a boyfriend," she says quickly.

"I usually date girls," I say.

"You *usually* date magical creatures—"

"I don't have a girlfriend, Penelope."

She looks at the wall. "I should probably add that to the list."

"What was your boyfriend like?" I ask, before I can process how stupid it is to bring him up.

"Micah?"

"Yeah." *Stupid, stupid.* "Was he a magician?"

"Of course."

I sigh. "Of course."

"We met at Watford. He was an exchange student. He was very bright."

"He'd have to be."

"And he was, um . . ." She shrugs. "Nice."

"Nice?"

"Oh, I don't know how to describe people." She frowns and twirls her licorice. "He was a good listener. He was never cruel. He was a very gifted magician. Good with languages, an excellent ear. He never seemed to get tired of me . . . Until he did, and then I didn't notice."

I'm wearing mint-green corduroy pants, and I run my thumb along my knee where the stripes are wearing off. These are the pants I was wearing in the desert. I still have these pants and one T-shirt and a few things I was carrying in my backpack that day. Everything else got left at our hotel in Vegas. Penelope had to buy me underwear and a change of clothes at the airport . . . Actually, she probably stole them.

I clear my throat again. "Were you in love with him?"

"I don't know." She seems irritated. I should definitely stop asking about her ex-boyfriend. (This isn't how I ended up going home with a fairy.) "I thought I was . . ." she says. "I definitely *cared* about him. But if I was in love with Micah, I'd miss him now, right?"

She looks up at me, like I'm supposed to answer. I stay quiet.

"I don't think I miss him," she says, still irritated. "I feel rejected and humiliated and lost. But I don't—" She shakes her head. "—*long* for him. Maybe I don't have that chip. Maybe I don't do longing."

"I probably wouldn't decide that after one boyfriend . . ."

"Have you been in love, then?" She says it like she assumes I have, like it's part of my whole insufferable package.

"Yeah," I say anyway. "Once, for sure. And then I think I've been at least half in love, twice."

"You can't be *half* in love, Shepard . . ."

"How would you know?"

Her face falls a little. I shouldn't have said that. We're going to need another chalkboard to keep track of all the things I shouldn't have said tonight. Penelope shifts her weight, so she isn't quite facing me anymore. "You probably don't believe in soulmates, then. Magicians usually believe in soulmates. And destiny."

"I believe in everything," I say.

She makes a judgmental noise in the back of her throat, then picks up the bag of licorice and spins it closed.

I want her to keep talking to me. Even if I keep saying the wrong things. "Did you think Micah was your soulmate?"

She makes another disappointed noise. This one is for herself, I think. "Micah made sense for me . . . So I plugged him into all of my important equations. It was like I solved wrong for x, and it threw off the other variables." She ties the top of the bag in a knot. "I must sound like a child to you."

"No . . . You sound like a person who doesn't know everything about love. That's most of us."

"*You've* got it all figured out. You've been in love three-point-five times or something."

"If I had it figured out, I wouldn't be alone and engaged to a demon."

"It's not a real engagement," she says softly.

"Thanks."

She turns her head towards me and looks into my eyes. Penelope only looks in your eyes when she expects something.

I wait for her to tell me what it is.

PENELOPE

I've been in this room too long with no one but Shepard.

He's starting to feel more real than everything else. He's starting to feel like the one thing that's supposed to be here.

It should be the opposite—it *is* the opposite. Shepard is

a Normal. And Normals don't matter. I mean, I'm sure they matter to other Normals—but they're not supposed to matter to me. They're supposed to be like ants. Or plants. Important to the overall ecosystem, but not *important*.

My mother always said there was no sense in making friends with Normals, because what could you even talk about, if you couldn't talk about magic? What's left?

(Have *I* ever said that?)

(Is that what drove Simon away?)

But Shep and I have been talking for days. And we've been talking *so much* about magic. And so much about *everything*.

And I know that he's a Normal, it's not like I ever forget, but I can't really imagine what would be different about being here with him if he had magic. I suppose he'd understand me a little better, he'd know what magic feels like . . . But magic feels different for everyone, even among mages. You can't ever really know what it's like to *be* someone else . . .

"Shepard."

He pushes up his glasses. "Penelope."

"Do you wish that you could do magic?"

He bites his lip. His bottom lip is pinker than the top, and there's a dimple in the middle, so that the top of his bottom lip is shaped like the top of a heart. I only noticed this yesterday, and now I can't stop.

"I feel sort of like you're asking me whether I wish I could fly," he says. "And the answer is—of course. Yes. I would love to do magic. But I don't wish that I was something else. Does that make sense?"

"Sort of . . ."

"Like, I wouldn't trade being who I am to be someone or something else that could do magic."

"You don't mind being Normal?"

He laughs at me.

"Don't laugh at me."

He smiles instead. "I don't mind being what I am. We don't call ourselves 'Normal,' you know?"

"But, Shepard, you spend so much time trying to get close to magic, you must . . ."

He looks like he's going to laugh again, so I stop talking. He's still holding the strawberry lace I gave him.

"Do you even like strawberry laces?" I ask.

"No, I'm sorry. They taste like cough syrup."

I take it from him and take a bite.

His elbow is on the back of the couch, and he leans a little closer to me. "The thing is, I don't feel apart from magic. The world is magickal, and it's my world, too. Just because *you* think I'm not magickal—"

"I don't . . ." I want to say that I don't think that. But I'm pretty sure I've said it out loud, multiple times.

Shepard's wearing his Keith Haring shirt again. He only has two shirts.

His face is long, and his eyes are wide. His cheekbones shine even by lamplight.

Whenever we leave the flat, strangers admire Shepard. He's tall and handsome. He looks kind and interesting. And then he starts talking to them, and they like him even more. Because he's even kinder than they were expecting, and he's as interested as he is interesting. Almost no one is that.

The man at the dumpling shop loves Shepard. My neighbours know his name. (My neighbours don't know *my* name.)

And all of these people don't even realize that it just keeps getting worse, the more you know him. That he just keeps getting better. There are no diminishing returns with Shepard—you just like him more and more until your head explodes. Until you actually die from liking him so much.

"Do you wish I was a magician?" he asks.

"No," I say, before I've even thought it through.

Shepard looks down. Like that hurt him. Why? How was that the wrong answer? He just said he didn't want to be—

"I wouldn't want to trade who you are," I say, "for someone or something else who could do magic."

Shepard looks up into my eyes. "Penelope," he says.

I push up my glasses. "Shepard."

He's moving his hand very slowly towards my face, and I know I've only kissed one person, but I know what this means. I know he's giving me a chance to say no. To sit back or turn away.

I bring both of my legs onto the sofa, and shift so I'm facing him. He still stops with his hand near my face. "Penelope," he says softly.

I raise my hand to his wrist and push his hand against my cheek. He smiles. The dimple in his bottom lip flattens out, and you can see almost all of his teeth. He could smile at anyone, and they'd want this. He could smile at anyone . . .

He's smiling at me.

What wouldn't I do to keep Shepard smiling at me?

He's tall—he can reach me without any work. He bends at the waist, and his smile gets closer. "Yeah?" he asks when his mouth is nearly touching mine.

"Yeah," I say, and it's more of a noise than a word.

Shepard kisses me.

He's still smiling.

His lips are soft. They cover mine. And it's so much better than I was expecting. It's better than I thought kissing was supposed to be.

It's magic.

It's *better*.

SHEPARD

Holy shit, this is . . .

This is not something I thought would happen. *Penelope* . . .

She's going to be mad about this, right? Like, this is *not* something she wanted to occur. But the way she was looking at me—like, if I didn't kiss her, she was going to turn me into a frog—what was I supposed to do?

Penelope . . .

We can stop if you want to.

She tilts her head and pushes closer. Our glasses tap against each other. I take mine off and set them as far away as I can reach, and then I bring my hand up to her shoulder. Her cheek is round and soft. Her shoulder is round and soft. I have a good feeling about the rest of her.

Penelope kisses like someone who hasn't done this very much. And that isn't to say it's bad—it's very *not* bad. She just doesn't seem to know what to do first. I hold her face in both hands and let her kiss me like she has a lot of questions about this whole scenario.

A long time passes before she touches me—one hand on

my shoulder—but then it's both hands on my shoulders, then both hands on my neck, both hands in my hair, both hands on my ears. I laugh, I can't help it.

"Don't laugh at me," she whispers.

I lick her mouth while it's open—and groan. *She tastes so sweet.*

Penelope has her hands on my shoulders again. She climbs into my lap and brackets my hips with her knees. She smooths down her skirt. And then she puts both arms around my neck.

I lean back against the couch and hold her waist.

I don't know how much longer this can go on.

I hope she doesn't regret it.

I'm glad she can't make me forget it.

PENELOPE

Nicks and Slick, I've been wrong about everything.

Wrong about love.

Wrong about kissing, for certain.

Wrong about Shepard—I was frightfully wrong about Shepard. And I'm so *glad*. What else could I have been wrong about? I hope he shows me. I want him to show me.

I've been sitting in his lap for what feels like hours. We're still kissing, and it's still so soft. And he's still smiling. I'm not sure he's stopped smiling. I'm smiling, too. Shepard looks different without his glasses—even more open, even more vulnerable. His eyes are smaller, his face has more space. I kiss the spot between his eyebrows, and he laughs.

My glasses are gone, too—Shepard took them off and set them somewhere. He tracks his thumbs along my eyebrows, down, over my cheekbones, and his smile fades. "Penelope . . . I need to ask you something."

I sit back a little on his thighs. "Okay."

He brings his hands to my waist, like he's holding me steady. "Are you going to regret this?"

"How would I know that now?" I ask.

Shepard bites his lip. His bottom lip is even pinker than before. "I guess that's fair."

"Are you?"

"No," he says.

"Well, you don't know that either . . ."

He sits up a little. "No, I do. Without a doubt. I am never going to regret kissing you. I'm never going to regret a moment we've spent together, even though I regret the mistakes I've made . . ."

"Oh," I say.

He pushes my hair out of my face. It falls back immediately. My ponytail must be nearly dead. "I need to tell you something," he says, "just in case this is . . . happening."

"What do you mean? Obviously it's happening."

He clears his throat. I reach down my T-shirt and find my gem, so I can summon him a glass of water. He just looks at the water for a second, then drinks half of it, and hands it back to me. I finish it, then disappear the glass. **"A place for everything, and everything in its place!"**

Shepard clears his throat again. "I need to tell you something, a few somethings. Because now is the time to tell you. Before we get serious. But it's going to make it seem like I think we're more serious than we are. I just don't want to miss my window for being honest with you."

"Shepard, you're making me nervous."

He groans. "I'm sorry. Don't be nervous."

My hands were on his shoulders. I drop them into my lap.

"Don't pull away," he says.

"Just tell me, Shepard! Are you engaged to more than one demon?"

"No! But . . . you know I've been in a lot of unusual magickal situations . . ."

"Right."

"And you know about my thirdborn . . ."

"I know that a giant you call a friend is going to eat your thirdborn."

He closes one eye and bites his bottom lip. "I may also have promised someone my firstborn."

"Shepard, your *firstborn* . . ."

He squeezes my waist. "It's all right, I told you—I'm not having kids."

"Who gets your firstborn?"

"An imp. Or three."

"Aren't imps the same as demons?"

"Never say that to an imp."

"How did this even happen?"

"We were playing impdice. I thought they were joking about the wager."

"We are going to kill these imps."

"Penelope . . ." He bites his lip again. "There's more."

"More? Your secondborn?"

"No, I've got dibs on that one . . ." He's grimacing. "But I did lose my last name."

Every time he talks, my jaw drops lower and my eyebrows

climb higher. "How on earth did you lose your last name?"

"Told it to the wrong fairy."

My hands are in the air. "How have you met so many fairies!"

"I fell in with a crew of them . . ."

"Shepard—hell's spells, is your name even Shepard?"

"Yes! I only lost my last name. And I only 'magickally and profoundly' lost it; I can still say it, I can still wear name tags. There's just one more thing—one more big thing . . ." He closes both eyes for a second. "I have a, um, well . . . I don't have a sexually transmitted disease. But I am a carrier. Only other merpeople can get it. So it's probably not relevant. Unless you want to sleep with a merperson. And also me. Me first. Which I'm not suggesting . . ."

Hell's spells . . .

Shepard.

I climb off his lap.

55

SHEPARD

Penelope has the refrigerator door open. "I knew that Simon left some milk . . ."

The kitchen is behind the living room. I'm kneeling backwards on the couch, trying to get her attention. "It sounds worse than it is—'mermaid venereal disease' . . ."

There's a succulent in a pot on the kitchen counter. Penelope dumps it in the sink.

"I'm sure I can't pass it to another human being," I say. "It's not even a disease, really—it's tied to how they fertilize eggs—"

There's a stack of mail on the table. Penelope picks it up and sets it on fire.

This is going so much worse than I expected, and I didn't think it would go *well*. I sit back onto the couch and look for my glasses. I find Penelope's glasses first and take them to her in the kitchen.

"Penelope," I say holding them out to her.

She grabs my wrist and jerks her fist over my hand.

"There will be blood!"

"What the *fuck*!" My hand is bleeding.

Her glasses are on the floor. She picks them up. "Hang on," she says, "let me get a teacup for you to bleed into."

"Why am I bleeding?"

"So that we can draw a door." She holds a teacup under my palm.

"What? No!" *No, no, no, no, no, no . . .*

"We'll have to move the sofa out of the way . . . How big was the door you drew the first time?"

"We can't do this, Penelope. We aren't ready for this."

"I'm ready," she says. "We've got everything we need— milk, soil, ashes . . ." She looks at the empty teacup and squeezes my hand. "Blood."

"But we don't have a plan."

"I have a plan."

"Are you going to tell me?"

She tilts her head up at me—"No"—then looks down at my hand—"Can you bleed faster?"

56

BAZ

I helped Simon pick out a sofa today.

One minute, we were eating toast in his bed, and he was wiping his hands on my pyjama bottoms, and I was wiping my hands on his pillow—and the next, he was practically daring me to go to Ikea with him. (He'd been in a such a desolate mood last night, after visiting Ebb's grave; I was relieved to see him so cheerful.)

He purchased: A navy-blue sofa. Four plates, four mugs, cutlery. Two sets of towels. Two pillows. A duvet. And two sets of bedding—one with thick purple stripes and one with giant green apples. (Who knew Snow was whimsical?)

"You should choose one set, Baz."

"They're your sheets, Snow."

"Yeah, but you're going to be sleeping on them."

(I would sleep on a bed of straw to be close to him. I'd sleep in the back of a truck.)

He found a kitchen table he liked, then got kind of

overwhelmed looking at chairs. "I need everything," he said. "This is going to take all day."

"We can come back," I said. "Ikea isn't going anywhere."

We ate lunch in their cafeteria, and Simon spent half his inheritance on Swedish meatballs and Daim cake.

He was wearing another Watford hoodie to cover his wings. One that he hasn't yet sliced to ribbons. I could tell he was overheated. (I don't know what the short-term solution for this is—a silk shawl? A lightweight poncho?) I noticed a few people noticing the hump on his back. But none of them seemed to think he was hiding anything.

We held hands the whole day. At lunch, he sat with his arm resting on the back of my chair. "If you can't be gay at Ikea," Snow reasoned, "where can you?"

Was this the best day of my life?

I'm nearly certain.

It was so good that I haven't come down yet, even sitting here in another one of Smith-Richards's meetings, this time in the very front row. Smith-Richards sent Simon a text this afternoon, making sure we'd be here—making sure *Simon* would be here. As if he'd miss it.

Daphne grabbed us as soon as we walked in and dragged us up front. The better to see Smith-Richards's pore-less skin, I presume. He hasn't come out yet. Daphne is on the edge of her seat, waiting for him.

I'm feeling too cheerful to harass her about calling home. At least my father seems to be doing better this week. I've been checking in. Vera, my old nanny, has agreed to come help with the kids. Her family is in Hampshire, so she won't stay for good, but maybe she can see him through Daphne's bout of madness. (I'm very relieved that my father doesn't need me in Oxford; it's very important that I stay in London and eat toast in Simon Snow's bed. On his new striped sheets.)

Simon squeezes my hand. "Do you see Jamie?"

We can't see anyone without cranking our necks around and calling attention to ourselves. "No."

"Maybe he's running late."

The show is about to begin. You can tell because they're playing Coldplay over the speakers, and everyone is getting jumpy. Daphne takes my other hand and squeezes it tight. She's beaming tonight—she looks like she spent the day shopping for dinnerware with her boyfriend at Ikea. (How doomed *is* my father?) (Maybe he can offer Vera an enormous raise . . .) (Maybe he can marry her.)

The room erupts when Smith-Richards walks in. He holds up his arms to acknowledge everyone. *"Thank you,"* he mouths over the applause. Simon lets go of my hand to clap.

Smith-Richards hops onto the stage. (Why step when you can hop.) When he sees Simon, his warm smile gets even more incandescent. "I'm glad you're here," he says to Simon, waving. We're sitting so close to the stage, we can hear him.

He's looking artfully casual tonight—white painter's trousers, a blue split-neck shirt, some sort of red and gold bandanna knotted at his throat . . . It suits him, loath as I am to admit it. It would suit Simon better.

An older man—the same one who was at the door the other night—hands Smith-Richards a microphone. "Hello!" he says into the mic. "Everyone! It's so good to see you . . ."

Smith-Richards goes right into his pitch: How much he *cares* about everyone in the room, how he wants to *help* them, how he *believes* he can help them. How they deserve *so much more* than life has given them so far.

It's not that he's wrong about all this, I suppose. It's just that he's *insufferable.*

I look over my shoulder. There are more people here tonight than at the last meeting. Smith-Richards is going to have to find a bigger pub. Maybe he should rent a church; the vibe would be spot-on.

I still don't see Jamie. There's a guy I recognize from Watford . . . Ian somebody, a few years older than us. And a woman who plays tennis at the club. Are all of these people low-magicians? Or are they just normal magicians who think they deserve better?

Alan, the man who got the power-up last week, was holding court at the back of the room when we came in, regaling everyone with stories about all the big spells he can cast now.

Smith-Richards is ratcheting up the intensity tonight. He's saying he wants to help more people, more quickly—that they shouldn't have to wait any longer for their birthright.

Daphne's enthralled. Her mouth is actually hanging open.

Simon is leaning forward, his elbows on his thighs, taking in every word. Does he truly *believe* all this? He keeps giving Smith-Richards the full benefit of the doubt, and more. It's like Simon *wants* someone else to be the real Chosen One— and he wants it to be someone like Smith-Richards, someone who'll wear the crown more comfortably than he himself ever did. I lay my hand on Simon's neck and scratch at the back of his hair, where it's too short to curl. He glances over his shoulder to smile at me.

We're going hunting after this. And then we're getting fish and chips. And then we're going back to Simon's apartment together. Tomorrow morning, we'll have toast in bed.

I rub his neck, and he doesn't shrug me off. (This must be another place where it's okay to be gay—or whatever Simon is.)

I look over my other shoulder, scanning the other side of the room for Jamie. I've seen most of these people before. Oh, there's Máire. I thought she'd already chosen a Chosen One. Hedging her bets, apparently. I wonder where Agatha's old roommate is tonight; I haven't seen her yet.

I look back up at Smith-Richards and cross my legs, trying to at least appear as if I'm paying attention. He's still being clinically sincere: "I've been consulting with some of my most loyal friends and looking at ways to expand my reach. If I can cast the spell on one mage, why not cast the same spell on two or three—"

My breath catches in my throat. *Agatha's old roommate!*

"Or six."

That's who she is.

"When we next meet, tomorrow, I'll be bringing six of my most faithful—"

The girl.

"—and steadfast supporters—"

The quiet girl. At the door. Pippa.

"—onto the stage, to stand beside me—"

It's Philippa! Agatha's old roommate, from Watford. She lost her voice.

"—and step into their destiny."

I stole her voice. In fifth year.

"My dear friends . . ."

I stole her voice.

"Patrick, Melinda—"

Miss Possibelf said it would come back. She promised.

"Eliza, Gloria, Daphne—"

Daphne shrieks and throws her arms around me.

"And you, Martin."

I stole Philippa's voice.

I was trying to steal Simon's.

It hasn't come back . . .

Daphne is weeping. I peel her arms away from me.

It never came back.

I lay a hand on Simon's shoulder. "I have to go," I say. It's not a whisper, because everyone in the room is shrieking and crying.

Simon looks concerned. "Go where?"

"I know this is your fault!" he shouted at me that day. Out on the Great Lawn. The day I stole Philippa's voice.

I'm standing up. "I'll catch up with you later."

He's standing, too. "I'll come now."

"I know you did this!" he cried.

I pat his back. I try to push him down. "No, you stay. I need—" I'm walking away. "You stay. I'll see you later." I'm running away. Out of the pub, onto the street. I need a car, a taxi.

Philippa.

I stole her voice.

I stole her voice.

And it never came back.

57

SIMON

I knew that Baz didn't like Smith—that he doesn't believe in him—but I didn't realize he was taking it so personally. I guess it's because of his stepmum and his dad. Maybe Baz thinks that if Daphne gets stronger, she won't want to go home.

At the moment, Daphne's crying like we've just won the World Cup. When Baz ran off, she threw her arms around me instead. *Six people.* Smith is going to heal six people, all in one night. How long before he's helped every magician in this room?

He's motioning for everyone to calm down, but I don't think they will.

"I won't be casting the spell tonight," he says. "I hope to spend the next day in meditation. Tomorrow we'll be meeting somewhere very special . . ."

The crowd gets quiet, waiting.

"Watford."

A few people gasp. A few people clap. And laugh. They're delighted.

"Headmistress Bunce has invited us to use the White Chapel!"

"I was married there," Daphne whispers to me.

I killed the Mage there, I decide not to say.

Smith steps closer to the edge of the stage. "If there are people in your life whose hearts are softening to our message . . . bring them tomorrow. Let them see the truth of what we're offering. And if there are people in your life who still harbour doubts, invite them, too! Invite everyone! Let's throw our doors open to the entire World of Mages and show them what equality looks like! That magic belongs to us all!"

The room goes wild for him. I'm clapping, too. Good for Smith. Good for Daphne. Good for everyone in this room who might have a chance at something bigger and brighter.

Smith sees me clapping and smiles at me. "Good night," he says to the crowd, "and see you tomorrow at Watford!"

He sets down the microphone and hops off the front of stage, reaching for my arm. "Simon, come quick, before I get mobbed." He pulls me towards the side door. As soon as we're through, he hugs me with one arm. "You came," he says.

"Smith, congratulations. This is really exciting."

He looks almost embarrassed. Nervous. "Yeah, I've been working on expanding the spell, and, I don't know, I'm tired of waiting. People shouldn't have to wait."

"It's so cool, I'm happy for you. Is Jamie meeting us back here?"

"Oh"—Smith's face falls—"Simon, I'm really sorry. I couldn't talk him into coming. He's such an introvert, and he says everyone treats him like a saint now. I told him it will get better after more people have been cured. Then he won't be such a curiosity."

I nod. I'm not sure what to say. I wish Baz was here to help me steer the conversation.

"If you want to talk to someone who's been healed," Smith says, "I could introduce you to Beth, from last week. I think she's here."

"Sure." I don't want to seem overly interested in Jamie. "I'd love to talk to Beth."

"Actually . . . are you coming tomorrow? I know she'll be at Watford tomorrow, and you can meet her family, as well."

I smile at him. "I'm definitely coming tomorrow. I wouldn't miss it."

"Cool. I'll save you seats up front. Simon . . ." Smith still looks nervous. "Would you mind going for a pint with me? I was hoping we could talk . . ." He laughs and rolls his eyes. "Chosen One to Chosen One."

"Smith, I'm not—"

"No. I know. I'd just really like to talk to you." He gives me the full serving of those blue eyes. "I feel like you're the only one who understands . . ."

A half hour later, Smith and I are sitting in a no-nonsense pub across the street from his building. The pub serves food, so I'm happy. (Baz and I were supposed to get dinner. I texted him twice before my phone died. He probably went hunting without me.)

Smith has a thousand questions for me about being the Greatest Mage—about the way people used to treat me, and why the Mage kept me hidden away . . . "They say that you had so much magic, other magicians would get drunk off it."

"Sometimes," I say. "Sometimes it made them puke. It used to give my girlfriend migraines."

I've got a plate of fish and chips with mushy peas. All Smith ordered was a lager. He plays with the glass, watching the bubbles roll around. "I've never had that kind of magic," he says.

"Count yourself lucky," I say, reaching for the vinegar. "It was unnatural. Impossible to control. Well . . ." I look up at him. "Maybe *you* could have controlled it. I could barely hold a wand."

"Do you miss it?"

I pick up a chip. "My wand?"

"Your magic."

"I mean . . ." The chip is burning my fingers. I drop it.

"You must," he says. "You had more magic than anyone, and then . . ." He swirls his glass. "*Phoof.* Nothing."

Do I miss my magic?

It wasn't mine, was it? And I was never any good at it—I regularly scorched the earth just trying to make it work.

Do I miss going off? No.

And I don't miss the way other mages treated me. They could never see past my power.

Do I miss casting spells? Merlin, half the time they backfired. I suppose the other half of the time, they didn't . . .

I could make fire. And air. And water.

I could melt butter and boil tea.

I could have wings when I wanted them.

I could protect everyone. Every time. Nothing was impossible for me when I had magic—no war couldn't be won.

Do I miss it?

"Yeah," I say. "Every second of every day. It's like I'm missing a hand. Like—I have two hands, and I should be happy about that, but I used to have *three,* you know? And now I can't even figure out how to tie my shoes. Fuck yeah, I miss it. All the time."

Smith is smiling at me. Which really doesn't seem appropriate, the bastard. He looks well pleased with himself. "Simon . . ." He's practically grinning.

"For fuck's sake, Smith, I just poured my heart out. Have some compassion."

He grabs my wrist. "No, Simon, I—" He shakes my arm, still grinning at me. "I can help you."

"I can tie my shoes. That was just hyperbole."

He laughs out loud. "*Simon,* I can fix your magic!"

My mouth is open, but I'm not saying anything. I sit back against the wall of the booth.

Smith moves his hand down to mine and clutches it. "I can make you a magician again."

"How . . ."

"My spell," he says. "I could cast it on you."

"But I'm not a mage—"

"You were the *greatest* mage—"

"That was never true—"

"It was *literally* true!" He squeezes my hand. "You may not have been the Chosen One, Simon, but you were the most powerful magician our world had ever known. Don't tell me you weren't a mage . . ."

"Smith . . ."

His eyes are shining. He's looking at me like we're old friends. Like he knows me inside and out. "I didn't cast the spell tonight," he says, "because I was saving it for *you*. I knew you wouldn't want to be part of the spectacle tomorrow, onstage . . ."

"I don't know what to say . . ."

He picks up my other hand and laughs. "Say yes!"

I shake my head. "I gave magic up to make things right."

Smith's face goes soft. He holds our hands between us. "Simon, you made the ultimate sacrifice so that our world could heal. Now let me heal you."

58

SMITH

One day at a time, Evander always says. One chapter.

This is my Simon Snow chapter. (*Simon Snow*, what a name! What an advantage. He even sounds the part, I'm almost jealous.)

This is where I heal him. Where I prove my power.

I'm not like those who have come before me. The false prophets. I'm not like *him*. He failed them. (Good name be damned! Good hair. Scarlet wings.)

My power won't fail.

My plan won't fail.

I'll fix their fallen idol, I'll show him every mercy—I'll restore him to glory.

I'll restore the whole World of Mages to glory.

I'm the one the prophecies are all about. I'll make this place like it was in the legends. With heroes. With miracles. With *magic*.

This is my story.

This is my Simon Snow chapter.

Once upon a time, I met an injured soldier.

Once upon a time, I took his hands in mine.

He'll look very good standing next to me in the White Chapel.

He'll sound very good spreading my good news.

59

SHEPARD

There's a doorway to hell on Penelope's floor. She pushed the couch aside to make room.

I rub my eyes. "I thought you said I was stupid to do this in my own house."

"This is a rental," she says. "Get started."

I told Penelope I wouldn't read the ritual out loud. And then she said, *"Fine, I'll read it."* And then I said, *"I'm not letting you propose to a demon!"* And she said, *"Then I guess you're reading it."* So here I am, standing above a doorway drawn with my own blood, holding the instructions Ken gave me two years ago.

"This is a very bad idea," I say.

"Your favorite kind."

"Penelope . . ."

She steps up to stand beside me, at the foot of the bloody door.

"You promised you'd stay in the kitchen," I say.

"No, you *asked* me to stay in the kitchen. Shepard, do you trust me?"

I look down at her. She redid her ponytail and cleaned her glasses to prepare for the ritual, and put on, I swear to you, a gray cape. Her brown eyes are set deep and pinched fierce, and her lips are still puffy from kissing me. She's got her purple gem in her fist.

"I do," I say.

She stands on tiptoe to kiss me again. "Summon the demon," she says, "and then stay out of my way."

It's different, speaking the ritual out loud now that I know it's a proposal. (It's embarrassing.) Maybe the demon won't come this time—maybe there's a different ritual for summoning your demon fiancée. I read the summons all the way to the end, then look down at the door . . .

And just like before, it opens.

The demon walks through like it's climbing up stairs. It looks the same as it did last time. Sometimes like a woman. Sometimes like a bear. Sometimes like a hole.

It steps into Penelope's living room, and there's a feeling in my head like a heavy bass note playing on cheap speakers. I try to shake it off.

"Shepard," the demon says warmly, and my head buzzes again, "my betrothed. Did you need to speak to me?" It looks very much like a woman at the moment. Smiling. Sincere. Its arms outstretched. It's wearing very expensive-looking stilettos and a silk pantsuit. (Is it really wearing that? Or am I projecting it somehow? When I try to focus on its face, my head throbs.)

"Hi," I say, "how are you?"

Penelope is already stepping between us. "Shepard doesn't

need to speak to you today. I do."

The demon stops short and frowns at her. "And who are you?"

"I'm his advocate."

It looks back at me. "You need an advocate, Shepard?"

"This is concerning the contract," Penelope says crisply. She sounds very officious.

"The contract . . ." The demon's eyes glow. (The woman's eyes, the bear's eyes; there's a pair of eyes burning red in a black hole.) My tattoos start to swirl and itch.

Penelope looks unfazed. "It's invalid, I'm afraid."

"You should be afraid!" The demon turns to me. "Who is this mortal, Shepard? Who dares question our engagement?"

"I—"

Penelope steps between us. "Your arrangement is with Shepard Love?"

"Yes," the demon growls.

"That isn't this man's name."

The demon lurches closer to Penelope. "He lied to me?"

Penelope presses her lips together and tilts her head. "He didn't fully disclose—"

"That is a lie!" the demon shouts. My head is full of static.

"Well"—Penelope shrugs, unimpressed—"whatever it is, it voids the contract."

The demon looks at me over Penelope's head. "I will disembowel you if this is true."

"You could disembowel him *after* the wedding," Penelope says, "*if* he is unfaithful; infertile; or if his face displeases you. The terms are clear. But providing false information merely invalidates the engagement."

"Where does it say that?" the demon asks.

"Right above his wrist. *'The agreement is null and void, and any favours or gifts shall be returned'*—"

It huffs. "He didn't ask for any favours!"

"That makes it easy, there's nothing to undo."

The demon looks especially bearlike and holelike for a moment. "This man called me of his free will!"

"I did," I say, "I'm sorry."

Penelope's elbow catches me in the stomach.

"There were no tricks," the demon goes on, "no entrapment! I wasn't even *looking* for a husband!"

"We don't dispute that," Penelope says.

The demon jabs a paw into Penelope's shoulder. "He summoned me with a time-tested, legally sound marriage proposal."

"We stipulate to that fact."

"He offered his name—and much else that I didn't require!"

"I'm surprised you didn't ask to see some identification," Penelope says. "Or attempt any due diligence."

The demon huffs white smoke into Penelope's face. "I could kill you both!"

Penelope, unbelievably, steps forward. "You could, but that isn't what you agreed to do in the case of inadequate disclosure." She takes another step. "You *agreed* to invalidate the contract!"

The demon points at me, right over Penelope's head. "I could elect to honour our covenant, regardless! I will come for you at the appointed hour, and take you on the long journey to my home, where we will be married for all my brethren to see. You will be immortal, because I will take you to a place where your kind cannot live or die."

Penelope folds her arms. "You *could* choose to flout the law and disregard the contract . . . Perhaps your word is as worthless as his."

The demon howls—the whole building vibrates—and then lumbers across the room to sit on Penelope's couch. It looks like a woman again. Beautiful. With skin a color my eyes can't see. And hair like horns, like hair, like a hole.

Penelope takes a breath to say something.

"Quiet," the demon says. "I'm thinking."

I really want to apologize or smooth this over somehow. Maybe I should offer the demon something to drink. Penelope must smell it on me; she presses her lips together and shakes her head, hard.

"We'll amend the agreement," the demon says, "clarifying his name and the consequences for further dishonesty."

"I'm not *your* advocate—" Penelope starts to say.

"Indeed you are not," the demon snaps. "I was not informed that I'd need representation."

"—but I'd advise you to take this opportunity to protect your assets."

"My assets are perfectly secure."

"I regret to inform you," Penelope says, sounding a lot like someone who works at the DMV and doesn't feel any regret at all, "that this man comes to you with many debts."

"He disclosed no debts!"

"He wasn't asked to!"

"Any debt he owes in this world will be meaningless in mine!"

"He has promised someone else his firstborn," Penelope regrets to inform it.

"His *firstborn* . . ." The demon widens into a hole that

consumes the couch. Its voice is a devastation. "Shepard, how could you!"

"I wasn't planning on having kids," I mumble.

"Also his thirdborn," Penelope adds. Crisp as hell. "As well as countless other debts and promises, some of them owed beyond death to creatures who live nearly forever."

The demon rises from the couch and seeps towards me. "I told myself I was done with this earth . . . When is it ever worth the trouble?" I can taste the demon's bitterness, like a mouthful of dirt, and my head won't stop ringing. Penelope is feeling it, too, I think. She keeps twitching her head when the demon isn't looking.

It's closing in on me. Penelope moves between us, but the bear*woman*hole*bear* passes right through her.

It looms over me. "But you . . ." the demon says, taking me by the chin. "You were different. You took me off guard. To call one such as me and ask for nothing more than my hand . . ."

It caresses my cheek. Claws*finger*emptiness. "I was moved."

"I'm sorry," I whisper.

"I would have given you eternity, Shepard," the demon thrums. "I would have built you a throne."

It sighs so low it feels like gravity. Like its breath is pulling us down, down, down. A ceramic dish on the table crumbles into dust.

"I should have asked to see some ID," it says. "I normally *do* ask for references . . ."

It looks up into my eyes. And down into them. Its gaze surrounds me. "The contract is void," it says. My forearms itch and tingle. I stand very still. "You are no longer my betrothed. Your debts are not mine. And you have no claim on immortality."

The demon turns its attention to Penelope. "You, however . . ."

Penelope doesn't flinch.

"You are very clever and very brave, and I like your knees." The demon's voice is honeyed now, like the lowest string on a double bass. "My powers are great," it hums, "and I'm pleased to inform you that my hand is available."

Penelope flinches. "Are you . . ."

"Is there anything you want in this world, young advocate?"

Penelope shakes her head. "No."

"Very well," the demon says, turning heavily away from us. "Call me if you change your mind." It opens the door in the floor, and descends on two feet and four and like a sinking void.

I look down at Penelope. She's staring at my arms.

At nothing but smooth brown skin.

60

BAZ

It takes forever to get to my aunt's flat, even casting spells on traffic.

I run from the taxi, up the stairs, and open the front door with my wand instead of my key. Fiona's in the living room. She jumps up from the sofa when I burst in.

"Fucking hell, Basil!"

There's a man still sitting on the sofa—Nicodemus, the vampire. I run past them into Fiona's room.

"What are you doing!" she shouts after me.

Her room is a disaster. The whole flat looked like this when I moved in . . . Clothes up to your knees. Unopened mail in stacks. Teacups full of cigarette butts and ashed-out incense. I go for the closet.

"Baz, seriously, get out of my room!"

"Where is it, Fiona!" I'm throwing shit out of her closet. Shoeboxes. Tights. Cut flowers that have never wilted.

"It's still at Watford! I couldn't find it!"

"At Watford?" I look over my shoulder. Fiona has followed me into the room. "The tape recorder?"

She looks pissed off and confused. "The tape recorder? No—what tape recorder?"

I go back to her closet. Vials of oil. Boxes of herbs. Bras. A wand I've never seen before. A bong made out of a lamp. A lamp made out of a bong. She's pulling at the back of my shirt. I ignore her.

"What are you looking for, Baz!"

I wheel on her, pushing her off. "The tape recorder you gave me in fifth year!"

"Why would I give you a tape recorder? That's a shit gift."

Of course she doesn't remember. *Of course* she doesn't. "The one you gave me to steal Simon's voice!" I yell.

Fiona puts her hand on her forehead. "Ohhhhhhhhh, the *tape recorder*. Fuck, that took a lot of magic—and it didn't even work."

"It worked."

"Mmm." She clicks her tongue. "Don't think so. Your man was just here, and I heard him talk."

"It stole *a girl's* voice, remember? Philippa Stainton's."

"Philippa Stainton . . . She's not one of ours, is she?"

"FUCK!" I shout, kicking Fiona's bong. It shatters. "Just—where is it!"

She laughs. "Where's a tape recorder I gave you ten years ago?"

"It was five years ago."

"Well, I don't know, what did you do with it, Baz?"

"I gave it back to you, Fiona!"

She shrugs. "What was I supposed to do with some girl's voice?"

"Why . . ." I fall back against the wall, leaning over and holding my stomach. I think I'm going to be sick. "Why did you ever give it to me . . ."

"You know why—it was meant for Simon."

"I didn't know what it would do to him!"

"You knew we were at war!"

I look up at her. "He was *fifteen,* Fiona . . ."

"And the Mage was already using him against us!"

"*I* was fifteen, too!"

"Yeah, and you were five when they killed your mother!" She puts her hands on her hips and her tongue in her cheek and laughs one cold syllable: "*Hnnh.* Don't try to make me feel guilty about this . . . We were at war."

"I wasn't at war, I was at school."

"You wanted to help."

"I wanted to make you happy, I wanted to be a good Pitch! Whatever that means . . ."

"You know what it means, Basil. You always have, even when you were small. I could always trust you to keep an eye on the Mage."

"Fiona . . ." I'm holding my head now. "Anything I said when I was ten was just me parroting your words back to you. I wasn't being a good soldier or a good spy; I just wanted your attention!"

She shakes her head. "I don't feel bad about giving you that tape recorder; do you want me to feel bad?"

"Yes!" I stand up. "I stole an innocent girl's voice! She lost her magic!"

"Shit happens, Baz!"

"*I* happened, Fiona! *I'm* the shit!"

"Well, I'm not sorry!" she shouts.

"You should be!" I scream back. "I was a child, and you used me!"

"And it fucking *worked*—it was children who brought down the Mage!"

"It was *Simon* who brought down the Mage! And it wouldn't have happened if I'd stolen his voice . . ." I kick at a pile of clothes.

There's nothing here. Not for me.

I leave Fiona in her room.

Nico is still sitting on the sofa. He jerks to his feet when I come in.

I snort. As if I'm going to open that box right now, the one labelled, *My fuckup vampire-hunter aunt is hooking up with a vampire fuckup.* No, thank you. I have enough on my plate.

I'm not a child anymore.

Fiona doesn't get to tell me what it means to be a good Pitch.

I don't think I care.

61

PENELOPE

The tattoos are gone.

Shepard holds out his arms, and I run my fingertips up the inside of one forearm. They're gone.

"Penelope . . ." he says. "You did it."

I did it. Shepard isn't going to hell . . . At least not that version of it.

"Penelope!" Shepard sounds a little delirious. He picks me up and spins me around. "You did it!"

"I mean"—I hold on to his shoulders—"you did *help*."

"You're an absolute madwoman! You summoned a *demon* in your *living room*. You're an entire crazy train!"

I frown down at him. "I wouldn't say *crazy* . . . I had a plan."

"A crazy plan." He sets me down, still holding me. "What if it hadn't worked?"

"I was pretty sure it was going to work."

"Yeah, but it might not have . . ."

I shake his shoulders. "Stop second-guessing me, Shepard!

The proof is in the pudding."

"You're the most dangerous thing I've ever seen," he says, kissing me. "You're an F5, easily. Maybe an F6."

I let him kiss me. I like it when he kisses me. "We broke the curse . . ." I murmur.

"You broke the contract," he says.

"It was never valid."

He pulls away, grinning down at me. "Should I be hurt that you got me out of this by convincing that demon that I was more trouble than I'm worth?"

"I merely presented the facts."

He kisses me soundly, then starts laughing, purely from joy, I think. "I'll never be able to thank you enough for this."

"Don't thank me yet, Shepard."

"Why not?"

"Because I'm probably going to slay your friend Ken."

Once we've cleaned up the doorway and moved the sofa back, it's imperative that I talk to Simon.

I try to text him, but his phone is dead. (It only holds a charge for a few hours—he needs a new one.) "Come on, Shepard," I say.

Shepard's standing in the middle of the living room, looking down at his arms. "Where are we going?"

"To talk to Simon."

"I thought you didn't know where he was."

"Pfft. It's almost impossible to hide from someone you love."

Shepard pulls on his black-and-white shoes without unlacing them. He reaches for his denim jacket, but I catch his hand. He looks at the jacket, then laughs. I may never get over how good it feels to know I'm largely responsible for this.

There's a picture of me and Simon on the refrigerator. I hold my fist over it, cast **"Winter, spring, summer or fall!"**—and my gem starts tugging me out of the kitchen before I've even said his name.

We end up in another taxi—cabdrivers really hate taking directions like this—and a half hour later, we're in Hackney Wick. We get out at a terrace house that's been split into flats.

"I'm not getting into any more taxis with you unless you show me cash first," Shepard says, as we walk up to the house. There are two buzzers by the door. "Which apartment is it?"

"I'm not sure," I say. It's so strange to think of Simon living here, of him having his own place. Without me.

"Bunce, is that you? Are you all right?" Baz is coming up the walk behind us. His hair is dishevelled, and he looks like he's been weeping—his eyes are shadowed and shot with grey.

"I'm fine," I say. "What happened to you?"

"Me," he says. "Nothing. I'm good as new. Snow won't let you in?"

"I hadn't tried yet."

"Come on up, I have a key." Apparently he and Simon have patched things up. We follow him upstairs, and he lets us into the flat, switching on the light. "Simon? Are you home?"

Baz looks even worse under the light.

"Are you *certain* you're all right?" I ask him.

"I'm fine, Bunce. Snow will be home any minute, I'm sure. He was—"

There are footsteps on the staircase. All three of us turn to watch the door.

Simon comes in, looking even worse than Baz. Like he's just lost a fight with an ennuisel.

Baz rushes towards him. "Simon?"

Simon is staring at me. "Penelope?"

I rush towards him, too. "Simon, what's wrong?"

He doesn't answer me. He collapses in my arms instead.

I hold him. I think he's crying. Baz is standing over us, looking wretched and concerned. "Snow, what happened?"

"Nothing," Simon says, gulping. "Nothing happened. Just . . . I'm a fool."

Baz curls his lip. "Did Smith do this? What did he say to you?"

"Who's Smith?" I ask.

"You don't want to know," Baz says, at the same time that Simon says, "He's the new Chosen One."

"*Stevie Nicks and Gracie Slick.* I let the pair of you out of my sight for a week . . ."

There are brand-new dishes from Ikea sitting on the counter. I rinse off some mugs, while Baz tries to make tea without a kettle. He can't manage the spell. "You are *not* all right," I say to him. "And you're going to tell me why, as soon we have Simon sorted."

"So . . ." Baz rubs his eyes. "That's never, then."

"*Rosie Lee!*" I cast.

We take the tea out to Shepard and Simon. They're sitting on the floor in Simon's empty living room. Simon's leaning against the wall, wringing his hands in his hair.

"Here," Baz says, holding out a cup. "Drink."

"All right," I say, sitting next to Simon. "So there's a guy named Smith who claims to be the Greatest Mage . . ."

"It isn't just a claim, Penny—he's the real deal." Simon's being especially strident. "He has a spell to help people reach their full magickal potential."

I balk: "What does *that* mean?"

"Magickal power-ups." Baz sits down at Simon's other side. "Like Super Mario mushrooms. He's promised to turn my stepmother into Baba Yaga."

"Well," I say, "that can't be real." Baz's stepmum couldn't spell her way out of a wet paper bag.

"We've seen him cast it," Simon insists. "It works."

"Yeah, but . . ."

Simon huffs so hard he nearly spills his tea. "Why is this so difficult for you guys to accept? You all believed I was the Greatest Mage when I showed up out of nowhere!"

"You grew on us." Baz lays a hand on Simon's shoulder. "Snow—what happened tonight, after I left?"

Simon looks into his cup. "I went out for a pint. With Smith."

"With Smith," Baz repeats.

"And he . . . Well, he offered to fix my magic."

Baz shoves Simon's shoulder back, splashing his tea all over. "He *what*?"

"Great snakes," I say, mopping at my knees. "Could that work? Would you even *want* it to, Simon? He could fix you right back into Humdrum territory!"

"Which is why you said no," Baz says. "Correct?"

"I . . ." Simon looks at Baz's face, then at mine, then back at his lap. He sets down his half-empty cup. "It doesn't matter. It didn't work."

Baz is livid. I think his fangs may have popped. "Are you telling us he tried it?!"

I'm livid, too; I let Simon out of my sight for *a week*, and—"You allowed someone to cast an experimental spell on you!?"

"It doesn't matter!" Simon not-quite-shouts. He's tearful again. "It didn't do anything! I'm not a mage! Smith couldn't fix me because there's nothing to fix!"

That shuts us up for a minute. I look at Baz, and Baz looks at me. I'm not sure what we're trying to tell each other. Maybe just, *Well, fuck.*

I look back at Simon and try to be gentle. "How do you know? Have you tried casting a spell?"

"Yeah . . ."

"With whose wand?" Baz wants to know.

"With Smith's."

"With *Smith's.*" Baz is rubbing his forehead. "I'm going to eviscerate him."

Simon shakes his head. "Smith didn't do anything *wrong.* His spell didn't hurt me, Baz—it just confirms what I've known all along. I think I knew it even when I was full of magic. I'm a Normal. I'm nothing . . ."

As soon as he says it, his head jerks up to Shepard, who's been sitting quietly beside me. "Oh God, Shepard, I'm sorry, I didn't mean . . ." Simon's eyes get wide. He sits up straight. "Shepard . . . your tattoos!"

Shepard looks, for once, like he doesn't want to interfere. He smiles and holds out his arms. "Yeah," he says softly. "Gone."

"But what about the curse?"

"What curse?" Baz asks.

"Shepard's cursed," Simon says. "He made a deal with the devil."

"It wasn't exactly a *deal*—" Shepard says.

Baz looks offended. "Why didn't anyone tell me we brought home a cursed Normal?"

"It wasn't my secret to tell," Simon says. "I don't tell

anyone about *your* curse . . ."

"Everyone already knows about my curse," Baz says.

"I'm not cursed anymore." Shepard rests a hand on my shoulder. "Penelope fixed it."

Simon and Baz both turn to me.

"You fixed it . . ." Baz looks wary.

"How?" Simon asks.

"I'll explain later, it's really not that—"

Shepard literally leans in front of me to interrupt: "She summoned the demon and browbeat it into letting me off!"

"You did *what*?" Baz says, in the same tone he's been using on Simon for ten minutes.

"You should have seen her," Shepard says. "It was insane!"

"It wasn't insane," I correct. "I had a plan."

"It was more of a hunch," he says, "but it worked! She Matlocked this demon into submission. It was like watching someone play chess with Death."

"What's Matlock?" Simon asks.

Baz is still shocked. "You summoned a *demon*?"

"I executed a research-based plan," I say.

"She *summoned* a *demon*!" Shepard looks so proud, it's making me blush. "In her *living room*! And didn't even blink!"

Simon leans into me, knocking my shoulder with his. "That sounds like Penny."

"So no one is cursed . . ." Baz says.

"Just you, babe," Simon says.

Baz shakes his head. "We left you alone for a *week*, Bunce . . ."

Simon grins at Shepard. "This calls for a celebration! We need to celebrate."

The rest of us frown at him. "We don't need to celebrate,"

I say. "We need to get to the bottom of this spell that was cast on you."

"There's no bottom to get to." Simon is emphatic. "I'm already there. Smith cast a spell on me, it didn't work—end of story. Literal, actual end of story. I'm not a mage."

"Snow—" Baz chides.

"Seriously, can we focus on someone else for once?" Simon looks at Shepard. "Shep! You're not going to hell anymore! And you don't have to wear a jacket in the middle of June. Do you know how jealous I am?"

Shepard smiles at Simon. Baz and I are looking at each other cryptically again. I think we're agreeing not to let Simon change the subject like this . . . (We should really come up with some hand signals or something.)

"Perhaps Snow is right . . ." Baz says carefully.

I shake my head.

Baz goes on. "If you really outwitted a demon, Bunce, that's one for the history books." The corner of his mouth quirks up. It's very nearly fond.

I roll my eyes. "It wasn't that impressive."

"Balls to that," Simon says. "They're going to teach a class about you at Watford someday."

"To Penelope," Shepard says gently, holding his teacup in the air. "My hero."

Simon raises his cup. "Mine, too!"

"A very fierce magician," Baz says, toasting. "I don't mind saying."

My cheeks feel very warm. And my eyes are burning. This really isn't the time for this. "It was no trouble. I didn't even have to get out my gem."

62

BAZ

We celebrate by ordering pizza and listening to Penelope and Shepard argue about exactly how she managed to get him out of what was apparently a beastly awful engagement.

I'm not surprised that Bunce vanquished a demon with only a Normal for backup, but she still should have asked for our help. We definitely could have used hers. Keeping Snow out of trouble is a two-man job. I can't do it by myself—look what happened tonight.

What *did* happen?

Simon doesn't seem . . . materially damaged. But he was already emotionally compromised; the last thing he needed was the shiny new Chosen One kicking him while he was down.

What a feather that would have been in Smith-Richards's cap—if he'd patched up the old golden boy and paraded him in front of the entire World of Mages. What an endorsement.

Now no one will know that Smith-Richards failed. Only Simon, and *he* blames himself.

Thank magic Bunce came back when she did. Snow is soaking her up like sunshine. It's going to take them two weeks to catch up on the week they spent apart. After an hour or so, I excuse myself from the merry reunion to hunt. Simon attempts to come along, but I don't want to pull him away from Penelope. "Stay. I'll be right back."

I don't have to go far. Snow lives near a canal now, and the rats are abundant. I may even catch an otter. I decide to stuff myself while I'm out here. Sometimes, if I fill myself to the brim, I can skip hunting for a whole day. I can pretend I'm still human.

It doesn't *really* mean anything that Smith-Richards's spell failed . . . We don't even know what his spell does or how it works. This isn't conclusive proof that Simon was never a mage . . .

As much as he'd like that, I think. It would help him settle into this Normal life he's trying to build for himself. He's got me playing Normal, too. I've already stopped offering to cast spells around the flat.

Bunce hasn't got the memo yet. She's had her gem out every five minutes since she arrived. She tried to spell the pizza delivery person, but I insisted on paying. ("Thank God," Shepard said. "She's gone full Butch Cassidy this week.")

When I get back to Snow's flat—after seven rats and a badger—Bunce has spelled the floor soft and conjured up sleeping bags. "Penny and Shepard are staying over," Simon says. Shepard is already curled up in the corner sleeping the sleep of the recently uncursed.

"I think I'm going to bed," I say. "I'm clapped out."

"Oh, so you stay the night now . . ." Penelope teases.

I cock an eyebrow. "Oh, so you fraternize with Normals now . . ."

"I—"

"We're not blind, Bunce." She's been blushing at Shepard all night, and he's clearly had a crush on her since Colorado.

Simon grins. "Wait, really?" he whispers. "You and Shepard?"

Apparently, *I'm* not blind. I leave them to it. I take a quick shower, then spread Simon's new striped sheets on his bed. He's not in here to feel oppressed by my magic, so I cast a spell to quickly wash them. It takes me three tries. My hands are trembling, and I can't say the spell with any conviction . . . Maybe it's good that Simon doesn't want me casting spells in his flat. I'm too rattled to get one out.

I crawl into bed, pulling the sheet up over me.

I'm cold. And unpleasantly full. And I feel like there's a car parked on my chest.

Since we left America, I've been trying to decide what I'm culpable for . . .

I don't feel bad for killing the vampires who took Agatha. (They were a nasty bit of work, good riddance.)

But what about those vampires at the Renaissance Faire? I thought they were murderous—but at the time, I thought all vampires were murderous.

Were they really going to drain those women dry? Or were they merely going to tap them for a few pints, the way Lamb did to that man in the alley? And does the latter get a pass?

What if they were a group of bloodless friends enjoying a day out with their fully blooded girlfriends, sharing a consensual sip in the shade . . .

No, I don't think so. The girls screamed.

The point is—we killed those vampires without any sort of evaluation. We didn't hesitate. (Just like my mother didn't hesitate.) (Vampires are dead. They're *death*.)

Simon doesn't feel guilty about it; he's killed too many things to wear every soul around his neck like a stone. Penelope doesn't feel guilty; she'd raze all of Las Vegas if she had the chance. I don't know what I feel . . . I don't know what I'm *responsible* for, in America.

But I do know that I stole Philippa Stainton's voice.

She was just a girl, an innocent girl. And, yes, I was just a boy, but I was far less innocent—I knew I was carrying something dangerous that day.

I stole her voice.

And I stole her magic.

And I stole her life as a magician. That's on me.

And I can't *fix* it. I can't—I can't *breathe* under it. I don't know how to carry it. And it's only been a few hours. (For me. Years for her.) How am I going to get through the rest of my life feeling this way?

Simon comes into the bedroom after an hour or so, walking softly. He thinks I'm asleep. He pulls his Watford hoodie over his head and drops it on the floor. He isn't wearing anything underneath. He rolls out his bare shoulders, and his wings slowly loosen and unfurl, purplish black in the dark. He spreads them wide, arching his back, and lifting his chin to stretch his neck. He looks . . .

"Come to bed," I whisper.

He looks over at the bed, squinting. "I thought you were asleep."

"Not yet. Come to bed."

"Haven't showered yet."

"It's all right. It's your bed."

He unbuttons his jeans, still squinting at me. His eyes

aren't as good as mine in the dark. "Are you sure?"

I hold the sheet open for him.

He pushes his jeans down and kicks them away, climbing into the bed beside me. I bring the sheet back up over him, and he scoots closer, shifting a bit to get his wings settled behind him. He's warm, and he smells like a pub. Like cider and fish and a little like pizza.

I slide an arm around his waist. "Did you make up with Bunce? Has she moved in?"

He shrugs. He's still shifting and wriggling closer. "I apologized like you said I should."

"And?"

"And she said we don't need magic to be friends."

"Wise girl."

Simon brings a knee up over my thigh. "She said she only has two and a half friends, and she can't afford to lose any."

"Am I the half, or is Agatha?"

"You're both three-fourths."

"Fucking Bunce."

Simon touches my chin. "You smell good."

"Soap," I say.

"Where'd you go tonight?"

"Hunting."

"Before that."

I shudder, and he moves even closer, nose to nose, bringing a wing around us.

"Do you need a blanket?" he asks.

"I'm fine," I say. "Just stay close."

"Where'd you go, Baz?"

"I realized I'd left something at Fiona's . . ."

"What?"

I shake my head. "Can we talk about it tomorrow? I'm done in."

"Yeah." He brushes my hair away from my face. "I thought you were asleep."

I run my palm up his back and between his wings. He's so warm. He smells like blood, but I'm too sloshed for the smell to sting. "Did you feel anything when he cast the spell?" I don't feel like saying Smith-Richards's name right now, here.

Simon shrugs again. "I felt his magic. The way you do when someone casts a spell on you."

"What does his magic feel like?"

He nestles even closer, his chest rubbing against mine, through my T-shirt. "I'm so tired of magic," he says.

"Did it hurt?"

"No. It made me feel . . . full."

"Full?"

"Like I was a bubble popping."

I pull Simon in tighter. "I'm really angry with you for letting him cast that spell on you."

"You don't look angry."

"You can't see me."

"You smell good," he says again.

"It's soap. What spell did you try to cast? To test your magic?"

Simon twines his fingers in my hair. "I tried a few. It was humiliating."

"Which ones did you try?"

"I just said it was humiliating . . ."

"All right." I sigh. I'm wrung out. So is he. We can talk about this tomorrow. I'm glad to have tomorrow at least. I'm glad to be here tonight. It's just . . . "It's just . . . Simon, how do you *know* his spell didn't work?"

He makes a fist in my hair. "Because I felt it. I felt it not working."

SIMON

Smith's building was quiet. Everyone was still out celebrating his big announcement. He took me into his office, and we sat in two folding chairs, facing each other.

"What are you going to do first?" he asked. "When you get your magic back?" He was wearing a shirt the colour of his eyes, with a little scarf that made him look like he spent the day on a racing sailboat. Maybe he did.

"I don't know," I said. "I don't even have a wand anymore."

"I have an extra you can have."

"You have an extra wand?"

"I inherited my grandfather's—and both of my parents'. I use my mother's." He flicked his wrist, and his wand slid out of his sleeve into his palm. That's how Baz wears his wand sometimes; he has a holster that straps to his forearm. It's dead sexy when he takes off his shirt.

"Are you nervous?" Smith asked.

"Yeah," I said, "I suppose I don't want to let you down."

He laughed. "You won't let me down, Simon. This is about helping you. Are you ready?"

"Sure." I was as ready as I was going to get. "Yeah, Smith. Let's do it."

Smith sat a little straighter. He held out his left hand to

me, and I took it. (I'm not used to touching someone who's as warm as I am; he felt almost feverish.) Then he pointed his wand at my chest.

Even in that moment, I was telling myself not to get my hopes up, that the spell wouldn't work. But I'd *seen* Smith cure other people. I couldn't help but think it *might* work . . .

"Simon Snow," Smith said in his onstage voice, like I wasn't his only audience. "You've given so much to the World of Mages. Too much. It's time for you to step back into the light. *Let it all out!*"

I felt it right away. Smith's magic hit me at my core and then moved outward. It was like a bubble growing in me, filling me up, pushing against my skin, then popping.

He was smiling at me. "How do you feel?"

"I don't know . . ."

"Here." He handed me his wand. "Try a spell. Start with something simple."

"Um . . ." Was there anything simple? Was there a spell I could count on? I let go of him to shift the wand into my dominant hand. It was pale wood with some sort of stone inlaid in the handle. It looked like a pool cue.

I pointed the wand, and Smith laughed, moving my wrist, so that I was pointing out into the room and not directly at him.

"*Light of day!*" I cast. That was a spell I could usually cast before; it's one of the first spells they teach kids. Nothing happened. I tried another children's spell. "*Sparks fly!*" Nothing.

"Let's try . . ." Smith stood up and walked to his desk. He unlocked a drawer and pulled out a different wand, made of milky green glass. "This."

I traded him for it. It was heavy. "I've never seen a glass wand before."

"It was my father's. Now, take a deep breath, Simon. Remember that intention counts. And conviction."

I got to my feet and pointed the glass wand away from us. I tried to believe in it. In me. In Smith. I imagined the end of the wand lighting up like a candle. *"Light of day!"*

Nothing.

I took a deep breath. I held the wand more firmly. I pictured Baz back in Magic Words class, standing with his chin up and his shoulders back. I pictured every consonant as I pronounced them—*"Fire burn and cauldron bubble!"*

More nothing.

Right, I thought, *that's that. That settles it.*

Smith was rubbing his chin. "Let's try . . ."

"No," I said, turning the wand and holding the handle out to him. "It's not going to happen."

"Maybe you just need to get your confidence back—"

"No." *No, no, no.* I set the wand on his desk and ran my fingers through my hair. "It didn't work, Smith. I don't feel anything."

"Nothing?"

"Not a spark."

Smith was frowning. Thinking. "What did your magic used to feel like?"

"Like a forest fire," I said quickly. "Look, I'm sorry—"

"Let's try again, Simon."

"Smith, no—"

He was already pointing his wand at me. ***"Let it all out!"***

I didn't even feel the bubble popping the second time. I think Smith could feel the spell fail on his end, too. He looked down at his pool-cue wand, then let his arm drop to his side. "Simon . . . I'm sorry."

"It's all right, Smith." It would be all right. It *would.* I tried to smile at him, so he didn't feel bad. "Maybe this is useful. Now you know how it feels to cast the spell on a Normal."

Smith's face had completely fallen. He was in shock, I think. "I really believed you were a magician, Simon . . ."

"You weren't the only one."

"You gave yourself *wings* . . ."

"I should go." I started for the door.

"Wait—" He reached out to me. "We should talk."

I sighed. "No offence, Smith. But you don't have to comfort me. I've been living like this for more than a year. If anything, I should thank you. This confirms what I already suspected: I was never a magician. I don't need to be healed."

I was never a magician. Never magic.

I was just some kid the Mage picked out, with no family who could object. I think I must have been part of an experiment—like one of those swords the Mage tried to enchant. He used me. *He lied to me.*

I was never the Greatest Mage. I didn't belong at Watford. It was all a fluke. Worse than a fluke—a plot.

"Simon!"

I'd already left Smith's office at that point. I was walking out of the building, running down the steps to the street. Smith was standing up in the doorway, under the HOME FOR WAIFS sign. There was just enough light to make his eyes shine blue.

"Are you coming tomorrow," he asked, "to the meeting at Watford?"

Oh God, no . . . No.

"I'll try," I said.

"It would be great to see you, Simon. To have you there."

I nodded. Then I ran away from him. I ran all the way home.

Baz is rubbing the patch of real skin between my wings. I have extra bones in there. Even after Niamh cuts the wings off, I'll still have two lumps, empty sockets. There might be some nerve damage—Dr. Wellbelove is hoping it will respond to magic.

My bedroom gets pitch black at night. I can just barely see Baz's face, even though he's right in front of me. Even though we're chest to chest. My thigh is resting on his, and he's tucked his knee up between my legs.

I'm stroking his hair. It's still wet. He smells so good, and it isn't just soap—it's Baz. He smells cold and clean. Like running water. Like damp wood. He doesn't smell like anything living, but he doesn't smell like anything dead either. I'll never get enough of it. My lungs won't hold on to it—they betray me every time I exhale.

Baz scratches between my wings like he's scratching a dog between its ears. It sends a shiver down my spine. I try to move closer. Our chins bump.

"I'm done with Smith-Richards," I say.

"Good," Baz says. His voice is soft.

"But what will we tell Lady Ruth?"

"We'll talk about it tomorrow."

I nod. I'll worry about it tomorrow. All of it: Smith. Jamie. Me. The thing Baz isn't telling me.

The bed feels good. Feels clean. "I like these sheets."

"Me, too." Baz scratches my back. "Good job, Snow."

"I like finding you here," I say. Very quietly.

I can hear him breathing. "I could always be here," he says. Very, very quietly.

I nod my head again. Our noses bump. Baz works his left hand under my neck, pressing and holding me there. I want to kiss him—but I don't want to barrel through this moment. I think this might be a moment. And I don't want to knock over whatever it is we're building. Here in the dark.

"Baz . . ."

"Hmm."

"Is this what people do?"

"What do you mean, Snow?"

"I'm not sure . . ."

He tightens his grip on the back of my neck. His fingers are cold. My fingers are cold, too, in his wet hair. I bring my other hand up to his throat; it's cool. There's no warm place on him. If I dip my tongue into his mouth, it'll be cold there, too. If I want Baz warm, I have to do it myself.

I'll do it myself.

I kiss him, and he hums again.

I kiss his mouth open. Cool, cool.

"Mmm," he mmms.

I can still see him, even when I can't, even with my eyes closed—I know his face too well.

Is this what people do? Get as close as they can and then push closer? Burn each other's faces into their eyelids? Let each other into every gap? And then what? Then just tomorrow, and more?

I want something.

I don't know what I want.

I don't know what I'm supposed to take.

"Snow . . ." Baz's voice is soft.

I kiss him. I kiss him.

"Simon . . . just kiss me for now."

"All right. I am." I kiss him.

"Just kiss me for the sake of kissing me."

I kiss him. "Baz . . ."

"Mmm."

"I want my sheets to smell like you."

"I smell like you, Snow. I used your soap."

Between kisses: "You smell like a cave."

"That's romantic."

"You smell like a hidden waterfall."

"Better . . ."

"I can't get enough of you," I kiss.

"Just kiss me. Please . . ."

I kiss him. I push my chest into his. I knot my fingers in his hair—

"No," he whispers.

I pull my mouth away. "No?"

Baz rubs his nose into my cheek. His voice is barely there. "Be gentle with me . . . Even though you don't have to."

"I—" My hand goes slack in his hair. "Gentle?"

"Please, Snow."

I let some air between us. "Don't say 'please,' Baz."

"Why not?"

"Because you don't have to," I say. "You don't have to, I'll give you whatever you want." I stroke his Adam's apple with my thumb. I slowly move my other hand back through his hair. "Was I hurting you?"

"No . . ."

"You want me to be gentle?"

He nods his head.

"All the time?"

"Now."

I nod my head. I kiss him. Gentle. Gentle. For the sake of it. He smells so good. Like rushing water. Like something underground. (I found a hidden waterfall once. There was a key there. I took it.)

Baz holds the back of my neck. He presses his other hand between my wings and drags his fingertips down my spine. I kiss him. I kiss him. Like I'm lapping up water from a stream. *Is this what people do?* I'm gentle, I'm so gentle.

Baz holds me fast. He moves his body in a wave against mine, moves against me like a serpent. "Just kiss me," he says between kisses. "Mmm," he mmms between breaths.

Is this what people do? At night? In the dark?

I was never magic.

I hitch my knee higher on his hip. He pushes his palm down my back. I wrap my tail around his forearm, and I'm gentle. He isn't. And I am.

"Kiss me," he says.

I kiss him.

"Please," he says.

"Baz, don't—"

"Please . . ."

"I will." I do.

He doesn't have to beg. He never has to beg. I'll give him whatever he wants. Can't he see that, here in the dark—that I'll give him whatever he wants? My hand is gentle on his scalp, gentle on his throat. I couldn't break him if I tried. I won't try.

"Baz." I kiss him. "You can have whatever you want."

"I want to always be here."

"I want that, too. I love you."

He's moving against me in waves. I hitch my knee higher. He's wearing pyjamas. I'm wearing boxers. We're both hard. I'm being gentle, he isn't. I was never magic. He was human once. My fingers clench in his hair—

"*Simon*," he says, and it isn't good.

I let go.

"Simon . . ." he says. That's better.

My wings spread out of their own volition.

Baz. Like a wave, against me. Like a serpent moving through the sand. (The Humdrum sent a three-headed snake once—I chopped all three of them off.) I hold Baz's face in both my hands. Like he's made of glass. Like he'd break. He won't. I kiss him. And it's cool. I kiss him like he's cold water, and I'm drinking.

He wraps his palm around the base of my tail. He holds me by the neck. He rocks and rocks and rocks into me.

"Baz . . ."

"Please, Simon."

"You don't have to . . ."

Is this, is this, is this what people do?

Is this what he wants? Is this what I'm allowed to take?

He's rocking into me, and I need this to happen again someday in the light. I don't know what Baz's face looks like, like this, when he's coming undone. And I can't keep my eyes open anyway, when I'm coming against him.

Is this, is this, is this . . .

Is this magic?

Is this enough?

63

BAZ

Simon is breathing hard.

At some point he stopped kissing me, but his head is still resting on my face.

Is he okay? Was that okay? Are we okay?

I can't ask him, I don't want to say the wrong thing. So I lie very still and try to read his heavy breath, his dead weight. I'm still squeezing the blood out of the base of his tail, so I unclench my fingers one by one. The length of it slips away from my arm, uncoiling and falling onto the bed.

Is Simon okay?

I mean, obviously, no, never. The real question is—what kind of not-okay is he at the moment? And what do I need to do to deal with it?

Is he scared? Embarrassed? Overwhelmed? Did he even want that to happen? He's never been with a guy, maybe he didn't like it. Maybe it wasn't what he was expecting. It's messier than being with a girl. (Isn't it?) (I don't know anything about being with girls.) (I don't know anything about being with guys.) (I know a lot about furtively bashing one out while my roommate is off fighting magickal crime, then hoping he doesn't wonder why I'm taking a shower in the middle of the afternoon.)

Simon's still got both hands on my jaw and cheeks. His fingers have come to life a bit. Tensing. I can practically hear the gears turning in his head. (Never a good sign. His brain is an engine that only overheats.)

In a minute, maybe less, maybe in a second, the wind is going to change. We're deep in the minefield now, with no safe path out. My hand is still on the back of his neck. All I want is to ride this out. To show him we can keep getting through every sort of breakdown together. (Is that what this was? A breakdown? Is that how I'm going to have to file it away? Because that's going to kill me a little.) (A little more.) *Is Simon okay?* His fingers are awake on my face, gently stroking my cheeks. And he's lifted his head a bit.

"Baz?" His voice is all breath.

I've still got him by the back of the neck. I think of minefields. I think of those mechanical bulls. Are those real? We didn't see any in America. I squeeze his neck. I'm going to ride this out, we're going to—

"Baz? Are you okay?"

I . . .

I nod.

"You're still cold," he says, and he brings a wing over and around me.

"I'm fine. Are—Are you okay?"

He pets my cheek. His thumb ghosts over my bottom lip. "If you are."

I squeeze his neck. "That's not how it works, Snow."

"Isn't it?"

Is it?

He hasn't moved his leg. I haven't moved mine. We're slotted together and sticky. I put my arm around his waist, carefully, and flatten my hand against his back. I've been biting my lip. "I'm okay."

Simon kisses me. He's still being so gentle. Maybe I'll have to tell him that he can stop now. (Maybe I'll never tell him.)

"You're being quiet," he says.

"Only because you're kissing me."

"You're being *weird*."

"You're not . . ." I shake my head. Our lips brush. I shiver. He tightens his wing around me. "You're not freaking out."

"Did you want me to?" he asks. "It's probably not too late."

"No . . . I . . ."

Simon slides one hand down to the back of my neck, and wraps the other arm around me. He's mirroring me. He's gentling me. He whispers, "I don't know what you're thinking. I can't tell whether I should be embarrassed or sorry or . . ."

"Or what?"

His mouth is close to mine. "Happy?"

I close my eyes and let out a breath. "Is that on the table?"

"Baz . . . we kinda sorta had sex. And I didn't cry or break anything."

I laugh. It sounds wet.

"Babe . . ." he says. That's new. That's extraordinarily stupid. "Are *you* freaking out?"

I hold him a little tighter everywhere that I can. He does the same.

"I've never done that before," I say into his chin.

"I know."

"I think I probably did it wrong."

"There's not really a *wrong*—"

"I know that's not true, Snow."

He's nosing at my cheek. "Did something happen that you didn't want to happen?"

"No."

"Did you feel good?"

"Yes, obviously."

"Me, too. Hey—" He tries to find my eyes in the dark. His pupils are wide as saucers. "Me, too."

I swallow. "Yeah?"

"Yeah . . ." He kisses me. "So good, Baz."

I hear him say it. And I feel him say it. And I feel something in my stomach clenching around it. "I'm a mess," I say. "I should—"

"You should stay right here with me. It's not like you're gonna get a UTI . . ."

"A what?"

"Do you need to get up?"

I don't need to. I just—"No."

His arm goes snug around my middle. "Then stay . . ."

"All right."

He kisses my mouth. And then my chin. And my nose. And there's something easy about him that I'm not used to. That I didn't expect.

"Snow . . ."

"I kinda want to tell you that you have to call me 'Simon' when we're covered in spunk, but I don't think I actually care anymore."

I move my fingers up into the back of his hair until I find some long enough to tug. "Snow . . . *why* aren't you freaking out?"

He sighs. "Honestly?"

I pull his hair again.

"Because you told me what you wanted, Baz. I liked feeling like I was doing something for you."

"You weren't doing it for you?"

"No, I *was,* sort of in the background. Up front, I was doing something for you. I had a mission."

"A *mission* . . ."

"You're making it sound bad. It wasn't bad. It was good, the best it's been so far." He kisses me. "Don't make it bad."

Is that what I'm doing? Making it bad?

I'm lying in bed with Simon Snow. No—I'm lying in bed with Simon. With Snow. He's holding me. Kissing me. He said he loves me. He's trying out pet names. That's all I've ever wanted. How could I make this bad?

I tuck my head into the crook of his neck and shoulder, and let my arms move into a hug. "Simon . . ."

He hugs me back; he's taking all of his cues from me.

"It was so good," I whisper. It comes out as a concession, even though I meant it as a compliment.

He laughs a little, just enough to make his chest hitch. "Yeah," he says, like he's agreeing with me. "Next time will be even better."

"Next time you can do it for you."

"No way," he says. "We've finally figured this shit out—you're driving from now on."

"I wouldn't say we've figured anything out; we didn't even get undressed."

At that, he pushes away from me and manhandles me onto my back, straddling my thighs and scrabbling at the bottom of my T-shirt. He's laughing, so I laugh, too.

"A *mission* . . ." I say.

His wings are spread above us. Simon's chest is wider than mine and softer, and his pectoral muscles actually bulge—it used to be from all the sword work, but now I think it's the wings. His chest hair is so sparse, it looks accidental.

He gets my shirt off, then grabs my hands, holding them over my shoulders. "Next time we go to Ikea," he says, "we're getting a lamp. I can hardly see you."

"I could use my wand . . ."

"Keep it in your trousers, Merlin."

I laugh, genuinely. He laughs, too. It makes his wings flap.

"I love you," I say. I may as well say it, I'm thinking it. It's all I ever think. I'm an *"I love you"* gun with the safety off, a finger constantly on the trigger.

Simon lets go of my hands and settles down on top of me, his head on one of my shoulders, his hand on the other, his fingertips gently drawing circles. "I love you," he says. "It's good."

I wake up to someone knocking on Snow's bedroom door.

"Baz? Are you in there?" It's Penelope. She's whisper-shouting.

"Yeah," I say. My voice is rough. I try again. "Yes."

"Your aunt is here."

"*What?*"

The door opens a crack. "Your aunt Fiona," Penelope hisses.

Fiona. What is Fiona doing here?

I climb over Simon, sticking a knee in his wing. He groans, rubbing his face. His bedroom is dark, even at—I check my phone—10 A.M. Fuck. Where's my shirt? Where's my *wand*? There it is. I point it at myself. ***"Clean as a whistle!"*** (Uch. I despise "Clean as a whistle." Now I feel grimy and metallic all over.) Where is my *shirt* . . .

"Basil!" someone shouts. That is definitely my aunt.

"For fuck's sake, Fiona," I mutter.

"Fiona?" Simon croaks.

"I'll be right back," I say, grabbing one of his hoodies off the floor.

I walk through the living room, where Shepard seems to be eating a dozen Pret a Manger sandwiches. Bunce is at the front door, frowning at my aunt, who's standing just inside the threshold. Fiona waves her fingers at me. "Good morning, Nephew. I'm taking you to get a cuppa."

"How did you even find me here?"

"I found you when you were buried under a bridge in a numpty den—did you think you could hide from me in Hackney Wick? Come on." She looks serious. "I'll bring you back soon."

"All right," I say, glancing back at Bunce and nodding like, *It's fine, I'll be fine.*

As soon as the door is shut behind us, Fiona smirks. "You live in some sort of unfurnished commune now?"

"Are we really having tea, or do you need me for a crime? I can't be your getaway driver if you won't let me sit up front."

"We're really having tea," she says. "There's a café up the street."

There is. I let Fiona buy me tea and banana cake. We find a table, and she casts a spell so no one can hear us talk. I haven't said anything yet.

"I know you want me to apologize . . ." she says, pushing

her hair behind one ear. "And I don't think I can."

Colour me surprised. Why am I even here . . .

Fiona holds her paper cup in both hands and frowns down on it. Her hair falls back over her eyes. My aunt's hair is the same colour as mine, nearly black, with a skunk stripe at one temple—I'm not sure if it's natural or if she did it with magic to look cool. She's normally wearing too much eyeliner and bright red lipstick, but not today. She looks tired without it. And less sure of herself.

"When your mum died . . ." Fiona shakes her head, then looks up at me, her eyes shining. "Your mum was the better of us, she always was. She was clearly our dad's favourite"— she huffs a laugh through her nose—"and it didn't even bother me, because she was my favourite, too. She was just so *class,* Basil. Smart, powerful . . .

"She always *did* the right thing, and she always *said* the right thing. The only time she ever pissed off our parents was when she married your dad—a lowly Grimm!—but that turned out to be the right thing, too."

Fiona smiles at me, the very picture of rueful. "Do you even know how cool that was? That Natasha married badly, for love, and then proved to the whole World of Mages that she and Malcolm could be unstoppable together?"

I didn't know that. I pick at my banana cake.

"And then she had *you,*" Fiona goes on. "And you were exactly the sort of child your mother *would* have—Crowley, you were such a charmer. Curious and headstrong and thoughtful. So thoughtful, even as a toddler. I remember looking at you and thinking, *Well, of course Natasha has had the best possible baby. Isn't that just like her?*

"She was so good at *everything* that I had to go all the

way to China to get out from under her shadow . . ." Fiona looks down at her tea and laughs again. Her eyes are brimming. "I suppose it did bother me sometimes."

She bites both her lips and looks lost for a moment.

"When your mum died . . ." she says again. She wrinkles her nose, shaking her head. "I knew that I'd never be able to replace her. No one would."

She looks up at me, wiping one eye with her thumb and the other with her knuckle.

"You had the *best* mum, Baz—you *lost* the best mum—and I knew that your dad and I would never make up for it." She smiles, her lips tight and twitching and trying to turn down. "But we had to *try*, right?

"When I hear you tell me what a shit aunt I've been, I think, *Well, yeah, I've always been shit compared to Natasha.* If she were here, she would have done a much better job with you!

"But she isn't here." Fiona's voice breaks. A tear slides down her cheek. "She isn't here," she says more softly.

"And I'm not sorry that I tried to be . . ."

I look down at my tea and wipe my eyes on Snow's sleeve. "I'm not sorry either," I whisper.

Fiona sniffs. She blows her nose into a napkin. "All right," she says, sounding more like her cock-of-the-walk self. She leans over and picks up her handbag, a giant, black leather thing with fringe. She opens the flap, and takes out a vintage tape recorder. She sets it on the table between us. "Found this under my bed."

I sit up straight and reach for it. "Is that—"

"That's it, all right. Don't push any buttons until you find the girl."

I pull my hands back. "Is there a spell?"

Fiona shakes her head. "The original spell should still be working. 'Caught on tape.'"

"Fuck, that's savage."

"It was a real chore finding someone who could cast it."

"So I just take this to Philippa and . . ."

"Push play."

I can't believe Fiona has had this under her bed for years . . .

No. I can believe it.

I gingerly lift the tape recorder off the table and look up into my aunt's eyes. They're brown. My mother's were grey, like mine. "Thank you," I say.

"Nah, don't thank me. I mean, really, considering the circumstances." She reaches over and takes a chunk out of my banana cake, narrowing her eyes at my chest. "'Watford Netball'? Do boys play netball at Watford now, or are you shacking up with a bird?"

I look down. Fucking Snow. Did he steal every one of Agatha's school jumpers?

"I have to get going." Fiona is standing up, brushing crumbs off her T-shirt.

I stand up, too.

She ruffles the top of my hair. "I won't let out your room right away . . ."

"Fiona . . ."

"Seriously, Baz, don't thank me. I already feel like a twat."

"What were you looking for that day at Watford?"

She looks at me for a second, then rubs her face with both hands and sighs. "I was looking for my mother's wedding ring. Your mum used to wear it, on her pinkie. I didn't figure she'd miss it now."

"A wedding ring . . ."

Fiona folds her arms, like she's ready for me to lay into her, and she doesn't fucking care.

I do just that: "Are you serious? You're marrying that sleazy Kurt Cobain wannabe?"

"That's not how I'd describe him . . ."

"His name was stricken from the Book, Fiona!"

"Well." She shrugs with both arms. "I'm not the Book, am I."

"You called him a 'two-bit gangster.' You said he was shitty, even for a vampire!"

"I was angry," she says. "But the truth is . . . he makes me happy. He always did." She huffs. "Are you going to turn me in?"

"Does he still drink people?"

"No . . ." She rocks her head from side to side, like she's equivocating. "Not in the traditional sense."

"Are you going to let him Turn you?"

"Are you fucking kidding me? Your mother would roll over in her grave!" As soon as she says it, she winces at me. "Don't worry," she says gently. "I'm not going to cop your look."

"This is outrageous, Fiona, even for you. Is it happening soon?"

Her hands are on her hips. She looks like she's trying to decide whether to be honest with me. "Yeah," she says, after a moment. "I think so."

"Well . . ." I shake my head and roll my eyes, giving in. "I won't tell anyone."

"Thanks, Basil."

"I can't believe you tried to rob my mother's grave!"

"Ah, she wouldn't have missed it! The ring wasn't there, anyway. Or at least I couldn't find it. Not in her rooms, either."

I make one last appeal: "I know I didn't know her, but I really don't think my mother would want you to marry Nico."

"I'm sure she wouldn't. But she isn't here, Baz. My mum and dad are gone, too. And I can't—We've got to make decisions for the living. You know?"

I do.

When I get back to Snow's flat, the new sofa has been delivered, and the three of them are christening it with sandwich crumbs.

Simon smiles at me. His hair is wet. "Shepard got breakfast. We saved you some."

I shake my head. "I have to go . . . do something."

"But you just got back."

"I know," I say. I can't talk to Snow about this. It's too much. "But I have something else now. To do. I just came back for my phone, and—"

"Great snakes!" Bunce exclaims. "That's the tape recorder, isn't it?"

I look up at her, speechless. *Fucking Bunce.*

"What tape recorder?" Snow asks.

She turns to him and points her thumb at me. "Don't you remember when Baz attacked you with a tape recorder? Fifth year. Out on the Lawn."

"Shit," Simon says to me. "That's it! The one you used on Philippa." He's on his feet, reaching for it.

"Simon, no!" I shout. "Don't touch it!"

64

SIMON

The tape recorder is sitting on the floor, where my coffee table would be if I had one. Baz is on the sofa, looking somehow paler than usual. I'm rubbing his back. I can't stop touching him, to be honest, even though this definitely isn't the time.

"But you *didn't* steal Philippa's voice," Penny says. She's sitting on his other side. Shepard moved to the arm of the sofa to make room. "Miss Possibelf said it would come back."

I nod. "The Mage said so, too."

"Right," Baz says, kneading his forehead, "the Mage *definitely, always* told you the truth. Philippa never got her voice back! She's living in Smith's compound, waiting for him to fix her."

"You saw her?" Penny asks.

"*Yes.*" He looks at me. "We both did—the girl who answered the door, the one who doesn't talk."

"The cute one? With the short hair?"

Baz groans.

"I thought her name was Pippa," I say.

"Philippa still can't talk?" Penelope's appalled. "Oh, that's awful. That means her magic never came back."

"Yeah, I *know*," Baz says, like he's in pain.

"Wait," Shepard says to Penny, "you can't do magic if you can't *talk*?"

"Well, you can't go to Watford," she explains. "In the old days, you couldn't even get in with a stutter."

Shepard shakes his head. "There must be magicians who do magic without speaking . . ."

"I've heard it's possible. I'm surprised *you* don't know a whole crew of them."

Baz is back to holding his head.

"Maybe Smith can help Philippa," I say.

Baz hisses and stands up. "*I* can help her." He looks down at the tape recorder. "Fiona never took out the tape."

I look at it, too. It's got to be older than we are. "So Philippa's magic is right there?"

"Her voice is." He swallows. "I'm going to give it back to her—and then I'm going to let her spell me into oblivion."

I stand up and take his arm. "Well, I'm not letting her spell you into anything."

Penelope stands, too. "Me neither."

"We'll have to hurry," I say, "if we want to catch Philippa before she leaves for Smith's meeting at Watford."

"'We'?" Baz pulls away from me. "There's no 'we.' You're not all coming."

"I can stay here," Shepard offers.

Penelope frowns at him. "Oh no, I'm not letting anyone in this room out of my sight, ever again."

"You know what? Fine. I don't care anymore." Baz leans

over and lifts the tape recorder with both hands, cradling it like it's a porcelain egg. "Let's just go."

He looks beaten. He's standing there with his hair all matted down on one side, wearing a Watford hoodie I never gave back to Agatha and his "Clean as a whistle"-d pyjama trousers.

I clear my throat. "Don't you want to, um . . . change?"

Baz looks down at himself and groans again.

Apparently this is another occasion that calls for a suit. Three pieces. A shade of brown that gleams red in the light. Baz buttons his white shirt all the way to the top, and puts on a shiny purple tie. (Why did he bring neckties and three-piece suits to my flat? What was he anticipating?) Then he dumps an entire duffel bag full of shoes onto the floor.

"Should we talk about this?" I ask.

"No." He lays the bag on my bed and carefully sets the tape recorder inside.

I keep trying: "We're about to do something huge; shouldn't we talk about it?"

"Who are you, and what have you done with Simon Snow?" He flicks his wrist, and his wand slides into his palm—he's wearing his holster. He points at the tape recorder. ***"Safe as houses!"***

I touch his arm. "Baz . . ."

He turns on me, eyes flashing. "*Simon.* She hasn't had magic. For five years. And it's my fault. I can't talk until I fix this. I can't even *breathe* . . . All right?"

I take in his wild eyes, his bloodless fists. "Yeah," I say. "All right." I squeeze his arm. "Let's go, then. Let's fix it."

I'm wearing a T-shirt with slits down the back for my

wings. I pick the Watford hoodie up from the floor. "It's too hot for this," I say. "Just hide the wings, would you?"

Baz has the duffel bag slung over his shoulder. "With a spell?"

"Yeah. I'm tired of wearing hoodies and trench coats, and it's not like I'm gonna fly to Camden . . ."

"All right," Baz says softly. He snaps his wrist, then aims his wand at my wings. ***"Now you see it, now you don't!"***

Baz's magic is hot, it normally burns a little bit . . . But not today. I don't feel anything. I glance over my shoulder—my wings are still there.

Baz frowns. He points his wand again. ***"There's nothing to see here!"***

Nothing happens.

"Sorry," he says. "I've been upset. My magic is . . . We'll have Bunce do it." He's already walking into the living room. "Penelope—"

Penny and Shepard are leaning against the living room wall, kissing. (I kind of feel like I've been cockblocking Penny all these years. As soon as I left her alone, *this* happened.)

"Spell Simon's wings away," Baz says.

She kicks away from the wall. "I thought we weren't doing that anymore."

"I changed my mind," I say. "It's too hot to hide them."

Penny fishes her purple gem out of her bra (we need to fix that ring) and holds it out to me. ***"There's nothing to see here!"***

Nothing happens.

Penny frowns. "Did you already try, Baz?"

"Yeah, I'm too upset to cast."

"Is that a thing?" she asks. "Maybe Simon moved to a dead spot." She points her fist towards the sandwich wrappers. **"A place for everything, and everything in its place!"** The trash disappears. "Hmmm . . ." She points at me again. **"Now you see it, now you don't!"**

Nothing happens.

Baz shoots his wand into his hand and points at my new sofa. **"Tickled pink!"** The sofa turns pink.

"Hey . . ." I say.

Baz points at me. **"Clean as a whistle!** Did that do anything?"

"I don't know," I say. "I was already clean. Should I feel dirtier?"

Penny has stepped closer to me. Her fist is still out. **"Float like a butterfly!"**

My feet stay on the ground. "Hey, you guys, slow down . . ."

"Roses are red!" Baz shouts.

Then Penny—**"Violets are blue!"**

Baz—**"Cat nap!"**

Penny—**"Cat got your tongue!"**

"For fuck's sake!" I grab her wrist.

"Simon . . ." she says. Her glasses have slid down her nose. Her eyes are huge. "I think you might be immune to magic."

Penelope makes me sit down. Like I'm experiencing a shock. I suppose I am—what does it even *mean* to be immune to magic?

She sits down next to me, rubbing her chin and staring at my wings. "It's got to be that spell he cast on you . . ."

Baz is pacing. "I'm going to murder Smith-Richards. I'm

already going to jail for Philippa's voice. I may as well add this to my crimes."

"Smith didn't know this would happen," I say. "Oh God—we have to tell him."

"Fuck *Smith*," Baz says. "He shouldn't be casting spells on people if he doesn't know how they'll work!"

"The spell works on magicians! He thought I was one!" I lean back on the sofa and fold my arms over my eyes. "I can't believe this . . . I'll never be able to hide my wings again."

Penelope pats my leg. "You're having them removed anyway."

Baz huffs. "Not helpful, Bunce."

"You're right, I'm sorry." She pulls my arms away from my face. "I'm sure it will wear off, Simon. I've never heard of a permanent shield. Even temporary shields are notoriously hard to cast."

"Do you think that spell would have the same effect on any Normal?" Shepard asks. He's been sitting quietly at the other end of the sofa, leaving us to it.

Penelope twists around to shout at him. "Oh my words, Shepard, I'm not letting you anywhere near that man!"

"I'm just saying, your mom spelled me unconscious five minutes after she met me . . . I wouldn't mind a shield."

Baz stops pacing in front of me. He looks agitated. "Simon . . . love, I'm sorry. I know this is serious. But I have to catch Philippa before she leaves. I just . . ." He shakes his head half a dozen times and hitches the bag higher on his shoulder.

"You're right." I stand up. "I'll get a coat."

"No—you don't have to come. Especially not now."

"Baz, I'm coming. This doesn't really change anything,

even if I am immune to magic or whatever. When was the last time you guys cast a spell on me that wasn't just to hide my wings?"

"We're coming, too," Penelope says. "I'm not letting you fall on your sword for this, Baz."

Baz looks frustrated. He's licking his bottom lip. "Neither of you are treating this situation with the gravity it deserves." He glares at us. "I've done something really bad, and you're just shrugging it off!"

"We're not shrugging it off," I say. "We're coming with you."

Penelope looks unimpressed. "Do you want us to say that you're bad? Fine, you're very bad."

"That's not—"

She rolls her eyes. "You did something unconscionable because an adult you trusted said it would matter. Join the fucking club, Basilton."

"You're not in this club, Bunce."

"No, but Simon is, and I was right there cheering him on, casting every spell I could to help."

Baz holds his bag out. "I was trying to *hurt* Simon with this thing." His voice is high and desperate. "Shouldn't you be angry about this?"

Penny folds her arms. "I don't believe you wanted to hurt Simon. I've never believed that."

It's true, she didn't. Even when I was the one trying to convince her.

"Why *not*?" Baz demands.

"Because if you wanted to hurt him, you would have! You had infinite opportunities! You've never cast a dangerous spell on him, Basil. At the height of the Mage's war with the

Old Families, you were tying Simon's shoelaces together and getting in shoving matches."

"I pushed him down the *stairs*!" he says.

"I always thought that was an accident," I say softly.

Baz wheels on me. "Are you fucking serious? You never shut up about it!"

I touch his arm. "I'm sorry."

Baz's grey eyes are wide and shining. He looks completely miserable. "I tried to take your magic, Snow! Your voice! It was supposed to be you!"

This is the confession I always wanted from him, and now that I have it, I just want to tell him that it doesn't matter. I lived. I lost my magic anyway. But at least now I have *him*. I know it wasn't a direct trade-off, but I still feel like I got the better end of the deal.

I touch his cheek. "I forgive you."

He just barely shakes his head. "How could you, Snow?"

I push my lips together. I shrug. "I just do . . ." I stroke his cheek. "Do you forgive me? For everything?"

He stares down at me, his mouth twisted to one side. "Yeah. I do."

We just look at each other for a minute.

"It *was* an accident," he says quietly, "when I pushed you down the stairs."

"I know," I say. "I always kind of figured."

"You fucking menace," he whispers. "You literally never shut up about it."

I rub my thumb along his cheekbone. "Let's go help Philippa," I say. "Yeah?"

Baz nods. He looks smaller than he did a minute ago. "Yeah."

65

AGATHA

It's a Saturday, so the clinic is only open for the morning. I haven't seen Niamh, and Dad's kept me so busy I haven't been able to look for her. She said she was going to check on the goats again today. What if the pregnant doe went into labour last night? Niamh didn't think the goat was *that* close, but it could have been. Did Niamh leave for Watford without me?

"Is Niamh in today?" I ask the receptionist when I get a chance.

"James Dean?" the receptionist says. "Just showed up. Not sure why. She didn't have any patients today."

I walk back towards the exam rooms, poking my head in every open door.

"Agatha?"

I spin around . . .

Niamh is standing in the hall behind me. *Not* dressed for the office. She's wearing jeans cuffed high over brown work boots, and a green T-shirt that clings to her shoulders and breasts. And . . . well . . . *and* . . .

She's cut her hair.

And combed it back.

Like she did at school. When she was Brody. (She's still Brody . . .) (Has been all along, I suppose.)

Niamh cut her hair the way I suggested.

Which means . . .

Well, it means that she knows good advice when she hears it.

Good for her. Good for Niamh. With her whole . . . face situation. The nose and the, um . . . chin, like a hatchet. The everything like a hatchet. Sharp. And heavy. I think she blow-dried her hair. Good for *her*. That's good. This whole . . . *thing* is good for her.

"I'm leaving," she says. She looks angry—which never means anything useful with Niamh, but it's honestly still a good look on her.

"You're . . ." I already feel ten steps behind this conversation. "What?"

"Are you coming or not?"

"Where?"

"To Watford? To check on the goats?"

"To *Watford*," I say, catching up. "To check on the *goats*."

Niamh frowns at me.

"Yes—Yes, I'm coming. I told you I wanted to help."

Niamh frowns even harder. Like she's really putting her back into it. "Well, I'm leaving now."

"Then let's go."

My dad needed his Volvo today, so we're back in Niamh's sti-

fling Ford Fiesta, with the windows down. We have to shout
to be heard over the wind. Well, I'm shouting. Niamh largely
ignores me. Are we back to this then, not talking?

We talked last night, *plenty*—until the pub closed.

Niamh told me about veterinary school. (She likes it.) And
living in London. (She doesn't.) About what she's learned
from my dad, and how she wants to start her own practice,
and how she's going to run for the Coven someday. Niamh
has a lot of opinions about how things should be done. And
what's practical.

I have zero opinions like that.

But I liked listening to Niamh's opinions and telling her
when they sounded impossible. (Less often than one might
expect.)

I laughed the whole night. At Niamh. And her straight-faced
opinions and strange pronouncements. At the way she lets the
whole world get under her skin. I never laugh that much.

Niamh never laughs at all, apparently, but I still think
she had a good time. She kept sitting there with me, when
she could have asked me to take her home. Morgana knows
Niamh wouldn't spend a minute in anyone's company just to
be polite.

We turn off the main road onto the sleepy little lane that
leads to Watford, leaving the noise and traffic behind us.

"I was right about your hair," I say, to break the silence.
And also to punish Niamh for the silence, I suppose.

"It's none of your business," she replies.

"And yet, you *did* get the haircut I suggested . . ."

"I've had this haircut before, Agatha."

". . . *and* I was right about it."

She pulls her eyebrows down so far that they disappear

behind her sunglasses. "Is it important for you to be right?"

"Not usually. But about hair, yes."

"It's more practical to wear it this way," she says.

"And it looks much better."

She shrugs.

"Hell's spells," I say, "you could just say 'thank you'! 'Thank you for the compliment and the good advice'!"

Niamh is squinting at the road. A lock of her hair has fallen onto her forehead. It's intolerable. She's intolerable. "I thanked the person who cut it," she says.

The road outside Watford is lined with cars. Dozens of them. "What's going on here today?" I ask.

Niamh parks the Fiesta in the grass. "Some sort of 'Chosen One' thing," she says, getting out.

I climb out after her. "What Chosen One?"

"The new Greatest Mage . . ."

"There's a new Greatest Mage?"

"Purportedly." Niamh is getting her gear out of the back of the car. She looks irritated.

"You're not convinced?"

She slings a bag around her neck. "I'm convinced that most magicians would rather let some mystical saviour solve their problems than do any work."

"How can there just be a new Chosen One all of a sudden . . . Do we get to vote on this? We should get to vote on this."

Niamh harrumphs and swings the hatchback closed. "There's no voting. It's prophecy."

"It's dogshit," I say, falling into step beside her.

"I thought you were just now hearing about it."

"I've heard enough about the Chosen One for ten life-times. It's *all* dogshit."

When we get to the Watford gates, they're hanging open. I can't remember them being open before. They usually swing shut on their own with a heavy clang. We walk through, and I close them behind us.

Niamh is carrying more supplies than usual, just in case the doe is in labour. I try to help, but she shrugs me off.

I've been reading about goat birthing online—it would be better if we could get the doe into a barn. Maybe Niamh has a plan. "Have you ever delivered a goat before?"

"No," she says. "But I've delivered a cow. And several dogs. And a gryphon."

"You did say you wanted variety . . ."

"I've also delivered a baby."

"What kind of baby?"

"A human baby. A magician."

"Well," I say, "aren't you useful."

"I'd be more useful if I had wings."

I frown at her. She's looking straight ahead.

"What does that mean?" I ask.

"It means . . ." She sighs. "It would be nice to have your—to have Simon here, to help us find the goats again."

"We don't need Simon," I say, striding purposefully ahead of her. "I think the goats are this way."

"You think?"

"I have a feeling about it."

"A feeling," she says.

"You don't have to follow me, Niamh. You don't have to listen to *any* of my suggestions."

I keep walking.

When I glance over my shoulder, Niamh is a few steps behind me.

66

PENELOPE

The new Chosen One has set up shop in old orphanage, apparently. We're standing under a sign that says HOME FOR WAIFS.

"Well, that's dramatic," I say.

"Wait till you see him," Baz mutters.

Baz has been hammering on the door with a brass knocker far past the point of politeness. There's no sign of anyone coming to answer it.

"Maybe everyone's already left for Watford," Simon says, trying to look in a window.

Baz drops the knocker in disgust. "Or maybe Philippa went home. Or out for brunch. Or to the moon. She could be anywhere."

"We could track her," I say.

Baz lowers an eyebrow. "How? We don't know her, we don't have anything that belongs to her . . ."

"We have her magic." I fish out my gem.

"Bunce, wait—"

My hand is already over Baz's duffel. ***"Find your way home!"***

The bag jerks away from his body. "Seven snakes!" he says. "What if you erased the tape?"

"I didn't erase anything. The spell worked—now follow it."

His bag bumps against the door.

"She must still be inside . . ." Simon cups his hands around his mouth and leans against the window. "Philippa!"

"She goes by Pippa now," Baz says.

"Pippa!" Simon shouts.

Baz's bag knocks harder against the door. He secures it to his chest with one hand and bangs on the door with the other.

"Honestly. Are you a mage or a mouse?" I hold my gem over the lock. ***"Open Sesame!"***

"Now she's breaking and entering," Shepard sighs.

"I didn't break anything," I say, shouldering Baz out of the way and opening the door. I step inside. "Hello? Is anyone here?"

My voice echoes. The foyer is empty, and it smells old, the kind of old you can never air out. There's a staircase leading to the next floor. I crane my head to look up.

The rest of them have come in behind me. Shepard moves to my left side and takes my hand. I like that he knows to leave my right free for casting.

"Hello?" Simon calls up the stairs. "Pippa?"

I turn to Baz. "Which way is your bag pulling?"

"I can't tell." He's frowning down at the bag, letting it float away from his chest. "Forward, I think, but also possibly—" His head jerks up, eyes sharp.

The rest of us go still, listening. There are footsteps some-where deeper in the building. A door creaking.

"Philippa?" Simon says, too soft for anyone but us to hear him.

"Come on," I say, pushing Baz forward. "Let her magic lead."

He lets go of the duffel, and it tugs him towards a door at the back of the foyer. Baz opens it, and the rest of us follow him into an abandoned hallway. We hear more footsteps . . . somewhere. I nudge him to move faster.

"Philippa?" Simon calls, more boldly.

"Hush," Baz says.

"Why?"

"Because we're trespassing now. If they wanted to let us in, they would have answered the door."

"Well, they've already heard us."

"Hush, Snow."

The duffel bag leads us past closed rooms and empty hall-ways, up to a wide swinging door. Baz has his wand out. I hold up my gem and push Shepard behind me.

Baz shoves the door open, and we both rush through, ready to cast.

We find ourselves in a big institutional kitchen—long wooden tables, ancient brown wallpaper, tiled floor. The room is empty, but there's a kettle heating on the stove. Baz lurches forward, the strap of his bag pulling at his neck. He leans over, trying to get his arms around it again.

"Are you okay?" Simon asks.

"I'm fine, Snow."

Shepard leans closer to me and whispers, "Is that Def Leppard?"

"What's deaf leopard?" I whisper back.

"Listen."

There's music playing. Somewhere close.

"*Ungh.*" Baz is struggling with the duffel now, scrabbling to get the strap off from around his neck. The bag looks like it's trying to pin him to the floor.

"Nicks and Slick!" I say, holding out my fist.

"I've got it," Simon says, grabbing the strap from behind.

"It's trying to get—" Baz drops to his knees. Simon is standing over him, pulling the strap with both hands away from the back of Baz's neck. The bag thumps to the floor, and the strap sags enough for Baz to slip free.

We all stare at it.

"The basement!" Shepard says. "There must be a—"
Right, of course.

It takes both Baz and Simon to lift the duffel bag off the floor. Baz wraps both arms around it and rushes back through the swinging door. "Come on!"

We run out of the kitchen, trying every door in the hallway. Some of them are locked. "Any of these could lead to stairs," I say.

"Here!" Simon's already at the end of the hall, shaking a door by its knob. "Listen. It's that music—"

" 'Pour Some Sugar on Me,' " Shepard says.

I frown at him. "*What?*"

"Come on, Penny," Simon says, rattling the door. " 'Open Sesame!' "

I catch up with him and hold out my fist. **"*Open Sesame!*"** The door swings open in Simon's hand. The music gets louder. It *is* a stairwell.

"Me first," I say. "I have magic."

"So?" Simon says, running ahead of me down the stairs.

"Simon!"

The music is thundering down here—and terrible, some old hard rock music from when my parents were kids. I glance over my shoulder to make sure Baz is still with us. He's coming down the stairs behind me, leaning way back so that the bag won't pull him into a dive.

"Is this where it wants to go?" I ask.

"I think so. It mostly just wants to get away from me. Keep up with Snow."

I nod and hurry down the stairs, pulling Shepard along with me. We end up in another hallway. Dark. Old. Walls of crumbling brick. We follow the music and find Simon standing outside another locked door, trying to muscle it open.

"Penelope!"

Morgana below, has anyone ever cast so many "Open Sesame"s? I hold my gem over the lock, and do it again. Simon wrenches the door open, and the music is suddenly unbearably loud.

There's a middle-aged white man inside the room, drinking tea and watching television. He's got stringy blond hair and a patchy beard. He fumbles for the remote. "Sorry! I thought everyone was—" He stops fumbling and stares at Simon. "Is that—Are you—*Simon Snow!?*"

Simon is staring back. "*Jamie?!*"

67

BAZ

Jamie Salisbury has been locked in a basement, listening to hair metal. He looks hale enough. He was sitting in an armchair, drinking tea when we barged in. Now he's standing and staring at Simon.

"How do you know who I am?!" Salisbury shouts over the music.

"We were looking for you!" Simon shouts back.

Shepard walks past them and picks the TV remote up off the floor. He turns the music down.

Salisbury looks at the TV, then back at Simon. "Why is *Simon Snow* looking for *me*?"

"Because your mum is worried about you," Simon says.

"My mum knows Simon Snow?"

"You can just call me Simon."

"*Really?*"

"Jamie"—Simon touches the man's shoulder—"who locked you in the basement?"

Salisbury pulls his head back, surprised. "They didn't. I mean, I'm *not* locked down here. I mean, well, I *am*—but not like that. Smith is *letting* me stay here. He's letting me lie low."

"Why do you *need* to lie low?"

Salisbury looks down at his feet and scratches the back of his head. "If I could talk about that, I wouldn't need to lie low."

Simon looks around the little room. There's a bed and the easy chair and a bare lightbulb hanging over our heads. The walls are brick and held together by spiderwebs. "If you *want* to be in here . . . why was the door locked from the outside?"

Salisbury shrugs. "Well, there *is* no lock on the inside, so Smith had to—Wait, how did *you* open it?" His eyes get big. "Did Smith fix your magic?"

"No," Simon says. "I—"

"Smith said he was going to fix your magic."

This is ridiculous. Jamie Salisbury hasn't been kidnapped. He's just hiding from his mother. I need to find *Philippa*. She's here somewhere—the bag is pulling towards the far wall of Salisbury's cell.

I step in front of Simon before he tells Salisbury the whole story. "Where's Pippa?" I demand. "Pippa Stainton?"

"Pippa?" Salisbury says. "She'll be at Watford by now, with Smith." He looks at Simon. "You're supposed to be there, too."

He's useless. I head for the door.

Once I'm in the hallway, I try to let the bag lead, but it wants to move as the crow flies, not down hallways and through doors.

"Baz, wait!" It's Penelope. I ignore her. Philippa is close. She must be—the bag is getting harder to hold on to. If I let go of it, it will smash into one of these brick walls and destroy the tape recorder. Fucking Bunce and her spells.

Most of the doors down here aren't locked. Most of the rooms are empty. When I get to the end of the hall, the bag pulls me flat against a door. I have to arch my neck up to breathe. I pry my arm free and try the door. It's locked. My wand is already in my hand. ***"Open Sesame!"***

I try the knob again, and the bag pushes the door open, hauling me in.

It's a dark room. Philippa is here. Her hands are tied. And a man is holding a wand to her head.

"Drop your wand," he says. "Now."

68

SIMON

"Honestly," Jamie Salisbury says. "I'm fine."

I suppose he looks fine. He's watching music videos. He's got a pot of tea and a stack of dirty dishes. There's a bed down here. "Maybe you could call your mum," I say, "and tell her that."

"I will," Jamie says, "as soon as Smith—"

"Smith won't let you call your mum?"

"It's not that simple—"

"Simon"—Penelope is pulling on my arm—"we can't let Baz run off."

I turn to her. "Where'd he go?"

Shepard is standing in the doorway. "Down the hall and out of sight."

"*Fuck*." I run after Penny—out the door, into the passageway. It's a properly creepy basement. One step up from the Catacombs. We run past a bunch of empty rooms and round the corner. Penny gets to the last doorway and stops—I run into her back.

There's an old man standing inside the room with a wand to Baz's head.

"Drop your wands."

69

BAZ

"Drop your wands," the man says.

And instead Penelope Bunce raises her fist. ***"K.O.!"***

The man slumps to the ground.

"Evander!" Salisbury shouts.

"For fuck's sake, Bunce, you could have killed me." I pick up my wand and rub my temple. I wonder if I have enough blood in me to bruise.

"But I didn't," she says. "Who's Evander?"

Salisbury's kneeling over the fallen man—who I'm fairly certain is the same person who runs the door at Smith-Richards's meetings. "It's Smith's godfather," he says, distressed. "Did you kill him?"

"No." Penny puts her hands on her hips. "Not intentionally."

Evander Feverfew is an older white guy, around 60 maybe, with longish grey hair, a diamond earring, and an elaborately tooled leather wand holster on his belt. Shepard stoops to pick Feverfew's wand up from the floor and hands it to Penelope. She tucks it in her waistband.

I let them fuss over him—I need to get to Philippa. The duffel bag is hauling me deeper into the room, where Smith's godfather shoved her. She's lying on her side on the floor, arms and legs tied. She's still so small. She still reminds me of a mouse . . .

When she sees me, she tries to squirm away.

"Pippa . . ." I say. Should I untie her first, or—No. I just need to—

I fall on my knees before her and unzip my bag. The tape recorder tries to sail out; I catch it. It pulls my arms straight and my body forward.

Philippa sees the tape recorder, and her eyes get wider. She's crying now. Kicking the floor to get away from me.

"I'm not going to hurt you," I say. "I promise!"

She twists her face away from me.

"I have your voice, Pippa. I—" Circe, what am I waiting for? There's nothing I can say or explain. I hold the tape recorder out and press play.

There's a staticky sound, and then Philippa's squeaky little voice rings out from the speaker. *"Hiya, Simoooooooooooooon!"*

The last syllable disintegrates into a long squeak. Then there's a sound like a record being played backwards. Like a little girl talking very quickly, in reverse.

Lying on the floor, Philippa gasps—and swallows and swallows. The noise gets higher and more chaotic, like a high-pitched waterfall.

Then the tape snaps to a stop. The squealing ends, and Philippa's head falls to the floor. The tug has gone out of the tape recorder. I drop it. "Pippa . . ." I say, scooting forward to free her hands. Simon is already working on her ankles.

As soon as she can, she sits up—and scuttles away from us. She's rubbing her throat.

"Are you okay?" I ask.

She doesn't answer. Her shoulders are shaking.

"I'm sorry," I say. "I didn't know, back at Watford. I thought it was temporary. I'm so sorry."

"Here," Shepard says. He's getting a bottle out of his backpack. "Have some water."

Philippa takes the water and swallows some.

"Philippa," Simon says, crouching next to me, "are you okay?"

She looks up at him, her eyes still wide, but no longer fearful. "S-Simon," she rasps. "We have to stop—stop Smith. His spell . . . is a *curse*."

70

SIMON

"Pippa, that's not true!"

"It—it is, Jamie! Smith lied to—to you."

We're in the kitchen again. I made them all come upstairs to sort things out. (I hate basements.) Penelope "Light as a feather"-ed the old guy to get him up here, and now she's tying him to the radiator.

"You can't do that," Jamie says, genuinely distraught. "That's Smith's *godfather* . . ."

"We don't have time—time for this," Philippa says. Her voice is still scratchy, like her throat isn't used to managing it, and she trips over every word. She hasn't calmed down at all since we untied her. She keeps pulling on my sleeve. "We have—We have to st-stop Smith!"

"We will," Baz says, standing on her other side. I think he'd give her anything she asked for right now. "Won't we, Snow?"

I'm not sure.

I'd *like* to believe Philippa . . .

No, that's not true. What I'd like is to know what's really happening here. Philippa would have us believe that Smith is a villain who tied her up and locked her in a basement. But *I've* tied things up and locked them away before, and *I've* always had a good reason . . .

I mean, we're tying up Smith's godfather right now. Is he a villain? Rather seems that way—he did have a wand to Baz's head. But Jamie Salisbury doesn't think so. He's been arguing with Philippa since she opened her mouth. (I think Baz is going to smite him if he doesn't stop.)

Who's good, who's bad—it's all about which side of the wand you're standing on. And who you're trying to protect.

I push Philippa's hand off my arm as gently as I can. "The thing is, Philippa—"

"She goes by Pippa," Baz interrupts.

"Right, sorry. The thing is, Pippa, we've *seen* Smith cast the spell. We've seen it work."

"It worked on *me*," Jamie agrees.

Pippa tries to argue, but nothing comes out for a few seconds. Then her voice kicks in, and she yelps, "—not true, J-Jamie!"

Penelope is looking between them, her hands on her hips. "Pippa, maybe you could explain what happened, from your point of view."

"There isn't . . . t-*time*."

"Well, we're just wasting time, arguing."

Baz looks like he might smite Penny, as well. "Lay off, Bunce. She was tied up in a basement."

"That's a good place to start," Penelope says. "How did you end up in the basement?"

Pippa holds her throat and swallows. "I—" She swallows again. "I—"

Shepard reaches out to her. He's holding a piece of yellow chalk. "Want to try writing it?"

She looks at his hand for a moment, then grabs the chalk, nodding. She turns to the wall and starts scribbling frantically on the wallpaper, as high up as she can reach.

I've been with Smith from the beginning, she writes.

We're all crowded around her, trying to read along. Baz pushes us back—"Give her space"—and starts to read aloud:

"He said he could bring back my magic . . . and I believed him . . . I worked for him . . . and for Evander . . . They trusted me."

Pippa glances back at us, like she's making sure that we're listening. We are. She goes back to writing.

"But today," Baz reads out, *"Beth . . . came to see Smith . . . She was afar*—no, *afraid . . . She told him all her spells . . . have stopped working."*

"Not Beth," Jamie cuts in. "She was so happy."

Philippa looks at him and nods. "Beth," she says. "Her magic—" She turns back to the wall, finding more space.

Baz leans over her shoulder. *"Smith told Beth that . . . she was just tired . . . That it was temporary . . . But . . . when she turned to leave . . . he cast a spell on her."* Baz shoots a glare at me, like this is my fault somehow.

"What spell?" I ask.

Baz looks back at the wall. *" 'Put it out of your head.' "*

"No!" Jamie is adamant. "Smith would never!"

"Yikes," Penny says. "That's like shaking up an Etch A Sketch inside someone's brain."

Philippa is still writing.

"*Smith didn't know . . . that I was watching . . . but he'd asked me to bring tea . . . I was standing . . .*"

She's running out of space. She gets on her knees.

"*In the doorway,*" Baz reads. "*With a tray . . . I dropped it . . . Then he cast a spell on me, too . . . 'Freeze' . . . and called for Evander . . . to take me away . . . I couldn't cry for help.*" Baz's voice cracks. He looks wretched. "*Smith told me he couldn't . . . have helped me anyway . . .*"

Philippa is kneeling on the floor, bent over. She's written herself into the corner.

"*That my voice was gone . . .*" Baz reads. "*Forever.*"

"She's lying," someone says.

We all whip around. Smith's godfather has come to. He's trying to sit up, but his hands are tied to the bottom of the radiator. Baz points his wand at him.

"She *attacked* Smith," Evander Feverfew says, furious. (He's an odd-looking duck for an old guy: shoulder-length grey hair, long sideburns, a pierced ear. I've seen him helping Smith at meetings. I thought he was a roadie.)

Pippa's eyes are wild, and her voice sounds bloody: "Why—Why would I do that?"

"Because he couldn't help you, Pippa. You didn't want anyone to have magic if you couldn't."

"Th-that isn't—isn't t-true!"

Evander looks at me. "She attacked him, and then she threatened to stop today's meeting! We couldn't let that happen. Smith is going to cure six people today. Six magicians."

"He's going to—to—curse them!"

"Liar!"

Baz is still pointing his wand at Smith's godfather; he looks like he's got a curse of his own at the tip of his tongue.

Penelope looks as confused as I feel. Jamie Salisbury has both of his hands fisted in his hair.

"Jamie," I say. "Did Smith fix your magic?"

"Of course he did!" Evander shouts. "Everyone saw it."

"I . . ." Jamie looks ashamed. "I hardly had any magic to fix."

"But Smith cured you," I say.

"He did," Jamie says eagerly. "And then . . ."

"He *cured* you!" Evander strains against the radiator. "First among his followers. It was a tremendous honour."

"It's true." Jamie nods. "I was the first."

"And it worked," I say. "You can do magic now?"

"Smith was still developing the spell," Jamie says earnestly. "He's already improved it since then."

"What does that *mean*?"

"It m-means," Pippa scrapes out, "his magic—his magic faded. Just. Like. Beth's."

Jamie looks embarrassed. He runs a hand through the top of his long hair. "*Pippa* . . ."

"Everyone who—who Smith—cured," she says, "has stopped c-coming to—to meetings."

"Did Smith-Richards take your magic?" Baz demands of Jamie.

"No!" Evander booms. "He made him a mage for the first time in his magic-forsaken life!"

"And now?" I ask Jamie. "Can you do magic?"

He's pulling his own hair. "It's complicated. Smith says—"

"Simon"—Baz squeezes my arm—"we *have* to stop Smith-Richards. He's going to cast that spell on Daphne."

"And Gloria Brooks," Pippa says, looking at Jamie. "And Eliza—Eliza Murphy. And Martin B-Bunce. And—"

71

SMITH

It's better than I hoped—every bench is full.

I've never been in the White Chapel before; I've only heard about it from Evander. The windows are disappointing, but the architecture is excellent. I can imagine how I look standing by the altar. I'm wearing white. My followers are fanned out behind me. I'm going to do Daphne first— she'll cry, but she won't wreck her face. Daphne has excellent presentation.

This is so much better than I hoped. There are hundreds of them here. All these weak wands. Perhaps some of them are powerful . . . That's all right. I expected that. It isn't meant to be a clean sweep, just a sweep. Just a winnowing.

I'll do Daphne first. She'll cry. She'll cast a spell. Another giant chocolate bar.

And they'll all believe it—because it's *true*. They'll believe in me.

And then I'll make my offer: I was only planning to help

six people today, but I could help them all . . . I could make every one of them more powerful, no matter how powerful they are now. Imagine it . . .

Who would say no?

I'll be standing at the altar. Daphne will be beside me in her flowered dress. There'll be cheers. And more tears. Laughter. I wish that Evander could be here to see it. My big moment. My leap into destiny.

That's all right.

I'll tell him the story.

It starts now, and it doesn't slow down until the world is new.

72

BAZ

There's no good way to get to Watford fast.

I won't let Simon fly. And none of us have cars. I probably should have thought of something before Penelope stole this builder's van—she's making Shepard drive it, while she casts frantic spells on surrounding traffic.

"I'm going to get arrested," Shepard says.

"I'll break you out," she tells him.

"That's not as reassuring as you think."

As soon as Bunce heard her father's name, she was on her way to Watford, whether the rest of us were coming or not.

"I can't believe you didn't tell me my father was wrapped up in this!" she shouted at Simon.

"I wasn't sure!" he said. *"Plus it didn't seem like my business!"*

"My business is your business, Simon!"

"I wasn't sure it was your *business either, Penny!"*

She cast a "Gentlemen start your engines" on the first van she found, and barely gave us time to climb in the back.

We're sitting on the floor now—there are no seats in the cargo area—Pippa and I on one side, Simon and Lady Salisbury's son on the other. The latter is still tearing his hair out, trying to defend Smith Smith-Richards, who may or may not have cast the magic right out of the poor sod.

Snow is still trying to sort everything out. (Smith-Richards is a villain; that's all I need to know.) He's sitting close to Salisbury, a hand on the man's shoulder. "Just tell us what happened, Jamie."

"This is all a misunderstanding," Salisbury says for the tenth time. He's huddled against the wall of the van. He's a thickset man. Broadly built. Big, open face. Heavy in a nearly-40 way. He scrubs his fingers through his collar-length hair. "Smith would never hurt anyone."

"So he didn't hurt you?" Simon asks.

"Of course not!" Salisbury looks anguished. "I don't think you understand what Smith did for me—what he's offering everyone."

"Mundanity," Pippa rasps. (I wonder if a body can reject its own voice. Maybe I can find a spell to help it stick . . .)

"Pippa, you've been with Smith as long as I have—you *know* the cure works." Salisbury turns to Simon, his face pleading. "Smith made me into a different person. It was like being a superhero. I could cast every spell I knew."

"That sounds wonderful," Simon says.

Salisbury huffs. "It was more than that—it was a *miracle*. You don't know what I was like before. I was rubbish at magic. I could only ever do really basic spells. Kids' stuff. But Smith . . . He made me into a real magician."

"That must have felt amazing," Simon says.

"Yeah." Salisbury nods. His eyebrows are pulled up in the middle. "It did."

"So what happened next?"

Salisbury looks down again, crestfallen. "Well, I should have known I wasn't a good candidate for the spell. I was practically Normal."

"But you said Smith's spell worked on you . . ."

"It did. At first. But then . . ."

"Then?"

Salisbury turns his face up to Simon, like he's looking for something there. "Maybe I was *meant* to be Normal."

"Jamie," Pippa whispers, "*no.*"

"Magicians don't have Normal children," I say.

"Maybe one of my parents was Normal," Salisbury says to me. "You never really know, do you?" (I hope he's never suggested this to his *mother.*)

"Jamie, what happened?" Simon pushes.

Salisbury looks at the floor. He tangles his hand in his greasy blond hair. "My magic started to get weaker, and once it started, well—it was gone in a few hours. Gone, completely. I couldn't even feel it in my fingertips anymore when I held my wand."

"What did Smith say?" Simon asks.

"He was frustrated, but he said we'd work it out. I was the first person he'd ever cured. He said he'd *learned* from me— that the spell was already stronger. He's going to cast it on me again once he's made more refinements."

"So you moved into the basement . . ."

"So that no one would ask questions. Or lose faith. Just because the spell wore off for me doesn't mean it will work that way for everyone else."

"It didn't just wear off," I say. "It took your magic completely."

"We don't know that," Salisbury counters.

"Jamie . . ." Pippa leans forward, trying to look him in

the eye. "Listen," she croaks. She clears her throat and tries again: "*Listen* to me. Beth said she c-couldn't cast a single—a single spell. Not—not even a 'Dust up.'"

Salisbury shakes his head, like he literally doesn't want to hear this. "That can't be right, Pippa. Smith said the spell was working better than ever."

"Why would I—would I lie to you? You're my friend! We've been—been in this to-together, all along!"

"I don't *know* why you're saying all this! Is it like Evander said? Are you jealous that Smith can't fix your magic?"

"No!" It comes out a painful squawk. Pippa leans back against the van wall, closing her eyes and clutching her throat. A tear runs down her cheek. "No," she whispers.

I wipe my hands on my trousers. "Pippa," I say quietly, "you don't need Smith-Richards to fix your magic."

She cracks her eyes open, but doesn't turn her head.

"There's no reason you can't do magic now," I say, hoping that it's true. *Desperately* hoping.

"I—" She lets go of her throat and looks down at her palms. "I don't have a wand."

I've never pulled my wand so fast. My holster kicks it into my palm as I'm reaching for her. "Take mine."

Pippa accepts it, fingers trembling, then looks at me for the first time since she got her voice back. She looks frightened. And angry. She points my ivory wand at me, her whole arm shaking. She looks into my eyes . . .

I close them.

"Wait!" Simon shouts.

Just as Pippa says, ***"Test the waters!"***

I open my eyes when the stream hits my chest. Pippa is staring down at my wand. Simon is holding her wrist.

"I—" he says, letting go of her. "Sorry, Philippa. Pippa. I just . . ."

"Good on you, Pippa," Salisbury says. He seems sincerely happy for her, despite everything.

She clings to the wand, watching it spill water onto the floor of the van.

"Baz!" Penelope is twisted around and shouting at me. "I need your help!"

I crawl up between the two front seats.

"Help me make the van go faster," she says.

I look out the window—the van might actually be flying. "It can't go faster without the Normals noticing," I say.

"We could cast spells so they don't notice."

We zip past a Volkswagen Golf. The driver nearly goes off the road, staring at us. "We really couldn't, Bunce."

Shepard is holding the steering wheel with both hands. "Penelope—are you steering, or am I steering?"

"You're steering, Shepard!" she says. "Obviously!"

"Do the brakes still work?"

"Obviously *not*. Why would the brakes work on a flying car?"

"You really shouldn't be allowed to use the word 'obviously,'" he murmurs under his breath. "That should *not* be in your vocabulary."

Penelope turns back to me. "Are you absolutely certain my father is caught up in all this?"

"Pippa says he is, and Simon saw him at a meeting."

She shakes her head. "I don't get it. My dad's at *peace* with his magic—he's a perfectly capable mage."

"Not compared to your mother."

"Baz!" She looks up at me, outraged. "What a thing to say!"

"I'm not insulting your father, Bunce. I just think it's easy for *us* to say he should be happy. That Daphne should be happy. We have all the power we've ever wanted. We don't know what it's like—"

"Shepard, here!" She points out the window. "Get off!"

"Where?"

"This exit! The one that says *Watford*—get off now!"

"I can't, there's a car!"

Bunce holds out her fist. ***"Sent to Coventry!"***

Shepard veers onto the Watford exit ramp at the last possible moment. We're still flying over the road. "Tell me you didn't just disappear that car," he says.

"I just *moved* it . . ."

"What's wrong?" Snow has come up to crouch beside me.

"Nothing new," I say, taking the opportunity to touch his arm.

He's antsy. He took off his coat, and he keeps spreading his wings out, then drawing them back—like someone clenching his fists. I don't say anything when they bump into me.

Bunce is navigating Shepard around the city of Watford and into the countryside. We've slowed down a bit . . . The wheels seem to be on the ground again. (Does Bunce really have a *flying* spell?)

"We're almost th-there," Pippa says. She and Salisbury have crept up behind us.

"Is that it?" Shepard asks. "Up on the hill?"

"You won't be able to see Watford from outside the gates," Penny says automatically.

"What's that thing up there? That kinda looks like a walled city?"

I look out the front window. At the fortress walls and the top of the Weeping Tower. Normals can't see Watford. It should sting Shepard's eyes even to look in that direction.

Simon is looking over my shoulder. "I can see it, too."

"This is—This is Smith's doing," Pippa says.

I turn to Snow. "Or is it the goats?"

"What goats?" Penelope asks.

"The Goats of Watford?" Salisbury chimes in.

"Just park the van," Simon says. "We have to get inside." There are more than a hundred cars already parked along the lane. Smith-Richards has apparently drawn quite a crowd.

"Fuck that," Penelope says, "take us through the gates!"

Shepard does just that. He drives right up through the Great Lawn.

"Over the drawbridge!" she commands.

"Your mother's going to kill you," I say.

The van goes tearing over the moat.

"Park here," she says, once we're in the courtyard. "Where's this meeting?"

"The Weeping Tower," Simon says. "The lecture room at the top. Jamie and I will stay here; we can't help you."

"Snow—" I squeeze his arm. I always want Simon's help. Even without magic, he's invaluable in a fight. But . . . now that my spells bounce off him, I wouldn't be able to heal him if he got hurt.

"Go," he says.

Bunce is already out the door. "Come on, Baz! You, too, Shepard!"

"I'll stay with Simon," Pippa whispers hoarsely. "Please— stop Smith!"

"I will," I say.

I *will*.

73

AGATHA

We find the goats in the hills behind Watford, almost completely scattered and in bad temper. They refuse to be herded, even with spells. They run from me and charge at Niamh—one of the old billy goats knocks her off her feet.

Niamh sits up, but doesn't get off the ground. "I don't know if we should bother rounding them up or just look for the doe."

"Let's look for the doe," I say, wiping my neck with a handkerchief and walking towards her. "I think they're all upset about her."

"Is that another of your 'feelings'?"

I cross my arms. "Do you want me to share my instincts with you or not?"

"Share them," she grumbles. "I don't have any instincts at all."

"Everyone has instincts, Niamh."

"Not me. I have . . . a university education."

"Oh, shut up." I'm standing over her, looking down. Her cropped hair looks even better brown than it did platinum. "I've seen you play lacrosse."

"You don't *remember* me playing lacrosse . . ."

"I've told you, I remember now. Do you need help getting up?"

She pushes herself up and brushes grass off her thighs and behind. She's very thick, is Niamh. In her cuffed jeans and her tighter-than-usual T-shirt.

I turn away from her—away from the school and the hills—and look out into the Wavering Wood. I start walking. I can hear Niamh following me.

"The goats don't like the Wood," she says. "I never find them there."

"I just have a—"

"I'm not arguing," she says.

"Good."

I find myself hesitating at the threshold of the forest. I don't like the Wood either. The last time I was here, I saw Baz drinking a deer. I wasn't frightened—I mean, I was a little frightened. But mostly I was excited. To share a secret with him. To be close to something thrilling and forbidden. He held my hand that day. I wanted him to kiss me.

It's mortifying to think about now, the way I felt *torn* between Baz and Simon . . .

I was just *standing* between them. And not even in a romantic, dramatic way. I was like a dead badger lying in the middle of the road, something they had to drive around to get to where they were eventually going.

I don't like the Wood. It's dark and full of magic. It makes me feel like I'm about to be kissed. And like I'm a fool to want it.

I walk into the trees. Between them. There isn't really a path.

"I've never been in here before," Niamh says. "It's darker than I expected."

"I thought you said you'd looked for the goats here."

"I said I'd never found them here."

I roll my eyes; Niamh must make an *effort* to be this difficult. "You never came to the Wood when you were at school?"

"No," she says, "the Mage always said there was dangerous magic here."

"Well, I suppose that's true." I get out my wand. I don't have a spell to cast, but I feel more in tune with .... *something* when I'm holding it.

"Why did *you* come to the Wood?" Niamh asks.

"Oh, you know . . . adventures, Chosen One dogshit."

"You really didn't like it?"

"What, the Wood?"

"No. You know . . . Being the future Mrs. Simon Snow."

I tense my shoulders up around my ears and clench my fists at my side. I think Niamh makes an effort to be *offensive*, too. "Well . . . I liked *Simon*. You'd like him, too, if you gave him a chance."

"I never said that I didn't like him . . ."

"But I didn't like being the centre of attention all the time. I didn't like being stared at."

Niamh makes a disparaging noise in her throat. "He's not the reason people stared at you."

I spin around, and she nearly walks into me.

"What does *that* mean?" I demand, even though I know very well what it means. I know why people stare at me. Of course Niamh would find the meanest *possible* way to say,

"You're beautiful." It's another thing I can't help that she holds against me.

At least she has the decency to look embarrassed. "I mean . . ." She looks at the ground. "I don't know what I mean . . ."

I step closer to her. "Don't you?"

"Sister golden hair," something says—something with a voice like crushed leaves, hardly a voice at all.

Niamh and I both freeze.

"Is that you . . ." the thing asks, lingering on every consonant.

I slowly turn towards the heart of the Wood. A nymph is floating there, half in darkness.

"It *is* you," she says. "The golden one."

She moves closer to us. Into the light.

I know this dryad. She's followed me through the Wood before. Watching, never speaking. She used to look very smart—in a yellow velvet jacket and green petticoats, her mossy hair pinned up with yellow ribbons.

Her skirts have turned to rags now, and the ribbons are long gone. Her hair hangs in her face and creeps down her chest and arms. She looks overgrown. Forgotten. More like a tree than a person.

"Golden one, golden one," she whisper-sings, "what do you seek?"

I walk closer to her.

Niamh catches my arm and tries to hold me back—I shake her off.

"I'm looking for a goat," I say.

"The Goats of Watford," the dryad says.

"Yes." I step closer.

She's hovering in the air. Trembling. The shadows of a thousand leaves dance over her. Her eyes used to glow, I think. But not now. Her face is scabbed over with bark. "The Goats of Watford are lost."

"Not yet," I say.

"Yet and yet," she singsongs. "They wander and roam . . . and fly."

"We're looking for them. We're looking for a doe."

The dryad is holding a parasol. She twirls it onto her shoulder and opens it. The silk is rotting away from the ribs. "Sister golden hair . . ." she says. "Your friends were here. I don't like them."

"My friends?"

She frowns. Pebbles and sticks whorl in the air beneath her. "Tell me now . . . What do you seek?"

"I told you—a goat. A pregnant doe. She's in the Wood."

"How do you know who walks in my Wood?"

"I have a feeling—"

The dryad bends at the waist to shout down at me, one hand clenched in her torn skirts. "The Goats of Watford are lost! They have no keeper! No hook, no crook, no one to lead them home!"

"We want to bring them home!"

"You?" She points her parasol at me. "You have failed them."

I put my hands on my hips. "To be fair, I didn't even know about them until last week."

"Mages," she hisses. "Treacherous. Traitorous. Takers! When have you ever protected anything good?"

I'm standing before her, below her. "I'm not here to defend magicians," I say. "I can't. We're terrible. Even the best of us are the worst. I'm just here to help this doe. She's scared and alone, and she's never done this before. We can *help* her. Take us to her—*please*."

The dryad is glaring at me. She draws her busted umbrella closed . . . Then she whirls around and sails off deeper into the Wood.

I snatch Niamh's hand and run after the nymph. Into the Wood, into the Wood. Into the murk. I push branches out of my way, and Niamh holds them back. It should be green and lush here. You should still be able to see the sun. This is dark magic, wild magic.

I keep an eye on the dryad flying ahead of us. She's hoping to lose us, I think. Hoping to leave us lost. We *run* after her. Niamh lifts me over a fallen tree that blocks our way—chest to chest, both our hearts clattering.

The dryad gets away from us. Disappears. We stumble around, looking for her.

"There!" Niamh whispers.

A clearing. Through the trees. Where sunlight falls in solid gold bars.

We move closer. This could be a trap—there are stories, about girls who enter the Wood and never leave. I'm holding Niamh's hand. "Can you hear that?"

Ahead of us—something is crying, bleating.

We walk into the light, into a circle of grass. There's a stone marker, and a doe lying on the ground before it, panting.

The dryad appears, hovering above the stone, watching us.

"There's a good girl," I say, kneeling in the grass next to the goat.

"How long has she been labouring?" Niamh asks.

The dryad ignores her. She settles onto the stone, sitting with her back to us.

It's a grave, I realize. A wide slab of marble, nearly as tall as Niamh, etched in a typeface I think of as Watford Gothic. EBENEZA PETTY, it says. SHE LIVED FOR WATFORD AND DIED DEFENDING IT. MAY SHE REST IN MAGIC AND SLEEP IN PEACE.

The doe moans. I shake my head and make myself focus: Her eyes are closed. Her body is limp. Her legs are covered in yellow gunk. "She's been in labour a long time," I say.

Niamh touches her belly, and the doe's eyes snap open. Wings unfold from her back, like magic. She tries to bite Niamh and fly away, all at once.

I dodge between them, wrapping my arms around the goat's neck and holding her against my chest. "Shhhhhh, it's all right, it's all right . . ."

The doe settles again, panting.

Niamh scoots back and opens her shoulder bag. "Let me see your right hand, Agatha."

I frown at her, but I hold out one hand, hugging the doe with the other. Niamh scrubs my hand with some sort of wipe. Then she squeezes clear jelly in my palm and rubs it through my fingers. She doesn't have to tell me what to do next; I've watched enough YouTube videos.

I shift myself around the doe—she doesn't fight me—and slide my fingers into her birth canal. She cries out. She's so tired, she's been here all day. We never should have left her.

The kid is right inside. I can feel it.

"It's backwards," I say. "Stuck."

"You'll have to get the legs," Niamh says.

"I know."

"All right, I'm right here."

I lean over the doe, holding her. Her wings beat against my face. I'm in her up to my elbow. Niamh is right beside me.

I can feel the kid. I can feel the legs.

"I've got them," I say.

"One at a time," Niamh says. "You're doing well."

Niamh's hand is between my shoulders. She's casting spells over the doe. The doe is crying. I have the legs—I have them. I'm pulling them out one at time. "Push for me, darling," I say. "I know you're tired."

Niamh whispers her spells. The doe pushes. The kid slides out into my hands, still in its sack. Niamh passes me a towel, and I rub the little goat clean.

"It isn't moving," I say.

Niamh presses her wand into the kid's chest. ***"The beat goes on!"***

It doesn't move.

Its mother cries.

The dryad is sitting on Ebb's grave, ignoring us.

"I'm sorry," Niamh says to me. "We were too late."

74

SIMON

We wait for Baz and Penny and Shepard to disappear inside
the Weeping Tower.

Then Pippa looks at me. "You lied to them."

"Yes."

"Are you going to st-stop Smith?"

"Yes."

"The White Chapel," she whispers. "Hurry!"

AGATHA

"It's all right," Niamh says.

It isn't all right. Nothing is all right. The kid is dead.
The mother is crying. And the fucking dryad is acting

like none of us are here.

"Why didn't you do something?" I shout at her. I stand up and walk around Ebb's headstone. The dryad is twirling her rotten parasol over her knees. "Why didn't you help it?"

"I'm not the goat's keeper," the dryad says, watching her umbrella spin.

"It came here for help!"

Her eyes snap up at me, flashing. "No. It came here to die. That's what this place is."

"The goats protect Watford—don't you know that? If they leave, the school will fall!"

"You care about Watford? Watford doesn't care about you, fair one! It doesn't miss you. It won't protect you." She runs one hand along the top of the stone. Caressing it. "She loved it, too, and all it gave her in return was a grave."

"Did you know Ebb?"

The dryad laughs. It sounds like wind passing through a tree. "Yes."

"Were you friends?"

She caresses the stone again. "No."

"I hardly knew her," I say, "but I know this—she loved these goats. If you let a goat suffer, on her grave, she will never forgive you. She'll haunt you forever."

The dryad laughs again. "Too late for that. Too late, golden one. You were too late."

SIMON

I'm going to stop Smith.

I don't know if he's the Chosen One. I don't know if his spell works.

But he can't cast that spell today—not on Penny's dad and Baz's stepmum. Not with Jamie hidden in his basement and a wand to Pippa's head. There are too many red flags here.

And I know that's rich coming from me. I'm wearing a suit made of red flags, metaphorically speaking, twenty-four-fucking-seven. But *this* . . .

(I *really* hate basements.) (You shouldn't hide people in basements. Even bad people. But certainly not your friends.)

I'm going to stop Smith.

I'm going to call a time-out. To keep him from making any more mistakes.

I get to the White Chapel first. (Pippa and Jamie are behind me somewhere—they're running, I'm flying.) I never wanted to come back here, but here I am. I land in front of the gilded doors and push them open.

The Chapel is full of mages, more than I've seen at Smith's meetings so far. Word must be getting out.

Smith is onstage, near the altar. So is Daphne. He's holding her hand. He's holding his wand. He's wearing a white suit—there's a microphone clipped to his collar.

I just have to *stop* him.

I don't have to figure it all out, I don't have to have any answers. I just have to stop *this*, today. For today.

Smith sees me. He says my name, but not loud enough for the microphone to pick it up.

I nod at him and raise my hand. Maybe it's all a misunderstanding. I keep walking down the centre aisle. I'll just ask him to step away for a moment, so we can talk.

"Simon Snow," he says again, and everyone hears.

They all turn to look at me. To gape.

"Is it really him?"

"Does he really have dragon wings?"

"How did he get through the gates?"

"Smith," I say. I'm more than halfway up the aisle. "I need to talk to you."

My wings flutter, and I fly forward a few feet. (That happens sometimes when I'm not focused on staying grounded.) The crowd gasps. It makes me anxious—instead of landing, I fly higher.

"Smith," I say, "don't cast the spell. We need to talk."

"Simon Snow," Smith says again, even louder, in his stage voice. "I know you're angry about being replaced. But you won't stop the good work we're doing here."

"What?" I'm hovering before him. "Smith, that's not—"

"Your years of deception have come to an end!" he shouts. "You've done enough to hurt the World of Mages!"

HEADMISTRESS BUNCE

Don't I have enough on my plate?

I know I'm not supposed to think that—I could never say it out loud—but for heaven's snakes, could I just have *one day* where nothing falls apart?

I have enough to manage, trying to keep the walls of Watford standing with scant resources and even less support. The Mage nearly ran this place into the *ground* . . . The library was empty. The curriculum was a shambles. I've got eighth years who can't cast a complete sentence and fourth years who only cast Internet memes. To think that my teachers thought *pop songs* were unstable—my own son brought down a classroom wall with a "Yeet."

It was Pacey. He's 17. And, frankly, the least of my problems.

I can say this with authority because I lie in bed most nights, ranking my list of problems—and ranking my list of problematic children. There are five of them; it's a dynamic list.

Premal, my oldest, usually owns the top spot. Holed up in his room back in Hounslow, still grieving the Mage, almost two years after the man's death—after Premal and I *found* him dead. I worry that Prem will never move on. I worry about what he'll move on *to*. I worry that no one is bringing him dinner when I'm here at Watford . . .

Alternately, I worry that his 12-year-old sister, Priya, *is* bringing him dinner, hovering over him and mothering him in my place. I know that she mothers Pip, the youngest. I worry about Pip, too, because I can't yet *see* how I'm failing him.

And of course I worry about Penelope—always Penelope. Attached at the hip to the most dangerous person in England. And now bringing home stray Normals. Morgana, I can't deal with it! I don't know where to start!

I need a break . . . I need some help . . .

I don't need *this* from Martin *now*.

He believes in *the Chosen One*?

When did this happen? Martin is a scholar, an academic. He's pragmatic. He believes in *facts*. It's why I fell in love with him. Partly, anyway.

We've always laughed at magicians who lived their lives by prophecy. People like Davy, who trusted every superstition more than his own eyes and ears.

Is this because I left Martin alone?

I left for Watford, and I left him with the kids, and we agreed it would be fine, that he could handle it, because he didn't have the Humdrum to track anymore. Pacey and Priya are at Watford with me for most of the year anyway—and Martin and I would still see each other on the weekend . . .

Martin and I have been married a long time.

We have a strong foundation.

Is this his midlife crisis? Joining a cult? Other people our age are coming out as bisexual or getting into Normal-style bread-making. (I would prefer either—or both.)

"Of course I'd like to be more powerful," he said to me on the phone this morning.

I'd been complaining to him about this Smith Smith-Richards meeting—I have to stay at Watford anytime there's an event here—and Martin said he knew all about it, that he was planning to attend.

"Why on earth?" I asked. *"Are you writing a paper?"*

"No." His voice was quiet, careful. Martin's voice is always quiet and careful. *"I've been following Smith-Richards for a while."*

"Following like 'keeping track' or following like following?"

"He's a good man, Mitali. He has extraordinary powers."

"We all have extraordinary powers, Martin. It's what makes us magicians."

"Not all of us, dear."

Then he told me that he's been going to these meetings for months. That he's befriended the people there—and befriended the man himself, the man who claims to be the Greatest Mage. (Martin and I don't have *friends.* We have colleagues. We have children. We have *each other.*)

"Did you bring the children?" I asked.

"No, they wouldn't be interested. They take after you— they don't need Smith's help."

"And you do, Martin?"

"Mitali . . ." He sounded hurt, that I would make him say this out loud. *"Of course I'd like to be more powerful. Do you think I don't wonder, what it's like for you?"*

We argued.

I hung up.

And now here he is, in my office, wearing the suit he only gets out for weddings and funerals. I hope he doesn't want my blessing in all this.

"Your meeting has already started," I say.

"I know. I thought—"

"I hope you don't want me to accompany you."

"No."

Martin is a small man. His hair was beige-blond when we were young. Now it's beige-grey. He has a squishy, nonde-script face. A soft voice.

It's his eyes that I fell in love with. Not their beauty. But the way they see everything. And feel everything. Martin takes the whole world in. That's a tremendous thing—to be able to hold the world inside of yourself, and still feel com-passion for it.

"Is it over, then?" I try to sound gentle. I don't have it

in me. "Did he spell you?"

"Mitali, I—"

He doesn't finish. The door to my office flies open, and Penelope and Baz—*and that Normal*—rush in.

AGATHA

"Agatha!" Niamh calls to me from the other side of the stone. "The doe! She's still going!"

I turn away from the dryad and rush back to Niamh's side. The goat is moving again. She's flapping her wings and arching her back. Her cries have grown more urgent.

"Here," Niamh says, making space for me on the ground next to her.

I crouch behind the doe.

"Let her work," Niamh says. "She may not need us."

I stroke the doe's flank. "You're all right, darling. We're here."

SIMON

I should have known it would end like this.

Two hundred wands pointed at me. Children crying. Parents running for the door.

These people don't know me . . .

The Mage never took me to their parties, never paraded

me around or made a spectacle of me. All they know about me is that I was a lie.

I was a trick the Mage played on them. A trained dog that turned on him in the end. They all know what happened the last time I was in this Chapel . . .

Smith is pointing his wand at me like he's Gandalf and I'm the Balrog. "I won't let you stand between these magicians and their destiny!" he calls out to me.

"Smith!" I fly to the altar. "Please listen to me!"

Someone in the crowd shouts a spell, and it connects with the window above me—a skylight that used to have a beautiful stained-glass design. I bow my head and spread my wings, but the glass still falls on Daphne and the others. A chunk of it gets stuck in my wing.

"This is a sacred space for mages," Smith shouts, "and I won't let you defile it any further! Leave now!"

"Smith, I can't let you—"

"Abandon hope, all ye who enter!"

His spell probably hits me. I can't feel it.

"Stone the crows!"

I don't even flinch.

"My spells aren't touching him . . ." Smith says. "What are you, Simon Snow? Are you the Insidious Humdrum after all?!"

"What? No!"

Other people start casting spells at me. From the audience. I can't feel them. I fly higher.

"You won't stop us!" Smith yells. He turns away from me and points his wand at the mages onstage with him. *"Let it all—"*

"What a tangled web we weave, when first we practice to deceive!"

AGATHA

The doe is straining. I cast a spell to give her strength.

There's a loud noise in the distance. An explosion? Niamh and I both look up. We can't see over the treetops. There's another loud bang. *Is that Watford?*

Niamh says nothing. She looks back down at the doe.

So do I.

SIMON

Smith erupts into goopy webbing. It's like it's coming out of his pores. His whole body looks a like a haunted house.

Everyone in the room turns to see who cast the spell.

Philippa Stainton is standing in the aisle, pointing Baz's wand. Jamie Salisbury is standing next to her, looking mortified.

"Pippa . . ." Smith says, his wand still hanging in the air. "Jamie?"

None of Smith's followers know how to react. On the one hand, Pippa just cast a nasty spell on Smith. On the other, she just *cast a spell*.

"Is that truly Pippa?"

"Did Smith cure her?"

"She didn't even have a tongue!"

"She had a tongue—she sold her voice to a sea witch."

"How did Smith do it?"

"He's the real fucking deal, that's how."

"No!" Pippa shouts in a gravelly voice, looking around the room. "Listen to me!"

Everyone stops to listen. Including Smith.

She looks him in the eye. "Smith Smith-Richards is a—is a fraud! His spell ruins people's magic! Ask Jamie and—and Beth!"

"*Beth? Where is Beth?*"

"*Jamie's right there. We saw him cured.*"

"*Smith's first miracle.*"

"*Beth hasn't returned any of my calls . . .*"

"Pippa," Smith says calmly, like he isn't dripping with cobwebs that prove him a liar. "Why are you so angry? After everything I've done for you."

"You? Y-you—"

"The prophecy says there will be false witnesses sent to tarnish me," Smith says. "I never thought it would be you." He turns his wand on her.

Pippa is already casting with Baz's. ***"Liar, liar, pa-pants on fire!"***

Smith's white trousers start smoking. Daphne quickly shoots a stream of water out of her wand to put them out.

I'm still treading air above them—my left wing is cut up, so I'm working hard with my right. When Smith points his wand at Pippa, I dive in front of it. ***"Cat got your tongue!"*** he hisses.

I'm sure the spell hits me. I don't feel it. "Enough," I say, scooping Smith up, my arms under his, and lifting him above the crowd.

"Put me down, you beast!" he yells. His microphone has come unclipped. "Put me down, Simon!"

The audience is casting at me again. I seem to be the only

thing they can agree on. Everyone is shouting now, spells or otherwise.

"*Take him down!*"

"*Protect the Chosen One!*"

"*Arrest the apostate!*"

"*But Smith must be deceiving us—*"

"*Crash and burn!*"

A stream of fire shoots over my shoulder. (That's concerning. I don't really want to see if I'm immune to magickal fire.)

"Stop!" someone shouts. I look down. It's Jamie. He's at the altar, holding Smith's clip-on microphone. "Everybody just stop. Please. Pippa's telling the truth—my magic *is* gone. Smith's spell wears off, and leaves you with . . . It left me with . . ." He looks miserably around the room. "With nothing."

"He's lying!" Smith screams. He's trying to squirm out of my hands, which won't be hard; I don't have a good grip on him.

"Calm down," I say. "I don't want to drop you."

Smith points his wand at Jamie, and I'm not sure how to stop him from casting. So I fly straight up, through the broken window—we break it a little more—and into the air.

BAZ

It was Bunce's idea to fetch her mother, when Smith-Richards wasn't where Snow said he would be.

We ran up the flight of stairs and burst into Headmistress

Bunce's office, interrupting what was clearly a heated conversation with her husband.

They stopped talking, red-faced, when they saw Penelope.

"Penny?" her father said.

Her mother looked at Shepard and put her hand on her forehead. "Penelope Bunce, *please* tell me you didn't bring a *Normal* to Watford."

"Daddy!" Penelope ran to her father. "You didn't do it, did you?"

"Smith-Richards!" I said. "Where is he?"

"They're all in the White Chapel . . ." Professor Bunce said, hugging Penelope and still looking confused.

I turned to his wife. "We have to stop him! That spell of his shuts off people's magic."

No one will believe me later when I tell them that Headmistress Bunce jumped from a window at the top of the Weeping Tower, but I saw it with my own eyes. She used the same spell I used once on the ramparts—"Float like a butterfly."

The rest of us could never manage that spell from such a height. We took the (damnably slow) lift.

When we finally got to the Chapel, Headmistress Bunce was standing in the doorway threatening to nullify anyone who cast a spell or tried to leave. Daphne was at the altar, with Pippa and Jamie.

Simon and Smith-Richards were gone.

75

SMITH

It wasn't supposed to happen like this.

I knew there would be challenges—antagonists, red herrings, *meaningful struggle*—but nothing like this. Not chaos and disgrace. They made a *fool* of me. How am I supposed to *redeem* myself?

And now him.

Hauling me around like a rag doll.

My Simon Snow chapter was over.

I'm clinging to him. He knocks my wand from my hand. (More disgrace.) (I'm *the Chosen One*. How do I bounce back from this? What is destiny *doing*?)

He drops me onto the flat roof of a nearby building. I hate to think about how good he looks doing it. Against the green hills, the castle walls. Those fucking red wings.

"Are you hurt?" he asks.

I refuse to answer.

He touches my shoulder, and I roll away. I'm not hurt.

I'm just at a loss. I hide my head in my arms. "That was a *debacle*."

"I don't know what you expected to happen," Simon Snow says. "People were going to figure out that your spell doesn't work."

I sit up to face him. He's standing over me with the sun at his back. One of his wings is pulled in; the injured one is hanging. It's asymmetrical. It works for him, damn it. "The spell *does* work," I snarl. "You've seen it with your own eyes, Simon!"

"Yeah, but you didn't tell me—or anyone else—that it wears off."

"That doesn't matter!" (It doesn't! It's practically irrelevant!)

"It matters to the people who lost their magic!"

"Oh, for Merlin's sake," I shout at him, "they hardly had any magic to lose!"

He puts his hands on his hips. He's wearing jeans. And an artfully torn T-shirt. "Did you steal it?" he demands. "Is that what this is?"

"*Did I steal it?*" I laugh, I sound hysterical—I suppose I am. Simon Snow is interrogating me. He looks like he just rolled out of bed. *I'm* the Chosen One. *I* am. "No," I say. "I *gave* it to them."

I gave them all of their magic, all at once. That's what my spell does. Draws their magic up, so they can reach it. And then . . . they run out. Sometimes in a month, sometimes in a week. It depends on how much they started with.

(I'd never cast the spell on a Normal before. I never will again, not if it makes them immune to me.)

"No one else can do what I do," I say. "*No one.* My magic begets magic. It's unheard of—it's a miracle."

"Yeah, but it's a lie!"

"It's not a lie!"

"Everyone was going to figure it out, Smith!"

"Not immediately!"

Not until it was too late to turn back!

I was going to give the people in the White Chapel the best day of their lives.

And then, tomorrow, their friends would line up at my door. All the weakest wands, all the weakest wills.

And the next day, more.

I'd clear them all out in the kindest way possible. I'd make some very strategic edits.

"They were going to see the truth in the end," the boy says. "And then what?"

And then, Simon Snow, a new age would dawn for the World of Mages . . .

A new *stage*, with only the most powerful and canniest players left standing. A new *era*. Of adventure, of high stakes, and glory—just like in the stories Evander told me.

All the best stories are old . . . Why is that? When did magicians stop doing anything worth writing down or repeating?

They wrote *me* down.

I was foretold.

I still am.

One day at a time, Evander always says. One chapter.

There's a scraping noise across the roof. A trapdoor opens. And the headmistress—Martin Bunce's wife—comes through it, wand first.

(She'll never line up for my spell. She'll stay in the narrative.)

"You're under arrest," she says to me. "And you . . ." She looks at Simon. ". . . will wait for me in my office."

I raise myself to my feet and put my hands in the air. I'm wearing white. I'm singed and sooty. It wasn't supposed to happen like this—but I don't fear destiny.

76

AGATHA

The second kid slides out, just the way it's supposed to. I catch it—I can already feel it squirming inside its bag. "It's alive!" I shout. "Niamh! Look!"

"You're doing so well," she says, handing me another clean towel.

The kid kicks its way out of the membrane, while I scrub at it. The doe cranes her head back, too exhausted to reach it. I bring the baby over to her face, and she licks away the gunk. "There you are, mother," I say. "Good work, darling."

I'm crying.

I'm laughing.

Niamh lays her hand on my back. "You saved them both, Agatha."

"I didn't—" I turn to Niamh. For once, she doesn't look angry. Niamh is looking at me the way lots of people do sometimes, but she never has. Like I'm . . . well, like I'm . . .

"You're amazing," she says.

I've turned right into her arm. Her hand stays on my back. Niamh's eyes are royal blue. Her eyelashes are short and dark. Her colour is high. Here, in the clearing, under the solid gold sun.

"Agatha," she says.

My hands are covered in goo and jelly. I lift up my chin, so it's there, if she wants it . . .

She does. She kisses me.

Niamh.

Her long nose in my cheek. Her chin as sharp as it looks. Her lips the softest part of her, surely.

Niamh.

I would like . . .

Niamh.

More of this . . .

Niamh.

Please.

Niamh kisses me.

"Agatha," she says, "you saved Watford."

77

BAZ

Smith-Richards has been arrested. He'll be kept in a tower until his trial.

There's an emergency Coven meeting; three members were already here for Smith-Richards's rally. (Which I find alarming.)

Headmistress Bunce makes everyone in the Chapel stay to give a statement. Even Penelope and me.

"I'm not telling you anything until you tell me where Snow is," I say when it's my turn.

"Easy, Baz. He's in my office."

"Is he under arrest?"

"Not yet." The headmistress narrows her eyes. "Should he be?"

"No. He should be given a medal. And a pension."

"We'll take that under advisement."

When the Coven is done with me, I go looking for my stepmother . . .

I find her on a bench in the courtyard, looking like she's run out of tears. I sit down next to her. "Are you all right?"

"In a manner of speaking," Daphne says, her eyes cast down.

I look more closely. She's wearing a lovely floral garden-party dress. High-heeled jute sandals. Her cheeks are red and chafed.

"Did you . . ." I'm not sure how to say it. "Were we too late?"

She looks up at me. "Oh. No. Simon stopped him. No one took Smith's spell today. But . . . I *would* have." She starts crying again. "Oh, Basilton, I've been such a fool."

I put my arm around her and fish a handkerchief out of my pocket. "There, there."

"I believed in him."

"I know."

"And now . . . oh, and now . . ." She sniffs. "Basil, will you just take me home?"

Thank fucking Crowley. "Of course. As soon as I've spoken to Simon."

Daphne nods, wiping her eyes.

A shadow falls over us. We both look up. It's Penelope's father, holding a stack of three empty glasses. "Hello, Daphne. Gin and tonic?"

She smiles up at him and nods her head, laughing tearfully. "Thank you, Martin."

Professor Bunce takes a glass and taps it with his wand. ***"Dutch courage!"*** He casts it again on a glass for himself. (In my good opinion, anyone who can cast that spell twice in a row doesn't *need* a power upgrade.) He holds the last empty glass out to me. "Basil?"

"No, thank you, sir. I'm driving."

"Could I trade places with you for a moment?"

"Yes, of course." I stand, and Professor Bunce takes my place on the bench.

"Shepard has lemonade," he says.

I nod and catch Daphne's eye. "I won't go far."

Shepard does have lemonade. And Penelope has tea and biscuits. They're moving through what's left of the crowd, offering refreshments. (Shepard may be the first true Normal on Watford grounds—it's a *spectacular* transgression.) (How many history books is Penelope going to end up in? And for how many reasons?)

I take the biscuits from Bunce and do my part to help. Now that the danger has passed, people seem glad for the chance to gossip. And now that Smith-Richards has been disgraced, people are quick to say they only came today out of curiosity, and didn't they get a show for their trouble. They're already talking about the other prospective Chosen Ones . . .

My own Chosen One has been in the headmistress's office for ages. We run out of tea and biscuits, and go to wait for him outside of the Weeping Tower.

I'm pacing the tiled pathway. Penelope is sitting cross-legged on a bench—never mind her short skirt—anxiously plucking leaves off a rosebush. Shepard is staring up at the Tower, probably wondering why it doesn't fall over.

"She won't hurt him," Penny says, to herself, as much as to me.

"But she doesn't like him," I counter. "He says she's never liked him."

"Oh, she likes him fine—she just thinks he's a bad influence on me."

Shepard and I both laugh.

Bunce frowns at us.

"Maybe we should leave before your mom comes down," Shepard says. "I don't want to be here while she's still putting people in towers."

"I'd break you out," Penny says dismissively.

"Almost nothing you say is reassuring," he says, somehow still smiling at her.

"Being reassuring isn't one of my core competencies," she tells him. "Breaking people out of towers is."

Maybe I should go check on Simon. I could wait outside Headmistress Bunce's office. She likes *me*, I think.

I was so terrified when I realized that Simon had gone to the Chapel by himself . . . Then I was irate that he'd lied to us . . . Now I don't know what I am. I'll decide after I see him again. After I've had a chance to inspect him for damage.

Someone pokes me in the back, and I whip around, reaching for my wand—

I find myself at the end of it.

Pippa is standing there, holding my ivory wand out to me. "Here you go." Her voice is rough, but it sounds like it's settled into her chest.

"Pippa . . ." I say.

She frowns. "I didn't mean to steal your wand. Not initially."

"You can have it."

"I—I don't need it."

I stand taller and adjust my cuffs. "Pippa, I'm ready to face whatever consequences I deserve. We can talk to the Coven right now."

"*Crowley*, Pitch. Just—*just shut up*." She shoves the wand into my chest and lets it go.

I catch it. "I don't expect you to forgive me—"

"Good!" she snarls. "I *don't* forgive you. I—" She shakes her head and presses her lips together, like she doesn't have words for how much she hates me. "I never want to see you again."

I nod.

Pippa stares at me for a second, with her arms folded and her face still hateful. "Tell Simon I said thank you," she says, then walks away.

Penelope touches my arm. She's standing just behind me, her right fist subtly pointed at Pippa's back. "All right, Baz?"

I put my hand on her wrist. "All right, Bunce."

78

SIMON

I wait for Penny's mum in her office. She sends the school nurse, Miss Christy, to tend the wound on my wing.

"There's a familiar face."

"Hello, Miss Christy."

"The headmistress says I'm not to cast any spells on you. Let's see that wing."

I spread it out and try not to flinch when she touches it. I trust Miss Christy. She's patched me up more times than I can count. And she never seemed to blame me for it.

"Ran out of bones to break, so you had to give yourself wings, is that it?"

"I reckon, miss."

"You won't need stitches, but this'll sting."

She cleans the cut and leaves me with a bottle of Ribena and two scones. "These are from yesterday, I'm afraid."

"I don't mind," I say. "Thank you."

"The headmistress says you're to keep waiting here for her."

I nod.

Miss Christy looks around the office. "Strange to think he's gone, isn't it?"

She means the Mage, but I'm afraid to acknowledge it. Is she angry with me? Were they close? Miss Christy was at Watford when I started, and she's at least as old as the Mage. How long did they work together?

I nod, carefully.

She pats my hand. "I was sorry for your loss, son."

Oh . . .

I'm still afraid to speak. I nod again. And watch her leave. The sun shifts, and the room falls into shade.

Penny's mum hasn't changed *everything* in here . . . There's still a painted Watford coat of arms hanging by the door. (I suppose those *could* be goats.) And a sturdy iron rack where the Mage used to hang his green woollen cape. An honest-to-Merlin cape.

I wonder where the Mage's capes went . . . And his knee-high boots with the big leather cuffs. Probably to his cousins in Wales. He had a belt I always coveted. Brown leather with a silver buckle that looked like a yew tree.

Siegfried and Roy, I'm losing my mind.

I eat the scones—sour cherry, you'll never find anything like them anywhere else—then pick up all the crumbs from the floor. I wonder what they've done with Smith. Am I under arrest, too? Can Normals be convicted of magickal crimes?

I take down a book about dragons and flip through it, looking for one with wings like mine. I'd call Baz—or Penny—but my phone is dead. (I need a new battery.)

When the door finally opens again, it's Headmistress Bunce and Jamie Salisbury.

"Wait out here a for a minute, would you, Jamie?" She pulls a chair outside for him, then closes the door. "Sorry that took so long, Simon."

She walks over to her desk and leans back against it, studying me through her thick glasses.

"The Coven may call for you to testify at Smith's and his godfather's trials, but I think I got the gist of what happened from Penelope and Baz."

I nod. "Can I go, then?"

"Not yet. I want to spend a little more time with the question of your magic . . ."

"There's no question left, Headmistress. I don't have any."

She moves behind her desk, taking a wand from a drawer and holding it out to me. It's bone with a wooden handle.

I take it. "This is my wand."

"You left it in your room in Mummers House."

"I didn't need it anymore."

She pulls her own wand from her waistband and comes back around to me. "Simon, it's one thing not to be able to cast spells. That's Normal. But it's quite another to be resistant to magic. I want to make sure there's nothing getting between you and the magickal atmosphere."

"Like what?" I ask.

She shrugs. "A curse, a dead spot . . ."

"You think I'm a walking dead spot?"

"I'd like to test a few things."

I do what she asks. I point and repeat. I let her cast spells on me that I've never heard before. Nothing happens—I'm inert.

But I'm not sucking up her magic; that's a good sign.

Eventually, she folds her arms. She's standing in front of me, frowning up into my face. Her hair is especially huge at the moment. "Martin has a theory," she says, "that Smith-Richards was allowing people to tap their magickal potential. The way you'd tap a birch tree. What did he tap in you, Simon . . ."

"I don't know, Professor Bunce—I mean, Headmistress."

She sighs. "You're cursed with usefulness, aren't you?"

"I don't feel very useful."

"Penelope says you have a new flat."

"Yes."

"I'd like you to go home to your new flat and get some rest." She turns away from me before I can reply, and opens the door. "Come on in, Jamie."

I get up to leave.

"Simon," Penny's mum says, "don't run off yet. I'd like you to see Mr. Salisbury back to London."

"Yeah, sure—I'll wait outside."

"You can stay," Jamie says. "Mitali's just going to test my magic. I don't think it'll be much of a show."

Headmistress Bunce and Jamie Salisbury seem to know each other. She's gentle with him, patient, running him through most of the same tests she did me. I wonder how they met. It couldn't have been at Watford—he never went here.

I don't know what Jamie looks like on a normal day, but he looks done in right now. His face is shiny, his eyes are puffy. He needs a shave. He's having trouble following Headmistress Bunce's instructions. "Sorry, Mitali. I'm so shagged out, I'm not sure I could cast a spell even if I *had* magic."

The headmistress lowers her wand. She looks apologetic. (I'm not sure I've ever seen Penny's mum look apologetic before.) "You should go home," she says. "I'll follow up in a few days—with both of you. Dr. Wellbelove will want to see you, as well. This could still all be temporary."

"I'll be at my mum's," Jamie says. Well, that's good news.

"I'll take you," I say. "We should get you something to eat first."

He nods. Headmistress Bunce walks us to the lift.

As we wait for it, Jamie says, "You don't hear from her, do you, Mitali?"

"No," she says quietly. "Do you?"

"Not once. My mum hoped that when he died . . ."

She nods. "Me, too." The lift arrives. Headmistress Bunce looks at me. "Simon, please tell my daughter not to leave Watford without me."

Baz is waiting in the courtyard. With Penelope and her dad and Shepard. Penny runs at me as soon as I walk out of the Tower, and wraps me in a tight hug. I'm just getting my arms around her when she shoves me away.

"What on *earth* were you *thinking*, Simon?!"

"Penny . . ." I say. Baz is just behind her. I reach for him. "*Baz* . . ."

His arms are folded, and his top lip is curled.

My wings flap out without my permission—it makes my cuts sting. "You guys can't be mad at me about this."

"Like hell," Baz says. "You lied to us!"

"I wasn't going to risk Smith casting that spell on you!"

"So you endangered *yourself*?" Penelope demands.

"He couldn't hurt me!" I say. "I knew his spells would bounce off."

"You couldn't have known that, Simon."

"Well, they *did* bounce off . . ."

Baz is still standing behind her, looking pale and furious.

"Baz . . ." I say.

"Are you hurt?" he asks.

"Only superficially; Penny's mum cast a thousand spells on me to make sure. I'm fine."

He shakes his head. "You lied to us, Snow."

"I . . ." I did lie. But it was the right thing to do in the moment. I couldn't risk either of them getting hurt. "I did what I had to do."

"Oh, *shit*," Penelope says. She's looking past me. Her mum is walking out of the Weeping Tower. Penny tries to head her off. "Dad," she calls over her shoulder, "don't let Mum cast on Shepard!"

Baz steps closer to me. There's a line between his eyebrows. He's unfolded his arms, only to put his hands on his hips. He doesn't say anything.

"Did you get your wand back?" I ask.

His shoulders drop a bit. He looks down. "Yeah." He runs one hand through his hair and sighs. I can't tell what the sigh means or what he wants from me. "Daphne's waiting for me," he says. "I said I'd drive her home."

"Oh," I say. "That's good."

"Yeah, it's a relief." He looks up at me, without lifting his head. "Do you . . ."

"I've got to get Jamie home. He's dead tired."

"To Lady Salisbury's?"

"Yeah."

"She'll be happy."

"She will. Baz . . ." I start, not sure how I'll finish.

He shakes his head again. "You can't lie to me, Simon."

"I—"

"Daphne is waiting for me," he says. He turns to go.

79

AGATHA

Niamh wipes my hands clean, finger by finger.

The doe has nursed her kid. Niamh says they're both doing well, though the mother is clearly exhausted.

"I wish we could take them back to the barn," I say.

Niamh lowers an eyebrow, thoughtful. "Let's try. I can carry the doe, with magic, if you can manage the kids."

I turn to the first kid, still lying where I laid it in the grass. The dryad is hovering above it. She looks meeker than she did before, her head down, her mossy hair hanging in her eyes. "I'll take care of this one," she lilts softly. "I'll find a place for it to sleep."

"All right," I say.

"Ready?" Niamh asks me. She's been ignoring the dryad; Niamh only has time for things that are useful.

I nod and pick up her bag. And then the little goat, the live one. Niamh lifts its mother in her arms and walks steadily back into the forest.

I feel like I should say something more to the dryad—

No. I feel like I should say something to Ebb.

I look up at her stone marker. There are flowers growing all around it, vines winding up and around the marble. I didn't notice that before.

The dryad is watching me from a few feet away.

I whisper to the stone: "I did what you told me to do. I ran."

The dryad drifts closer.

I drop my voice even more. "Thank you."

I leave then, before Niamh gets too far ahead of me.

"Do you know where you're going?" I call out to her.

"No!" she shouts back. "Hurry up, so I can follow you."

It's daylight again at the edge of the Wood. When we walk through the trees, the rest of the herd is waiting for us. They jump and bleat when they see the doe in Niamh's arms. A few of them spread their wings—they're feathered, just like a pegasus's.

I kneel and hold the baby out—a little doe—so they can see her.

"Careful," Niamh says.

"It's all right," I say. And it is. The goats nose at the kid and crowd around Niamh's legs to check on the mother. "You're very special goats," I coo, "aren't you?"

One of the billy goats flaps his wings and lifts off the ground, flying in a circle around us. A few of the others join him. I laugh and look up at Niamh. She's already smiling at me.

"Niamh," I say. "I wonder . . ."

I stand again, and start walking towards Watford. Niamh walks with me. The goats leap and bound and flit around us. Across the Great Lawn, over the drawbridge, through the courtyard. There are a few people milling around outside the White Chapel. They stop and stare. I keep walking, back to the barn Ebb shared with the goats. The doors swing open for us, and the goats follow us in, making themselves at home. Niamh casts a spell in one corner, to freshen up the straw, and we set the mother and child down together.

Niamh is beaming. At the goats. At me. When her hands are free, she gets them around me. I hook my arms behind her neck. More of her hair has fallen into her eyes, and it makes my knees weak. Thank magic she's holding on to me, holding me up. Niamh kisses me again, and I want to draw a line through everything I considered a kiss before. I never knew a kiss could ask this much from me.

80

SIMON

Jamie and I end up in the stolen van. He doesn't know how to drive, but I think I can manage. (Though my only practice has been on American highways.) He hasn't eaten all day, so we stop at a KFC and eat our chicken in the car park. Neither of us says a word till we're finished.

"What'll we do if we get caught with this van?" Jamie asks, shoving his rubbish into a paper bag. "Neither of us have magic."

"I guess we'll have to wait for Baz and your mum to come fix it."

"Well," he says glumly, "I'm used to that."

"Getting arrested?"

"No. Just my mum fixing things . . ." He glances over at me. "You must think I'm a right plonker. Letting Smith fool me like that. Hiding in his basement, just because he told me to."

I shake my head. "I don't think that—I believed him, too."

"Part of me *still* believes in him." Jamie sighs.

"I really am a plonker."

"I'm sorry," I say, "about your magic."

"Ah, it's all right." He throws a napkin into the bag. "I didn't have much to lose. Not like you. You must miss it like crazy."

"I do. But . . . if I'm being honest, I was never any good at it either. It's not just about power, you know—you have to have some skill."

Jamie buckles his safety belt. "My sister was a brilliant magician. She was so good, they sent her to Watford a year early."

"My friend Penelope started school early, too." Penny had to wait almost a year to go the pub with the rest of us.

"Mitali's daughter."

"That's right." I start the van—Penny charmed it to work without a key—and glance over at Jamie. "Were you jealous of her? Your sister?"

"Of Lucy?" He sounds surprised. "No. I mean, I missed her. When she left for school. We thought I'd be joining her someday. She used to tell me how she was going to show me around Watford once I got there, teach me all the tricks . . ." A wave of exhaustion seems to roll over him. He drops the rubbish onto the floor. "Nah, I wasn't jealous of Lucy. She was so good to me . . . I couldn't begrudge her anything."

I know what I want to ask him next, but I'm not sure that I should. I wait until we're driving again, my eyes on the road. "What happened to your sister? I hope that's not a rude question. Your mum showed us her picture . . . and the candle."

"Lucy ran away," Jamie says. "When she was about your age."

I glance over at him. "Ran away from what?"

"From *who*," he says, pushing a hand roughly through his

hair. "She got involved with a bad bloke. My parents reck-
oned she left the country to hide from him."

"Christ," I say. "He must have been terrible, if she had to
run away from the whole World of Mages."

Jamie's squinting out the window. "My mum doesn't like
us to talk about it . . ."

"Sure," I say, "I understand."

". . . because it was the Mage."

I turn my whole head towards him, then whip my eyes
back onto the road. "The *Mage*?"

"Uh-huh."

"Your sister dated *the Mage*?"

"They met at school."

"I didn't know the Mage *dated* . . ."

"My parents hated him." Jamie's voice is flat. This is all
old news for him. "They thought he was a nutter. My mum
wanted to send Lucy to Switzerland to get away from him."

"What's in Switzerland?"

"I still don't know. Anyway, Lucy didn't listen. She and
Davy ran off after Watford—maybe they got married. Whatever happened, it wasn't good. She used to write my mum
these letters . . ." He trails off. I give him a moment to go on,
but he doesn't.

"And then what?"

He shrugs. "Then she stopped writing. She disappeared."

I can't wrap my head around this. Not even a little. "What
did the Mage say about that?"

"Not much. He blamed my parents for Lucy leaving him.
My dad wanted to challenge him to a duel. My mum was
beside herself."

"You don't think . . ." I rearrange my hands on the steering wheel. "I mean, you don't think he . . ."

Jamie looks at his lap. "My mum believes Lucy's alive. You've seen the candle."

"Right," I say. "Cor. No wonder Lady Ruth hates the Mage."

"She practically threw a party when you killed him. I think she would have sent you roses if she knew how to get them to you."

We're both quiet.

"I suppose I have to tell my mum that I lost my magic," Jamie says after a while.

"I think she's just gonna be so relieved to see you."

"I still can't believe she sent *Simon Snow* after me . . ."

"It's kind of a long story—the Coven thought you'd been murdered by vampires."

"Vampires?" He laughs. "Imagine."

When we get to Lady Ruth's house, Jamie tries to get me to come up to the house with him—but it doesn't feel right. I stay in the van. (I'm going to abandon it a few blocks from here.) I watch him walk up to the big front door. I can see the candles burning in the upper window.

Jamie knocks. And after a few minutes, Lady Ruth comes to the door. She looks shocked to see him. He hugs her. I think she might be crying.

They go inside, and the door closes.

81

BAZ

It's an hour-long drive to Oxford. My stepmother cries intermittently for the first half hour, then goes pale and wrings her hands for the second. I think she would have turned back if she were the one driving.

When we get to the hunting lodge, I pull the car right up to the house and turn off the engine. She shows no sign of getting out, so neither do I. I tap the steering wheel and look up at the door.

Daphne and I don't talk about things. Not usually. Not *really*.

She'll ask me how university is going, and I'll tell her, and then she'll say, *"Good show, Basilton. You make your father so proud."* She used to ask for my help with the girls—but never in a badgering way. She used to take me shopping for summer clothes and sports gear.

I never rebelled against my father's remarriage. I just went to Watford and got over it. I got used to Daphne. Things got better after she moved in. (Even though she's the reason my aunt moved out.)

My father got very hard when my mother died—perhaps he was always hard, I don't know—but Daphne softens him. She's the reason I got a mobile phone when I turned 15. And the reason I got to go on school trips. And probably the reason my father didn't murder Simon after our ancestral home lost its magic.

She's a good person. A good stepmother.

"They're going to be happy to see you," I say softly.

She laughs, joylessly. Some of the tears come back. "How am I going to explain this . . ."

"You might not have to," I say. "My father is usually relieved when I don't explain things."

Daphne laughs again, less joylessly, and cries a little more. "Your mother never would have been such a fool," she says in a small voice.

My mother might have killed me, I think.

And then, *My mother isn't here.*

And then, *How did my mother feel about gay people, has Father ever mentioned it, maybe when George Michael came out?*

I get out of the car and walk around to Daphne's side, opening her door. She looks up at me, still hesitating. I hold out my hand. "Come on, Mum."

Mordelia is passing through the living room when we walk in. She doesn't look up from her phone.

"Delia," Daphne says.

Mordelia looks up. "Mum!" She runs at Daphne's middle.

I step out of the way. "Dad!" Mordelia shouts. "Mum's home!" She pulls away a bit to look at Daphne. "*Are* you home? Did you get the thing you needed?"

"I'm home," Daphne says, smiling, her eyes too bright.

"Mordelia, I've asked you not to shout in the—" My father is walking into the living room, holding Swithin. He stops when he sees Daphne.

"Mum's home!" Mordelia shouts again. (I never would have raised my voice in this situation, even at 8.)

"Hello, Malcolm," Daphne says.

"The twins . . ." my father says.

Her face falls. "Are they all right?"

"They're out back . . . I was just going to check on them."

"I'll do it," I say. "Mordelia will help."

Mordelia pouts. "Baz, no—"

"Come on, Mother's not going anywhere." I take Swithin from my father and haul Mordelia towards the back door. "Let them have a hug. You know they won't do it in front of us."

"Did Mum finish magic school?"

"Yes," I say. "All done."

"And she's really home?"

"Yeah," I say, hoping I'm right. We find Sophie and Petra in the garden, playing with the Tibetan mastiff my father bought when they moved to Oxford.

"Mum's home!" Mordelia tells the twins.

"That's Baz," one of them says, climbing up my leg. I sit on the ground, so that I have some lap for her. The dog edges away from me, growling. Good instincts.

When Daphne comes out, fifteen minutes later, all three of the girls run to her. Swithin starts crying. Daphne takes him.

My father is standing in the doorway, watching. "Help me with dinner, Basilton?"

"Of course, Father."

You'd never guess, at dinner, that Daphne has been gone for weeks. Which is a good sign, I think. My father treats her with as much polite tenderness as ever. He dotes on her, in his way. Caters to her every whim, without making a show of it.

I could get back to London before the trains stop, but Daphne asks me to stay the night. After dinner, I head to the attic to rummage through some boxes of my old things that were brought up from the house in Hampshire. Then I go hunting in the fields behind the house. (Two rabbits and a mole.)

Daphne makes a bed for me on the sofa. "You should have your own room here," she says.

"I'm fine. The twins are already doubled up." I've just taken a shower, and I'm wearing some old pyjamas I found upstairs—they're a bit short. Daphne hands me a wool blanket, and I spread it out over the cushions.

"We could add on," she says. "Your father could manage the spells. Or we could, you know, hire a builder."

"I don't think that's necessary—"

"Or we could convert one of the barns! So you could come home for holidays. And bring a friend."

"I . . ." I look over at her. Is she joking? My father would set me on fire if I brought Simon home. (Any boy, really. He'd set me on fire *twice* if it was Simon.) "That doesn't seem likely."

Daphne has just finished shaking a pillow into its case. She looks very sincere. And very cautious. Like someone who is very, very carefully stepping onto thin ice. "It's possible, I think. Basilton."

I nod. And take the pillow from her.

She touches my shoulder, just for a second. "Good night, darling."

"Good night, Mum."

I wait for her to leave, and then lie down, under the blanket. My phone is on the floor. I pick it up and open my text messages. I click on "SNOW."

All of my unanswered messages from last week are still there. I shouldn't reread them, it will just make me melancholy—I do read them, of course—and I definitely shouldn't text Simon right now. Simon hates texting, even when he isn't trying to ghost me.

"I'm staying in Oxford tonight. Did you make it home in one piece?" I send the text, then immediately set the phone on my chest, rolling my eyes at myself.

It buzzes, and I jump, knocking it to the floor.

I pick it up.

"3 pieces actually, do you know how to sew?"

I smile. And roll my eyes at myself some more. It takes nothing to please me. *"Did you deliver Jamie Salisbury safely home?"*

"yeah, you won't believe what he told me—his sister dated the mage!"

Aleister Crowley. The Mage? *"The actual Mage?"* I text.

"THE MAGE," Simon sends back.

"No wonder she fled the country."

"no wonder her mum hates him!! lady ruth already called

to thank us, for jamie and everything—she's making us lunch tomorrow to celebrate, will you be back?"

"*Yes*," I send.

He sends me back a thumbs-up.

I stare at the screen for a second, not sure what to say next. Simon and I don't have text conversations. Not usually. *Not really.*

Simon starts typing—there's a "..." on the screen—then stops. Then starts again.

"*you still angry with me?*" he finally sends.

I think about it for a second. "*Yes.*"

"*can it wait until you come back?*"

"*What do you mean?*"

"*be angry with me tomorrow, when you're here, not now*"

"*You want me to set it aside?*"

"*y*"

I think again. "*All right.*"

"*are you angry?*"

"*No*," I type. Honestly. It's easy to set my anger aside; I don't *want* to be angry with Simon. If anything, I want to apologize for being angry with him. Which isn't fair. He's the one who lied.

He doesn't reply right away. Then—"*you were right about smith.*"

Well, obviously. "*Yes.*"

"*i'm worried that I'm just going to keep falling for this bullshit*"

"*What bullshit?*"

"*first the mage, now smith*"

I frown at the phone. "*You* didn't *fall for the Mage's shit. You were a child.*"

"fell for smith's tho"

"Only for a minute. Then you brought him to justice. That's the important part of the pattern, I think—the bringing to justice."

"maybe"

Simon starts typing more, then stops. Then starts. Then stops.

I wait.

Finally he sends: *"i wish smith had been the real thing"*

For fuck's sake. *"Why?"*

"because then i could stop feeling bad about letting everyone down, they'd have a greatest mage to do all their great mage stuff"

I scowl at the phone and tap his name to call him.

He picks up after a few seconds. "Baz?"

"You have never in your life let anyone down."

Simon doesn't say anything at first. (I can hear the three dots.) "That's not true," he says. "I let you down all the time."

"It isn't 'letting someone down' to be depressed."

"You're literally still angry at me from earlier today."

"Because you lied to me, Snow!"

"Doesn't that count?"

"Fine," I whisper harshly, "you let me down all the time—I think that's just being in a relationship—but you've never let the World of Mages down. You don't owe the magickal community anything. You never did. But you've served it with unflagging honour."

"I liked it!" he says. I'm speaking softly, but Simon isn't—he's practically shouting now. "I liked every part of it! I know you think it was wrong that the Mage used me and made me fight, but I liked it. I miss it. I liked having a job, and I liked that specific job, and I liked knowing who I was. In a larger sense. I didn't know who my parents were, but I knew who *I* was. Who I was supposed to be. Who the fuck am I now, Baz?"

"You're the same person!"

"I was the Chosen One before."

"You were *you*. You still are."

He growls. "You're not getting it—"

"I *do* get it." I pull the blanket up over my head to muffle my voice. "I understand that you've lost something—a lot of things—but you're still the same person. I know, because I loved you then, and I love you now, and I know that's not enough to make you happy—to make anyone happy—but you're the same *person*, Simon. You're still you."

He doesn't answer me. It sounds like he's pacing. I can hear his wings snapping open and closed.

"It's enough," he finally grumbles.

"What is," I whisper.

"The fact that you love me. It does make me happy."

"Yeah?"

"Yeah," he sighs. "It doesn't fix everything. I still don't know who's looking back at me in the mirror. But . . . it makes me happy."

"You sound ecstatic, Snow."

He laughs.

There's a creaking noise, like he's sitting down—on his mattress or the new sofa. "I want to tell you that I'm sorry I lied to you," he says. "But then I think about you walking into the Chapel and getting that spell cast at you. That curse."

"Why would Smith-Richards have cast a spell on me that would immediately make me more powerful?"

"I don't know—to hurt you. He's a fucked-up person!"

"You'll get no argument there," I say. "But you can't lie to me every time there's trouble. You can't sideline me from every battle."

"Are you expecting lots of battles in the future?"

"You may have forgotten who you are, Snow, but I haven't."

Simon sighs. He sounds tired. "You said we could set this aside until you come back."

"You brought it up."

"I know. I'm sorry. About that, anyway. Are . . . Are you still coming back?"

"*Simon . . .*" I know he's damaged and insecure, but he keeps questioning the one thing I know for certain. It's insulting. "I'll always come back," I say.

He's quiet. I can hear him breathing. I can hear the three dots hovering over his head.

"Me, too," he whispers.

82

BAZ

I hunt before I leave Oxford. (Two more rabbits, a fox.) Then my father drives me to the station.

He doesn't say anything in the car, and I don't expect him to.

It's an hour on the train to London. When I get there, I go to Fiona's flat first. I let myself in. "Fiona?"

There's no answer. I suppose I could leave her a note . . .

"She went to get breakfast," someone says.

Nico is standing in the door to my aunt's bedroom, looking like he just threw on jeans and a T-shirt—and looking thoroughly displeased to be speaking to me.

"You could wait for her," he says.

"I live here."

"I know that, I just meant . . ." He smooths back his blond hair and sighs. "You want tea?"

I frown. And nod. I sit on the sofa.

Nico comes back from the kitchen with two mugs and a

pint of milk. He sits on the chair.

I cross one leg over the other and pick a piece of lint off my knee. "So you're going to marry my aunt."

"That's right." His chin is sticking out, like he's expecting whatever nasty thing I say next. I can't overemphasize what an unpleasant face the man has. Sour and smirking. Handsome in an angry way. Like the lead singer of a band who resents how popular his music is with teenage girls.

He must be nearly 40—he's Ebb's twin brother—but he looks like an unhealthy 20-something. His skin is grey, and his eyes are tired. Is this what I look like? Is this what I'll always look like? Like a 21-year-old who never gets any sleep?

Nico wipes his mouth with the back of his hand. There are gaps where his eyeteeth were. At least I still have my smile.

"Congratulations," I say. "Does this mean you're turning over a new leaf?"

"What's that supposed to mean?"

"I don't know whether you've noticed, but my aunt is a vampire hunter."

He smirks. "Yeah, I've noticed—have you?"

I find some more lint on my trousers. Perhaps I should just leave. Fiona doesn't need my blessing for this.

"I'm not gonna Turn your aunty," Nico says. "Is that what you're worried about? If I were gonna Turn Fiona, I woulda done it already. I wouldn't put a scratch on her."

"That's cold comfort for all the people you murder."

"I don't—" He sets his tea down, and pulls an e-cigarette out of his pocket. He takes a hit off it. "I'm done with all that. Fi's made me go vegan."

"Vegan?" I say, genuinely surprised.

He rolls his hand in the air. "You know . . . Rats, cats,

bats. Nothing that talks back to me. I feel like shit, and now I can look forward to losing my hair, but I reckon it doesn't matter. Don't wanna live forever without Fiona, at any rate."

I sit up. *What does he—*

Does that mean—

I refuse to ask Nicodemus Petty any vampire questions. But . . .

"Do you mean . . ." I say, "that it affects you? Not having . . . people?"

"You fucking with me?" He sneers. "You think you can find immortality at the bottom of, what the shit, a squirrel?"

"I—"

The front door opens, and Fiona walks in with a paper bakery bag and coffee. "Basil." She looks at me, then at Nico, then back at me. "Is everything all right?"

"Everything's fine," he says. "I made tea."

"I . . ." I stand up. "Fiona, could I talk to you for a moment?"

"I'll step out," Nico says. "Could use a nip anyway." He walks to the door, patting my aunt's shoulder on the way out. Her hand goes to cover his for a second.

Then she sets her breakfast down on the coffee table. She narrows her eyes. "Did you forget something? Come back to ransack the kitchen cupboards?"

I reach into my jacket and fish my grandmother's ring out of my pocket. It's gold, with a sapphire and three diamonds. I hold it out to Fiona in my palm.

"Mum's ring," she says, eyes wide. She looks from my hand to my face. "Basil, did you rob your own mother's grave?"

I shake my head. "My father gave it to me. Years ago, as a keepsake. He told me that my mother used to wear it every day . . ."

"She did," Fiona says, her voice breaking.

I hold my hand farther out to her. "Take it."

She looks away. "No. Your dad's right. You should have it to remember your mum."

"I'll see it more often on your hand than I will if it stays in a box."

She peers back at me, biting her cheek, but still doesn't take it.

I look down at the ring. "I think my father hoped I might give it to a girl someday . . ."

Fiona snatches it from my palm. "Simon Snow is *not* getting my mother's sapphire."

I laugh. "Homophobic."

"It isn't because he's a boy," she says. "It's because he's a pain in my arse." Then she screws up her face at me—like she feels guilty, and it's my fault. "Well, shit . . . Did you *want* to give it to him?"

"No," I say, still laughing. "Take it."

She beams at me. "Thank you."

"You're welcome."

She grabs me into a hug, rocking us back and forth. "Thank you, thank you."

"You're welcome, Fiona."

She pulls away and opens her fist, holding the ring so she can admire it. "I know you think I'm mad . . ."

"As a hatter. Are you telling anyone else about the wedding?"

"Can you imagine? Pitches on one side of the Chapel, vampires on the other."

"That would put me in a very awkward position."

She bumps her shoulder into my arm, smiling at me.

"Wasn't planning a wedding. But Nicky's going to move in."

"I figured as much."

"And we're going to make it legal the Normal way. *They* haven't stricken him from their books." She quirks an eyebrow at me. "We could use a witness . . ."

I consider knocking at Snow's door. But it's still early, and I have a key.

His flat's quiet. I'm quiet, too, in case he's sleeping. I've brought scones. I set them on the kitchen counter.

"I thought you were a goblin," Simon says. He's standing in his bedroom door, holding a dinner knife like a dagger. He slept in his knit boxers—he still looks half asleep.

"I'll take that as a compliment," I say. "Goblins are fit."

Simon rubs his face and walks back into the bedroom. When I get there, he's under the duvet again.

I sit on the edge of the mattress. "Are you sleeping with a full set of cutlery or just the knife?"

"Don't have a sword," he mumbles, like that explains it. "Come back to bed."

"I wasn't in bed."

"Don't be a dick."

I take off my jacket and waistcoat—the same thing I was wearing yesterday, maybe I should leave some clothes in Oxford—and look over my shoulder at Simon. He's tucked himself into a knot under the blanket and buried his face in his pillow. His hair is curling in every direction. Big, fat curls. He must have gone to sleep with it wet.

I look down at my shoes and quickly unlace them. I take off my socks and my trousers, my button-down shirt, and—after a second of deliberation—my T-shirt. It feels strange to get undressed without anyone requesting it or giving me permission. I suppose I'm requesting it. I'm the one who wants it.

I get under the blanket. Snow reaches out to me and pulls me against him. He's still sleep-warm. I feel his tail sliding over my thigh. We're face-to-face, but he's not looking in my eyes.

"Don't be angry with me yet," he whispers. His breath smells rotten. Maybe if he were someone else, I'd mind.

"When do I get to be angry?" I ask.

He knocks his forehead against mine, still looking down. "Later."

"All right," I whisper.

He brings his hand up, catches his thumb on my bottom lip. "You're pink."

"Breakfast," I say.

He rubs my lip roughly against my teeth. My jaw goes slack. Simon glances up, into my eyes, and then rubs my lip again, more gently. I shiver.

I touch his side, his skin, his ribs. He thinks he's fat—he isn't. He just isn't a starving teenager anymore. He's solid and stalwart. And so warm . . . His skin feels different when he's been sleeping, I don't understand why. Thicker somehow, more lush. I move my hand to the small of his back, just above his tail, and pull him closer—he grimaces.

I lift my hand away. "Are you injured?"

Snow shrugs. "A bit. My wing's cut up. From the glass in the Chapel. I have to heal the old-fashioned way."

I kiss his cheek, quickly. "What can I do?"

"Can you . . ." He pushes me onto my back (I let him) and rolls partly on top of me. It frees up his wings, and he relaxes them, half spread, above us. "Thanks."

I reach up to pet the edge of one wing. It twitches.

"Does that hurt?" I ask.

"No, it . . ." He wrinkles his nose, like he isn't sure. "No—it's sensitive; it doesn't hurt. The cuts are farther back."

I go on, rubbing the bony ridge of his wing. It's kid-glove soft and warm like the rest of him.

Simon relaxes into me, nuzzling his face in my cheek.

I'm going to miss these wings. This tail. I won't tell him so—I don't blame him for wanting them gone. But I love them now the way I love every part of him. I get my other arm around him, and rub his other wing, too. He groans into my neck.

"Okay?" I ask.

He nods. After a minute, he mumbles, "Do you feel like you're in bed with a dragon?"

"Not in a bad way," I whisper, feeling the thick cords that run through the top of his wings. (Simon Snow has muscles no one else does.) "Do you feel like you're in bed with a vampire?"

"Yes," he says. Then laughs.

I move my hands down to his sides, where it's safe to pinch him.

"Ouch," he laughs. "I'm injured."

I pinch him again, just above his waistband.

He's still laughing. He tries to push my arms away. "Ouch. Stop. I meant—'not in a bad way.'"

"There's no *good* way to be in bed with a vampire."

"I beg to differ," he says, biting my neck. "It's only been good so far."

I close my eyes and push my face into the side of Simon's head. I want that to be true. I want it to stay true.

"I'm sorry I lied to you," he whispers.

I wrap my arms around his waist. "Promise me you won't do it again."

"No."

"*Snowww,*" I groan. "I thought you didn't want me to be angry right now."

Simon lifts himself up, rests on his side, on his elbow, and takes my face in both hands. "I think I made the right decision. To protect you and Penny."

"We don't need protection."

"You do," he says, mulish. "Sometimes."

"What I need is to be able to trust you."

"You *can,* Baz. Trust me to make the right decision. In the moment. Trust me to think on my feet."

Simon's blue eyes are open, guileless. He isn't manipulating me now. His eyebrows are tense. His lips are parted. His teeth are very white.

"You can trust me," he says again. "You already do."

He's right . . .

But he's also *wrong.*

"You're infuriating," I say.

He kisses my cheek. Quickly. "Be infuriated later."

"No. You've run out of extensions."

He brushes my hair out of my eyes, runs his fingers along my scalp. "I think this is what people do . . ."

"What are you talking about, Snow?"

"You said last night that I disappoint you constantly."

I shake my head. "I didn't mean—"

He catches my chin. "You did. I do. I let you down. And yet you don't stop . . ."

"I don't stop?"

Simon swallows; it's my favourite show. "Loving me."

"Simon . . ." I kiss him. He kisses me back. My arms are tight around his waist. My head is in his hands.

I've wanted this . . .

With Simon . . .

Since I knew how to want.

But it isn't what I thought it would be. It's like I dreamed of kissing him in black-and-white, and now I'm kissing him in colour. And his mouth is sour. And his face is shining with summer morning sweat. There's hair under his arms and down his stomach, and the skin on his forearms is three shades darker than on his chest.

He still disappoints me sometimes. But not . . .

I pull my mouth away. "I'm not disappointed."

"I know," he says, kissing me.

"You don't let me down."

"It's all right, Baz." He kisses me. Then kisses me again.

"As long as you—"

He kisses me with his mouth loose and his tongue pushing fat into my mouth. My jaw drops open, and I move my hands to his hips, clutching him.

"As long as we—" I say when he takes a breath.

He pushes his tongue back into my mouth, and it's obscene. His mouth is getting wetter and sweeter. I groan and give up on my sentence. *As long as we keep on trying,* I was going to say. But now I'm just trying to keep my fangs from popping. Now Simon is fucking into my mouth again, and I'm pushing my fingertips down the side of his pants, because I want to, and this is what's happening, I think.

Simon growls and lifts up off of me.

"I'm sorry—" I say immediately, sitting up.

But Simon is pushing his jersey boxer briefs down, and kicking them off his ankles. Then he pulls the blanket back over us as high as his wings allow. "Okay?" he asks.

"Yeah, I . . ."

"I love you," Simon says, settling over me again, all skin and bones and belly. "I'll keep getting better for you, I promise."

What could be better than this?

"You don't have to," I say.

"Yeah . . ." He takes my chin in hand again. "I do."

SIMON

Baz looks so good right now, does he know it?

All that inky black hair curling on his paper-pale neck. He looks less grey than usual. Or maybe I've just acclimated to it. I like him grey. I like him.

I like his narrow shoulders—narrow compared to mine, anyway. All of him longer and leaner than me. I like comparing us. I want to lay myself over him elbow to elbow, hip to hip. I want to grow my hair out, so I can see what it looks like, twined up with his around my finger.

Baz came back. This morning. He was always going to come back. I think he always will, if I make it good for him. I think he wants this, wants me. And I'm going to make it so good for him. This morning. This life.

I'm being gentle—it's already easier, now that I know how much he likes it. The way he goes boneless when I hold him like china. When my hands are whispers not shouts. I'm going to keep finding out what he likes.

This is what people do.

They get close and try to stay there.

They stay.

They keep trying to hold on to each other, even though it's not really possible, I don't think. Because people are always moving, aren't they. But this is what they do. They keep trying.

I'll keep trying.

To keep him well.

To keep him happy.

Merlin, I'm too turned on to think. I love him, I love him. But I also want to *do* this, whatever it is that works between us. With Agatha, it—No, never mind, that doesn't matter.

I'm holding Baz's jaw and kissing him. I'm stroking his cheek like he'll break. My cock is in his hip. He's pushing his briefs off, he's trying to stay under the blanket—I help him.

This would be good enough. Just this. Baz. Finally. Beside me.

"You don't disappoint me," he says, reaching for me.

"It's all right," I say. "I knew what you meant."

He holds my face in both hands. I hold his like it's precious.

This is what people do. This is what we'll do. Baz and me.

His lips are pinkish grey. His tongue is nearly red. His fangs are down, I'll be careful.

"You smell so good," I say.

His eyes are half closed. "Like a cave."

"Like cold water."

"That's not a smell, Snow."

I lick his lips. "So good."

"Stay with me," he whispers. "Don't get lost in it."

"I won't," I swear. "I'm here."

He makes a fist in my hair. "Stay with me."

"I will."

BAZ

Maybe this is enough. Simon. Finally. Beside me.

Maybe it's too much.

Maybe I'm the one getting lost . . .

(This is what I wanted, but I didn't know what it was like. His heart is beating in my throat. His hands are everywhere. His tail. He has so many ways to hold on to me.)

I push his face away from mine. "I need—"

"What do you need, babe?"

I hold on to his cheeks. "I need you to know that I'm not disappointed in you."

"Baz, it's okay. I know."

"I believe in you." I cover his mouth, so he'll listen. "Simon, I believe in you."

He doesn't try to argue. Not right away. His face looks so red under my hands. My bloodless fingers. My blue nails.

Simon pulls my wrist down. "Do you trust me?"

He knows I do. That I did, even when I hated him. (I never hated him.)

"Yes."

"Can I touch you?"

I nod my head.

83

SIMON

I'm not crying. Neither is Baz.

My wings hurt. I lie on my stomach, so I can spread them out.

Baz sits beside me, and I know he's inspecting the damage from yesterday. They're just cuts, I'll live.

I feel his fingers on the back of my neck.

"You can be angry now," I say.

He pulls my hair.

84

SIMON

A few hours later, Baz is sitting on my bed with his violin, holding it like a guitar. He's not playing anything, really. Just making cheerful noises with it. I didn't know Baz's violin was capable of cheerful noises. At Watford, it always sounded like it was crying.

"Does that hurt?" he asks.

I've got my wings folded up as tight as I can, and I'm buttoning a shirt over them. "Yeah, but there's no way around it."

"You could leave them out," he says, "and I'll cast spells at everyone who looks at you."

"Seems impractical," I say. "I'll cope. I can spread them out once we get to Lady Ruth's."

"She'll like that." Baz stands up, leaving the violin on my bed, and comes over to me. He moves my hands away and finishes buttoning the shirt. It's his shirt, an olive-green cotton one with complicated stripes and short sleeves. (I've never even seen Baz wear short sleeves.)

"Are you going to dress me every morning?" I ask.

"If you allow it, absolutely."

I'll probably allow it, what do I care.

"I don't want to wear flowers," I say. Baz is wearing flowers. His button-down shirt is grey with sprays of pink and blue lilacs. He makes it look manly somehow, with his indigo trousers and grey lace-up shoes. I'd look like a sofa.

"No flowers." He kisses my cheek. "So noted, rosebud boy."

I look up at him. "That's what the ghost called me—your mother. That's what she said."

Baz is looking in my eyes. "I remember." He runs his thumb over my cheek. Then my bottom lip. "My rosebud boy."

Lady Ruth has the door open before we get to it. "Simon!" she says. "Baz! Come in, come in!"

She hugs us both. I try not to wince.

"Do you mind if Simon lets out his wings?" Baz asks. "They're injured."

"Oh, of course!" she says. "The wings are always welcome. I wish I could walk around with wings."

I take off my jacket, and Baz casts, ***"Like a glove!"***—which makes the shirt tailor itself around my wings. It's probably the best way to deal with them, but I can't count on Baz and Penny always being around to cast it for me.

"I hope you're hungry," Lady Ruth says, herding us into the dining room. "I may have gone overboard on the sandwiches, even for me—but we are celebrating. *Jamie!*" she shouts. "*The boys are here!*"

"Great snakes . . ." I say. The dining room table is cram-jammed with food. Finger sandwiches, little cakes and tarts, meringues. All on fancy pink and green pedestals and platters. It's like Wonderland. I half expect the dormouse to poke his head out of the teapot.

Right in the middle of everything, stuck right into the table, is a tremendous sword. An antique, it looks like, with a golden pommel.

"Tch, Jamie," Lady Ruth mutters. "He thinks it's very funny to leave his sword around. *Jamie! Come and move your sword!*"

"I've got it," I say, reaching for the sword and sliding it out of the table. It hasn't left a mark—it must be magic. It's got a nice heft. Well-balanced, too. "This is a hell of a blade."

I look up. Lady Ruth is staring at me like she's just seen a ghost. Jamie is in the doorway, looking just as shocked.

I turn the sword and offer him the grip. "Sorry. I shouldn't have, um . . ."

He doesn't take it.

"Sorry," I say again.

BAZ

Snow has apparently committed some massive sword faux pas. He's standing there, holding it out, and the Salisburys are looking at him like he just stuck his hand in the butter. Or worse, like he's threatening them.

"That's . . ." Lady Salisbury gasps. "That's an Excalibur!"

Simon looks down at the sword, his eyes goggling. "*This* is Excalibur?"

"It's *an* Excalibur," she says. "Made by Merlin himself."

"I don't understand . . ." Simon says.

Neither do I. But if this means Snow is the once and future king, I can't say I'll be surprised at this point.

"It's a family sword," Jamie says, still looking gobsmacked. "Made for the House of Salisbury."

"I'm not a Salisbury by blood." Lady Ruth's voice is trembling. "Once it's planted, I can't budge it."

"I . . ." Simon looks like he wants to set the sword down, but that seems like another faux pas.

Lady Salisbury rushes towards him, past the sword, to throw her arms around him. "Oh, my child, my child!"

Does this mean . . .

Could Simon be . . .

SIMON

Lady Ruth is hugging me even more tightly than usual. I move the sword behind me.

"I'm sorry," I say.

"You're a Salisbury," Jamie says, still staring at me.

"I'm certain I'm not. It must be a fluke—I'm not even a magician."

"Oh, my child," Lady Ruth says again. She's crying. "My child."

"I'm not—"

She pulls away from me and takes my face in her hands, like she's looking for something there. "I've waited so long for you. Where is your mother?"

"I'm sorry?" I whisper.

"Come!" She pulls me out of the dining room.

"Lady Ruth—" I say, letting her drag me. I look back at Baz, but he just shrugs, as confused as I am. He and Jamie follow us up the stairs, to Lady Ruth's bedroom, to the shrine she keeps by the window.

Jamie's candle burns bright.

But her daughter's candle has finally sputtered out. A thread of smoke curls above it.

"I'm so sorry," I say.

What have I done?

85

LADY RUTH

Lucy.

Her candle.

She's gone.

Or perhaps . . .

Simon Snow is standing before me, holding my husband's sword. I can see Lucy in the set of his shoulders. And Davy in the set of his eyes. Why didn't I see it before?

Lucy is gone. But perhaps . . . perhaps she let go.

I told her to bring the child home. I prayed and pleaded. *Bring it home. Let me help you keep it safe.*

And here he is.

Here he must be.

My Lucy's child, my flesh and blood.

My Simon.

86

BAZ

"I'm sorry!" Simon is looking frantically between Lady Salisbury and the candle.

"It's all right," I say, trying to get to him.

But Lady Ruth is hugging him again. "It's *you*. You've finally come *home*."

"This is a mistake—" Simon insists.

"My sister had a child . . ." Jamie Salisbury says, standing beside his mother. "She told us that she had a child."

"I can't be—"

"You *must* be," Jamie says gently, pointing at the sword. "Merlin, Simon, you even look like him."

Oh . . .

He does.

Doesn't he?

Those narrow eyes. That tilt of his head.

I thought . . .

I thought he'd learned it. Was imitating it.

Simon Snow is the Mage's heir.
He was.
All along.

87

SIMON

No.

No.

Because that would mean—

It would mean—

No.

The Mage found me in a care home. He said he followed my magic.

(But that was a lie; I didn't have magic.)

The Mage found me in care.

And he lied to me.

He used me—to what end, I still don't know. I was part of a plot, a plan. I was a vessel, he said.

He *found* me. He *made* me his heir.

He lied to me again and again.

(The Mage had a name. The Mage fell in love. The Mage ran off with a yellow-haired girl, and then she disappeared.)

It can't be true, I'm not what they say, because that would mean—

It would mean *too much.*

It would *be* too much.

The Mage lied to me. He lied to the whole World of Mages. He killed Ebb. He tried to take my magic. He hurt me. He hurt me again and again.

Then I begged him to stop.

And he did.

I can't be Lady Salisbury's child. Because I can't be Lucy's. Because I can't be the Mage's.

I killed him.

I killed him.

I killed the Mage.

I can't be—

88

BAZ

Lady Salisbury won't let go of Simon. He's collapsed in her arms. Sobbing without tears.

"My child, my child," she keeps saying. And I think she's right—I think it's undeniable. I'd cast "Flesh and blood" on them, but it would probably bounce right off of Snow like every other spell has so far.

I'm standing beside him. His wings are keeping me from getting close. "It's all right, love," I say, touching his back.

He keeps apologizing into Lady Ruth's shoulder. She's crying, too. Only Jamie Salisbury is smiling, standing at Snow's other side.

"Simon," Jamie says, "don't you know how happy we are to find you? This is, like, the best news we've had in twenty years. We're your family!"

Simon lifts his head. Confused. Like Salisbury is speaking Greek.

"*We're your family,*" Jamie says again, clapping Simon on

the shoulder. "We've been looking for you for so long, and now you're here. We're well chuffed!"

Simon is looking into Salisbury's eyes. They're about the same height. The more I look at them—at Lady Ruth, at these photos of Lucy—the more I see. The more he seems to belong here among them.

"He's right," Lady Ruth says wetly. "We're so happy to have found you."

"But what if . . ." Simon shakes his head. "What if it isn't true?"

Something cold whips around us—I'd call it a draught, but the window is closed, and it's June—and Lucy's candle flames up one last time, then fizzles.

None of us say anything.

That was better than a spell.

Or even a DNA test.

After a moment, Lady Ruth pulls away from Simon and takes his hand, the one not holding the sword.

"Come downstairs, child. There's cake."

89

SIMON

There's chocolate cake with chocolate-orange buttercream.

And cherry Bakewell tart. And purple-iced éclairs with sugared violets.

There's tea. And milk. And lemonade.

And big pink meringue kisses that look like clouds.

Plus Lady Salisbury made a *thousand* sandwiches . . .

How many have I have eaten, I don't know—I've lost count. Cheese and pickle. Ham and mustard. Cucumber and cream cheese with sprigs of mint.

"The curry chicken are the best," I say.

"Wrong again, Snow," Baz says. "It's the lemon and prawn."

"I make those with magic." Lady Ruth smiles.

"You'd have to," he says.

"Nothing beats Mum's egg and cress," Jamie says.

"I can teach you that recipe," she tells me. "There's no magic at all."

We don't talk about Lucy. Or the Mage.

But we stay at the table till we're hungry again, and every time I try to hand the sword to Jamie, he shoves it off. "What do I need with a sword?" he says.

What do *I* need with a sword, I wonder.

I've never seen Baz eat at a table like this. With people. Every time he laughs—Lady Ruth makes him laugh, and I do, too, sometimes—I look for his fangs. I don't see them.

Could this be real?

Is it something else that will blow up in my face?

Does everything I believe in fall apart?

Jamie boils more water. Baz refills the milk jug. Lady Salisbury shows us this trick, where she makes roses bloom from the end of her wand. She tries to teach Baz, but he can't match it.

I turn my chair around and sit on it backwards to make room for my wings.

"Have more cake," Lady Salisbury says, cutting another piece of the chocolate.

"All right," I say, and I do.

90

PENELOPE

Shepard has a new T-shirt—GOG & MAGOG: WORLD TOUR 1993. It's something to do with giants; my dad gave it to him.

We went back to my house for dinner last night. I was worried about Shepard learning too many magickal secrets—our house is full of magic, my mum keeps her scrying glass in the kitchen—but it was the other way around. My dad spent the whole night asking Shepard questions. About magickal creatures and America. Even a few about the weather. Dad thinks Shepard is marvellous.

(Shepard is a bit marvellous.)

Mum was more cautious. She at least didn't cast any more spells on him.

"A Normal, Penelope," she said, when it was just the two of us setting the table. (We ordered takeaway kebabs, with tabouleh and labneh and lentil soup.)

"I don't want to hear it, Mum."

"You'll only be able to marry him in three dimensions."

"That you know of," I said.

She sighed. "Micah was at least a skilled magician . . ."

I dropped the last plate onto the table. "Honestly, Mum. Can you hear yourself? Can you hear yourself in the context of *this* day?"

She frowned at me. "Fair point. I just . . ." She shook her head. She looked tired. Mum looks like she hasn't had a full night's sleep since the Mage died. "I want you to have a rich and challenging magickal life, Penelope."

"I want that, too," I said, and then I smiled like—well, like someone I'd mock, like a twitterpated pixie. "Give him a chance, Mum."

After dinner, Shepard came back to my flat with me and slept in Simon's old room, and then we woke up and went to the British Museum and Westminster Abbey, and now we're taking an Overground train to check on Simon. (*"come hungry,"* he texted. *"i've got 1000 finger sandwiches."*)

"I'm going to miss the Overground," Shepard says. "And the Underground." We're sharing a pole. He towers over me.

"No subways in Nebraska?" I tease.

"We barely have buses."

"Sounds terrible."

"It's not so bad," he says, smiling.

"No public transportation, no pie . . ."

"We have excellent steaks."

"I don't eat steak."

"Hmmm . . ." He looks thoughtful. "We have pretty good tacos."

"We have tacos here," I say.

He laughs. "Is this like your pizza? Because I've tried your pizza."

"You should stay!" I blurt out. Too loudly. A man standing next to us scowls at me.

Shepard tilts his head and looks down at me. He bites his bottom lip.

"You should stay," I say again. More sanely.

"Penelope . . ." he says quietly, "I'm not even here legally."

"You know that's not an issue, Shepard."

"It never seems to be for you . . ."

I'm holding on to the pole with both hands. "There's still so much you haven't *seen*. Piccadilly Circus, the Tower of London. There are magickal swans in Oxford, we could take a day trip. And then Scotland—great snakes, you could probably bond with the Loch Ness Monster!"

The whole time I'm talking, Shepard looks like he's getting ready to tell me no. And then he does. "I can't stay," he says, his forehead all wrinkled and his eyebrows pulled up in the middle. "I didn't bring any money. I only have two pairs of pants."

"So you could get a job," I say.

"Not legally."

"Or you could go to uni."

"How would that work?"

"You're getting hung up on technicalities, Shepard. If you don't want to stay, just say so!"

He frowns. He's holding on to the pole with both hands, too. He slides one hand down, and catches my thumb with his pinkie. "I *do* want to stay."

I hook my thumb around his finger. "I like you so much," I say. It comes out resentful.

Shepard smiles. But his brow is still furrowed. "I like you, too, Penelope."

"I don't want you to leave."

He bends closer. "Come back with me."

"*What?*"

"Come back to Omaha with me. I'll get a passport, a real one—it only takes a few weeks. You can meet my mom, I can get my truck back . . ."

"Maybe you shouldn't try to get your truck back."

"*Come home with me.* Or just wait for me. Let me come back to you on my own two feet."

"Shepard, the last time I was in America, things didn't go so well."

"Are you kidding me? The last time you were in America, you kicked ass."

Could I do that? Go back to Nebraska with Shepard? As what, his girlfriend? His dread companion? "I suppose you could introduce me to Ken . . ."

Shepard is smiling at me.

"Come," he says.

"Are you going to tell me that Nebraska is beautiful in June?"

"Nebraska is miserable in June; you've already been there. But it *is* tornado season . . ."

91

BAZ

Simon has finally found someone to talk to about sandwiches.

"It's like your apartment is a Pret a Manger," Shepard marvels.

Lady Salisbury sent us home with all the leftovers from lunch. It took two giant hampers. (The woman has top-level picnicking gear.) And now Snow has everything spread out all over the kitchen and living room. "It's way better than that," Simon says. "Have you tried the cake?"

"Not yet."

"You have to try the cake—all of it."

"What about you?" Bunce says. She's sitting next to me on the sofa.

"Me?" I say. "I've tried the cake. I've eaten more cake than Mary Berry today."

She laughs. Bunce is in an uncharacteristically laid-back mood. I suppose she's had a pretty successful week: She bested a demon, won the heart of a handsome Normal, and helped keep Simon Snow alive and kicking through another harrowing adventure.

She doesn't know his latest news. He asked me not to tell her.

"I thought you and Bunce didn't keep secrets," I said.

"This isn't a secret," Snow said. "I just need to sit with it for a while."

Penelope cast a spell on him the minute she walked in the door. *"A horse of a different colour!"*

"Still nothing," Simon said.

"We'll keep trying," she replied.

"I'd rather we didn't."

Penny scoots closer to me now to make room for Shepard. It's a three-person sofa. Snow plops down at my feet. "I got enough to share," he says, holding up his plate.

I groan. "I'm still so full . . . I'm too full to hunt."

"That's how you're going to kill your vampire boyfriend, Simon," Penelope says. "Sandwiches."

Snow barks a laugh. "He'll be fine. He's always got room for four to six rats."

She pushes his knee with her socked foot. "How'd Baz spell that shirt around your wings, if you're immune to magic?"

I cock an eyebrow at her. "The spell is on the shirt, Bunce."

"Oh," Penny says. She really is in a mood. "Well, it looks nice."

"Until I have to tear it off," Snow says.

"Just let Baz reverse the spell."

"I don't like being dependent on him."

I kick him. "Magic forbid you rely on me."

"That's not what I meant—and everyone needs to stop kicking me. I'm injured."

"You could have some shirts made," Shepard offers.

All three of us turn to him.

"Magickal shirts?" Snow asks.

"No—regular shirts," Shepard says. "But with openings that button closed around your wings."

I try to picture it. "Buttons?"

"Or zippers," he says. "I've seen people use buckles, but those seem fiddly."

"People?" Bunce asks.

"Well, fairies . . ." Shepard sweeps his arm, expansively. "Harpies. Gargoyles . . . Lots of things have wings."

"That's not a bad idea," I say. "Why didn't we think of that?"

"Because you think with your wand," Snow says.

I kick him in the side again. (It's hardly a kick.) (I can't stay off him.)

"I didn't mean it in the dirty way!" he objects. "Penelope does, too."

"Where are we going to find a magickal tailor . . ." Bunce wonders aloud.

Shepard grins at her.

When I get out of the shower that night, Snow is wearing my pyjama trousers and practising sword manoeuvres. I hang back in the bathroom door to stay out of his way.

"You're not supposed to do that on my side of the room," I say.

"You haven't got a side of the room," he says, letting the sword drop.

"We'll have to negotiate that." I walk past him to the bed. My violin is still sitting there. I pick it up and rest it on my shoulder. Simon swings his sword again, watching me. "Are you going to tell me I can't play violin on your side of the room?" I ask.

"I would never tell you that," he says, pointing the sword. "You can play violin wherever and whenever you like."

"Your landlady might disagree."

"I'll cut off her ears."

"That sword is already a bad influence."

He climbs onto the bed next to me, still holding the sword. (Is he going to sleep with it?) "I should give it back," he says. "To Jamie."

"Snow, he insisted that you keep it."

"Yeah, but what do I need with a sword?"

"What does *Jamie Salisbury* need with a sword? I'm surprised he still has all his fingers. You, however, have spent your whole life wielding one."

"Yeah, but . . ." He shrugs with the sword. (I really think he might sleep with it.)

"Just keep it for now," I say. "It's like the smallest thing in your life that you need to figure out."

He laughs. "You sound like my therapist."

"A lot of your insults are compliments, I think."

Snow leans back on the headboard. "You're both always telling me that I have bigger things to worry about."

"Or—" I rest my chin on my violin and pull the bow over the strings. "—maybe we're both telling you to worry less, in general."

"I don't think that's what she meant."

"You should call her and ask."

He narrows his eyes at me. "You're not clever."

I play another note. "I am."

Simon holds the sword out in front of him, twisting his

wrist, then tossing the hilt gently, switching his grip.

"Does it feel like handling an incredibly rare and precious antique?"

"It feels fucking solid," he says. "Maybe even better than the Sword of Mages."

"I wonder if it has a name . . ."

"They said it's Excalibur."

"They said it's *an* Excalibur. Like, that's the brand name. It might have a family name."

"Yeah . . ." He's looking at the sword, frowning.

I play the beginning of a song.

After a minute, Snow brings his free hand up and wipes his cheek with the back of his wrist.

I keep playing. He wipes his eyes again. I pull the bow away.

"Don't stop," he says.

"Is it making you cry?"

"Partly. Isn't that what it's for?"

I laugh. "No."

He elbows me, so I start playing again. I suppose I have picked a melancholy song . . . (I like melancholy songs.) Snow messes about with the sword, occasionally wiping his cheek on his bare shoulder.

When I'm done, I lay the violin in my lap. Simon passes the sword to his left hand and slumps into my side.

"Do you think it's real?" he asks.

"The sword?"

"Do you think I was a magician? All along?" His voice is rough, and his cheeks are flushed. There's one damp curl hanging over his forehead.

"Yes," I say. "That's clear now."

He hides his face in my T-shirt. "It's too much for me."

I set the violin on the floor by the bed, then rest my hand over his on the hilt of the sword. He lets go. For a moment, I wonder if I'll be able to lift it, but I can. I set it by the bed, too.

Simon crawls half into my lap, burrowing his face into my chest.

I lay my cheek on top of his head and hold him behind his ears.

"It would be too much for anyone," I say.

EPILOGUE

ONE YEAR LATER

AGATHA

I could leave the goats to themselves all day. They'd be fine, and there's plenty for me to do back at Watford. The goats know their own way home.

I still end up out in the fields with them most days . . . I have my favourite stones and stumps to sit on. I've traded my wand for a walking stick.

I like to be the one who brings the goats in when the sun sets. Over the hills, across the Great Lawn, over the drawbridge—the merwolves are gone, thank magic (thank Niamh)—and into their clean barn.

I sleep above them in the loft. It's not half bad. There's a huge wheel window and a claw-foot tub.

I'll probably stay awhile.

ACKNOWLEDGMENTS

I WROTE THIS BOOK at a time when the entire world was afraid and uncertain. I was so grateful to have something I could work on every day—a way to move forward and make progress. And I was so grateful to spend these months with Simon and Baz, the characters I know best.

I never expected to write a trilogy set in the World of Mages, and the task would have been immensely more difficult without the help of Ashley Christy, my friend and continuity editor. She is incredibly sharp and kind, and I am lucky that she replies to my texts.

Over the last five years, I've exhausted all my British friends with my endless usage questions. (They probably wish I would have warned them at the beginning that it was a trilogy.) (I would have, if I'd known.) Thank you, Melissa Cox, Susie Day, and Keris Stainton. I am in your debt and available for questions if you're ever curious about Nebraska.

Thank you, especially, to Melinda Salisbury, who answered literally thousands of my questions with such grace and humor. (Melinda, what will I do now when I want an excuse to talk to you?)

Thank you to my UK agent, Nicola Barr, my UK editor, Rachel Petty—who you can thank for all those gorgeous special editions—and the entire team at Macmillan Children's Books, who enthusiastically welcomed the World of Mages.

ON THIS SIDE OF THE ATLANTIC, I'm very lucky to work with Wednesday Books, St. Martin's Press, and Macmillan Audio. From production to publicity to marketing, the whole team works with so much care and thoughtfulness. Designer Olga Grlic has put her whole heart into these wonderful covers. (With the help of super-illustrator Kevin Wada.) Everyone at Wednesday Books refers to Baz and Simon by their first names.

I GET STUCK and tied in knots when I'm writing. And in those moments, I was so glad that I could ask for help. Thank you to Joy DeLyria, Bethany Gronberg, Flourish Klink, Photine Liakos, Tulika Mehrotra, and Christina Tucker for helping me get untangled. (As I typed each of these names, I felt a specific rush of ardor and gratitude.)

I also sometimes fall flat on my face. Thank you to Leigh Bardugo, Alicia Brooks, Margaret Willison, and Elena Yip for helping me back on my feet.

MY REAL ACTUAL KIDS have grown up while I was writing these books. Thank you, Laddie and Rosey, for being so encouraging and for putting up with all the cardboard Bazzes— and for helping me come up with spells. ("Let it all out" was all Rosey; he saved my shirt!)

And thank you to my husband, Kai, for forever talking me into happy endings.

I CAN STILL HARDLY BELIEVE I wrote a trilogy. I can't believe I wrote a book about these characters in the first place! It was such a weird idea . . .

I am beyond lucky—maybe actually blessed—to work with people who love weird ideas. Who encourage me to take risks, and then have my back every step of the way.

I am profoundly grateful for my editor, Sara Goodman, and my agent, Christopher Schelling. They make my books and my life immeasurably better.